THRESHOLD

THRESHOLD

ERIC FLINT
RYK E. SPOOR

THRESHOLD

A Baen Books Original

Baen Publishing Enterprises
P.O. Box 1403
Riverdale, NY 10471
www.baen.com

ISBN 13: 978-1-4391-3360-6

Cover art by Bob Eggleton
Interior Illustrations by Keith Morrison

First printing, June 2010

Distributed by Simon & Schuster
1230 Avenue of the Americas
New York, NY 10020

Library of Congress Cataloging-in-Publication Data

Flint, Eric.
  Threshold / Eric Flint & Ryk Spoor.
      p. cm.
  "A Baen Books Original."
  ISBN 978-1-4391-3360-6 (hardcover)
  1. Life on other planets—Fiction. 2. Women paleontologists—Fiction.
I. Spoor, Ryk E. II. Title.
  PS3556.L548T47 2010
  813'.54—dc22

                                                      2010009368

10   9   8   7   6   5   4   3   2   1

Pages by Joy Freeman (www.pagesbyjoy.com)
Printed in the United States of America

This book is dedicated to Kathleen.

We'd also like to thank several people for their help:

The real Hank Dufresne, and his real financial wizardry.
Dr. Robert Sheldon, who took the time to explain the
operation of a dusty-plasma vessel. And James Nicoll, for
Enceladus (and for inspiration in the saga of Joe Buckley).

Liberties are often taken with physics to permit the story
to move forward. Don't blame our scientific consultants for
deliberate, or accidental, mangling of reality or practicality
that may have resulted from theory contacting story.

Finally, Ryk would like to thank his beta-reading group,
especially his Loyal Lieutenant Shana, who poked holes
in the rough draft before other people got the chance.

THRESHOLD

Cast of Characters

Ares Project

Baker, A.J.: Sensor-system specialist for the Ares Project, with a specialty in micro/nano technologies, especially in the area of independent networked sensor nodes called "smart dust"; married to Helen Sutter.

Buckley, Joe: Electromechanical engineer for the Ares Project; married to Madeline Fathom.

Conley, Larry: Astronomer/astrophysicist for the Ares Project; formerly with NASA; discoverer of Bemmie Ceres base.

United Nations, Interplanetary Research Institute

Fathom, Madeline: Chief of security, Interplanetary Research Institute (IRI); formerly an agent for the United States Homeland Investigation Authority; married to Joe Buckley.

Glendale, Nicholas: Paleontologist; director of the IRI.

Irwin, Bruce: Captain of the IRI vessel *Nobel*.

Sutter, Helen: Paleontologist; discover of *Bemmius secordii*; chief xenobiological researcher for the IRI; married to A.J. Baker.

Secord, Jackie: Chief engineer of the IRI vessel *Nobel*.

European Union

Bitteschell, Helmut: Vice-president of European Union's European Commission and Commissioner for Enterprise and Industry; the effective head of the E.U.'s space program.

Eberhart, Horst: Chief engine and control systems programmer for the E.U. vessel *Odin*.

Fitzgerald, Richard: Chief of security for the *Odin*.

Hohenheim, Alberich: General in E.U. space program; captain of the *Odin*.

LaPointe, Anthony: Astronomer/astrophysicist; part of the *Odin's* scientific contingent.

Modofori, Leo: One of Fitzgerald's security team for the *Odin*.

Osterhoudt, Goswin: Chief operations officer, European Space Development Company.

Svendsen, Mia: Chief engineer of the *Odin*.

United States

Hathaway, Ken: Captain of the U.S. vessel *Nike*.

Hughes, Andy: Director of the Homeland Investigation Authority.

Jensen, George: National Security Advisor of the United States.

Other

Gupta, Satya: Scientist in American space program; U.S. citizen of Indian descent; scientific advisor to the Indian space program.

PART I: POLITICS

*Political Compromise, n: an arrangement
to solve some complex problem which
is satisfactory to no one except the
politicians who arranged it.*

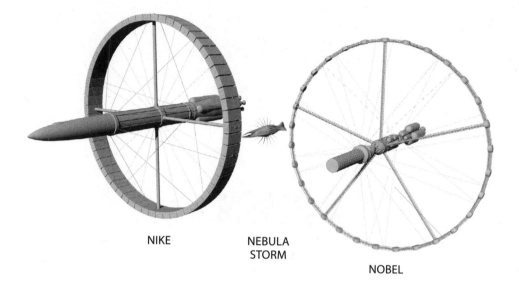

NIKE   NEBULA
STORM

NOBEL

Chapter 1

"I'll sue all of your asses, you little bastard! I didn't invest my money in your pie-in-the-sky operation to—"

"—get only a two hundred percent gain in ten years? Well, tough, that's what you're getting." A.J. rose, mirrored-VRD gaze two inches higher than Anton Margulis' angry brown eyes. "Take it or leave it. But let me guarantee you that if you sue us, even if you win, you'll wish you'd lost. Please, though, go ahead, try it. You've been such a prick ever since you invested, acting as though you thought your money made you a goddamn expert, I'd almost think it was worth it. And I'll enjoy every minute of making you look like the class-A jackass you are." He saw Margulis' fists tightening. "Or you could take a swing at me, and I could hand you your ass in a sling. Any way you want it. So, do you want your money, or do you want a fight?"

Margulis glared up at him for a moment. A.J. kept the sneer carefully fixed on his face. He knew the advantage his blank mirrored stare had in this situation, and liked it that way. Finally the speculator's gaze dropped, he snarled something that A.J. deliberately did not let his sensors enhance to comprehensibility, and he grabbed up the settlement form and scrawled a barely legible signature across it. The smart-paper form recorded Margulis' retinal for verification.

"Thank you, Mr. Margulis." Hank Dufresne took the form. "And if you will check your designated account, you will find I have just authorized the transfer."

Margulis grunted something that might, charitably, have been described as a version of "thank you" and left the office with considerably more noise than was necessary.

A.J. collapsed back into his chair, feeling the weight of Earth's gravity crushing him down. He'd worked hard to keep in shape back on Mars, and overall he thought he'd done fairly well, but there was a big difference between keeping in shape and *living* in a 1-g environment after being on Mars and similar low-gravity settings for two years. "For a minute I thought he was going to call my bluff."

"So did I, and not the part involving a fistfight, either." Hank shook his head. "Can't you find a more diplomatic way to do this?"

"Look, you want diplomatic, you get Joe here. Better yet, Glenn."

Hank favored him with a sour look. "I would have, if it wouldn't take another six months." He relented slightly. "Actually, I guess it was a piece of luck that any of you three were here when it came to a head. Some of these guys—like him—won't take anything that isn't said face-to-face seriously."

"He *was* the last, wasn't he? Because that was one hell of a chunk of change we had to hand him."

"The last one of any note. And I did get one piece of good news: Your TV-host girlfriend—"

"My wha— Oh, you mean Myranda." Myranda Sevins, one of the daytime talk mavens, had allowed A.J. to basically use her show as a publicity platform in the days after the big accident that had nearly cost A.J. his life. To their surprise, she'd actually become something of a convert, investing a moderate (for her) amount in Ares. "What about her?"

"She sent us another check instead of asking for her money back. Said she figured we'd find a way to make money out of the deal somehow, so if we'd just give her stock she'd back off on the county-sized Mars homestead."

A.J. gave a tired grin. "Thank all the gods for that. I know my limits, and I couldn't outfight *her* on the publicity front, even with Helen and Maddie helping."

"So . . . you're not broke, are you?"

A.J. tried to look nonchalant, then shrugged, looking down. "Not exactly. Liquid assets are pretty much tapped out, though. I've got a bunch of options and locked-in investments of other sorts at Dust-Storm that I could liquidate at a terrible loss, but I'd also lose out on my position there. Which was really what I came here to solidify."

Hank nodded. He knew A.J. had made the trip back from

Mars specifically to work on major advances to the "Faerie Dust" sensor motes and use his unique talents and access to the alien-technology discoveries made by NASA and Ares to finish acquiring a major stake in Dust-Storm Technology. It just so happened that a week before A.J. landed, the U.N. finished its acrimonious arguing over how the entire "Mars situation" would be handled. That had set off an awful lot of political and business landmines, including the current crisis at Ares.

A.J. brushed back his unruly blond hair. "Anyway, that puts Ares back in the black, or at least enough in the gray that we can operate on for a while, right?" He felt his gut tighten as he saw the older man's normally cheerful face go carefully neutral in expression.

"Well, A.J., yes and no. That takes off the immediate financial pinch, but we have a major issue that's only partly to do with money and investors. If we actually had been granted title—or, let's be accurate, since there wasn't any way we'd actually be granted *ownership* of a planet—right to exploit for some reasonable time on all of Mars, we'd have kept our investors. Or even if we got a really big chunk of it."

"Hey, we *did!*" A.J. said. "Joe's stunt made it so that we didn't lose out!"

Hank shook his head. "We got lucky, yeah. The Buckley Addendum was rammed through, but even though the administration claimed that was to ensure 'fair treatment' of Ares, it was just taking advantage of the situation to make sure that there was some mechanism to allow *other* government and corporate agencies to claim rights on extraterrestrial territory by allowing the first person to set foot on an extraterrestrial body to have a ninety-nine-year no-holds-barred lease on some portion of that body. The wording, of course, allows them to decide how much you can claim. Anyway, the problem is we've got a lot of good territory, by Martian standards, but only about nine percent of what we hoped to get—which is not 'a really big chunk' to the investors. What would your reaction be to someone who got you to invest in new sensors, and the sensors only did about one-tenth of what they claimed when you invested?"

"But..." A.J. shut up. He knew that *he* could clearly differentiate between the scenarios, but what Hank was telling him was, basically, that many other people couldn't, and to them Ares was already a failure.

"Let's get to the point, Hank."

A.J. jumped. He'd forgotten Anne Calabrio was present. She was the only other Ares board member currently on Earth.

"We've ditched the whiners and the guys who somehow ignored all our warnings about speculation and so on," Anne said. "We aren't broke, and we've got, what, five million square miles of mostly prime Martian real estate. We're helping build Phobos Station along with NASA, our own colony is starting up fairly well for something so early in the development stages, so what's the problem?"

"The problem is that we're about to be left out in the cold," Hank said bluntly. As Ares' financial genius, his job had always been to look ahead and find innovative ways to keep the perennially cash-short speculative venture afloat. A.J. couldn't ever recall a meeting where he'd looked more grim. "The presidential election ended just a little before the Mars-Phobos Treaties were finalized, and the president wasn't happy about the results of the treaties. Sure, anyone with sense would have realized that something like it would be the end result, but I think you people know that our president hasn't always been sensible unless what you said agreed with what he wanted. My contacts say he's going to be pulling in the wagons and focusing on purely U.S. interests—which means the government and large businesses. From his point of view, Ares really stole a march on NASA even though we were working together, and we've already been paid for our efforts. He probably doesn't think he owes us anything, and like most people he doesn't have any real gut grasp of the demands of space travel. So he won't think twice about doing things that can cause us one hell of a lot of problems."

"Like...?" A.J. prompted.

"Like starting to make us pay our own freight. Yeah, we've started our colony, but it'll be a lot of long, hard years before we can even dream of them being fully self-supporting. If everyone's playing nice, they recognize that helping us stay established helps them with our expanding resource base and so on, but I don't think a lot of these guys will get that angle."

Anne sucked in her breath as the implications sank in. "Oh, hell."

"No kidding," Hank said.

A.J. turned the implications over in his mind. His gut churned as the situation clarified. "You mean we'll have to pay full price for launch capacity. When our own launch capacity never got developed outside of NASA because of the emergency get-to-Phobos-*now* project."

"It gets better. You know, I wasn't stupid when we got sucked into this. One of the deals I cut was that after the *Nike* mission was finished—and by the contract I negotiated, it was finished once we'd gotten to Phobos and provided a few months support—Ares could have any available launch capacity basically at cost of launch, no more. But..." Hank ran a hand through his prematurely white hair. "The treaty divvied up Mars, and for political points the U.S. used NASA's foresight in making the *Nike* engine-rocket assemblies detachable to offer each of the other space-capable nations—China, the E.U., Japan, Russia, and India—one pre-tested, functional, high-power NERVA engine to 'help bring all of Earth into the true Space Age,' as the president's one speech put it. The extra engine they agreed to give to the U.N. so they had something to use for their administration of the 'common property of the human race.'"

"So? That should help us, right? More people have a reason to get into space, and—"

Anne shook her head, and A.J. felt his face flush with embarrassment as he saw Hank's almost pitying look. "You're such a genius with your stuff that I keep forgetting that you're also as clueless as a kid sometimes. No, it hurts us. Because all the countries involved are now going to be using *all* of their available launch capacity to start building their own ships so they can hopefully find something—like another Bemmius base—that they can claim for their own use under the Buckley Addendum. So..."

Now he got it, and A.J. cursed aloud. "Son of a bitch. So there *is* no 'available' launch capacity for us to use! That means that we'll be competing directly with the government for its own launch capacity. They'll sell it to us, probably, for 'humanitarian' reasons—translated: they won't let us starve to death, probably—but they'll make it so expensive that we'll eventually have to give up and come home."

"Bingo."

He slammed his fist on the table. "Dammit, they can't do that! We fucking *gave* them Mars! They wouldn't even have *found* that stuff without me! If Ares hadn't shown them up early on, they wouldn't even be landing there now!"

Hank shrugged. "Fair doesn't mean much in politics. We aren't getting anywhere with that line of thought. We need a solution."

"Sure, I'll just cover myself with Faerie Dust, think a few Good Thoughts, and *fly* my ass back to Mars!" A.J. knew he shouldn't be directing his anger at either Hank or Anne, but he ached all over and this new turn of events was...well, just too much. He'd spent most of the last month working like a demon at Dust-Storm, only to be pulled out by an emergency call from Hank, leading to him spending almost everything he had to save Ares from a bunch of idiots...And now another bunch of idiots was threatening the whole project. "Sorry." He thought for a moment. "What about the U.N.?"

"Talked with Glenn and Joe on that a few hours ago," Hank answered. "Our guess is that since the U.N. doesn't have any launch capacity of their own, they'll be a long way from building anything. Their best bet will probably be to use the reactor as a power source for Phobos Station or something like that. The countries agreed to let the U.N. be the arbitrator because that was the only deal everyone could live with, but don't think any of them like it. We also don't know yet who's going to be in charge of the Interplanetary Research Institute, which is the body that will be running that part of the show. A couple of candidates could be useful, but a few of the others would be actively hostile to us for a lot of reasons."

Something was nagging at A.J.'s subconscious. Something about the mission to Mars...the original crew of *Nike*...things said... that argument he'd had with Jackie, back in the restaurant before the disaster...Taken off the crew...Dammit, what was it?

"So, you think the space-capable powers will be competing?"

"Right now it looks like it. Maybe the other four will form some kind of temporary alliance to catch up with the United States, but in any case they'll be using everything they've got to make parity. Nothing left for us."

The idea was right there, almost in his hands. "So...," he said slowly, "we need more launch capacity. We can't build it, right?"

"You know *those* numbers, A.J. Yes, we could, if we had time. But...I'm guessing we can keep things running for a year or two on Mars, drawing on the credit we've got and so on, but if we have to build our own launch capacity, that goes way down. And of course then to reestablish ourselves we'll need *more* launch capacity—assuming that someone doesn't find some legal wrinkle to use that makes our *leaving* the area weaken our claim. Which they might."

Launch capacity. Outside launch capacity. Outside launch capacity that wouldn't be focused on building other people's ships. Why did he keep thinking of Jackie? She was a great engineer, but—

And then it hit him, in a blaze of inspiration. An ally, a reason, something that only one man would both understand and be able to make work. Somehow he *knew* this was the only chance they had.

Feeling his tired muscles scream in his thighs, A.J. stood. "I think there's a way. *We* can't do it, no. We need to keep our money for surviving long enough. But if we can convince one of the other countries to help us directly..."

Hank and Anne looked at him quizzically. "At their own expense?"

"No, for their own benefit. Oh, don't look at me like that. I'm not stupid enough to think that I could convince any politician of anything like that. But I know one guy who could convince anyone of damn near anything. And he would understand exactly what has to be done, too. If I can get him to come here..." He almost ran out of the room, wireless processing already showing a search for the fastest way to contact his target.

Chapter 2

The message ended. Madeline Fathom Buckley stared at the screen blankly.

"Oh . . . Jesus, Maddie . . ." Joe put his hands gently on her shoulders.

Without a word she turned and pressed into him, letting his arms enfold her. For the first time since . . . since she could remember, all she wanted was someone to hold her, tell her it would be all right, and make things better.

"That son of a *bitch*," she heard Joe growl, even as his hands gently stroked her back. "After everything you did for him!"

She pushed away, jaw setting. "Don't you dare blame him!"

"Huh?" Joe looked puzzled, then apologetic. "Not *him*," he said, nodding at the now-dark screen where Director Hughes' face had just moments before finished speaking. "The president. That rat bastard. Our mission—carried off on his timetable, so we could be doing our stuff right around election time—practically *gave* him the election. And now he turns around and does *this*?"

Madeline couldn't help it. She laughed. Then she hugged Joe so tightly that he grunted in discomfort. "You and your friend A.J. are such sweet little idealists. Every time I think you're not quite as innocent as he is, you say something that shows me you are. That's exactly *why* he's doing this, you silly man. He may have built the election on what we did, but in private, we—and especially I—embarrassed the hell out of him and his administration. Once he got the election in the bag, there wasn't any way he'd forget that. No politician likes getting put over a barrel. There wasn't any way he could get rid of the boss, though, so I knew—we both knew—he'd come after me. But I thought he'd do it differently."

She frowned, tapping her foot—a motion that, in one-third gravity, tended to slowly cause her to rotate in a lazy circle around her other foot. Director Hughes' message—delivered across the two hundred million miles that currently separated Earth and Mars—was of course couched in the most positive terms. Given that the president and National Security Advisor George P.D. Jensen—two of Madeline Fathom's least favorite politicians—were also in the message, Hughes had probably had no choice but to transmit it that way. She knew the director well enough, however, to know that the very exuberance of the message was his way of apologizing in public. The director had thanked her for her stellar service on the *Nike* mission, her courage and resourcefulness in the crash and survival thereof, et cetera, et cetera, and all the long hours she'd spent trying to maintain the balance between the needs of security and the practicalities of mankind's first sustained space exploration and colonization effort, et cetera, et cetera, and now said the time was right to reward her for this effort by promoting her. She was hereby relieved of her responsibilities as the representative of the United States' security interests in the Mars system. A new security representative had already been selected and was on his way. Madeline and Joe were welcome to take passage home on the *Nike* when she left, and the president had personally authorized a large baggage allowance so that they would have to leave nothing behind.

There was more, including fatuous congratulations from both the president and Jensen, but what it boiled down to was simple: now that the president no longer had to worry about elections, he was yanking her back to Earth and sending out someone who'd do what the president said instead of thinking for ten seconds about consequences.

She stopped suddenly and stomped her foot, sending her a short distance into the air. This startled Joe, who'd been watching her with both concern and admiration; the slow rotation made for an excellent view, and in private Maddie preferred pretty minimal clothing. Maddie was of course aware of Joe's scrutiny, but didn't begrudge him the view.

"You okay?"

"I'm okay, Joe. I . . . I just don't want to go. Even with you."

"We don't have to. You can stay here. I know Ares isn't exactly in the best shape, but we don't have to leave just because you're not working here."

That's true, she thought with a sudden moment of wonder and fear. She stared at Joe. "I don't *have* to work for the HIA?"

Joe knew why she phrased it as a question. "No. You don't have to go back and push papers. You can stay here—at least as long as Ares manages to keep operations running." He studied her sympathetically. "But I know it might be hard to do that with some other guy trying to play super-security man."

She managed a slight laugh. "Oh, I think it would be at least as hard for my replacement, whoever he is. Remember, I happen to have a rather inflated reputation."

She tried to sit next to Joe with her usual relaxed intimacy, but despite all her years of discipline and training, she suspected Joe could sense her tension. She wondered if this was what a zoo animal would feel if someone just took away the cage. She'd always thought her attachment to the Homeland Investigation Authority was just loyalty on her part, but she now realized it had also been habit and psychological safety.

"Can we drop this subject? Maybe...there was something you were going to tell me, I think, before the call came in?"

As usual, Joe—bless him—didn't try to keep on the topic and press for a solution like ninety percent of the men she knew would have. He simply leaned back and smiled, almost naturally, as though nothing had happened. "Well, yeah, there was. You've been working so hard on the Mars Base—setting up stuff for the U.N. to take possession—and then running over here and helping A.J., me, Glenn, Reynolds, and the rest put up our own colony, that I think I've gotten a piece of political news ahead of you, while you were out there working."

That *would* be something of a little coup for Joe, given that Maddie usually paid far more attention to the news than he did. "Okay, give."

"They've announced the director of the Interplanetary Research Institute."

Maddie sat up. "You win, Joe. How'd you hear this before I did?"

"Because I got it from Helen just a little bit before you came in, who got it in a private message from A.J., who I guess was at the U.N. for some reason."

She laughed. "Four degrees of separation? All right, tell me, who is it? Pelletier? Markovny? Shah?"

"Nope. Nope. Nope."

Madeline raised an eyebrow. Those had been the three leading contenders. The remainder was a morass of a dozen names, none of them thought to be likely choices. "Okay, give."

"A very good friend of ours."

She felt the grin start automatically. "Not—"

"Dr. Nicholas F. Glendale, yes—and from what A.J. said, Nick was as floored as the rest of us. He was sure he was way back in the pack of also-rans. And they'll be sending him out here as soon as *Nike* can restock. He'll be here in, say, four months—and A.J. probably will be, too." Joe looked momentarily depressed. "Though it's anyone's guess as to how much longer we can stay here after that."

Maddie knew exactly how difficult things were going to get for Ares. A year, two years, but if a solution wasn't found... Even if one *was* found, it would likely take time to implement. They needed something that would give Ares more breathing space right now. Even just one more load, even *half* a load on *Nike* or one of the other similar vessels being constructed, and Ares could make three or four years—enough to probably get past the pinch. But half a load was over seven hundred tons, far beyond Ares' means....

Suddenly she was on her feet, bouncing across the room to grab her uniform and pull it on.

"Where are you going, Maddie?"

Madeline smiled, all her momentary uncertainty gone. Hughes' overly genial communication had sent a message as clear as if he'd recorded it straight out: *do whatever you have to.*

"Not far at all. Just got to send a few messages. But I have to look my best for the job interview."

"She can't do that!"

Director Hughes had to restrain a rather unprofessional grin. Truth be told, he had been anticipating this moment ever since the president, through Jensen, had revealed their plan to perform a genteel railroading, followed by a private tar-and-feathering, of his best and favorite agent.

"I'm afraid that's not true, Mr. Jensen. She's a free woman in a free country. There's nothing in her contract that requires that she accept a promotion to assistant director of the HIA. True, it's a hell of a career move, but if she wants to stay on that godforsaken rockball as a glorified security guard, there's nothing I can do to stop her." He was very deliberately exaggerating his sympathetic tones. Jensen was the National Security Advisor he had come to detest more than any other who'd held that post in twenty years.

George P.D. Jensen's long, narrow features were twisted with sour anger. His eyes narrowed. "Don't you get cute with me, Hughes! She knows way too much—"

"It doesn't work that way, Mr. Jensen, and you know it perfectly well. Americans don't give up their rights when they go to work on behalf of national security. They do accept certain practical limitations, but they are neither slaves nor indentured servants. Intelligence agents can quit or retire anytime. They just have to keep the secrets they've learned and return any government property they have. Which Madeline Fathom did. I have her letter of resignation, her Official Secrets certification, and all her equipment accounted for. She's now a private citizen and completely within her rights to take a job with anyone she likes."

"But for a foreign power—"

"The U.N. is not exactly a foreign power, in the normal sense of that term. Lots of Americans have worked for U.N. agencies over the decades. Besides, Nicholas Glendale is an American citizen. And he's the one who offered her the job."

Jensen practically snarled. "A *security* job—on Mars! Where she'll be on the inside of the U.N. installation and I'll bet will be doing her best to stonewall Keld—ah, our new agent."

"Keldering, eh? A better choice than I might have expected, even if he is a major-league political ass-kisser. Madeline might actually have to think around him once in a while. But that's just as well. I wouldn't want her getting too bored out there."

For a moment, as the implications sank in, Jensen just gaped at Hughes, open-mouthed. "You...you *told* her to do this!"

Hughes' expression became very lugubrious. "Mr. Jensen, how could you suggest such a thing? I've sent her just one message since that decision was made, and you were sitting right there with me when I sent it. In the most enthusiastic terms I could think of. Exactly, I will note, as you instructed me to."

He managed to avoid the temptation to say anything further.

Easily, even. Hughes was a veteran of decades of Washington's infighting and turf wars—a veritable Achilles, one might say—and he was far too smart to say openly what he felt. Thought they could jerk him and his top agents around, did they? Damn fools. In their eagerness to get rid of Fathom, all they'd done was leave her right where they didn't want her, on Mars—and now with absolutely no control over her at all. For anyone who knew Madeline, that outcome had been a foregone conclusion.

Still, it was hard not to let any traces of his gloating show openly. He turned his chair so he faced away from the National Security Advisor, as if admiring the view of the capital through his window. It was a fairly spectacular view, actually.

Chapter 3

Satya Gupta paused by the doors a moment, gathering his thoughts. A.J. Baker's hasty and intense conversation had indeed helped, but there was still resistance to be dealt with. He hoped that the new factors, however, would be enough to sway opinion in his favor. Then he nodded to the guards outside and strode in.

The president of India, Goutam Gaurav, rose respectfully, as did the other men and women of the Space Development Committee. "Thank you for coming, Dr. Gupta."

"The pleasure is entirely mine," Gupta said, aware of the atmosphere in the room. They were very doubtful. Yes, he had supporters, but most were afraid of the imponderables of perception as well as the practical difficulties of the project he proposed. "It has been some time since I initially made my proposal. I trust you have had the opportunity to consider it?"

"We have," the president answered. "And it is a . . . very interesting idea, Dr. Gupta. Speaking for myself, I would be inclined to follow your advice. But as you are aware, I am but one member of the committee. Many other members have questions and objections."

He nodded slowly, taking in the entire room. The president was being a bit evasive. True, looked at from one angle, Goutam Gaurav was just one member of a committee. Since the very same person was the head of the state of India, if not the head of its government, however, the difference was obvious. But he did not say anything aloud. The president was simply using the evasion to defer making a decision. Gupta had not expected anything different.

"Indeed, indeed it must seem risky, Mr. President." He let his sonorous voice roll about the room. He was aware—none better—that his voice was in some ways his most potent weapon of debate; here he must employ it to the full.

"With India being only newly come to space capability, in comparison with the United States, Russia, and even China and Europe, I can understand that it must sound strange for me to urge you to *not* develop a NERVA-style spacecraft such as *Nike*, especially when you have been given an engine and reactor capable of driving just such a vehicle. Yet I tell you that this is an opportunity—a *great* opportunity—which I can see propelling India to the very forefront of space commerce."

"That is what you said in your original proposal," Madhuri Ganeshan pointed out. The speaker for the Lok Sabha, the House of the People in the Indian parliament, was an intensely political, though scrupulously honest, member of the committee. She would be most concerned about the potential for political gain or loss from decisions made here. "We have seen the proposal. And make no mistake, sir, we do appreciate what you have done for us—advocating our side in the debates on the Mars Treaty, and in other ways showing you have not forgotten your heritage. We have read your proposal very carefully. You advocate building a so-called 'space elevator'—something no country has yet attempted—rather than build our own interplanetary vessel, when we are already being given one of the key components for nothing. I can see that such a course appeals to a gentleman such as yourself, Dr. Gupta, since you are well known as a visionary. It may be a bold and daring move to take this course, but many of us are elected to be reasonable, not risky. Convince me that it is more *reasonable* to do this, and you will have my vote." Her sharp, severe features, framed by pure white hair, were like a sword upraised in salute and challenge.

"I do indeed have additional facts to present, Madame Speaker. And I will attempt to convince you that it is reasonable. Indulge me, however, by allowing me to restate what I think are the compelling reasons why it is *not* reasonable to follow the current course."

Speaker Ganeshan glanced at the president and the other members. "I have no objection."

"In building a ship like the ships that all the other spacegoing powers either have built or are building, you are attempting to compete with them in the area where they are strong and you are weak. We all know how this reflects a lack of wisdom, if an alternate course exists. And there is such a course.

"Instead of a ship, which transfers people and materials between the planets, I say that you should instead make a better way to transfer these people and materials from Earth to space. Build an elevator to space, a tower stretching thousands, *tens* of thousands, of miles, provided with power to draw up almost limitless material for construction, and to return safely to Earth, people and goods from space. Consider that the major limitation on the construction of *Nike* according to its schedule was the severe lack of launch capability—pushed to its limit, perhaps six hundred tons per month, far less in ordinary times. With even the simple, single elevator proposed as the beginning of this project, India will immediately *double* the launch capacity of the entire Earth, and by building additional cables we can increase that capacity, almost without limit. A similar design that rotates may be used as a mighty slingshot, to cast cargoes of nearly any size across the solar system to their final destination. You will need no ships. The ships and colonies, instead, will need you."

They stared at him, caught momentarily in the spell of his voice. "But if this is so obvious and easy, why are the other countries not pursuing it?" The question came from one of the other members of the committee—Singh, from the Rajya Sabha, the Council of States, which was the upper house of the parliament of India.

"Obvious? Perhaps. Easy? I said nothing of easy. No project so grand will be easy. Yet it is within India's ability to do, with the right allies." Gupta made a wide, sweeping gesture. "There are many possible reasons they may not be following this course. Perhaps, as all the other space-capable powers are to the north, they see more of the problems of a space elevator. For example, it must be anchored to the equator if it is desired that one minimize its tendency to sway, and they have no direct access to the equator as we do."

That was fudging a little. The southernmost tip of India was eight degrees of latitude north of the equator, not directly upon it. But eight degrees was close enough, as a practical matter.

"But that is probably not the main reason," he continued. "If need be, they could certainly find an area they could lease for the purpose. To name one, the Galapagos Islands are situated directly on the equator. The government of Ecuador has made it quite clear that it would be delighted to provide any spacegoing nation which wished to use the islands as the anchor for a space elevator with a ninety-nine-year lease. Even at a reasonable price."

He shook his head. "No, I suspect the main reason is the simplest. A man with an existing skill will invariably seek to apply it to new work before he concludes that he must undertake the more difficult task of learning a new skill altogether. You, on the other hand, do not suffer from that handicap for the obvious reason that you have no significant commitment to the traditional methods of space travel. Why not take advantage of it?"

Speaker Ganeshan spoke. "You mentioned the 'right' allies, Doctor. This is also in your proposal, but you give little guidance as to who these allies are. You also mention that the ships and colonies will need us. All well and good, but before embarking on such a project I would want to see at least one specific need— a customer, in short, for what we would offer." She held up an imperious hand as a few other members began to speak. "I am not unreasonable myself, Dr. Gupta. I do not expect you to have a market which will make the project profitable in the next five years, not in an area filled with so much risk and speculation. Give me one real customer, one group which I can believe as needing our assistance in this specific way. Give me a name or two that specifies these 'right allies' that we will need to construct your space elevator. No more generalities."

Inwardly, Gupta smiled. He had left those broad statements in to allow one of the members to bring up just these points, in just this manner.

"I will answer your second point first, Madame Speaker," he said. "While we have our own space program, it is quite limited at this time. To construct the elevator, therefore, we really require two things—the materials from which it is constructed, and additional people with experience and expertise in the construction and maintenance of reasonably large space facilities who are, themselves, not already going to be devoted to their own country's spaceship projects. Now, the creation of such an immense structure can only be done through the use of carbon nanotube materials."

The president's eyebrows rose. "I see."

"Indeed. The Tayler Corporation has established considerable manufacturing ties with India in the past decade, as have many other manufacturing corporations in the past several decades. Tayler is the primary—almost, in fact, the only—source of the material needed. Their work has been well-proven in the *Nike* mission—as spectacularly shown by Ms. Fathom's exploits, among others. I have taken the liberty of approaching them confidentially on this matter, and they were very receptive. Based on that conversation, I have brought with me a sample agreement which, I believe, will suit Tayler's needs.

"Manpower would seem to be a difficulty, as all the space-capable countries are already working as hard as possible to create their own—or in the case of the United States, additional—vessels. But there is one other source of such expertise—the one other organization which already is established on Mars. I was contacted earlier by Mr. A.J. Baker of Ares, who has supplied me with this letter of support and commitment." He placed the document on the table. "If you undertake this project, Ares will not only assist you in the engineering of the elevator and all associated infrastructure, but will also contract with you to construct a similar elevator for Mars itself. They are very much in need of launch capacity themselves, and so, Madame Speaker, they may also be considered to be a customer as well as an ally."

The committee seemed nearly convinced; a faint murmuring of intense conversation began. Ganeshan's smile, however, was wintry. "I will agree that you have supplied the allies in specific, and sufficiently so for now, but let us not attempt a magician's trick in making one appear to be simultaneously the other. I cannot speak for my learned colleagues, but I have been following Ares' activities quite closely in the past few months. They are essentially bankrupt, are they not? Oh, if they somehow manage to establish themselves and survive the next ten years, they may amount to something, but is it not true that it would be quite ludicrous for us to consider them a significant customer at the present time?"

"Madame Speaker, you are entirely correct." The murmurs turned to a hush. "I do believe that in the future you will find them excellent customers, but it is undoubtedly, *undoubtedly* true that you need another customer, one in the here and now. One which has considerable monetary resources, yet no space capability of its own. One which has pressing reason to enter space in a wide and diverse capacity but which at the present time cannot do so itself." He saw her eyebrows rise as the thought struck her an instant before he spoke his next words. "Such a market, such a customer, exists already: The Interplanetary Research Institute.

I have spoken with Director Glendale on this matter, and he was willing—I will even say, enthusiastic—to commit the IRI to supporting this enterprise." He placed the final document on the table like a poker champion laying down his hand, and looked calmly into the Speaker's eyes.

After a moment, she smiled more broadly. "Dr. Gupta, I withdraw my objections and offer my support. This project is visionary, risky, and bold. But—in the context of history as we are seeing it—it is, indeed, reasonable." Her smile widened momentarily. "And I believe we can all find profit in the publicity."

Gupta laughed. "Indeed, *indeed* we can, Madame Speaker!"

He heard and answered additional questions, but the expressions on the faces, the way in which the questions were phrased... The conclusion had already been reached. They would try. They would at least try. If they could manage to see this project through, the results would transform the world.

He thought back to a conversation he'd had years earlier with Jackie Secord where he expressed his lack of complete enthusiasm for the Ares Project's intended approach to space exploitation. One of his major concerns was, and had always been, that the benefits of extending humanity's reach into space be brought to all of humanity, not simply to its wealthiest and most privileged classes and nations. Brought, not in some fuzzy handwaving sense, but in the hard and practical ways an engineer could appreciate.

Despite all the economic shifts of the past decades, the United States had always managed to stay—sometimes just barely—ahead of the other countries in its influence and power. Gupta didn't begrudge them that status; he was an American citizen himself, after all. But he felt it was far past time for other countries, especially his native land, to step forward from the red, white, and blue shadow by taking the best that America had to offer and making it their own. The alliances he proposed here would do just that. And regardless of what some of the current crop of politicians might think when they realized that he was helping India "steal a march" on the other countries, including America, he felt that this was actually a quintessentially American direction.

The thought came with great satisfaction. *Let my native land follow the best of my adopted homeland's methods, and there will be a victory that we can all feel pride in: a victory for the whole world.*

Chapter 4

Nicholas Glendale leaned back in his chair, relishing the lightness of one-third gravity—though not quite as much as he was enjoying the majestically rotating view of the Red Planet through his office window.

Phobos Station was shaping up nicely. Basically the habitat ring of a *Nike*-class vessel with a docking hub, the station was one of the subsidiary conditions of the Mars Treaty, a centralized location where missions to and from Phobos and Mars could be launched or concluded. Nicholas had wasted no time in making it clear that he intended to permit ships of any and all types to avail themselves of the station's amenities, so long as they were willing to help support the station—or to put it more crudely, pay for the privilege. True, such use was implied in the nature of the Interplanetary Research Institute, which essentially owned Phobos Station. But by making it explicit and enthusiastic, Glendale hoped to ensure that the IRI would be not just an overseeing body, but an active force in the exploration of the solar system.

And, as Madeline pointed out, it would also make it a lot easier for us to keep tabs on all the other players. It was a bit of a jarring shift of gears to start thinking in those terms. While you did try to keep an eye on other scientists' work in academia, the level of paranoia and security needed for his new job as director of the IRI was something entirely different, and one of the least-pleasant parts of that job.

Having Fathom as his new head of security, however, certainly made it easier. As he thought that, he heard the faint chime from his door announcing her arrival. "Come in, Madeline."

"Good morning, Director. Or is it afternoon?" Madeline glided in, every golden hair impeccably in place as usual.

Easier on the eye as well as on my schedule, Nicholas mused. He was quite honest about the fact that he thought both Joe Buckley and A.J. Baker were exceedingly lucky men. Or perhaps just much easier to live with, he corrected himself. As an admittedly handsome and very well-known figure, he'd been "lucky" that way four times, each time ending with a divorce: one friendly, one neutral, two savage. He'd been single for some years now, and suspected he'd be smart to remain that way. For whatever reason—probably flaws in his own personality, he'd readily admit—Nicholas Glendale and marriage just didn't seem to suit each other.

"I suppose it depends on your preference," he said, in answer to her light question. "The standard Martian time is early morning. Hopefully we should be concluded by the time Joe is ready to call you."

She gave a slight frown. "I shouldn't be that transparent."

"Madeline, my dear, you *should* be that transparent about something that isn't at all a secret. You have to bounce constantly between here, Phobos Station, and Mars—the last thing I want to do is cause you to miss out on whatever you married Joe for. This may be a mystery to the rest of us, but as long as it keeps you happy..."

Fathom grinned, sticking her tongue out.

Glendale smiled in response. "Always glad to be of help. It's time for the general briefing, is it?"

"With new wrinkles and info, yes. I've sent it to your e-mail, too."

"Which I will file with the others after I get the live presentation, yes."

Maddie sat down across from him. "Well, I'll try to make it fast. First, Ares. I am required to give you a big thank-you once again from everyone on Mars. Yes, I know that's the fifth time, but they'll probably send the same message five more times anyway."

"And tell Glenn, Joe, A.J., and the others they're all welcome. Again." Nicholas had stretched several points to have a considerable portion of the shipment he'd brought with him from Earth, ostensibly intended to help set up the IRI, delivered to Ares at a very reasonable price. That wasn't, in his view, charity. The division of Mars had given Ares essentially all of the Melas Chasma area as well as a number of other notable claims elsewhere—except for, of course, the Bemmie base on Mars. This made the IRI a political and economic island with exactly one neighbor: the Ares Project. It only made sense to be neighborly. The fact that many of the people involved were his friends just made it easier.

Maddie consulted her notes. "Walter Keldering is requesting another meeting with you. Probably wants to try to push for more U.S. direct access to the research."

"Of course he is." Nicholas sighed. "I suppose you'll have to set one up. I don't have any reason to antagonize the United States, even if I'm going to have to once more refuse him special privileges—whatever justification he's come up with this time." Nicholas' hopes had been that whoever was sent to replace Madeline would be a pure political yes-man, someone who just did exactly as he was told. Keldering was political, but unfortunately was very competent indeed. The former CIA operative had not attempted any bluster or bullying, as might have been expected from the current administration's attitude. Instead, he seemed to be almost infinitely inventive at finding legal and practical arguments that would lead to preferential treatment of the United States with respect to any new discoveries in the alien bases. Even Maddie had more than once voiced a grudging respect for Keldering's unfailingly polite, doggedly resourceful approach.

Privately, Nicholas suspected part of Madeline Fathom was actually pleased with the situation; she enjoyed having an adversary who might occasionally test her steel. For Nicholas himself, however, Keldering was just an annoyance. "Put him down for an appointment in a week or so."

"Yes, sir. On the positive side, the finalized cooperative agreements with Ares have arrived and the Ares board of directors just signed all of them. Once you countersign, all our arrangements will be in place."

"Good."

"Let's see . . . America's got the second engine built and tested for *Nike* and is building two more for *Athena*. Europe's keeping tight lips on the *Odin*. They're making some major design changes, and I think what they're planning is something more suited for outer-system exploration. Based on preliminary hints and the fact that they've hired a number of people in a couple of related specialties, Jackie Secord and Dr. Gupta have both told me they suspect *Odin* will be designed to use a mass-beam drive as well as the NERVA rocket and standard electric ion drives." She glanced at Nicholas to see if he understood.

Nicholas nodded. "Ions or small particles fired at the ship, which catches them, probably magnetically, thus transferring the momentum directly without need for using fuel. Very power hungry, however, yes?"

"I think they're also planning on attempting solar powersats to run the thing. Do it far enough away from Earth to be no particular danger or nuisance, and once you've proven the reliability you can also then market the satellites to supply energy. We'll have to keep a close eye on them. Japan's well along in the construction of *Amaterasu*, and current buzz is that they're planning to also build a real orbital colony. This has been a perennial favorite of Japan's space enthusiasts, so that's no real surprise.

"China, unfortunately, had their engine go bad—you heard about all that. I think what's going to happen there is that the U.S. will apologize, promise to repair the thing at no cost, and probably sell them or give them another engine eventually. It'll still slow down China's deployment significantly, probably putting them last in terms of getting a functional reusable interplanetary craft going. They may benefit to some small extent from watching other people's mistakes along the way, but overall it's a bad break for them.

"India's moving forward with the creation of the space elevator. They've named the project Meru, by the way, after Mount Meru, the legendary world pillar in Hindu mythology. Preliminary calculations show that their proposed design will come in under a thousand tons total mass. Modifying the NERVA reactor to act as a power generator—not the best design if you start from scratch, but having the reactor already up in the sky counts for something—they'll have plenty of power for dragging cargo up and down and keeping a station above the world running. You asked me about anchoring the thing down last time—something I didn't know much about—so I checked into it. The design they're using doesn't really require much anchoring force—about as much as the designed transport capability, actually. They're going to be splitting the base and anchoring it to several nearby ships, so it doesn't have a single simple point of failure. Time to completion, about another year."

"One year?" Nicholas sat up straighter. "That seems awfully fast!"

"Apparently it's within reason. And building up its capacity will be built into the design. In a few more years they'll be able to send a thousand tons per week up or down. With the IRI and Ares having first call on much of that capacity, we will be a lot more comfortable. And after you made sure Ares got a cheap shipment"—she gave him a grateful smile on behalf of Joe and his friends—"they'll definitely make it long enough to survive the crisis."

"Which means we're missing just one element—how are we going to get the stuff from geosynch orbit around Earth to here?" Nicholas said. "Slingshot?"

He was referring to the fact that if one placed a load farther out than geosynch, one could literally let it "fly out" like a slingshot, propelled in essence by the Earth's rotation, just like a real sling spun about someone's head.

"Possible—and, once *Meru* is fully operational, I'm sure they'll be building some orbital slingshots anyway. But using *Meru* itself as a slingshot is limited by a lot of factors of timing and relative position between Earth and Mars. Some packages could be shipped up with their own little electric drives—once you're in geosynch, it's a lot easier to get elsewhere—but that'd cut down on the actual cargo arriving here and make it a *lot* more expensive. We really do need our own ship."

"Well?"

She grinned. "Bruce Irwin's willing to be the captain and pilot if we get one built. As you know, Jackie Secord's already offered to run the engineering side, and she's keeping the reactor-engine assembly maintained now. Pricing on the standard *Nike* or Phobos Station habitat ring segments, though, is totally out of our league, even if we could get them to slow down their build schedule to supply us."

"We really do need something like that, though, don't we?"

Maddie nodded. "Anything much less than one-third g as constant living conditions will cause a lot of health problems. In fact, I'd really feel more comfortable if we could push that up, and on some of the new ships like *Odin* they might well. They'll have more time and luxury for crew selection, so they won't have to worry about spin disorientation as much."

"Does Ares have a solution in mind?" This was one of the major reasons for establishing cooperation between the IRI and its closest neighbor. They were, as India had already recognized, the only talent pool of space-qualified experts who were not currently committed to a specific country's space program.

"Since the full agreements haven't been signed, I can't officially say anything, but Joe told me to tell you 'Damn straight we do.' If it's what I think, it will work, too."

Nicholas leaned back slowly. "Then get me those originals pronto, so I can sign them. Let's get to work!"

Chapter 5

"I can't believe this," said the national security advisor. "First Fathom turncoats, and now the U.N. is going to steal a march on us. You want to explain this particular mess, General?"

Ken Hathaway kept his expression respectfully neutral. Despite his dislike for the current administration, he had no intention of torpedoing his own career as the first and, currently, only military commander of a major space vessel. "I wouldn't describe this as a mess, sir. There are actually some advantages for us in this situation."

Jensen looked at him incredulously. "You—along with my other analysts—assured me that there really wasn't a chance that the IRI would be able to build a ship around that engine. You all told me they'd probably just use it as a portable power source, or maybe a Mars-to-Phobos transport. And now Walter tells me that they're about six months from launching their own version of *Nike*!"

Ken issued a chuckle, which he hoped looked spontaneous. He'd planned this sort of reaction, and Jensen had obliged him with precisely the kind of line he'd been hoping for.

The national security advisor's face darkened. "Would you like to tell me what you find amusing, General?"

"Sorry, no disrespect meant, it was just ... You haven't seen the thing. Saying they were ready to launch their own version of *Nike* ... Sir, that's like saying Huck Finn was launching his own version of *Old Ironsides* when he pushed his raft into the river."

Jensen slowly leaned back, the anger shifting toward a hard speculation. "Go on. Are you saying they're not really making an interplanetary vessel?"

"Well . . . No, sir. They are, in one sense. I mean, their ship *does* have a real nuclear engine on it, and that can sure push it around the solar system. But . . . Here, *look* at it."

Ken sent a command to the White House network, which acknowledged he had authorization to trigger image presentations, and the far wall lit up with a picture of *Nobel*, the interplanetary vessel Glendale was having constructed.

Jensen snorted. There were a few other grunts or chuckles around the table.

The *Nobel* looked very little like *Nike*. Both had a central hub where the main engine sat, and other parts about four hundred and fifty feet from that center which would serve as living quarters. But where the *Nike* was a shining vessel, an integral structure of smooth components and clear functionality, *Nobel* was . . .

Clunky, Ken thought, was probably the most charitable term you could use. "They've had to make do with whatever they could get," he said. "They don't have manufacturing capability of their own, and all the aerospace resources we have—all the aerospace resources any country has, for that matter—are tied up in building our own ships and bases. So they had to go to the one group of people who can somehow manage space construction and who don't have their own ship—Ares. But Ares doesn't have the money or the manufacturing capability to crank out things like *Nike*'s habitat sections. So what do they have? Speaking as a military man, they've got Tinkertoys, Legos, and an Erector Set to hold 'em together."

He pointed. "Look at their so-called 'habitat ring.' Looks like a bunch of tuna cans linked together with duct tape and silver straws. That's because what they've got are basically just standard Ares habitat cans, not all that much different from the ones Zubrin first drew up almost half a century ago. The whole central body there"—he pointed at the boxy gray skeleton in the middle of the screen—"that's just some beams to hold all the pieces together. They'll be using something like an inflatable tank to hold their fuel together, I'd guess, or maybe some reusable solid tanks. The point is, sir, that thing can't match *Nike* in any respect. Especially since you got us a second engine."

The sight of the *Nobel*, looking rather like the result of a high-school science project to create a model of a space station, had thawed the atmosphere considerably. Ken no longer felt that his job was immediately in jeopardy.

"You mentioned that you thought this situation offers advantages, General Hathaway?" Jensen said. "Explain."

"If that thing actually works, sir, it takes a big load off of us. We've been committed to being their long-range support since the Institute got established, because there just wasn't anyone else available. Once they have their own ship working, we're free to work more for the United States' direct interests. Sure, we'll still be doing runs to Phobos Station and the Institute. We've got plenty of reasons to do so, and we'll have to help with the short distance ferrying anyway."

Hathaway flashed a momentary smile at the realization he was now calling Earth-to-Moon orbit hops "short."

Before he could continue, one of Jensen's analysts spoke up. "What you're saying is they won't *need* us just to survive any more. They can send their own ship on their own errands, ferry their own supplies back and forth, and in general deal with all the logistical headaches we've had to handle the past few years. And welcome to them."

Jensen nodded. "All right, General Hathaway. I understand your points. The reports from Mr. Keldering were perhaps overly alarmist. So you don't see anything to worry about in this situation?"

"Nothing whatsoever, sir," Ken said. "We have a battleship and they have a rowboat. Let's just hope they don't spring a leak rowing back and forth—that would require us to rescue them."

PART II: ALLIANCES

Plausible Deniability, n: positioning oneself such that one can permit actions to be taken which would be politically damaging, but in such a manner as to allow one to deny any knowledge of, or connection to, the actions in question.

Chapter 6

"Prepare for spin-up. *Nike*, are you on station?" Jackie waited for the response.

"*Around behind Phobos in case of disaster, yes, ma'am,*" Ken Hathaway's voice responded.

"I don't think you had to get *that* far away, Ken!" Jackie responded in a nettled tone.

"*Probably not. But probably nothing bad's going to happen, either, and we're not betting on that. Nike is the U.S.A's only major interplanetary vessel, and Uncle Sam isn't paying me to take risks with it.*"

"Especially," she said, "for a rowboat."

Hathaway clucked his tongue. "*Look, I don't control what the NSA says in public. Been me, even if I thought that, I'd have kept my own counsel.*"

"'Even if I thought that,'" Jackie jeered. "Ken, I'll bet you're the one who first coined that charming term. Applied to us, anyway."

A diplomatic silence followed. Jackie smiled. She was pretty sure that Hathaway had, in fact, been the one to put the idea in Jensen's head that the *Nobel* was a "rowboat." He'd used the derisive term himself in private, after all, when joking with his friends in Ares.

He wasn't going to admit it, of course. Jackie was quite sure that if Hathaway had done so, he'd been aiming to relieve or at least deflect tensions between the current U.S. administration and Ares and the IRI. But the same political skill that would have led him to do so—you didn't get to be a general in the U.S. armed forces without such skills—would also keep his mouth diplomatically shut.

"*Sticks and stones may break my bones...*" came Ken's singsong voice.

Jackie chuckled. "Yeah, sure, I know. 'But words can never harm me'—and people who aren't really familiar with space travel usually don't realize how little appearances matter when it comes to deep-space craft that don't have to penetrate an atmosphere. Still, I didn't like having my baby called ugly."

"*Well, sure. Are you ready?*"

"Almost. A.J.?"

The sensor specialist's confident voice rang out. "*Every inch of* Nobel *is wired, Jackie. If anything happens, you'll be the second to know.*"

"After you, of course."

"*Glendale squeezed a guarantee out of us on workmanship. I get the bad news first by a millisecond if we have to pay out.*"

Jackie took a deep breath. "Fire laterals."

The side reaction thrusters fired. They were powered by the central reactor, as long as reaction mass was available. The wavering pale line of superheated gases stood straight out at a tangent to each "tuna-can" chord. To protect the bottom of the cans, the side thruster vents were actually mounted a short distance farther out.

Slowly, majestically, the *Nobel* began to spin. "*Rotation started. Stresses all at predicted levels. No unexpected readings. Keep it going, guys.*" A.J. was in his professional voice now, which she found immensely comforting. A pain in the ass he could be, but his skill and his ego combined to make him the best man for a job like this. He wouldn't *let* anything go wrong; it would be a personal insult.

"*Up to an interior acceleration of one-tenth g... closing in on a revolution per minute... still all green, no signs of stress. Wobble within acceptable limits. Might need to trim weight a bit on one side, though, I think someone missed a couple kilos somewhere... almost there... now!*"

The superfluous command coincided exactly with the automated cutoff of the thrusters. *Nobel* spun with massive dignity, generating exactly one-third gravity within its linked habitat cans. "How are we doing, A.J.?"

"Nobel, *all green. You're well within tolerances. Minimal precession at this time. Orbital alignment optimum for main drive test.*"

Jackie took a deep breath. The next set of maneuvers would

stress the *Nobel* to the maximum that any ordinary conditions would demand. If she survived that, she'd be fully spaceworthy and Jackie Secord would be the chief engineer for the only independent nuclear-powered vessel in existence. "Captain, all systems appear to be ready. We are going to try a main-drive burn."

"Very good then, Chief," came the cheerful Australian tones of Bruce Irwin. As the first man to ever land (however disastrously) a manned vehicle on Mars, and one of the few interplanetary-qualified pilots, he'd been top of the list when Glendale was looking for someone to command *Nobel*.

Well, actually, second from the top. Glendale had first offered the job to Jackie, to which she'd replied: "Jesus, no. I'm an engineer, and I don't want to move to management. I'll stay here in charge of keeping everything running."

Jackie brought her focus back to the here-and-now. "Right, let's see what our lady's got. *Nike*, now that we're spinning fine, *Nobel* is going for a full main-engine burn. Figuring on one to lift us up in orbit a bit, say twenty seconds at full."

The entire set of maneuvers was meant to take only about sixty seconds of full burn. *Nobel* was lightly fueled right now, with only about a hundred tons of reaction mass—enough for two hundred seconds of *Nobel*'s maximum million-pound thrust at an ISP of around one thousand. The light load was important; by having a minimum of reaction mass on board, the effective acceleration of *Nobel* was maximized, which maximized the strain of the maneuvers. There was no point in testing her at low thrust if she'd break at high thrust, especially since high stress would, obviously, occur when the vessel was low on fuel—toward the end of a journey and therefore potentially as far away from help as it was possible to imagine.

"*Understood*, Nobel. Nike *is standing by to initiate rescue in case of emergency.*"

"We surely do appreciate that, mate. Not that I have any experience with emergencies while flying, mind." Bruce's tone sobered. "Check course vector."

"*On target, Captain,*" A.J. said after a minute. "*Radar scans show all clear, not that there's ever anything to hit out here. And Joe isn't on board this time to jinx everything.*"

"True enough. All stations, report in. Everyone strapped in for full acceleration?"

The full acceleration wasn't actually the problem, as even with a million-pound thrust the *Nobel* couldn't exceed about a quarter-gee. The concern was if something went wrong. There were only five people aboard, but that was still a major portion of the skilled space personnel available to the Institute.

"Good," Bruce said after everyone had confirmed readiness. "*Nobel*, as programmed: all ahead full, twenty second burn."

When you were used to weightlessness, a quarter-gravity acceleration was actually pretty impressive, Jackie thought. *Nobel* seemed to lunge forward, the hissing rumble of the NERVA-derived engine transmitting itself through the main supports of the ship. A few seconds later, the jets cut off. In the rear-view cameras, Phobos Base was shrinking. By space standards, of course, the *Nobel* was barely moving at all; that burn had added a puny forty-nine meters per second to her orbital velocity of over two kilometers per second. Still, it had stressed the entire ship along its main axis as much as anything ever should. "Anything to report, A.J.?"

"*Minor tightening and tweaks will probably be needed later,*" the sensor specialist answered a few minutes later, after examining the data. "*I'm seeing nothing to worry about on any important components, though. I think we're go for Operation Cartwheel.*"

"Then Cartwheel it is. *Nobel*, initiate."

"Operation Cartwheel," as A.J. had whimsically termed it, was the major active structural test. Since the habitat sections were spinning, any attempt to turn *Nobel* would be fighting against the gyroscope effect, causing a lot of stress across the entire ship. *Nobel* would be using several short periods of vectored thrust from the main engine to attempt to turn in different directions while the wheel spun.

A few minutes later, A.J.'s voice reported with great satisfaction, "*Everything important's intact. Might want to shore up some of the connecting areas—I've highlighted them in the model—but unless you plan on flying like that a lot, I don't think it's necessary. Congrats, Jackie, Bruce—you've got yourself a ship!*"

Jackie let out a whoop of relief and exultation.

"*Congratulations,* Nobel. *A lovely test flight, even if you didn't get to go very far, and that tail-shaking maneuver looked kinda fun. Maybe I'll have them do it on* Nike *before we head back.*"

"It probably looks more fun than it is."

"*Yeah, probably helps if you already look like a Ferris wheel.*"

"Watch it, Captain Hathaway!"

"Sorry, sorry. Really, it's a great ship."

She gave him a chuckle. "You're right there, Ken. So, when are you heading out?"

"A couple of weeks. We're waiting for some artifacts they're shipping back, and I have to send a couple guys over to Nobel *to do the inspection."*

"Oh, come on, Ken!" A.J. grumped. *"Do they really think we're putting super-duper deathrays on this workhorse?"*

"No, not really. But the regs clearly state what you can have as armaments in any space vehicle, and that at least one of the major powers has to inspect any new space vehicle after construction to ensure it meets those regs. And since I have every intention of keeping my job, I'm going to make sure the inspection's done."

"No worries, mate. I don't have any guns, bombs, missiles, or even loose sharp sticks on this crate." Bruce said. "Come on over and we'll have dinner."

"That sounds like it could be an attempt to bribe an officer of the United States."

"Righto, I'll just offer you some vegemite."

"Ahh," said Hathaway in a tone filled with grim vindication, *"I knew it. Biological weapons hidden on board. I may have to have my inspectors confiscate any and all biological products connected to Captain Irwin."*

Jackie giggled. "Heard about Bruce's interplanetary beer stash, sir?"

"Pressurized containers. Very dangerous. Could be classed as explosives, Mr. Irwin. I'm afraid I will have to inspect some of them. In person."

Bruce gave a heavy sigh. "Yeah, that'd be right. Suppose you'd better just come over an' get it done, then. Eight tomorrow all right?"

"My inspectors and I will be ready."

Chapter 7

Helen unlocked the pressure-cooker cover. A hiss of fragrant steam billowed out as she took the cover off, filling the dining room with the warm brown scent of...

"Pot roast!" exclaimed Nicholas, leaning forward in astonishment. "With ... actual vegetables. Cooked right here. I'm utterly astounded, Helen."

"You should be," A.J. said with reflected pride in Helen's achievement. "Not only have Helen and Joe been spending off-hours time trying to figure out ways to duplicate the effects of on-Earth cooking in our habitats—which carry a lot less pressure for a lot of reasons—but also a lot of the rest of us have to put in hours getting those greenhouses to work."

"First major crops grown in Martian soil—or mostly Martian, anyway." Helen started serving. "Some of these are imports—besides the beef, I mean—but this is a special dinner. And when A.J. says 'us,' he means it. Not that his sensing and tracking talents aren't pretty much omni-useful around the colony, but the colony still needs plenty of good old-fashioned pioneering muscle. Which," she continued, giving A.J. a kiss on the cheek as she passed, "my trophy husband here happens to be willing to use even if it does make him in danger of being viewed as a real worker instead of a lab geek."

Nicholas laughed. "Helen, A.J., thank you so much for inviting me. I can't tell you how happy I am that both of *you* still seem happy."

A.J., just recovering from grinning rather fatuously at Helen, nodded. "Yeah, I guess you might have wondered how long this odd couple would last. But we've both got so much to do, and what we do . . . Well, we do it best together."

Helen sat down. "Shall we eat?"

A few moments passed in appreciative chewing. Helen could see, however, that Nicholas was also studying the Baker household. "Like the house?"

"Quite a bit, yes. From the outside it looked like almost a pair of domes under the Martian soil . . . but I had to step quite a ways down. And these walls certainly aren't rock."

"Basic structure's two hab cans buried for insulation and sealing support," A.J. supplied. "Plus we've done some extension underground. Digging's a pain, but it's really worth it—oh, and lemme say thanks again for the help there."

"And for the thousandth time, it was our pleasure," Nicholas said easily. "We knew getting settled was a major proof-of-concept priority for you, and it would help us out in the long run."

A.J. grinned. "Yeah. And survival priority, since we weren't sure we'd be able to count on any of the governments giving us a hand. Power was actually the first priority, and with things getting competitive we couldn't rely on doing things the fancy way. Yeah, Ares has got a couple small nuke reactors for the colony, and we're hooked in, but solar is much more the way to go here. LED lighting indoors, when there isn't a way to pipe in sunlight. I've spent a lot making it comfortable, and it's roomier than I thought it might be. Now that *Meru*'s cranking stuff up, we'll be a lot better off."

"Not luxury accommodations, perhaps, but I've stayed in much, much worse." Glendale surveyed the curved dining/living area. It was clearly heavily modified from the base hab can, but the underlying structure was the same. He took a bite of potato and chewed thoughtfully. "Interesting. There's a subtle difference of flavor . . . almost peppery, but not like the pepper I know you used in the roast."

Helen nodded, remembering the first hesitant tasting of the Mars crops. "Joe's positively ecstatic about that. The gourmet in him was afraid that we'd be barely able to raise stuff that's edible, and now he's finding some subtle changes in taste that he can use. Possibly, if things get to the point of routine travel in the next twenty years, we'll have a small export trade in food—not that it would counterbalance the imports."

"But we do intend to be independent, even if it takes a long time. As you well know," A.J. added.

"Yes. I am glad that Ares and the IRI were able to reach an accord."

Helen smiled. Despite the inherent friendliness between some of the principals, A.J., Glenn, Hank, and Joe had spent a lot of tense days trying to hammer out all aspects of that agreement, and she'd had to absent herself from those discussions since she herself was, naturally, an employee of the IRI. With the tiny pool of skilled people on and around Mars, it was actually more the rule than the exception for the formal, or informal, families that existed to include rather divided loyalties. This did make it awkward when there were potential conflicts of interest, and both the Institute and Ares knew they had a lot of legal landmines to negotiate around when they were trying to arrange a deal that would keep Ares mobile and independent, maintain the IRI's reasonably neutral position, and yet make it possible for both groups to get most of what they wanted.

In this case, though, the small number of people worked to their advantage. Everyone knew everyone, and respected their needs and goals. Off the record, Nicholas knew perfectly well what Ares intended to do. Off the record, Glenn and the rest of Ares knew that they had to be willing to hand over considerable control to the IRI of certain assets when conditions warranted. So when it came time to negotiate, it was mostly a matter of getting on record with hard-nosed noises of negotiation for the investors and watchdogs back home and then coming to a good gentleman's agreement and finding the most ironclad legal terms to nail it down, and thus see to it that it wouldn't be broken if one side or the other eventually ended up with less cooperative and cordial people in charge.

"How does it feel to be on Mars, Nicholas?"

"Absolutely wonderful, Helen. I cannot even begin to describe it. How very strange it is, though, that I'm here, running some kind of interplanetary research organization that has hardly anything to do with paleontology. Not a career course I could have expected."

"I'll drink to that. I'm not even sure *what* I am right now. Paleontologist, partly, but now it's more biology...with some guesses at behavior of alien species. A sociologist of the alien? Xenopaleo-archaeological-sociological-reconstruction-and-analysis specialist?"

"And interplanetary supermodel, too," A.J. inserted.

Helen poked him. "Which I suppose is the more important point to you?"

"I can't complain," A.J. answered equably. "And for our bank account it is arguably the most important point."

Nicholas nodded. "While there's obviously a certain element of crude sexism about it, Helen, I think it's still a rather positive thing. And there is not a man within, um, a hundred million miles that does not envy A.J. and Joe whenever one of yours or Madeline's advertisements appears."

"They do make us look good, I admit. And I can't say that I don't feel some pride in managing to break into a business usually reserved for those half my age." She raised her glass. "To changes!"

The two men joined her. "Changes!" they echoed, and drank.

There was a muffled thumping at the door, and then the intercom came on. "A.J.! A.J.! Hey, let me in, man!"

A.J.'s brow wrinkled in confusion. "Larry? What's the big fuss? I've got company right now. Can't it wait?" Regardless of the answer, Helen could see from the door telltales that he'd opened the outer lock and the cycle had started.

"No, really . . . Well, maybe, but I think you'd kill me if I just waited on this." The lock finished cycling, and the tall, massive frame of Larry Conley entered. He took off his helmet. "I—holy sheep, something smells great!"

"First Martian frontier pot roast," Helen said, folding out another chair. "Want to try some?"

Larry looked torn. "Hey, I wouldn't want to deprive you of the leftovers. . . ." His eyes wandered longingly to the steaming pot. "But, jeez, that looks a lot better than the package I was going to have later."

"Sit. Eat. But talk," A.J. said. "If it's that important, you can even talk with your mouth a little full."

"Mmm. Thanks, guys. Hey, Dr. Glendale, sorry to go busting in like this. But I think you'll be interested too. It's Ares business, though. I don't—"

Nicholas stood. "I perfectly understand. Even if we are going to be working together, there may be some things you don't want me to know right away." He turned to Helen with the same courtly grace he brought to almost any occasion. "Helen, my dear, why don't you show me around the other parts of the house? With the connecting doors insulated as they are, I'm sure it should be private enough."

A.J. looked at him gratefully. "Thanks, Nick. We really do appreciate the IRI's cooperation with us."

"And we the help of Ares. As I'm sure Jackie and Bruce have told you more than once."

Helen was obviously bursting with curiosity about what Larry found so important, but if the director wasn't going to eavesdrop, neither would she. Instead, she took Glendale into the second hab can, where the bedroom and home offices were, and took care to shut the door behind her.

"Okay, we're secure. Give."

To A.J.'s resigned frustration, now that everyone else was gone, Larry seemed to have lost his initial excitement over whatever it was that he'd discovered, and was much more excited by the pot roast and gravy. "Now, this is a meal. Y'know, I really ought to . . . mmm . . . learn to cook."

"Larry," A.J. said threateningly.

"You don't think I should?"

"Keep it up, *Doctor* Conley. Just remember who's in charge of your data feeds."

"Okay, okay. It's worth a little wait. You'll remember that I've been working with the IRI and our own departments in trying to match up Bemmie astronomical information with ours? Correspondences of various objects, trying to figure out orbits, all that kind of thing?"

"Yeah. Cosmological importance for you guys, I guess."

"Oh, there's all kinds of great data we're getting, and if we can get enough out of that oversized DVD and the other stuff we've found, we could learn a hell of a lot. But I was going over a bunch of data on the asteroids—finally got it separated out and decoded with our in-house programs a little while ago—and I found this."

Larry tied his personal VRD to A.J.'s with a standard signal. A.J. saw an image come up of a generally spherical object, sketchily drawn as the Bemmies often represented things. At first he didn't see what had excited Larry, but then he saw a small ripple-shaped line of Bemmius-style writing. Studying it he had a feeling he'd seen some of the symbols before. "What is it?"

"Don't recognize it? From the lecture a few months back with Jane and Rich? No?"

"Missed that one. Glanced over the notes. Anyway, get to it."

"Well, when Jane and Rich were analyzing the data on the images they could match between the Phobos records and those on the Rosetta Disc, they noticed repeated symbols on the labels for the Phobos base and for the one here. Long story short, they think—and so do I—that those symbols stand for *colony* or *base*."

"A third..." A.J. stared at the image, almost in awe. "Damn, they were busy. Um, there's an awful lot of asteroids, though. How are we going to figure out which one?"

Larry grinned. "They do show a few surface features on here. And I know it's pretty spherical, which not very many are. And I know our friends were very much into water. A quick comparison, and *voila*! Ceres, no doubt about it." An image of a dusty-gray scarred marble appeared next to the sketchy image.

"Water and *Ceres*?"

"Jesus Christ, A.J., you have so many blind spots it's amazing you can find your way to the can without some of your damn sensors to guide you. Yes, water and Ceres. We were pretty sure even thirty years ago that a really large proportion of Ceres was water ice—maybe more than all fresh water on Earth combined."

"Can you tell where on Ceres this base is supposed to be?" A.J. said, ignoring the (to him) irrelevant shot at his lack of knowledge outside of his specialty. "Compared to a planet, Ceres is puny. But after working on Phobos for months, I've gained a lot of respect for how much even puny space rocks can hide. And Ceres is far bigger than Phobos."

"If we assume the markings are accurate, yeah. So far all the Bemmie maps we've seen have matched up pretty well."

"Okay. I don't remember, but do our resident linguistic geniuses have anything to say about whether the labels discriminate between the owners of the bases? That is, can we tell if the base belonged to the Bemmie group that ran Phobos, or the one that had the base here?"

"Hmm. I dunno. Lemme check." A few minutes later Larry and A.J. were studying the still-sparse translation archives. "Yeah, though it's pretty tentative. If I'm reading this right, looks like the Ceres base belonged to the other side, the Phobos gang."

"Okay," A.J. said. "Have we got decent imagery of that side of Ceres?"

"Not tremendously good. Two probes were sent out that way, but there were a couple of accidents that screwed the chances of getting good Ceres images. We've got better pics of Vesta. Still, here's the best of what we've got."

"Good enough . . . excellent. Double excellent!"

"What's the deal?"

"Well, except for the Vault—which seems to me to be the kind of thing you'd only do once, in one location, given the extreme effort involved—the guys down here on Mars cleaned up everything on the base before they left. They obviously won the conflict, or at least didn't lose and chased off the others. They had the time to build and fill the Vault, seal it off, and do cleanup. Which would mean that their other bases in the solar system, I'd expect, will either have been smeared by the Phobos group, or they've been carefully and completely evacuated.

"But they *didn't* clean out Phobos. And that means that I'd bet that if we find a base from those guys even partly intact, like Phobos, it should have lots of goodies inside. And judging by these images"—he pointed to the critical area of Ceres—"no one nailed this base with an impactor or mega-huge bomb. So double good—the base is probably intact, and if so, it's probably not cleaned out."

"*Sweeeeeet,*" Larry said appreciatively.

"Yep. Now we have to tell Glenn and get together with Nick once we've figured out the approach." A.J. was practically bouncing in his chair with excitement. "Time to get that cooperative agreement working for *all* of us."

Madeline watched Glendale pace the Phobos Station room with slow one-third g steps. She shook her head slightly, noting that his temples looked more gray than they had just a year before, when he first arrived. He seemed unaware of her presence, which was possible, as she hadn't made much noise entering. Finally he turned. "I'm terribly sorry, Madeline. Woolgathering again."

"Woolgathering," she repeated with a soft laugh. "Director Hughes used to use that sometimes, too. Do you know, I never actually looked up where that term came from."

"Really?" Nicholas smiled, looking momentarily younger. "Then allow me to enlarge your education. In the fifteenth or sixteenth centuries, the poorer folk who owned no sheep would search the areas where the sheep belonging to others roamed. Some of the fleece would come off naturally—get snagged in briars or bushes, that sort of thing—and they would gather this wool, eventually hoping to have enough to be worth weaving or selling. As this took a lot of time and effort wandering about, the term 'wool-gathering' soon came to mean occupying oneself in wandering unproductively at apparent random—especially within one's own head."

"You are a well of knowledge, sir."

"A sink of trivia, mostly, I'm afraid." His gaze wandered back toward the black-starred window.

"You sent for me, sir?" she said quietly.

"Yes. They're off, now. I suppose . . . I want advice. Or another reassurance. Is this the right thing to do?"

Madeline knew exactly where his concern came from. "Director, whether it really *was* the right thing to do we won't know until a long time from now. But I know the reasons *you* would be sending out this mission so fast, before anyone else gets wind of it. And I agree with them."

"Should you be going along?"

Maddie took a moment to consider that. "I honestly don't know. I suppose it depends on if anyone else decides they want to play hardball, and if they can get there in time. But it's not really worth it, given that we can track anyone in the system fairly easily. Stealth technology is pretty damn tough to manage in space. I don't think it's an issue that way, sir. So offhand I don't see a good reason I should go, especially since I'd really hate to go trucking off into the outer solar system without Joe. I'll do it if I have to, of course, but it's not my preference."

"Naturally not, and I'd try never to ask that." He made a visible effort to relax. "Besides, Bruce and Larry assure me that none of the other ships in the system, except maybe *Nike*, are in any position to compete, and if they don't react immediately, *Nobel* will get there first."

She nodded. "And the real thing to worry about is the shortage of equipment downstairs."

"Ah, not for long, however." Nicholas gave her a more natural grin. "As we are to receive a deputation from our Indian allies via *Nike*, I had already arranged for some of *Nike*'s cargo space to include additional equipment. I admit I had originally intended that equipment to be used for expansion in our own interests, but it will serve just as well in this situation. What do you think the United States will do when they figure it out?"

Madeline shook her head. "They won't be happy. In fact, I'm reminding you to make it an absolute priority—once they've found the base on Ceres and gotten the essentials set up—that Helen and the others send *Nobel* back right away, unless we can arrange something else with one of the other space-capable nations. And I don't think *they* will be happy with us, either, so I wouldn't bet on getting any other arrangements. We'll need *Nobel* to do at least one supply run for us if the other countries decide to get grouchy with the Institute." She gave a predatory smile. "But, if you'll pardon me for saying so, sir, I'd just love to see their faces when they figure it all out."

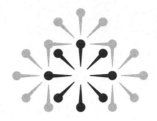

PART III:
ACCELERATION

Oberth Maneuver, n: a method of drastically changing a spacecraft's velocity by performing a rocket burn within a gravity well near perigee. The spacecraft gains or loses velocity according to the equation:

$$\Delta V_{total}{}^2 = (V_{esc} + \Delta V_{burn})^2 - V_{esc}{}^2$$

Where ΔV_{total} is the total change in velocity, V_{esc} is the escape velocity from the gravity well at perigee, and ΔV_{burn} is the change in velocity resulting directly from the rocket burn. The Oberth Maneuver can thus be used to greatly increase or decrease the velocity of a spacecraft.

Chapter 8

"I don't know about you blokes," Bruce said, a subdued tone in his voice, "but 'asteroid' don't seem to do this bastard justice."

The vast gray bulk of Ceres covered most of the forward viewing area, a titanic object that showed none of the fuzziness of living planets like Earth and Mars, but also none of the human-scale, comprehensible irregularity of Phobos. Instead, it had the cold, crater-scarred sphericity of the Moon, and with nothing else around to compare it to, seemed to be at least as large, especially in the light of the clearly-shrunken Sun, more than two hundred and fifty million miles away. Helen thought it looked less hostile than Phobos had on first approach, but a lot more lonely.

Jake Ivey, the mission archaeologist, shrugged. "It's still nothing even compared to the Moon, let alone any decent planet." This was a typically Jake comment; he had a focus on his specialty that was like A.J.'s with respect to sensors. Rumor had it that absolutely nothing impressed him unless it was in a properly labeled dig site, which Ceres obviously was not, at least not yet.

"Poor Ceres," Larry Conley said. "Always the little guy. Every debate on what should and shouldn't be a planet has always kept just on this side of letting Ceres into the club. He's a little shy of a thousand kilometers wide, so people always proposed that as the cutoff."

"Right now I wouldn't be inclined to argue with Ceres," Jackie said. "It's got an actual gravity well that we're going to feel, not like Phobos, where we could shuttle back and forth without hardly noticing the cost."

Jake brightened. "But that's *good*. Phobos had so little that you couldn't rely on anything having remained in place for you to study properly. Ceres will have kept things where they belong. Hopefully they had disposal areas, and there will be remnants of their entire range of activity."

Helen nodded. Even more in some ways than her own paleontology, archaeology relied on the forensic approach of examining objects in context; said context was hard to verify in microgravity. "Good in some ways, bad in others, Jake. As you probably know."

She glanced over at the others. "What's escape velocity from Ceres?" She knew she'd heard the answer before, but it hadn't really registered.

A.J., predictably, answered first. "About half a kilometer per second. Not much compared to Earth or Mars, but definitely not irrelevant like Phobos. Unless and until we can get things set up down there to produce us extra fuel—probably from the water, if there is any—we'll have to be very, very careful about how many trips we make."

"I could try to land 'er," Bruce said, grinning.

A.J. shuddered. "No, thanks. I know you and I set up that sim, just to see what would happen, but there's many things that could go wrong. And *did* go wrong in the sims, early on."

"Are you serious?" Larry demanded, staring across the bridge of *Nobel* at A.J. and Bruce. The bridge, unlike *Nike*'s photo-op–ready installation, was just a control room with viewscreens, safely buried in the middle of *Nobel*'s blocky central body. "You could land *Nobel* on Ceres?"

The Australian captain of *Nobel* flashed Larry a devilish grin. "Well, like A.J. says, mate, too many things could go wrong to risk it if we don't have to, but the sims show that this old girl could take the strain. She's built for accel up to a quarter-g under the right conditions, remember, and Ceresian—"

"Cererian or Cererine, if you please," the astrophysicist corrected pedantically.

"Cerelian, whatever, mate, gravity is only about a ninth of that—about one thirty-sixth Earth's. But the landing would be dicey, I admit, so I'm not quite so keen to try it as I might have sounded. Nice to know we could if we had to, though."

"I suppose," Helen agreed. The idea that the fourteen-hundred-foot ship could land and take off from the miniature planet below was, indeed, oddly comforting, despite the obvious risks in ever actually trying it. "So are we go for scouting the target area?" Helen asked.

"By remote at first, as usual," A.J. said breezily. "Once more, you will all be hanging on my every word, awaiting my blessing on your perilous enterprises."

"Hey, Mr. Ego, we're not a whole A.U. away this time," Larry pointed out. "At this distance I can do an awful lot with the sensors on *Nobel*."

"Which I designed, programmed, tested, and helped install. OW!"

The "OW" came as a result of Helen kicking A.J.'s shin. "You are getting too old to act the *enfant terrible*, A.J., and try to one-up everyone. And that wouldn't have hurt if you'd been wearing your suit."

A.J. tried to look loftily defiant and only succeeded in looking like a three-year-old being scolded. He opened his mouth to say something but reconsidered under Helen's watchful eye.

"We'll still want A.J.'s remotes to pave the way," Jackie said finally. "I'm sure we'll be able to pinpoint good target locations from up here, but the fact is that there's only a few of us, and so we're going to be pretty dependent on remotes and robots to keep things running."

"At least we've finally got a power source with a density that makes it really feasible, thanks to Bemmie and Barb Meyer, bless her stubborn heart."

"Power *carrier*, A.J., not source," Jackie corrected automatically. "But it is nice to not be worrying so much about how we can cram enough power into one of your gadgets to let it pull off its tricks, and instead spend a lot of the space on more gadget."

What A.J. and Jackie were referring to, Helen knew, was one of the first major fruits of the Bemmius explorations. The material Barbara Meyer and her colleagues had discovered—and whose attempted transmission had revealed Madeline Fathom's covert mission—had indeed turned out to be the holy grail of electrical work, a room-temperature superconductor. The existence of such a material had sent both physicists and chemists running back to their theories to try to find a way to explain the stuff; the engineers had turned instead to discovering how to manufacture it. It had taken a few years, because it appeared that the stuff's unique properties depended both on its odd composition (carbon, boron, silicon, gold, and a smattering of rare-earth elements) and its microstructure.

For energy storage, a room-temperature superconductor with high current capacity offered a near-perfect battery; in essence, one shoved electrical energy in and it stayed there, chasing its tail near the speed of light, until you took it out, with minimal losses in either direction. There were some issues with magnetic fields and so on, but after the engineering was done, the result was a battery with an energy density a couple of orders of magnitude greater than even the best chemical fuel cells or batteries. These super-batteries weren't generally available quite yet, but the Institute and Ares had managed to get a cooperative contract with the manufacturers in exchange for a small custom run. So far, Jackie had been ecstatic over the results.

The other major advance from the Phobos/Mars expeditions was in the area of nanodesign. A.J.'s conjecture about the noteplaques had turned out to be correct, and analysis of the plaques, the precise structural design of the superconductor material, and other unusual features of Bemmie design had given nanodesigners (including Dust-Storm Technology) a major leg up in that area. Helen knew A.J. had a large batch of the latest "smart dust" with him; from some of his comments, she suspected that he'd have married these sensor motes if they came with more attractive exterior construction.

A.J. was agreeing with Jackie. "Ceres is actually going to be a major pain in some ways. It's not small enough to treat as basically a weightless spinning rock, like Phobos, and it's got none of the good stuff of a planet like Earth or even Mars. I can't walk normally there, but I also can't float along without worrying about maintaining altitude." He leaned back, wiggling his fingers in that rippling motion that showed he was controlling something through his VRD. "So instead of Faeries, this time I had to make Locusts."

Having seen the squat, squarish-bodied drones with their spidery legs, Helen still thought "Toads" would have been a better name for the Cerean...no, Cererine exploration vehicles. But like any parent, A.J. had the right to name his creations. "So they'll bounce over the surface, right?"

"Sort of. That sounds like something bounding along going real fast. I really want them to use the legs mostly as altitude maintenance. They can do a pretty good jump if they have to, of course, but an even glide is more what I like to see for surveying places.

At least this time I can also scatter Faerie Dust in appropriate locations, now that we've licked the vacuum issues. And with the power storage capabilities on the Locusts, we've got more direct physical options for exploring recalcitrant alien installations."

"You mean we can bust open doors if we have to."

"Within limits, and 'bust open' sounds awfully crude. I would prefer to use more subtle means for many reasons, not the least of which being that we might break something worthwhile."

"We will most definitely be using more subtle means," Jake declared darkly. "No more of this Indiana Jones breaking and entering."

"Yeah, yeah, Jake, we know, you already got your changes logged into the procedure book. And I still might have to use force in some cases. You guys have been known to use bulldozers." A.J. was studying readouts in the thin air before him. "No immediate signs of the base. It was, I suppose, too much to hope for that there'd be a clear landing area with markings. We know the general location of the base from the Bemmie data, but on the scale of Ceres that's still a lot of territory to search."

"How much, mate? I saw your maps—looked like you'd got her fairly well locked down."

Larry gave a slight laugh. "Yeah, that little circle-cross does look pretty small. But on a thousand-kilometer sphere, we're still looking at a search area about twenty kilometers across. That's about as far across as Phobos—over three hundred square kilometers of surface."

"Well, A.J. found Bemmie's base on Phobos his first time out. Why not again?"

"If only it was so easy," A.J. said. "We were lucky as hell that time. Phobos was leaking water vapor, which of course turned out to be coming from Bemmie's combination mud bath, sauna, swimming pool, and water supply. So all I did was follow the water. I'm picking up hints of water vapor around Ceres, but it's pretty damn thin, and it looks like it's all over the place. So probably what's happening is that if there are cracks that go down far enough to reach the water ice Larry and the others think is there, they're *all* subliming into vacuum. Meaning, of course, no trail of breadcrumbs leading to the target."

"Still, that's a pretty small area to search with modern tech."

Larry, Helen, Jake, and A.J. winced. "Small? Look, Bruce, what you're trying to find is about the size of a house, probably, on the surface. But there are a *lot* of holes, canyons, valleys, crags, and so on that are in that size range. First, of course, I'm going to try to spot it from up here. I've deployed a couple of Beholders already." The Beholders, named for some many-eyed creature in one of the many games A.J. played, were compact multispectral sensor and communications satellites, allowing *Nobel* to maintain both constant radio contact and constant visual surveillance over Ceres. "But if that doesn't work out—and I'm not seeing an encouraging trend here—then it'll be down to probe search on the ground, which will be at around walking speed. I've got quite a few Locusts, but still . . . Why don't you do the math? How long will it take to search an area three hundred kilometers square for probably one entrance no more than twenty meters wide? When there's going to be a bunch of holes *just like it* all over the place that I have to poke into, maybe quite a ways, before I can tell for sure whether I've got the right one?"

Helen didn't need A.J.'s lecture, unlike some of the others. She'd done fieldwork where she might be looking for something smaller than that. She caught Jake's frown, saw that he was thinking along the same lines. Even with the almost supernatural capabilities of some of A.J.'s technology, the thought of trying to find something the size of a single T. Rex skeleton in the middle of a hundred square miles of poorly lit, pockmarked rocky badlands gave her a headache. It wasn't made easier by the fact that the Bemmies appeared to prefer to keep the entrances looking "natural"— something which, given the war they'd obviously fought, might have been done for more than aesthetic reasons. She looked down at A.J.; his face was shadowed with uncertainty. She gave his shoulder a squeeze. "You'll find it."

A.J.'s face lit up at her touch, something only visible from her angle since he was currently facing his console. She restrained a grin; there was, indeed, something childlike about the man which she found irresistible, and that quick flash of simple joy was part of it.

"Find it? Of course I'll find it," the blond sensor expert said, the momentary drop into negativism over. "I didn't say I couldn't find it, just that it's not going to be easy. Unless I get lucky. Which, since Helen's here, I just might." She gave him an affectionate poke at the mild double-entendre.

"You know, A.J., you actually discovered Phobos Base before the Faeries ever went inside," Jackie pointed out. "The internal-structure map showed a lot of the tunnels. You—and the rest of us—just would never have thought of what they really were beforehand. That's not true now, though. So why not just do the same internal mapping for Ceres?"

"Because Ceres is big. Big. Big-biiiig-big. Big—BIIIIIG!" A.J. did a Warner Brothers' set of caricature gestures showing how BIIIIIG he meant while he voiced the sentiment. "I could, with a lot of pulses and overpowered emissions and processing, manage to map out a lot of the interior of Phobos, yeah. Using all the Faeries and several hours. On a chunk of rock about one-fiftieth as far across. Even with the better power and sensor capacity I've got here, there's no *way* I'm getting a signal through Ceres." He looked momentarily abstracted. "Well, not a wireless one. If I put some sensors down and start doing impact events on the other side I could get seismographic and vibration data . . . but that'd require having a lot of spare stuff to throw, or a lot of explosives—a lot more than we have. Anyway, I'm going to do my best—GPR data and all that might help, depending on what stuff they made their installation out of here. Remember that some of their stuff was practically invisible to me, and other parts blocked everything. But we might come down to a remote foot-survey. Still, no point wasting time. I'm already on it."

A.J. turned back to his console; Helen could see him getting ready to settle in for one of his legendary marathon sessions.

"I'll bring you something for dinner later," she said, glancing at the others. They all clearly recognized the symptoms. "That good?"

"Yeah, that'd be great. Haven't done this for a while. Time to get really down to business." Thin screens rose up around his station, blocking him from view.

"Why does he stay there?" Jackie mused as they climbed to the hab ring. "I mean, he could control all that stuff from your cabin, or even one of these connecting shafts, just as easily as he could on the bridge."

"Because he's A.J. Baker, certified genius at work," Helen answered with a laugh. "No, really. Partly he does it because he finds it too easy to be distracted in more comfortable surroundings. But . . ."

Jackie smiled in understanding. "But he's also a show-off, and no one will see how hard and dedicated his work is unless he's somewhere public." Her tone was more amused than critical; Jackie liked A.J., no matter what his faults.

"You've known him as long as I have. Never thought about dating him?" Helen asked suddenly, curious.

"Date A.J.? God, no offense, Helen, I'm glad you're happy and all, but Jesus Christ, no. It'd be like dating my hyperactive little brother. Aside from being admittedly very cute, I can't understand what you see in him—romantically, that is. Joe was much more my speed, but it never really jelled."

"And once Madeline showed up, that was it."

Jackie grinned. "Oh, I wasn't possessive over him. Like I said, it never jelled. But I admit that trying to compete with Maddie would be a lost cause anyway."

"So...no one serious in your life?"

The younger woman shook her head, dark hair restrained in a tight ponytail. "Not really. Well..." She looked slightly embarrassed. "I did have a crush on Dr. Gupta for a while."

"No need to be embarrassed about that. The man has presence." Helen stepped off the central ladder and made room for Jackie. "I admit to having had some rather nonprofessional thoughts about my mentor, too, from time to time."

"Dr. Glendale? Can't fault your taste *there*, even if you seem to have gone downhill since." Helen snorted. "But..." Jackie looked pensive.

"What?"

"Oh, I don't know. I suppose I'm still looking for that perfect guy, as silly as it sounds." She looked dubious.

Helen tried not to look dubious herself. "I'm sure there's just such a guy out there, waiting for you."

"Well, he'd better not wait too long," Jackie said emphatically. "Or I'll end up marrying this ship, and *Nobel* just never *talks* to me."

Chapter 9

"You found something, A.J.?" Bruce asked, floating quickly up. "Bloody hell, mate, you look awful."

"Huh? Oh, just a little tired, I guess." The blond sensor expert's eyes had dark circles, visible even behind the VRD glasses, and he spoke with the heavy tones of someone almost asleep on his feet. "Found something, yeah. Larry made the suggestion, after I hadn't found anything in the past couple of days, to look for really deep straight holes."

"You haven't been up for five days straight, have you?"

"No, no, I slept a full eight hours last night."

"The hell you did," Helen said, concern in her voice. "A.J., it's Tuesday evening."

"Uh? Oh." A.J. gave a jaw-cracking yawn. "Um, yeah, that'd mean I slept, umm, two and a half days ago. No problem..." He turned back to the console. "Anyway, Larry gets credit. I was wrong. They did get creamed, just not with a big rock. Something hit hard with a lot of smaller things, made holes that looked"—he yawned again—"um, looked like a lot of the other craters, so it didn't stand out. Punched straight down. Found 'em because they were all in a pretty close group, and so they made parallel holes right around the target area."

"And can you show us where that is, exactly?"

"Oh, yeah, stupid of me...right here." The larger image of Ceres on the main screen suddenly ballooned upward as though *Nobel* were plummeting straight toward the surface of the miniature planet, then halted. A pattern of little circles in bright green suddenly appeared in the center of the screen, with a brilliant red X to the left and below the middle of the pattern. "X marks the spot I think you'd best land at. . . . Looks to have slightly higher, um . . . what the hell is it, I can't think . . . Oh, higher water readings."

He's practically dead on his feet, Jackie thought, and moved forward. "That's it, A.J., you're going to bed. Jesus, you're going to make yourself sick. You're not twenty anymore. In fact, you've seen the other side of thirty already."

"Not thirty, refuse to believe it." Helen helped A.J., still mumbling in a disjointed way, out of the control room, while the others watched.

"Right," said Bruce as the doors closed. "Time to plan the landing."

Jackie nodded. The reason that they hadn't landed anyone on Ceres yet was simple: they wanted there to be absolutely no chance of any creative interpretation of the Buckley Addendum that would remove the Cererian Bemmie base from the control of the joint IRI-Ares mission. Unless the Addendum was interpreted very broadly, they wouldn't be awarded the leasehold on the entire miniature planet, any more than Ares had gotten all, or even a majority, of Mars.

The Addendum and its current interpretation, of course, was very clear: the claim would be based on the location of the first *person* to "set foot"—i.e., land and leave the landing vehicle—on the object in question. Thus, they had to wait until they could determine exactly where the Bemmie base was, and land *directly* above it. If another ship, like *Nike*, *Amaterasu*, or *Odin* had gotten close, the crew of *Nobel* might have had to just go for it anyway. But now, fortunately, it wouldn't be necessary.

"A.J. won't be available for a while, obviously," Bruce said. "Still, I don't see it should be a problem. I'll be flyin', of course, so me, you, Larry, Jane, and Jake are doing the landing."

"You sure you want to send both the top pilot and chief engineer down?" Jackie asked, startled. She'd already resigned herself to waiting until later.

"Sure am, luv. Let's face it, this old wheel of tuna cans and duct tape is doing just fine, and if they have to coast home without us, well, that doesn't take fancy flying, and they're none of them stupid, so if they have to fix something they'll figure it out. Landing *Feynman* on a new rockball, that's not quite so simple. And A.J., Helen, and Rich all got their chance to land on a brand-new world, so I think they can wait for trip two."

She hadn't realized how much she'd wanted to be "in" on that first landing until she found she was giving Bruce an emphatic hug. "*Thank* you, Bruce!" She kissed him on the cheek.

"Hold on with that stuff, mate—Tammy might not approve," Bruce said, grinning. "Not that I mind, mind."

"How does she put up with it?"

"Knowing me, wouldn't you wonder how she'd put up with me if I was there all the time?" Bruce answered lightly.

"No, really. How can you both stay married and so far apart?"

Bruce grimaced, seeing she was serious. "It's been a fair dinkum problem, or was. See, she knew I was a pilot and I'd be going off for weeks at a time, but months—that was pushin' it. Speakin' honestly, we damn near didn't stay married. But Tammy, she's the practical sort, too. My pay's good, an' being out here I don't spend much of it, and little Stevie loves seein' her daddy on TV. Very proud of me, she is." Jackie could hear the affection in his voice, the rough edge that was like a tiny hint of tears. "Stevie was sorta an accident, but the best kind."

"Still... how? I mean, I know you send them long letters, video, things like that, but..."

"Oh, no doubt it's tough. But that's why we've made the decision that it ain't going to be that way anymore—thanks to Nick."

This was something new. "Director Glendale?"

"Yeah. You remember he called me aside a little before we left? We had a long talk. Well, actually, he did a lot of talking, and I did a lot of listening. If the IRI were a regular military or government agency, things'd be different. But Nick basically told me that there was a better way to do things. He's authorized it all. Tammy and Stevie are coming to stay."

"*Here?* You mean, on board *Nobel*?" Jackie demanded incredulously.

"Well, not right this minute. But yeah, after we get back to Phobos Station, from then on they stay with me when they want to. And if I'm taking a long trip, like something to the outer part of the system might need, they get to come with me."

Jackie knew her face reflected her astonishment. It wasn't the idea that Nicholas Glendale might have thought that far ahead for the welfare of his most important employees; that was characteristic of the charismatic and razor-sharp former paleontologist. The real issue was expense. On Earth, it was much easier to give the family of critical employees appropriate living quarters; but in space, where every ton of food, water, or air cost someone *something*... and that issue was ten times more important on an interplanetary ship. And there were other problems, too.

"Bruce, you know that at least some people can't take weight-lessness at all, even for short periods."

"Right, which is why ol' Nicky didn't even call me over until the family'd passed preliminaries. Tammy kept the whole thing a secret from me, too. Coulda knocked me over with a feather when I found out. Tammy wasn't too keen on it to start, but after these years seein' each other for a couple weeks at a time, and knowing how there just ain't going to be *any* jobs like this any-where, ever again, she changed her mind. Because, funny thing, I still love her—more'n I did when I married her, strewth!—and hard as it is to believe, she loves me."

"Not hard at all." Jackie said, smiling wistfully. "She's a lucky girl."

"I'm the lucky one." He saw her half-sad smile. "Don't you fret, Jackie. There's plenty of guys out there for you."

"Yeah," she said, turning to the console to start making up the manifest for the landing. "That's the problem. They're out *there*, while I'm out *here*."

"...and that is why, Director Glendale, I want to assure you that the European Union is not only going to back Ares' claim along with you, but also, as *Odin* is now fully operational and tested, we would be happy to assist you in maintaining supply lines for both the Martian and Ceres operations." After he completed the sentence, Vice-President Bitteschell studied the impeccably dressed yet exhausted-looking figure across from him carefully.

Bitteschell was one of the twenty-seven commissioners who made up the European Union's executive body, the European Commission. In addition to his largely formal post as one of the vice-presidents of the Commission, Bitteschell also held the portfolio of Commis-sioner for Enterprise and Industry. Since the European Space Agency had been absorbed by the E.U. some years earlier, that made him the effective head of Europe's space program.

He could see Glendale's face relax slightly as he gave his famously brilliant smile. "Commissioner, I won't conceal from you that this is a considerable relief. The current American administration is... somewhat less happy with the situation."

How very unsurprising, he thought to himself. Aloud, he said "I would be less than honest, Director, if I were to say that everyone in the Union is precisely *happy.* Naturally there is some jealousy. But if we were to push in a manner that might limit your rights, we simply make it less likely that we could benefit from any discoveries we might make in the future. And there are few enough vessels in space that I believe that we should all be helping one another. In return, I would hope that we might be able to arrange some cooperation in the dissemination of research results?"

Glendale's nod and smile were slightly... off. Too heavy, Bitteschell decided. The director had spent most of his time in the past year in one-third gravity. He'd clearly kept up on his exercise, but still there was a major difference between spending an hour or three in a centrifuge each day or two, and spending days in a gravity field three times greater than you'd become accustomed to. "I am sure something can be arranged. Certainly we would like to encourage cooperation rather than competition at this stage."

"Excellent. If you like, *Odin* can begin by transferring a full load of supplies from Earth to Moon orbit, where *Nobel* is allowed to approach. We can then take another load in *Odin,* assuring that instead of falling behind, you will be somewhat ahead of your support schedule."

"We would like that very much indeed, Commissioner. I am sure that Ares, as well as the Institute, would be very grateful for this." The gratification on Glendale's face was clear. Unsurprising, in that one of the major distinguishing facts of *Odin* was that the E.U. vessel was nearly twice the size of *Nike* in terms of cargo capacity. While there had been considerable debate as to the wisdom of modifying the design that extensively, in this case there was no doubt of the advantages.

"Then consider it done." He shook hands with Glendale, who had risen from his chair with some momentary difficulty. "I can see you are tired, Director. The rest of the arrangements can be done at a later time. I mostly wished to assure you that not all of us are either shortsighted or petty."

"In that case, I thank you again, Commissioner. I admit that my homeworld's gravity appears considerably heavier now than I used to find it." The difficulty was evident in Glendale's almost cautious walk out the door.

After a few minutes, Bitteschell said, "Send in the general." His desk pinged, acknowledging the command and that the appropriate individual had been alerted.

The door opened a short while later, admitting General Hohenheim. The general was an imposing figure, tall and square-shouldered, with a neatly trimmed blond beard and blond hair that seemed to always be just *this* side of being too long for regulations. However, he was also well-known for getting results, even under the most difficult circumstances, which made his tonsorial preferences irrelevant. Bitteschell nodded and gestured for Hohenheim to sit down. "General, thank you for waiting. I had to be sure that everything would work out as we expected."

"Then...?"

"The Institute will be more than glad of our assistance. This will give us significant access to their information. I want that access maximized for our benefit. We need to get our own source of extraterrestrial knowledge, and this appears to be by far the best opportunity we have."

"Can you explain that, sir?" the general asked. "I have my own ideas on the subject, of course, but why can we not proceed independently, as America, China, and Japan are doing?"

The commissioner gave a very undignified snort. "America, independently? Despite their very shortsighted fits of pique, the American government is in a much better position. It is beyond belief that none of the former governmental personnel now working with the IRI and Ares would be passing at least some information back to their government. Moreover, as America had a stranglehold on the last mission, the major profits from it are clearly already going to American companies. Look at Tayler, Ares, and, of course, the Maelstrom Power Systems startup that is exploiting the super-conductor technology. As far as China and Japan"—he grimaced—"China is undoubtedly looking for similar opportunities, as is Japan, but the Japanese have already started building to construct a colony in orbit. They've also contracted with India for materials shipments now that *Meru* actually is completed. The Japanese plan appears to be to offer space residency and tourism, and comfortable research-and-development locations near microgravity facilities.

"So. The Americans are currently doing well by secondary means, the fact that the majority of the important individuals involved are American helping to compensate for the fact that America itself doesn't control the alien installations. India has chosen to attempt to become the heavy-shipping focus of this new space age, and from all indications this project will succeed. Japan has its own niche that would be difficult to compete with. Only we and China have no clear 'direction,' so to speak. We are really in competition only with China in this matter, and—fortunately for us—they are still having problems with their own interplanetary vessel."

Hohenheim nodded. "Understood. What of the IRI and Ares?"

"The IRI and Ares have forged an alliance of convenience and necessity which, unfortunately for us, appears to be founded actually on direct personal understandings as well as business sense. This means that I do not foresee a likelihood that we might be able to separate the two." Bitteschell frowned. "In addition, I am reasonably certain that, barring sheer good fortune, no one will discover additional alien artifact sources without their assistance."

"Why is that, sir?"

The commissioner gave a slight laugh. "There is an old expression, General, which I'm sure you're familiar with. 'Once is happenstance, twice coincidence, but three times is enemy action.' The people currently working with Ares and the IRI discovered the alien base on Phobos. They then discovered the alien base on Mars. And they have now, apparently, located another on Ceres, an asteroid hundreds of millions of miles away. Despite the IRI's status as a supposedly independent and disinterested organization, they have had to arrange various business interests to ensure that they are not dependent on the whims of the American—or any other—government. This would seem to have included making arrangements that permit cooperative research and discovery with Ares. This was undoubtedly a result of Ares' own strategies, and cleverly done. The simple fact is this, General—all the new discoveries on the aliens are being done by members of those two groups, who are mostly friends, and who undoubtedly are doing their best to ensure that both organizations benefit first from their discoveries. Not illegally so, though possibly skirting the edge of the law in places, but still more than enough to make it virtually certain that any new alien finds will only be made through them."

The general nodded. "I agree. So, to summarize, sir, you want us to cooperate with them so as to get access to their data and find another alien installation—'get the jump on them,' as they might say it—which we will then proceed directly to and claim for the E.U.?"

"Precisely. Undoubtedly they will be expecting something of the sort. I want you to select the right crew—engineers, scientists, and security—to ensure that anything they do, we can counter, all while maintaining civil relations."

"If we take their information—especially on the location of some other installation—and use it to beat them to the site, civility may not be possible."

The commissioner shrugged. "At that point, civility is not the issue. It would of course be nice if everyone could remain happy, but I am sure that harsh words will be said. Once you have a clear target, however, you may disregard the need for civility, as long as the indications are clear that the target will be a *valuable* one. We do not want a crater with a few traces of old ruins, as I am sure you understand."

"I understand perfectly, Commissioner. I also understand that I did not hear such instructions from you."

Bitteschell grinned. "Always a pleasure to work with such thoughtful men as yourself, General Hohenheim. As you are commanding *Odin*, everything you need is easily authorized under that budget."

The big man rubbed his beard thoughtfully. "Given the nature of this mission, I hope that we might be able to authorize additional, hmm, research equipment?"

"Oh, undoubtedly. Our scientists and engineers should not be completely dependent upon our prospective partners. I would recommend you allocate significant cargo to whatever additional equipment you, or your selected personnel, think might be helpful. I will authorize all reasonable expenditures."

"Then," General Hohenheim said, standing, "I will begin at once. If we are to leave for Mars soon, I have little time to waste."

They shook hands. "Good luck, General."

After Hohenheim left, Bitteschell resumed his seat behind the desk and stared out the window at the city vista beyond.

Which was that of Brussels, unfortunately. While the capital of the E.U. was an interesting city from a professional standpoint—even an exciting one, at times—there was no denying it lacked much in the way of scenic splendor. That was especially true for someone like Helmut Bitteschell, who'd been born and raised in the very picturesque Bavarian town of Bamberg.

But the commissioner had never regretted his decision. He

hadn't come to Brussels many years ago for the scenery, after all. He was today one of the most powerful and influential figures in the European Union; which, if it still lacked the political cohesion of the United States and had only a small portion of its military power, had a larger population, the largest gross domestic product in the world, and a currency which rivaled the dollar and occasionally surpassed it.

Good luck.

Bitteschell had no great faith in luck, actually. But he was a strong adherent to the old saw that one creates one's own luck, with the proper preparations.

Should he employ Fitzgerald or not on this expedition? True, there were potential risks. Judging from the extensive files that the commissioner had studied, Fitzgerald was prone to... Well, not recklessness, exactly. That would be too strong a term. But there was no question that the mercenary from Belfast tended to take an expansive attitude toward his instructions.

On the other hand, that might very well be what was needed. There would be no way to micromanage—even to manage at all, really—an expedition such as this one, from such a great distance. And Hohenheim's weakness was the opposite. The man was undoubtedly capable, but prone to...

Well, not timidity, precisely. That would be a rather silly term to use with regard to one of the most experienced and accomplished members of Europe's Astronaut Corps. Still, in Bitteschell's opinion, Hohenheim was not the man to place in charge of *Odin*. He'd have preferred Joachim Blücher, or even the Frenchman Duvalier.

However, there was no point in fretting over the matter. Hohenheim was popular with the public—always a major concern when dealing with an expensive project—had strong support in the German government, and unlike Blücher had not aggravated the French and the Italians. Even the British thought well of him.

Bitteschell's decision, in the end, came down to the need to keep Europe's powerful industrial corporations satisfied. That was always a major political concern also. One of those corporations, the European Space Development Company, had strongly recommended Fitzgerald. The ESDC was centrally involved in Europe's space program, one of its few truly critical players, and their recommendation had come with the support of several other important corporations as well.

He pressed the button which communicated with his personal assistant. "Francesca, please get in touch with Richard Fitzgerald and ask him to come for an interview tomorrow."

Best to err on the side of caution. Bitteschell didn't think the risks were that great, anyway.

Chapter 10

"What is *that, Helen?"* A.J.'s disembodied voice asked over the suit radio.

"I'm not quite sure," she answered, staring at the objects in front of them.

Ceres Base was big—probably as large as Phobos Base—and undoubtedly they'd be finding new weird stuff in both of them for years. A.J.'s Locusts were demonstrating the advantages of a few years of design improvements plus Maelstrom's superconducting batteries, gaining them access to the interior of the base and opening even severely stuck doors with levering components similar to the old "Jaws of Life" design; even so, it would be a long time before all of the base was mapped.

There had been signs that parts of this base had been evacuated in a more orderly fashion than Phobos, which appeared to have been "evacuated" mostly in the sense of "suddenly exposed to vacuum." While the areas where the house-sized holes had been punched through had clearly lost their atmosphere instantly, other areas had apparently maintained pressure. But Ceres Base hadn't been cleaned out, like the Mars Base. It appeared that the conjectures were correct: whoever ran the Mars installation had won, and their opponents kicked out with barely the clothes on their backs or whatever they could drag out in a few minutes. Why the winners hadn't felt it worthwhile to rebuild or loot these bases, however, remained a mystery.

The tubes in front of Helen were another mystery. They were behind walls of glass, or a glassy substance, which had gone rather milkily translucent over the years; the tubes seemed to be made of the same stuff, so that all they could make out were tantalizing hints of shapes inside the tubes. Helen shivered as she suddenly remembered an old sci-fi movie with similar tubes.

A.J. apparently thought the same way. *"If anything down there looks like an egg, I'm sending a Locust in to stomp it."*

"Shut up, A.J.," Helen said, repeating one of the constant phrases of the universe. She turned slowly in place, surveying the whole huge room. "See all that? This is a major control center, or something. There must be a dozen of those computer stations with the ramps that we found in Phobos control. And a bunch of noteplaques."

"It's a lab," Larry said firmly. "Chem or bio, maybe. Bio, if those fuzzy shapes in the tubes were living. Can we get a better look at them?"

"One thing at a time." A.J. said. He was sitting comfortably in *Nobel*, watching through telemetry, as he had another task to help with. *"Bruce and Jackie are coming up on the reactor placement. Helen, Jake, Larry, you guys keep looking around, but follow protocols, okay? I have to pay attention to this."*

"Understood, A.J.," she said. The idea of Bruce and Jackie having an accident at this point wasn't a pleasant one. The nuclear reactor, a twenty-megawatt design, massed seventy tons and was derived from a combination of nuclear technologies, including the "town-sized" reactors manufactured by Toshiba in the early part of the century, and the thorium breeder design used in the *Nike*-style reactors. It would provide power for almost thirty years before needing a core replacement, and the core itself could be sent back for reprocessing to recover fuel and cleanse the reactor of waste products. Ares and the IRI had a total of five of these reactors on Mars, one on Phobos Station, and one in Phobos Base. They were as safe and reliable as any such design could be, but anything could be broken by accident... and this was to be their main power source for Ceres Base.

She continued to cautiously circle the oval room with its curved window—containment area, perhaps? Larry was carefully imaging the noteplaques as they lay before attempting to move them aside, very gently, so as to look at the ones underneath. Like those on Phobos, the plaques were locked in whatever their last display state was, and were probably very vulnerable to impact—as Joe had demonstrated once. The fact that A.J. had been able—just barely—to recover the apparently lost data from some of the incidental imaging scans had led to the current requirement to thoroughly image all finds before even attempting to move them. There'd been a general requirement like that in the original expedition notes, but there'd been some fuzziness as to what constituted proper imaging.

Now there was no such debate, especially after Jake Ivey got through lambasting the prior expeditions for their criminal sloppiness. Jake had grudgingly agreed to certain shortcuts when compared to normal Earth fieldwork, acknowledging that even with modern gear there were a lot of constraints on safely exploring an airless rockball with an average temperature of –106° C.

"Lowering... Support and locking plate is holding well. Keep her centered, Bruce.... Jackie, keep an eye on line 3...." She heard A.J.'s instructions dimly in the background.

"Hey, Helen, take a look at this one." Larry flashed an image of one of the plaques before her. "Is that Bemmie?"

She studied the semi-streamlined, tri-armed creature. "No... no, definitely not. That looks like one of the creatures they'd left as a model in the Vault, the section clearly showing their homeworld's native species." She activated her data retrieval. "Hmm... Yes, here it is. We named it *Bemmius symmetrius minor*, the small symmetrical alien creature. See how it's rounder in cross section and more symmetrical than Bemmie? And it's about the size of a housecat."

Scientific naming conventions for the species of another world was a subject that was going to be hotly debated eventually, she suspected. Right now they were using *Bemmius* as an overarching tag meaning *alien creature from Bemmie's home ecology*, but if they managed to learn enough about the taxonomy of the creatures, they'd probably have to develop a much more detailed and discriminatory nomenclature. For now, though, the only agreed-upon change made to any of the names was to the original: no longer merely *Bemmius secordii*, he was now *Bemmius secordii sapiens*.

"Yeah, now that you mention it, I can see that. Did Bemmie actually have that third eye?"

"In a somewhat degenerate form. It's there, but much less developed than the other two."

"In the hole now.... Going smoothly... Okay, Bruce, detach. We have impact... well within tolerances... Triggered the locking clasps,

all on cue.... Lockdown. Jackie, if you want to go and start her up, I think we're good to go. Start laying your cable, and pretty soon we'll be in business." She heard A.J. give a sigh of relief. *"Okay, I'm back. What do you need?"*

"The tubes?"

"Right. Let me see.... Oh, screw them! It's some of that damn composite stuff that eats a lot of the wavelengths I scan on. I'll have to make do with enhancing the visible. Hey, can you find a way into that glassed-off area?"

"I'll take a look." There were two other doors leading out of the room, one of which seemed to be closer to the side of the sealed location. She pointed the Locusts in that direction; a few minutes later, the door ground slowly open. "Yes, I think this goes around the side."

She bounced with dreamlike slowness down the corridor, her suit's lights reflecting a rippled gold and gray pattern from the walls. The corridor ended in a rounded door with a familiar long bar arrangement in the center. "Pressure or seal door. I think this *is* a containment facility."

Having already made his little joke earlier, A.J. managed to resist making a similar remark now. Clearly he was getting older and more responsible. Possibly, she mused, he'd reached high-school–level maturity by now.

"Well, after sixty-plus million years of vacuum, plus your being in a suit capable of withstanding small-arms fire, I don't think we need to worry about whatever they were containing. Nothing showing on the sensors I've got around you, Helen."

"Okay. Try the door?"

"You can try, but I think you'll be waiting for the Locusts. Readings show it's vacuum-cemented at points around the door seal."

"How long, A.J.?"

"Hard to say. I'll give it a quick try, but I think I may have to make several attempts to commit a Lara Croft on this one." She heard a growl of protest from Jake.

"That bad?"

She could see A.J. grimace in the miniature screen. "Yeah. Remember how well these buggers built, and with what. I don't think I'm going to *quite* have to call up Maddie for advice on demolitions—this isn't as bad as the first Vault door, but it's close."

"Then I won't just hang around."

"If you want to help out," Jackie's voice broke in, *"you and Larry can come join me and start laying down cable. The reactor's powering up beautifully. The more of us who get cracking on this, the sooner we'll be able to set up our real Ceres headquarters!"*

"On our way, Jackie," Larry said as Helen emerged from the tunnel. "Jake, you're staying?"

"Well, first of all she didn't invite me, and second, there's plenty for me to sort through here without the amateur bulls in the china shop around." Jake's tone wasn't as hostile as the words could have sounded. "I'll keep my lines open and keep an eye on the Locusts when they arrive. I might as well supervise the vandalism if I can't prevent it."

"Sounds like a good idea to me," A.J. said cheerfully. *"I'll start loading* Feynman *with the first set of base supplies, including the fuel maker. That'll be a serious load off of Bruce's mind."*

"You got that right, mate. Once we're makin' our own fuel, I'll be a lot happier."

"And we'll have a lot wider options. I'm on it. With any luck, I'll be seeing you guys down there soon!"

She cut in a private circuit. "Looking forward to it," she said, and winked.

Chapter 11

"Please have a seat, Mr. Fitzgerald," said Goswin Osterhoudt. The chief operations officer of the European Space Development Company motioned toward a chair positioned near one corner of his huge desk.

Osterhoudt did not do Fitzgerald the courtesy of rising to greet him. But Richard managed to contain his dismay. Actually, he had to struggle a bit to keep from smiling. People like Osterhoudt were so predictable.

Two other people were already seated in the office, in chairs positioned near the opposite corner of the COO's desk. One of them was a paunchy middle-aged man with hair that was almost pure white; the other was a somewhat younger woman with dark hair, dark eyes, and a narrow face. Both of them were wearing business suits, as was Osterhoudt. The man's suit was expensive; the woman's more expensive still.

Neither of the suits was as expensive as Osterhoudt's. And where Osterhoudt had taken off his jacket and loosened his tie, neither of his subordinates had done the same. It was all delightfully predictable.

"Florian Lejeune, Chiara Maffucci," said Osterhoudt by way of introduction.

Maffucci nodded, her face expressionless. Lejeune half rose to his feet and extended his hand. "Pleased to meet you," he said.

Richard shook his hand and took his own seat. Both Osterhoudt and Lejeune had spoken in French, so Fitzgerald presumed that would be the language for the occasion. That was a bit of a relief. His French was excellent. His German was almost as good, but when he and Osterhoudt met privately the COO insisted on speaking in Dutch, a language with which Richard was only passably familiar.

Osterhoudt's accent was pronounced whenever he spoke in a foreign language, but his French and German were quite understandable. In English, he was almost incomprehensible.

Lejeune's French had been smooth and fluent, as with a native speaker, but with a trace of an accent. Between the accent and the given name, Richard assumed he was Belgian.

"Very well, Mr. Fitzgerald," Osterhoudt said. He nodded toward his two associates. "I've given them a summary of what I propose to make your assignment, and they have a few questions they'd like to ask."

There'd been a slight emphasis on the word "few." Richard suspected that neither of Osterhoudt's underlings was happy with the situation—but Osterhoudt was making clear that he'd made up his mind already.

Richard gazed at Maffucci and Lejeune, his expression as bland as he could make it. Which was surprisingly bland, in fact—he'd practiced in front of a mirror—given that Fitzgerald's face was composed of harsh planes and angles and decorated with three scars, one of them quite visible.

Lejeune cleared his throat. "Mr. Fitzgerald, I'm puzzled as to the reason you're requesting so many people for this assignment. Nine people besides yourself, given that the entire company of the *Odin* isn't much more than a hundred people, seems an exceedingly large security force."

Richard was tempted to point out that in his negotiations with Osterhoudt, he hadn't "requested" a team of ten people. He'd insisted on it. In fact, he'd made approval of that number a critical item in the dickering.

But there was no reason to rub a flunkey's face in his own status. So, politely, he replied: "Yes, I realize that the number must seem unnecessary—and, if this assignment were anywhere on *this* planet, I wouldn't have asked for more than five or six. But we're to be engaged on an interplanetary mission, Mr. Lejeune. Furthermore, we have no clear idea how long the assignment might last. It could go on for years before we return."

"Oh, nonsense!" snapped Maffucci. "Months, certainly. One or two years, perhaps."

Richard transferred the bland gaze to her. "Or three years, Ms. Maffucci. Or four years. The truth is that we have no idea how long we'll be gone. If we turn up evidence of another Bemmie base somewhere in the asteroids or the outer solar system, we could be gone for a very long time indeed."

"The projections—"

"*Projections,*" Osterhoudt interrupted, "are even more apt to go astray once you leave the Earth's atmosphere than they are on the planet itself. And they're quite apt to go astray here. Leave this be, Chiara. Fitzgerald is just being realistic."

"And given that the length of the mission might become very protracted," Richard continued smoothly, "I need a large enough security force to handle attrition. I won't be surprised at all if one or two—possibly even three or four—of my people become incapacitated at one point or another. Possibly permanently. I have to make allowance for that."

"I can understand the need for some redundancy," said Lejeune. "But this still seems excessive. Let's assume that you lose as many as four of your people. That leaves you with a security force of six people, including yourself. For a ship with a crew of not more than a hundred people, Mr. Fitzgerald? All of whom are either experienced and thoroughly vetted astronauts or prominent and almost-as-thoroughly vetted scientists. I'd think yourself and one other person would suffice." He smiled, almost sweetly. "I realize you do need to sleep on occasion."

Richard wondered why Lejeune and Maffucci were pressing this issue. He would've expected their questioning to focus on some of the details of the mission itself, given that many of those details were stated in exceedingly fuzzy language in the contract.

They were probably just covering their asses, he decided. If they pressed him on the operational specifics of his assignment, they'd risk getting too close to knowledge that might someday—if things went badly—wind up being embarrassing. Embarrassing, at best. At worst, such knowledge could potentially even lead to prison sentences. That was very unlikely, of course. Still, it wasn't impossible.

By making a fuss over the crude issue of the size of his security force, on the other hand, they avoided that problem—while still, if it ever proved necessary, being able to claim they had raised objections and reservations from the beginning.

It was all *so* predictable. The only somewhat puzzling thing was the reason Osterhoudt was letting them go on as long as they were. Richard suspected that was because neither Lejeune nor Maffucci was entirely under the COO's authority. Though officially his subordinates, they probably had other patrons in the hierarchy of the huge corporation—or its board of directors, more likely—and were acting on their behalf here. As much as Osterhoudt might like to squelch them, he simply couldn't.

On the other hand—as he made clear that very moment—the COO didn't have to tolerate them for very long, either.

"I think that's enough, Florian. Mr. Fitzgerald has explained his reasons for wanting a ten-person security force, and they seem quite sensible to me. So let's move on. Do you have any other issues to raise?"

Lejeune hesitated, and then shook his head. Osterhoudt turned to Maffucci. "Chiara?"

The woman was made of sterner stuff. She proceeded to waste Richard's time with pettifogging quibbling over some of the equipment he proposed to take aboard the *Odin.* It was all quite pointless, since nothing on Richard's list came close to violating the prohibitions in the Mars Treaty concerning weaponry in space.

True, combined with some of the equipment already on board or soon to be loaded on to *Odin,* and certain . . . enhancements that had been carefully introduced into the ship's design, the stuff being brought by Richard and his team would allow them to construct several quite effective types of weapons. But that sort of arcane military use of seemingly innocuous equipment was very specialized knowledge. Richard was confident he could smuggle the stuff on to the ship without alerting even the U.N.'s professional inspectors. There was no chance that either Maffucci or Lejeune would be able to spot the potential violations of the Treaty. In fact, Richard was pretty sure he could assemble a complete weapon system right in front of them and they wouldn't realize what it was unless it was put into operation.

Which was quite unlikely also, of course. Richard did not expect to have to actually use any of those military options. He simply wanted them available, just in case. Careful planning for all contingencies, he had found, was the key to success in his line of work.

Finally, they were done. Maffucci and Lejeune rose and left the room. The Belgian nodded politely on the way out. The woman didn't.

"My apologies for putting you through that silliness, Richard," Osterhoudt said. He waved his hand. "Corporate politics, you understand."

The chief operations officer leaned forward on his desk. "I stress that nothing has changed in the basic parameters of your mission. Whatever nervousness may exist on the part of some of the company's directors, everyone who really matters is entirely behind this project. We *must* get our hands on at least one major alien installation. Exclusively in our hands, that is. That is absolutely imperative. The benefits of this new Bemmie technology are literally incalculable. There's been enough of this 'sharing' that we've had to tolerate because of the unique position enjoyed thus far by Ares and the IRI. Now it comes to an end."

Richard smiled and said nothing. The smile was mostly to cover what would otherwise have been a derisive jeer. It was typical of people like Osterhoudt to toss around expressions like "Now it comes to an end."

Really? When the shortest transit time to Mars would take months and there was absolutely no way of knowing when, where, and how the *Odin* and its crew might discover the whereabouts of another Bemmie base? Assuming one existed at all, beyond those already known. That was quite likely, but it was hardly an established fact.

Ah, well. People like Osterhoudt also paid extremely well. Which was all that really mattered, when you came down to it.

General Hohenheim found himself shaking his head slowly in disbelief. "I knew it was going to be big, but..."

"The largest mobile object ever built by mankind, General Hohenheim," Francesca Castillo said proudly, "though not, of course, the most massive." She gestured toward the nearly completed E.U. vessel *Odin*. "She masses as much as a modern missile cruiser."

Hohenheim shook his head again. *Ten thousand tons.* It would have been impossible to move that much mass into orbit only a year or two ago. Fortunately, the EU had been quick to invest in India's *Meru* project once it became clear that they were going to succeed in becoming the source of mass transport to orbit using the space-elevator approach.

Odin loomed before the transfer vehicle, ever larger, surrounded by what seemed to be delicate spiderwebs but which were massive cables providing anchors, support, power, and access for workers and automated assembly vehicles. It looked, in some ways, similar to the United States' *Nike*, a generally cylindrical central body with a large hab ring set outward from the body near the center, to provide a substitute for gravity when spinning.

Sweeping back from *Odin*'s rear, however, were four great arching tendrils, delicate compared to the more massive main body but extending an almost incredible distance. They were surrounded at intervals by circular bands that bound together and supported the slender ribs of composites, until at the far end was a circle a full kilometer across. The entire vessel, from the point of the bow to the end of that wireworklike cone, was nearly four kilometers in length.

She is, of course, mostly empty space—cargo, fuel, consumables. Still...!

"That structure is the mass-beam drive," he said, pointing to the kilometers-long tendrils and their accompanying circular bands. "I notice, however, that especially along the base there are additional pieces that I don't recall from my briefings."

Castillo, the chief engineer directing the assembly of *Odin*, pushed a strand of graying black hair into the hairnet she wore while in microgravity. "Additional...oh, yes, I see." She studied the symmetrical long blades, like fins, that stretched for a considerable distance along the mass-driver support ribs. "Heat sinks and radiators, General. The *Odin*'s reactor generates an immense amount of heat, and for some maneuvers may need to even store some of it and dissipate it even more quickly. As there is no water or air in space to help by evaporating or carrying away heat by convection, radiation is really the only option. It is of course possible to dump heat extremely quickly in an emergency by sacrificing water or, if you had it, another fluid, boiling it off and throwing it away. But such an approach would waste a huge amount of such resources, something you could likely ill-afford where *Odin* will eventually go."

Hohenheim nodded. "Yes. The outer planets, not the inner ones." Jupiter was uppermost in his thoughts there. The huge gas giant was the largest object besides the Sun in the solar system, and it was attended by the largest and most diverse grouping of satellites. More to the point here, it also presented the largest

danger, overall, of any location in the system to a large ship...
outside of diving down for a close encounter with the Sun itself.
"Has the shielding been fully tested?"

Castillo snorted, a perhaps not very respectful way to address
the man who would be commanding the *Odin,* but clearly express-
ing her opinion. "Sir, you couldn't *fully* test this shielding unless
you had Jupiter's magnetosphere and accompanying radiation to
test it with. But we have conducted extensive tests on both the
general ship shielding systems and on those in the excursion suits
and the *Hugin* and *Munin.* They have all passed all tests." She
pointed. "If you look along the hab ring, you can probably just
make out the coil sections. The radiation shielding design is made
with redundancy in mind. It shunts radiation around sections of
the ship to pass down what amount to magnetic...tubes, I suppose, though they're not really tubes and certainly aren't physical.
Those go between the spokes of the hab ring and pass onward
either forward or backward from the vessel."

"I would suppose, then, that anything lying along the centerline
of those 'tubes' would be subject to very intense radiation—even
greater than ambient?"

"Quite so. And true to an extent with the suits. The field does
not focus the beam very far, of course, and once the deflected
particles leave the field they may be dispersed by the main
magnetosphere, which will of course predominate away from the
immediate area of the ship."

"The suits appear to have a rather nonsymmetric field, however."
Hohenheim gestured, and an image of the *Odin*'s outer-system
worksuits appeared. While not very different from traditional suits
of this kind, there was one obvious change: a hole, about the
diameter of a man's fist, running through the area where many
older suits simply had an oblong backpacklike box to carry air
supply. In these suits, that area was divided by the hole.

"Magnetic metamaterials work has allowed us to effectively
shape the fields to some extent. The radiation would normally
pass through the center of a symmetrical field—which would,
unfortunately, include a large part of the astronaut. By biasing
the field, the deflected radiation can be sent through a less...
crucial location." She smiled at him. "And the Bemmies themselves
gave us the superconductor that makes it possible to build the
shielding this small."

"And to do much of the other work involved," agreed Hohen-heim. He didn't follow the exact details of the sciences involved, but he didn't need to. What was important was understanding how the changes in technology affected capabilities and approaches. Metamaterial sciences, which had really taken off in the late part of the twentieth century, involved studying how specific variants in the structure of a material, rather than its precise composi-tion, could affect its physical properties. Metamaterials in optics had demonstrated bizarre properties, including negative indices of refraction, optical magnetism, and others, and it was clear that something of the kind was responsible for the operation of the Bemmie room-temperature superconductor material. Similarly, magnetic metamaterials had shown the ability to affect magnetic fields in ways simple changes in composition couldn't.

"There will be some effects on the drive in the deep magne-tosphere," Castillo noted. "Well, to be precise, not on the drive itself, but the deflected particles will be imparting some sort of thrust. You must make sure this is taken into account at all times."

"Understood. It is something of a magnetic sail by default—no action without an equal and opposite reaction. If we are deflect-ing and redirecting energetic particles, their deflection exerts a force on us." He pointed to the rear of the main central body. "The main nuclear rocket nozzle—"

"Ah, yes. Because the *Odin* may wish to use far more power in bursts from the reactor than *Nike* did, we have had to build a better cooling and protective system for the nuclear rocket's exhaust. It cools itself to some extent, but there is much heat in that area. Also, the main water tankage is spaced around the base of the mass-driver ribs and around the main engine area to provide additional radiation shielding. The wide spacing of the hab sections from both the main body and the active drive areas of the ribs minimizes any exposure to hard radiation from either the nuclear reactor or the mass-driver."

"Hard radiation from the mass-driver?"

"Most likely not much." Castillo blinked and for a moment her eyes didn't seem to want to meet his, but she continued before he could be sure. "Still, as they say, it is better to be safe. Magneti-cally accelerating material to high speeds can produce X-rays or even gamma radiation, depending on how much mass, how high the acceleration, and other factors."

Hohenheim wondered what she wasn't telling him. The general was no political innocent and did not doubt his instincts. At the same time, the regulations were clear, and he knew the United States had been carrying out its inspections with clockwork regularity and undoubted thoroughness. There should not be any major surprises hidden on his ship.

Chapter 12

"Bioforming colonization?" Bruce repeated. "I dunno that one, Helen."

"It's sort of the reverse of terraforming," A.J. said. "Dunno who was the first to come up with it. The oldest story I read based on the idea was something by James Blish. *The Seedling Stars*. Basically, instead of trying to change the world you're going to, you change the lifeforms you're bringing to the world to fit the environment."

"So *that's* why they had the big bio labs all over the place?" Jackie asked. "Trying to make an entire biosphere for Ceres?"

Helen nodded. "Actually, they had to be doing some terraforming—xenoforming, I suppose I should say—on Ceres as well as bioforming on the various species. Ceres is frozen and would normally stay that way."

Jake took up the narrative. "Right. While results are very preliminary, we've also located several places where it appeared they were doing excavations and, possibly, waste disposal. That's given us a general timeline of the Bemmie presence on Ceres, at least in the sense of a knowledge of what events came first. Exactly what attracted them here we don't know. Helen presumes that they were interested in the high water content and could somehow determine that from a distance."

"We'd already guessed how much water was here years ago," Larry reminded him. "So it's no stretch to assume that Bemmie could do it at least as well or better."

"Okay, then we'll assume that. Where was I? Oh, yes. The damage this base suffered in the war, unfortunately, appears to have been in the area of the original Bemmius landings. However, they first tunneled down a kilometer or so, as you know, and reached the water-ice layer. The crust of Ceres is astonishingly thin, at least in this area. Larry"—he nodded to the astrophysicist—"says it's just enough to keep the water from all subliming away."

"Actually, my guess is that it's at least half the stuff that's left after it's done a lot of subliming away—the dirt and so on, plus whatever's accreted on the surface since," Larry put in. "Wouldn't be surprised if Ceres used to be a few kilometers bigger and had an ice surface, then lost it over billions of years. Sort of a very, very slow-motion comet."

"Anyway," Jake resumed, "they set up and started doing a lot of excavation. It looks to me like they were pretty clear what they intended to do from the start. There are signs that expansion of the underground areas was essentially constantly ongoing. The bioengineering labs were actually laid out a long time beforehand, but not equipped and used until a lot later. Jackie looked over a lot of the things we found in some of the other chambers, and she thinks that a large amount of their engineering was going into making something to melt the ice."

Bruce sat up suddenly. "That'd take one bloody lot of power, mate."

Jackie nodded. "And there's a lot of machines down there that might be generators. It'll be a long time before I'm sure, but... we might finally be able to say fusion power is less than twenty years away and mean it."

"Hot damn!" A.J. said. "That'd pay for this little junket, all right."

"They'd been working on that area for a pretty long time—must have been years—before the war hit. The bioengineering labs had only been going for a considerably shorter time."

"They managed some impressive work in that time, too," Larry said. "According to some scans I had A.J. run in the critical underground areas, I think they managed to liquify something close to a cubic mile, as well as several much smaller volumes, and were using them as a testing ground for the products of the labs."

"Were they working just on what we might call 'lower' lifeforms, or were they engineering themselves, too?" A.J. asked Helen.

"The labs we've found so far seem to have been working only on things ranging from microscopic to, oh, maybe the equivalent of fish. But I wouldn't be surprised if they eventually intended to make modified versions of themselves. It's one of the obvious ways to colonize." Helen looked abstracted. "Some of the modifications are interesting. There's a whole class of creatures that appear to be adapted to sessile forms from forms that were not originally sessile. It's going to take a lot of biologists to figure out exactly what they were doing, but this is a bonanza for us. We may be able to derive a significant portion of their genome from all this material. They're not using DNA or RNA as we know them, exactly, but they have similar self-replicating molecular blueprints, and the work they were doing here indicates they understood that blueprint very, very well."

"Sounds like we've got a fair dinkum of a report to send back home. Anything else?"

"Jackie and me found what looks like another ship or shuttle bay," A.J. said. "There's something in there, all right, but I'm still trying to figure out what. I mean, it's got to be a ship of some kind, but it's not the same as the model we found on Mars, or the damaged whatever-they-weres on Phobos. Once I get done I'll be sending the data to Joe and the others to see what they can get out of it."

He looked annoyed. "What's the problem, A.J.?" Helen asked, knowing that look of frustration.

He shook his head. "I think...there's something almost *familiar* about the damn thing, but I can't quite put my finger on it."

She laughed. "Don't worry about it. If you stop trying to remember it, maybe it'll come to you. Anyway, Bruce, Jake, and I will finish up a report—Jackie will provide the tech appendices—and you can encrypt it and send it off to the IRI and Ares."

"Great!" Bruce gave a wide grin. "Tell you what—everyone's got shore leave for a day after that."

They stared at him wryly. "We're already *on* the shore, if that's what you want to call it."

"Oh, right then. How about just celebratin' with an extra Joe dinner all around?"

"Now *there's* a treat, Captain!" Helen said, grinning back. Joe Buckley's spacegoing cuisine, suitably enhanced by Maddie's input, had become the standard for good food in space. Given that the other spacefaring nations were adopting his menus, Helen suspected that Joe was probably starting to see some considerable income from the use of his processes and recipes. One couldn't carry only "Joe" dinners for supplies, though, so they tended to be kept for special occasions and perhaps once or twice a week, like old-fashioned Sunday dinner.

"With that as motivation, I'll get this report finished today," Jake concurred. "Jackie?"

"The technical appendix is almost done. So start thawing out the Lobster Supreme—I'm hungry!"

"Righto," Bruce said. "Now, you blokes know I have to take *Nobel* back real soon—like as soon as we've topped off her tanks?"

"Yes, we do," Helen said, glancing at the others to make sure they all remembered. "Who's going? You and Jackie, I know."

"I am." That came from Tim Edwards, another of the original *Nike* crew who'd become a part of the IRI as a technician and all-around handyman. He formed part of the semipermanent crew of *Nobel*.

Josh Saddler raised his hand. "I'm going, too." Josh was the youngest of the group to visit Ceres, an environmental engineer with an artistic bent who kept an eye on the life-support systems both here in the Ceres base and on *Nobel*. His decorative wall paintings also tended to brighten any place he visited, and were always signed with a cartoonish sketched face of the type that A.J. called "bishonen" ("pretty boy"). The image was appropriate, Helen thought. Josh looked something like A.J. had when he was twenty-five (and to be fair to her husband, he still looked rather like that).

A couple of others acknowledged that they'd be going. "Still . . . that's going to be quite a few months knocking around that ship mostly alone. And we'll be pretty thin around here, too."

"Can't be helped, mate. The IRI needs us back home, an' I can't run the Tuna Wheel by my lonesome." Jackie tried to kick him under the table, which he managed to avoid. "Besides, you'll need me to go out an' bring you some more helpers, right?"

"That would be a good thing. And other replacement luxuries, for sure."

"Then just look at it as a chance to get shut of my Strine for a while," he said, grinning.

Helen and the others laughed. "Hell, that's one of the things we'll miss," she said. They knew that Bruce deliberately exaggerated his dialect, but that was part of the fun.

"'Strewth. You blokes just need to learn how to sling the lingo."

"No," A.J. said, "there's something just not the same. I wouldn't hang a faked da Vinci on the wall, and a phony Aussie just won't cut it, either."

Bruce blinked and then chortled. "Well, I'll be blowed. Never thought I'd be compared to a priceless piece of art."

"Well," A.J. said with that sideways grin that showed he'd gotten the response he wanted, "you certainly are a piece of work, anyway."

"Ouch. Now I know why I'm leavin', mate. In fact, I think I'd better go right now. And I'm takin' all the Joe Dinners with me."

Helen and Jackie gasped in mock horror. "Someone block the exits!"

NEBULA STORM

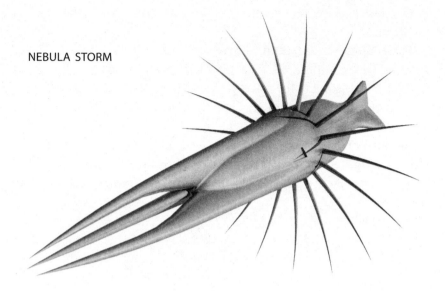

Chapter 13

"All *right*, all right, I'm awake," Nicholas Glendale grumbled at the insistently buzzing door as he dragged himself to consciousness. Usually he could wake up immediately, but whoever this midnight caller was, they'd caught him on one of the deep-sleep cycles.

He glanced at the clock as he rose from the bed. No, it was past midnight. It was 2:00 A.M., Phobos time. *This had better be worth it,* he thought and palmed the door open.

"I'm terribly sorry, Dr. Glendale," Madeline said, barely before the door finished opening, "But Joe insisted he talk to you right away."

It was a slight shock to see that Joe Buckley was, in fact, right there with her, along with Reynolds Jones, the tall, prissy-looking materials expert. "Well, I admit I prefer a bit of warning. If it's that important or exciting, though, I would hate to put a crimp in our relations over a few hours of desperately needed rest."

"Sorry, Nick," Joe said. The apology sounded genuine but rushed. "Take your time waking up."

That did deserve at least a slight smile, which Nicholas managed. "Why don't you take our late-night visitors to my office, and I will join you in fifteen minutes. Madeline, you don't have to stay."

"Actually, I think she should," Joe said firmly.

"I'll get them to the office and have Joe make us all some coffee," Maddie said.

As the door closed, Nicholas could hear the conversation continuing, "Only if you have the right beans..."

He took a quick shower, which was one of the luxuries really only possible with artificial gravity. He had experienced extended weightlessness, and while there were a number of attractive features of that condition, the methods needed to maintain proper hygiene were not one of them.

The shower cleared his head, setting off the usual cycle of waking-up routines. By the time he set out a few minutes later, dressed in comfortable clothing and with hair damp but presentable, he felt almost human.

The scent of brewed coffee greeted him at the office door. "I see you found my beans satisfactory, Joe?"

The gourmet engineer grinned. "I found your stash."

Glendale couldn't quite restrain a slight wince. "Were it anyone else, Joe, I would be a bit annoyed. But I think you can truly appreciate Jamaica Blue."

"I know *I* do, Nicholas," Maddie said appreciatively. He noted that Reynolds Jones was apparently drinking tea rather than coffee.

He took his own cup—pure black, no sugar—and sipped at it. "My God, even better than I make it."

"Well, I *did* design the machine myself," Joe said, bowing modestly, "to deal with the problem of good brewing in differing pressures and so on, so I probably just have a better touch with it. And with these beans to work with, well, you just can't go wrong." He sat down, having finished cleaning off the critical components of the coffee machine, and took his own first sip.

"Now that we're settled and we're using up—at a conservative estimate—about two hundred dollars' worth of coffee, taking into account the rather extravagant shipping expenses, would you like to tell me what this is all about?"

"Thought you'd never ask, Nick," Joe said. "It's about the ship on Ceres. I know what it is. And between me, A.J., and Reynolds, I think we can make it work again."

Nicholas found that he had stopped with his cup halfway to his lips, staring at Joe. "You're joking. That vessel is sixty-five million years old."

Reynolds shook his head. "Yes, yes, of course it is, Nick, but we can do this. It's really an *amazing* combination of serendipitous events, absolutely amazing."

Nicholas blinked. "All right, let's start from the beginning. What *is* that ship? From what A.J. said, it had what appeared to be some kind of fuel tanks, but ridiculously small for any reasonable range, and the places it connected to didn't look anything like rocket exhausts or ion emitters. But the layout of the interior—inhabitable areas, storage spaces, power—all pointed to something that had a pretty long range. A.J. said that he would have thought it was maybe some kind of trailer, a cargo/passenger pod or something of that nature, except that something kept nagging at him, especially one area where a lot of the controls went to which seemed to have a lot of that superconductor material."

"And A.J. was damn right to have that nagging at him," said Joe. "That's a dusty-plasma-sail ship."

"A . . . *what*?" Nicholas glanced at Maddie and saw that she was as much in the dark as he was. "I've heard of solar sails, and I think of something like a magnetosail, but—"

"A dusty plasma sail combines the ideas of solar sails with magnetosails and gets most of the advantages of both," Joe answered. "A researcher at *NASA*—Dr. Robert Sheldon—first came up with the idea. Basically, a properly ionized plasma can be used to guide and expand, or inflate, a core magnetic field outward, and the plasma can be pretty darn thin—basically the equivalent of hard vacuum on Earth—and still achieve the results. The field confines the plasma and acts as a sail, catching the solar wind, without needing any physical structures like some of the magnetic-sail designs—the force is exerted on the ship through the magnetic field. Then Sheldon noted that if you were to add dust with the right characteristics, the dust, too, could be confined by the ionized plasma and magnetic fields."

"That increases the mass of the whole system," Nicholas pointed out. "I understand how the first part works—and it seems a quite elegant solution to the problem of needing multi-kilometer lengths of superconducting cable—but what's the point of the dust?"

Joe grinned. "Dust reflects sunlight. The solar wind pressure is puny, while sunlight pressure is a hell of a lot more powerful. If you can get just a few percent reflection or absorption, you increase the effective thrust many times. An even more important point is that this system is effectively constant thrust—you'll be accelerating just as fast at the orbit of Jupiter as you were here at the orbit of Earth."

"Now, wait, that doesn't make sense," Maddie said. "The sun's light, and I'd bet the solar wind, is a lot weaker out there. It *can't* be getting the same amount of thrust."

"You would be completely correct if you assumed the sail is a fixed size," Joe agreed. "But that's not the case. The sail will expand and contract in size depending on the magnetic conditions surrounding it, like a balloon rising higher and higher into the air and expanding as the pressure around it drops. The solar magnetic field decreases as you get farther away, until you hit the magnetopause somewhere out past Pluto. So as you get farther away, your sail just keeps getting bigger, catching a proportionately larger amount of sunlight and solar wind, essentially maintaining a constant thrust. Yeah, at some point you have to dump more gas and dust into the mix, but overall it turns out to be reasonably constant thrust."

Madeline looked impressed. Nicholas certainly was. "What sort of thrust are we talking about?"

"Nothing immense in terms of acceleration. You wouldn't feel it, not unless you're awfully sensitive and looking for it, so to speak. But *any* constant-thrust vehicle will kick the crap out of any limited-delta-V system over the long haul, and I'd bet that this ship can at least equal *Odin*'s mass-beam approach—and it doesn't need some linear accelerator at the other end being constantly fed. The sun's doing all the work."

"Nice." Madeline's expression showed she was thinking about the implications of the design. "Another nice thing about it, I imagine, is that the drive system itself would serve as a magnetic shield. Remember how much engineering had to go into *Nike* in order to make it safe, and how we had to design special shields for the Mars rovers and shelters?"

Nicholas nodded. That was another area where the Bemmius superconductor was making things much easier. Before, they'd had to maintain liquid nitrogen around sets of isolated magnets, which then generated a magnetic field surrounding the habitable areas—especially a pain in the original *Nike* habitat-ring design. Now they could just put the superconductor in appropriate configurations and charge up the field, removing a huge, huge parasitic mass cost from the system. "I certainly do. So this dusty-plasma drive protects the ship from cosmic radiation?"

"And from some other sorts, too," Joe confirmed.

Nicholas frowned, musing. "With all these benefits, why haven't we ever built one?"

Joe laughed. "Kind of my reaction, really. But, first off, the theory never got a lot of play. Why, I don't know, but even though Dr. Sheldon did several papers on the basic concept and even did some simple but effective demonstrations in the lab, no one was ever really willing to put the money into a test. That might partly be because in order to really test it you needed something to go out past the Earth's magnetosphere, which was a major operation to contemplate back in the beginning of the century. It was pretty easy, relatively speaking, to get something up in low Earth orbit, but tens of thousands of miles up was a whole different ballgame. And controlling the sail was another sort of sticky point. There are ways you might do it, but they were never clearly laid out in the initial research. Also, it really *does* require superconducting magnets to work, and those have always been a pain. What happens if your liquid nitrogen pops a leak and you're out by Jupiter? And there is the eternal question of 'How do I stop this crazy thing?'" He looked at Nicholas with a raised eyebrow.

"And how *do* I stop the crazy thing?" Nicholas asked, obliging him.

"Very carefully," Joe said with a smile. "Seriously, it's a bit of an issue. There are a couple of ways. With just the ship itself, basically you have to be willing to stop accelerating before you reach too high a speed—basically solar escape velocity—and then tack such that you're using the pressure to oppose part of your own vector. In a way it's like regular sailing, but you don't have a water surface to play with. You can also swing around a planet large enough to permit a good-sized Oberth maneuver, but you'll want some rockets for that, because the major slingshot effect comes from dumping mass at an advantageous moment. Then you take a course which opposes your current orbit to enough of an extent that you effectively slow down. It can get pretty tricky, actually, because you'd have to choose your course such that you'd end up at an appropriate planet when you wanted to slow down, *and*—here's the really tricky part—you have to be ready to deal with your sail doing weird things to you when you get close to the other planet."

"Why?"

"Because a lot of planets, like Earth and especially Jupiter, have their own magnetic fields, and when you go through their magnetopause it'll be like suddenly diving underwater. Your fifty-kilometer sail will suddenly squeeze down to five kilometers, or something like that. All of a sudden you've got a lot less thrust—and you might start picking up small but noticeable thrusts from other directions if there's a lot of charged particles being guided by the planetary field. And of course as a magnetic sail, cutting through another magnetic field is going to have an effect on you as well. Even very small thrusts will have a major effect on whether you actually arrive at your destination or wind up a few tens of thousands of kilometers off.

"That's if you're a singleton ship. If you're already spacegoing, you can set up a bunch of stations that are sort of like the *Odin's* mass-drivers except they might fire high-energy particles or light at your sail, slowing you down. You might also use these ships sort of like one-way shipping containers, and when they got to the end destination you might send them back in using a mass-beam or just a long-time ion drive that will get them home eventually."

Nicholas nodded. "Interesting. Combining the problems of a sailing ship and a riverboat on a current. But eliminating the problem of carrying a gigantic sail or many tons of fuel." That struck another chord. "You do need to supply the gas and dust for your sail, and a thirty-kilometer sphere is an awfully large volume. How much gas and dust are you going to need?"

"A few hundred kilograms. A hell of a lot less than you'd need for an even vaguely plausible solar sail, let me tell you."

"I see." He turned to Reynolds, who had just finished his tea. "What's your role here?"

"Mine? Well, material sciences, of course. Reconstructing the ship will require just tons of work making sure we get the materials correct. We think that some of the components are designed to help guide and perhaps even shape the magnetic fields—you know, tacking back and forth, that sort of thing." Reynolds gave an expansive gesture that somehow conveyed the impression of billowing sails. "So much easier to sail when you have rigging, if you know what I mean.

"Now, Bemmie did all that marvelous work with materials that has frustrated A.J. so much when trying to scan through it both by finding *just* the right combination of elements *and* by tremendously careful work on the microstructural end, to the point that it's really quite a job to figure out which characteristics of the material are coming from its composition and which ones are from the unique microstructure. This is still an expanding field, you know, and it's just not something that you can hand to a computer. Even with someone as good as A.J. doing the data-collection work, you need a real expert to make the judgment calls. And, of course, material design and synthesis are my major specialities, Dr. Glendale. So naturally I'm going."

"Going?" He looked up. "You want to *go* there?"

Joe nodded. "I can't supervise this at a distance, really. I have to see it. And A.J. can't do it all himself."

"What's A.J. got to do with reconstructing a ship?" Nicholas found the question coming out more sharply than he'd intended. If Joe left, Madeline would almost certainly want to go, and he really didn't want her just leaving; nor, however, did he want to keep her there against her will. "I'm sorry. Obviously he's the one providing you with data, but—"

"No, I understand, Nick," Joe said. "Actually, it's the damn Faerie Dust again. A.J. has several new designs, and one of them—based partly off some of the Bemmie concepts we've managed to derive, and partly on our own experiences—is meant to literally go through something almost a molecule at a time, rearranging stuff according to a prior pattern. A reconstruction expert's dream. He wanted something to test this on, and while this is a lot bigger than he originally thought, he probably won't have to do that kind of thing on most of it. The main hull and structural members are made of the same carbon-metal composite-ceramic stuff the Vault was armored with. I suspect the best use of the Faerie Dust will be reconstructing the superconducting components."

"Could we just build one of these ships from scratch, rather than trying to rebuild something older than humanity?" Nicholas asked reasonably. "There's a certain poetry about some ancient alien ship being brought back from the grave, so to speak. But won't it be just far more work to reconstruct this one?"

Maddie answered that, somewhat to his surprise. "Probably not, Dr. Glendale. First, I don't think Joe and A.J. would have neglected to think of that, so they wouldn't be proposing this if they didn't think it would be the right course. But more importantly, while I think that we—as the human race—probably could build one more easily, I doubt seriously that we—as the IRI and Ares—can. It's a matter of what resources we have and how we can apply them. In Joe, Ren, and A.J. we have the resources to reconstruct this ship, though it will undoubtedly take time. We simply do not have the resources to build an entire ship from scratch. If we did, you wouldn't have had the trouble you did getting *Nobel* built in the first place."

"She's got it," Joe confirmed. "Sure, we could just hand over the discovery to everyone, and I'll bet that the United States or the E.U. would build at least a test ship in a few years without any strain at all, but then we don't get any real benefit out of the deal."

And that's the real rub, Nicholas thought. The whole point of the cooperative agreement was to let both parties get some use out of the deal, and with Ares personnel making the discovery, they did, indeed, have the right to profit from it. "Madeline?"

"I think I have to go with them, sir."

The tone of voice surprised him. So did the formal address. He had known she'd want to, but Madeline would never try to justify it without cause. "What is the problem?"

She gestured out the window. Glancing out, he saw the massive habitat ring of *Odin* gliding by in stately fashion. The E.U. vessel was currently docked to Phobos Station, transferring supplies it had brought from Earth, and was preparing to make its return journey. The *Odin* had made the trip entirely under the mass-beam system and was to return using mostly the fuel it had captured from the beam, thus proving both components of the system. The E.U. was also constructing a second mass-beam unit near Mars, a move which would permit extremely quick transits between Earth and Mars in both directions.

"That's the problem, sir. I know that the E.U. has been very accommodating, and that as a U.N. agency we can't very well forbid them from going anywhere. None of us want to be unfriendly, anyway. But if we're trying to keep secrets from them on Ceres, it's going to be a hell of a job. *Odin* carries a crew of slightly over one hundred people, and we're going to have—even if all three of us go—a total of less than twenty people on Ceres to keep an eye on them."

Nicholas shook his head in chagrin. "You know, I hadn't even thought of that. And they are of course going to Ceres as soon as they finish this return trip."

"Of course," Madeline acknowledged. "Not only have they already been implying that, but with Ceres now an established base that has some resources of its own, it makes an absolutely ideal destination for a longer-range test of the mass-beam, especially the self-guiding components. They have at least some hope of getting help if something goes wrong, and they'll be the first people outside of our group to get to see the material on Ceres firsthand. They will expect—and have to be given—some considerable access to the base. The Mars Accords make that very clear. And in any case, even with Ares' claim verified, it's a matter of good strategy to not annoy organizations a thousand times your size. Playing that kind of handicapped chess game is something I absolutely do *not* want to do by remote control."

She chewed her lip. "Also, I've looked over their personnel lists. There are some people there that make me nervous, especially their chief of security."

Nicholas sighed. "I won't say I like the idea of you leaving, Madeline, because I don't. But I would be doubly a fool if I hired the best security specialist in the solar system and then ignored her own advice. If I said that I was not going to approve Joe and Reynolds going to do this reconstruction, would that change your mind?"

"No. It would make it a much more painful decision, sir, but I really think that Ceres is going to be our vulnerable area for a while to come. Especially since we have two major secrets there at this point."

"So they are convinced it was fusion?"

"Ninety percent, anyway," Joe answered. "If it gives us enough hints, this would be a bigger jump forward than even the superconductor."

Nicholas brought up the orbital application he'd come to rely on over the past few years. "The real question is whether we can make this work. *Nobel* will be getting back here soon, but it will be *very* tight. The only launch window we will have for a reasonable transit time to Ceres—say, six months—is going to be in two months from now. If we're right that *Odin* will set out for Ceres shortly after she gets to Earth, then she'll be launching for Ceres—using mass-beam for constant acceleration—just about the time you get to Ceres. And that means you will have only a few weeks to prepare. I suggest strongly that you have A.J. do as much as possible via remote, even if it means that he'll do things more slowly than you would. Otherwise you will lose at least eight months of work."

"I was planning on that anyway, but I'll make it a priority," Joe said. "I guess we'd better get planning. Sure don't want to leave the wrong stuff behind."

Nicholas sighed. Obviously he wasn't going back to sleep tonight.

"No. And I have to get other things moving. I was originally planning on having *Odin* ferry some of our personnel out there, but if I'm sending *Nobel* back out right away, it makes more sense to send anything I can back that way. And a good thing that *Odin* brought Tammy and Stevie out as a favor. I'd hate to try to tell Bruce that he was going to have to wait another year or more to see them."

"You're going to send them out with us?"

"That'll be between them," Nicholas answered. "They'll have more than a month to work that out, but I'm not telling them what to do."

Joe shook his head dolefully as he got up to leave. "I dunno, Nick. Now we've got the last element for disaster—a cute, perky little girl to be shipped off to the isolated space colony."

"Funny," Nicholas said with a smile as they were exiting. "According to Bruce, the recipe for disaster is to have a gentleman named 'Joe Buckley' on board his ship. So I suppose you're right in either case. Make sure your insurance is up to date, Maddie."

She looked concerned. "Bruce does have a point. Maybe I could go out on *Odin* a little later—"

"Maddie!"

"—but then, who'd be there to rescue him from the inevitable disaster?" she finished, grinning. "I'll be back later to help start the planning, Dr. Glendale."

"Thank you, Madeline."

Nicholas gazed out at the *Odin*. *How easily the universe gets more complicated,* he mused. *I wonder if it will ever get simpler?*

Chapter 14

"—and that should catch anyone trying to sneak in, no matter how smart they think they are, or how advanced they think their skills and gadgets are," A.J. finished.

Maddie couldn't restrain a smile. "I seem to recall someone who used to tell me how free information wanted to be and was the kind of guy I was afraid I'd have to have arrested just to maintain security."

A.J. returned the smile. "Yeah, I remember him. In this case, the information wants to be expensive. Instead of fighting against that evil government witch who wanted to allow the government to take our hard-won data, I'm simply protecting Ares' God-ordained profits. Completely different."

"No similarity at all," she agreed gravely. The smile came back. "Anyway, let me say I'm a lot happier working with you than against you."

"Same here. Neither one of us was enjoying that part of the first trip. And I'm glad it never came down to a real argument, because I'd have lost."

She was startled by A.J.'s candid admission—the more so because it was, in her experience, only the first or second time he might have been underestimating himself. "You know, I think you're growing up despite yourself." She leaned back until her chair bumped the wall of the Ceres control center.

The sensor expert's face gave a reflexive twitch, then settled back into a smile—but one with a startlingly sad edge. "Yeah. I try not to let anyone else see it, and sometimes I even fool myself. But I'm not the same A.J. Baker, not really. Not the guy who couldn't keep from throwing an annoying photographer through a window, or who had to show off every six seconds to everyone, or who thought he was an unstoppable supergenius."

"That bother you?"

He shrugged. "Sure, some. But he also wasn't the kind of guy who could really have appreciated Helen, even if that was the way I was when I first fell in love with her. You know, I think the whole crash-landing-and-survival bit really helped. Nothing like a little life-and-death peril to focus a guy on what really matters." He studied her a moment. "You, though, you're more yourself than you were before. I'll bet that's another reason they let you go."

"You could be right." She thought back to various conversations she'd had with Director Hughes over the years. He had always been very careful to maintain a professional quality to their relationship, but it was clear that he cared very much what happened to her. "You probably are right. I think he didn't really like the idea of my continuing on as an agent until I was old enough for retirement. The administration just gave him a good excuse to get me to move on."

"And Joe gave you motivation to move on. Well, enough psychology. Are we set?"

"I think so." Madeline went over the security contingencies in her mind one last time. *Odin* would be arriving at Ceres soon, and while they'd spent months en route debating and rehashing the various means by which they could satisfy treaty obligations and still not give away everything the IRI-Ares group had discovered, it was now down to the actual event. There was no telling how long *Odin* would remain on-station. The current friendly relationship between the IRI and the E.U. made it a matter of obvious policy to encourage them to stay and assist, and the E.U.'s own interests would obviously be served by being able to study another alien installation.

She had also finally managed to confirm something she would rather not have had confirmed: the Richard Fitzgerald who served as *Odin*'s security chief was indeed the same person she'd feared it was. The man from northern Ireland liked to call himself a "commercial and industrial expediter," but he was really just a mercenary. He'd gotten his start in one of the elite British military units and had left that service under vague but apparently cloudy circumstances. "Cloudy," in this instance, being indistinguishable from "unsavory."

She'd had one brush with him before, and she hadn't liked what she'd seen one bit. Fitzgerald was undoubtedly intelligent and competent. But, so far as she'd been able to determine, he was also a man without a conscience beyond a determination to finish any job he started. For all practical purposes, a functional sociopath.

What was even more disturbing was the fact that he'd been selected—from a very wide field of candidates—to be in charge of *Odin*'s security. Why? And that gave rise to other serious questions, the most important of which was the sheer size of the E.U. ship's security force. Why would anyone in their right mind think they'd need almost ten percent of a large crew on an interplanetary ship to consist of security people? Did they think there might still be some live and hostile Bemmies lurking about, sixty-five million years later? That made as much sense as worrying there might still be dinosaurs roaming around loose.

She realized she had been gazing into space while A.J. waited patiently. "Yes, all set, A.J. I know you want to get back to working on the ship with Joe and Ren, so go to it."

"Cool. But actually, I'm going to go see Helen first. She's just decided to take a break."

Maddie raised an eyebrow. "How do you know that? I didn't hear you call her."

A.J. grinned. "Look down."

For a moment Maddie didn't understand what he meant—which was an unusual experience in itself. Then her gaze fell on her own pair of rings. "Ahh . . . she's still wearing a Faerie Dust ring?" She frowned. "And how would she feel about you spying on her?"

"Very hostile, if I actually used it that way. We had quite a talk on the subject—she's way far from stupid, so she figured out what I could do with it if I wanted to. But she doesn't mind if I have it just give me alerts on important general events, and she can always shut it off if she wants to. I gave her a general shutdown code that will force the motes to basically do nothing other than sit there and glitter. And some important general events, besides injury and so on, include detecting when she's 'on work' and 'off work.' I got an 'off work' ping just a little bit ago." He pulled on his Tayler-built suit as he spoke; this portion of the base wasn't connected to the others by pressurized corridors yet. "So I'm off to see my wife before I go geek with my friends. Is that grown-up or what?"

"With you, that's a scary thing, A.J. Have fun." She watched him leave and then turned back to the security consoles. She caught her own reflection in one of the panels. Grim.

"Yeah, me, too," she said wryly. She was keeping a reasonably positive face up for the others, but her instincts were screaming at her. The whole setup made her nervous. *Odin*'s design bothered her. The fact that the massive E.U. ship carried a hell of a lot more personnel than *Nike* ever did bothered her. The existence of a ruthless mercenary like Fitzgerald as chief of security got her hackles up, as did the fact that he was in charge of a grossly oversized security force. This, with two separate secrets they were trying to hide, and gods alone only knew what *else* might be here to protect.

Rationally, her worries made no sense. Oh, there were security issues, and it was quite possible that one, or both, of their little secrets would be blown. But that was just a professional worry, and nothing that should be causing her this level of concern. She usually trusted those instincts, but cloak-and-dagger stuff just didn't make *sense* this far out. Everyone knew where everyone was. It wasn't like you could sneak onto Ceres, steal the top-secret plans, and get away without anyone noticing. Spaceships weren't stealthy objects. Compared to the solar system they were small, yes, but they behaved so differently from everything else, radiated energy in such characteristic patterns, and were so very rare that everyone knew the location of everyone else's ships and there was no way to hide.

Yeah. There was no reason to get all nervous, like that time in Ecuador. Those people really *had* been up to something. She rubbed the almost-invisible white scar on her upper arm, almost unconsciously. No reason to worry at all.

PART IV:
ORBITS

Espionage (industrial), n: the use of spies by a corporation or the like to acquire the plans, technical knowledge, etc., of a competitor.

ODIN

Chapter 15

"Ceres Base, this is *Odin*," Hohenheim said. "We are preparing to take up orbit around Ceres. Please advise us as to any particular orbital vectors you wish kept clear."

"The sky's wide open, Odin." That was the easy-to-recognize Australian-accented voice of Bruce Irwin. *"Just make sure you don't cross over Nobel's path, and you're good. Welcome to the outer system, mates."*

"Thank you, *Nobel*, and it's good to be here."

"Congrats on how well that mass-beam is working, too. I think we might all have to start changin' over to those. This six-month ferry deal is getting a mite old."

Hohenheim laughed. "I admit, Captain Irwin, I much prefer going straight from here to there. Our engineers have been working on a design which might work to retrofit *Nike*. I would not be surprised if it could be adapted for *Nobel* as well."

A female voice responded. *"Really? Dr. Secord speaking. I'd be very interested in looking at those."*

"I will of course have to clear it with my superiors, but in the current spirit of cooperation between our groups, I feel sure that can be arranged. Now, on another subject, Ceres. Is Madeline Fathom available?"

The unmistakable harmless-sounding soprano voice answered. *"Fathom here, General. How can I help you?"*

"Well, let us be completely honest—off the record, so to speak. We at the E.U. are quite sure that you have found some items or data of interest already in your stay—the sudden reassignment of two of Ares' finest engineers was a strong hint, you see. I also

am very much aware that there are at least five times as many
of us as there are of you, and you haven't the space to house us,
let alone maintain security. So I would like to have you give me
specifics on where we may and may not go, rather than have us
pretend that this really is a totally open and public installation
of the U.N. with nothing whatsoever to hide."

There was a light chuckle following his speech. *"I see. And in
return we can then feel free to give you the ability to explore other
areas with us?"*

"Joint cooperation and expansion of the base in areas you have
yet to reach does sound more interesting than playing a game of
shadow-chasing, doesn't it?"

*"It does, General. Let me discuss details with our staff here, but
I thank you for your candor. While I have played that game often,
I don't particularly like it."*

"No more do I. We shall speak later, then."

The immediate pleasantries concluded, he cut off communication with the IRI/Ares base and turned to face Horst Eberhart.
"I would like an immediate conference with you, Dr. LaPointe,
Mr. Fitzgerald, Ms. Svendsen, and Dr. Meyer," he said. "Please
gather everyone in the conference room—meeting to begin in
one-half hour."

Hohenheim unstrapped and floated himself to the exit, then
drifted/slid his way "down" to the habitat section, stopping briefly
to use the facilities and then to grab a sandwich from his room.
Long experience had taught him to always start a meeting with
an empty bladder and a full stomach. That removed all pressures of urgency except those of the actual issues, and—in more
competitive meetings—often gave you a small but significant edge
over the less prepared.

He entered the room, which had not the one-third gravity of
the *Nike* but instead nearly normal gravity. That could be done
because of *Odin*'s larger radius and the increased rotation speed
of the habitat ring. The general saw that the others were already
waiting. Good, no delays. He disliked wasting time in meetings.

"Thank you all for coming so promptly. As you know, we are
entering Ceres orbit and will be shortly in position to join our
colleagues of the IRI and Ares." He saw Richard Fitzgerald give
a momentary smile at the wording, but no one else was looking

in that direction. "Obviously, they will have things they wish to keep from us, and, eventually, we hope to be in the same position. Right now, however, I am interested in conducting our presence here with the least possible amount of friction. Ceres Base is putting together a list of places we may go and places they prefer we do not go. I intend to accommodate them, even though legally I might be able to argue that we have the right to go anywhere other than, perhaps, life-supporting control areas. The European Union is currently interested in cultivating the friendship of certain people who have, shall we say, unique advantages and resources.

"That said," he continued, "I am sure that everyone here knows that one of our major goals is to obtain information which will be of material benefit to the Union—and which, I assure you, will be of material benefit to all of us as well. As I recall, Dr. Meyer," he said, addressing the tall British woman on his left, "you were rather annoyed by the severe information restrictions the United States attempted to impose on the *Nike* expedition."

Barbara Meyer nodded shortly. While she had gotten along with most of the *Nike* crew, she had never quite gotten over being shortstopped and silenced by Madeline Fathom. This had eventually led to her leaving the original Phobos crew and signing up with the E.U. once the *Odin* was clearly well along.

"While I would not encourage any of you to attempt to directly violate the rules," he said smoothly, "I do wish to emphasize that in this case I *want* you to find out everything you can, especially when it comes to new and interesting scientific and technical information. Anything of real value will be credited to you, of course. Dr. LaPointe."

Anthony LaPointe looked up alertly. "Sir?"

"You will be working very closely with Dr. Conley, I am sure. You and Horst Eberhart have shown excellent teamwork already in the development and implementation of our navigation systems. You will continue to work together, although Mr. Eberhart's talents as a programmer and system engineer may of course be requested by other members of the crew as needed. You have what may be the most uncertain, yet potentially most important, mandate. Your main task is to keep an eye out for any trace—however small—of data which leads us to *another* alien installation. I will point out that the restrictions we agreed to only apply to this base on Ceres."

He turned toward Horst. "Mr. Eberhart, while again I caution you against directly violating any of the guidelines set down by the people from Ares and the IRI, I would like you to devise methods whereby if we are, in fact, the first to find certain information about another Bemmie base, we can eliminate direct references to this information from their systems. At least, for long enough to enable us to reach such a base before our competitors. Is this possible?"

Horst frowned. The general knew that the earnest young engineer did not really approve of such maneuvers. It was those same misgivings that had led Hohenheim to see to it that some of the security preparations under Security Chief Fitzgerald's direction were not known to Eberhart, who otherwise had a hand in the software engineering of virtually every system on *Odin*. But Hohenheim felt that Horst's loyalty would outweigh his personal issues.

It was therefore mildly gratifying to see the young man respond with a nod, after a brief hesitation. "Yes, General. Not easy, though, and I'd rather not have to do it if we can avoid it. A.J. Baker's down there, and hiding stuff from *him* isn't going to be easy."

"But he is not a programmer like you?"

"In his specific area, he's very good. But no, he's not a programmer. If he's not directly watching us—and putting bugs on us would be a direct privacy offense we could take action against—I think I can pretty much hide anything."

Fitzgerald's eyes narrowed. "Bugs? You think he could do that without us knowing?"

Horst laughed. "Baker didn't get his reputation for nothing, Mr. Fitzgerald. Sure, he *could*. Those motes he uses are microscopic. But he's also very close to an anarchist in some ways. He might spy on people, if he had to, for his own personal reasons, but he wouldn't ever try to be Big Brother. And if he tries to work through more normal distributed systems, I can detect him."

The security chief settled back, looking only partially convinced.

"Mr. Eberhart, you and Mia"—the general nodded to Mia Svendsen, sitting just across from Fitzgerald—"will also likely be working with *Nobel*'s engineer if, as I expect I will, I get permission to give them information on upgrading their vessels to mass-beam designs. You are the expert on the control systems while Mia is the actual expert on the engine systems themselves. This will be a profitable exchange for both sides, as the various E.U. corporations involved will be building the driver systems, so you may enjoy full openness on that little aspect of our visit.

"Other than that, our people are to explore where they're allowed, find out what we can, enjoy the limited amenities, help expand the working and living areas of Ceres Base, and in general be helpful, friendly, and alert to any interesting tidbits of information. Follow all the directions of our hosts except where I have noted otherwise, and we may find this to be a quite enjoyable little jaunt."

"Do we know how long we're staying?" Mia asked.

"That is indefinite at this time. I would expect at least several months."

He answered several more minor questions and then, after giving everyone another chance to ask questions, dismissed the meeting. He caught Richard's eye as the security chief stood. "A moment, Mr. Fitzgerald."

Once the others had left, he closed the door. "How are your preparations?"

"All set," Fitzgerald said with satisfaction. "Testing the hidden control layers worked fine. Was a little dicey with Eberhart always nosing around, but I don't think he's seen anything."

"Well, with any luck, all your preparations will be a waste of time."

"We can hope." Fitzgerald's tone was not precisely in agreement with his words.

The general gazed levelly at the Irish mercenary. "Please understand that I really do wish to avoid conflict. And that means I want you to work very hard to do that. Including getting along with your opposite number."

A muscle in Fitzgerald's cheek twitched, but his voice betrayed nothing. "Fathom."

"We knew she had been sent out with her husband. It's clear that she's running security here."

"Then—meaning no offense, sir—you're a real optimist if you think you're going to pull off something under her nose and not get into a spitting match. She doesn't trust anyone on Earth except her darling boss—I pity her hubby, if he ever gets seen with anything else vaguely female—she doesn't miss the smallest thing, and she lives for the payback if something ever goes wrong." Fitzgerald shook his head in cynical satisfaction. "No, we'll be needing my 'preparations' before this is all over, you can bet on it. But you're the boss, General. I'll make nice with her. She's still easy on the eye."

And I suspect you just described yourself a lot more than her, Hohenheim thought. Not for the first time, he found himself wondering if Bitteschell had made a misjudgment in choosing Fitzgerald. The man was a professional, good at his job, flexible, and didn't question the goals of his employers. But he seemed a bit too eager to be the one to solve problems with his own personal approach. And that speech about Fathom didn't make the general at all comfortable; it sounded very much as though Fitzgerald had a score to settle with Fathom. "See to it that you do. Politely, and watch your approach. Don't give her the slightest excuse to complain."

Fitzgerald nodded. "I'll be the soul of courtesy, I promise. We don't want to give her any excuses, you're bloody right on that. And I think I'll keep most of my men well out of the way up here. Some of them aren't the best at keeping their mouths shut, at least around someone like her."

"That's probably a good idea. Thank you." He watched his security chief exit. And felt his misgivings intensify the moment the door closed and Fitzgerald was out of sight.

Chapter 16

"So, how much power are we talking about here?" Jackie leaned forward, studying the modifications which reflected the wide-flung rings that had been visible behind *Odin* when the huge E.U. vessel was approaching. "Accelerating a ten-thousand-ton vessel at a hundredth of a g is a million newtons. That's not so much. But I know that building the driver for the mass-beam was a major effort, and it uses a lot more than that."

Horst Eberhart smiled. "You know the NERVA drive well, and some others, but I'm guessing not so much the mass-beam?"

She glanced at him sharply, but then saw that the smile was a purely friendly one, the smile of one engineer to another, saying: *I've got some cool stuff to show you!* It was not at all sarcastic or derisive.

And that's what he's here for, she reminded herself. Whatever cloak-and-dagger might be going on, here at least they could be straightforward. *And that's a really, really nice smile.* "No, I didn't study anything on mass-beams except the basic concept—throw stuff from way over here to hit something there, to push it on its way."

"Yes, that's the basic idea. But as you say, the devil is in the details. That million newtons is what has to actually be *delivered* to the ship."

"Inefficiency in the driver makes that larger in actual cost?"

He shook his head.

Jackie frowned. "No, I'm missing a fundamental issue, and I know I'm going to kick myself when you tell me."

"Probably. I did." He activated a little animation showing a simplified mass-beam driver and a cartoon ship. The driver threw little balls at the ship and bounced them off a plate on the ship's base. "See, I throw the mass at the ship, it bounces off, ship moves forward. Keeps moving forward. Then I have to throw next mass, but ship is moving faster now. The best momentum transfer is when the speed of the mass is about twice the speed of the ship, so to make the best transfer throw my mass must be a little faster this time—"

Jackie smacked herself on the forehead. "Of course! When you start the ship going, you only have to accelerate the particles to twenty centimeters per second, but by the time you hit thirty kilometers a second you need to be throwing them at *sixty* kilometers a second. Basically since you're using them as the ship's fuel, you have to do what the ship would have done if it was carrying them along—spend the energy to first accelerate the fuel to your speed, *then* give it that extra oomph for the hundredth-g. So that means that you're using..." She did some quick calculations. "Wow! I get over a hundred gigawatts constant?"

"You *are* good," Horst said, his tone very respectful. "You picked up on the whole thing much faster than I did. I can't tell you the exact numbers for our assembly, because that's restricted information. Which is silly, in my opinion, since if we push *Odin* to the limit, you will know the numbers anyway."

"So, you could actually get a little more acceleration speed out of it to begin with by cranking up the wattage, though it'd be less efficient."

"Not much point, though. Constant acceleration builds up quickly enough. Good for launching things and getting them out of the way, I suppose."

"How exactly do you stop, though? It's like a solar sail that way."

He shook his head. "Not quite, Ms. Secord."

"Please, call me Jackie."

He flashed a white-toothed grin. "And please call me Horst. The idea is to build many collectors and accelerators and put them around the solar system, eventually. But if you know where you are going, you can send some slow stuff ahead of you. Catch as much of the regular beam as you can to store for fuel, use that, then—"

Jackie laughed. "Oh, that's clever! You can either bounce the particles off, or catch them as fuel. So after you empty your tanks on the first decel, you start slowing down using the slower cloud of stuff sent before you left. That refills your tanks, so you can do *another* stop burn, after already doing one and having the slow cloud slow you up more. Hmmm...and the slow cloud can be more concentrated—massive—because you have the energy to send the stuff faster. So you send more stuff slower. There'd be a lot of fancy tradeoffs, but I can see that would work nicely. How do you keep the beam focused, though? At a few hundred million miles I'd think it would be, well, a *lot* of kilometers across."

"I thought that, too. But look, here is an image of one of the fuel particles."

The image that popped up was surprisingly recognizable. "Faerie Dust? You're sending tons of Faerie Dust?"

"Faerie...? Oh, yes, Mr. Baker's nickname for it. Not nearly so complex. It has to be simple. Tons of fancily designed material would be expensive, and you need many, many tons. There is a special plant dedicated to the whole operation. Very simple overall design, with just enough capability to home on target signal."

"Signal? Oh, I see. You use something like a laser pointed toward the driver, and the particles use that as a homing beacon—they can use sunlight and the solar wind to steer themselves toward you. Very nice. And they'll really concentrate down this far?" She indicated the large ring designs, which extended to a maximum diameter of about four times *Nobel*'s habitat ring, or somewhat over a kilometer across.

"Yes. Not a problem. The swarm of particles tries to stay concentrated. Uses very little power and only needs small corrections every few hours."

Jackie studied some of the parameters. "It's still going to be expensive. I find it hard to believe so much has happened that makes all this possible."

"A few years makes a big difference. You left Mars two years ago for Ceres."

"God. It really has been that long." She shook her head. "If they're making superconductor cable that large, it'll be a great investment. Right now I guess your accelerator must spend a lot of time idle, so if other people were paying you for it that would defray costs."

He shrugged, something very noticeable with his wide shoulders. He seemed far more athletic than the average engineer. That piqued Jackie's interest, which had already been aroused. She was quite athletic herself and always had been.

"The money side of it doesn't interest me," he said, "but I would guess so. Do you want to go over installation details?"

"No, not right now, Horst. I know more than enough now to be able to inform Dr. Glendale and let him know that I think it'd be a great idea. Until I find out whether we're going for it, details would just be more of a tease than anything else. Besides, we've been at this for five hours."

He blinked. "Really that long?"

"Check for yourself." An impulse came to her, which she began to stifle from automatic reflex. Then . . .

Well, why not?

"We could quit for the day. *Nobel* just finished downloading our copies of the new films you brought with you. Would you like to watch one with me?"

She bestowed her own white-toothed grin on him. Which, she knew, was quite a gleaming affair, especially against her complexion. Her mother had been Indian in her ancestry—American Indian, mostly Choctaw. Judging from the evidence, at least some of that ancestry had been of African origin, too, although that showed in her dark skin, not her features.

Horst Eberhart's eyes widened, and for a minute she thought he'd refuse. But then she realized his hesitation was simply the natural shyness of someone who, like herself, was normally cautious in personal relations. She thought of it as the Cursed Wallflower Syndrome.

"Well . . . yes," he said. "I would enjoy that very much."

She shut down the engineering station and floated up, grabbing his arm. "Then let's be off." She felt a delicious pang of self-conscious worry and anticipation she hadn't felt in years.

Chapter 17

"I swear, these guys were animated by the Japanese," A.J. growled to himself. "*Hentai* Japanese animators. Everywhere I go in this ship's design, I find tentacles."

"That's your dirty mind reading into things. Just because the control cables are long, slender, flexible things that extend outward from the—"

"Bah, Joe. I say again, bah. Just don't blame me if Bad Things happen to our female crewmembers if we get any on board." A.J.'s real annoyance, he had to admit, was due to the sheer volume of superconducting material he kept finding—to a great extent in the apparently extendable field-control and shaping units that lay coiled and quiescent in the alien vessel's hull. Dust-Storm's best new Faerie Dust had performed magnificently, but the job was far bigger than he'd ever imagined, and they had had to ask for a number of additional supplies since. Even the highest technology couldn't fix the superconducting cable if all the materials weren't there to fix it.

"And," he muttered, "we're gonna need a buttload of power to run this thing, even if we get her working."

"If?" Reynolds' voice responded from somewhere inside the ship. "You know, that doesn't sound at all like you, A.J. Since when did you start doubting we could do anything?"

"He's in a bad mood because he met Jackie's new boyfriend last night."

"Joe," A.J. said calmly, "remind me to kill you after the shift."

"Jackie has a boyfriend?"

"Horst Eberhart," Joe answered, ignoring A.J.'s threat of mayhem. "One of the *Odin*'s crew members,"

117

"You'd better not say *that* in front of Jackie, or *she's* likely to kill you," A.J. pointed out. Then he added: "Jackie's insisting they're 'just friends,' Ren. Which is probably true, technically speaking, given that the cramped conditions we're living in make going beyond 'just friends' pretty tricky. My guess, though, is that Jackie would be quite happy to see that status change before too long. So would Horst."

"What do think of him?" Ren asked.

"Seems like a nice guy. He's smart, that's for sure."

Ren's puzzlement was clear over the link. "But then, A.J., I don't understand why you aren't in a good mood. You aren't jealous, are you?"

"It's *Joe* saying I'm in a bad mood!"

"Well, you are. I heard you cursing at your sensors not long ago."

"I'm certainly not jealous." A slight pang of guilt. "Well, no more than I am of any other pretty girl I know well."

"*Any* other pretty girl? I really must warn Helen of your approaching midlife crisis."

"Killed after the shift, Joe! Remember that!"

"Mars couldn't do that—what makes you think you can?"

A.J. tried to glare at him, but couldn't really keep it up. He sighed. "I guess it's because I like him, Ren."

There was a slight silence. "You *do* know that makes absolutely no sense whatsoever, A.J."

He sighed and rolled his eyes, putting down the imaging probe he had been using. "Maybe not. But that's the truth."

He wasn't even sure he could explain it to Joe. Not without sounding silly, petty, childish, or all three. Helen might understand.

The Bakers had invited Jackie and Horst to have dinner and visit with them the prior evening. A.J. had been ready to be suspicious and to even put the fear of God—or A.J. Baker—into Horst if necessary. Instead, just the way the tall, muscular, handsome Eberhart entered, a little bit behind Jackie with a friendly but almost apologetic look on his face, put A.J. off his stride. That was the look of a man meeting his date's parents and worried he might not make a good impression. Given that Jackie was only a little younger than he was, that seemed pretty funny. Of course, Helen was older than Jackie—not that she looked it much—and her real parents were hundreds of millions of miles off, so maybe it made sense. Sort of.

Then, during dinner—Joe Dinners, of course—Horst had responded quite openly to any questions they had. He didn't seem to much like the security chief on board *Odin*, but other than that he just admitted straight out he was supposed to watch for useful stuff but mostly just work with them. Which was only fair, A.J. supposed. The E.U. had to be going nuts trying to find a way to get what they'd see as their fair share.

Horst was also very impressed by A.J., which made it even harder to be hostile to him. When a man's telling you how much he admires your work, it's awfully difficult to maintain the right level of paranoia and suspicion.

So Horst had talked. And they'd watched a movie, and talked some more, played some four-way Trivia, and somewhere in there A.J. had realized that he really did like Horst Eberhart...

Partly, he supposed, that was because Eberhart was like him. Except he was several years younger, taller, probably more athletic and certainly better looking. And apparently without A.J.'s ego problem. In his entire life, A.J. couldn't ever remember meeting someone who made him feel like he could fade into the background. Eberhart was like...like Glendale. Without knowing it, and that made it worse.

A.J. rolled his eyes, grumbled another curse, and cut off outside communication except for emergencies. "Fine, so I really *am* starting to feel kinda old. Stupid. And anyway, as long as he cares about Jackie, assuming something gets rolling there, that's really what matters."

He began to direct the work of a new batch of Faerie Dust motes along the next section. "Helen was right—time for me to stop acting like the brainy kid genius and instead just be who I am. And that's a guy who's got a hell of a lot going for him—not the least of it being that he's married to Helen." He grinned. "And there's one thing Horst can't compete with!"

"What exactly is bothering you, Mr. Fitzgerald?"

Hohenheim saw Fitzgerald grimace. "Nothing in particular, General. It's the waiting. Most of the jobs I've been on in the past, I was the one in charge of the timing. Bloody annoying to be sitting here waiting for one of our eggheads to find what we need."

"Other than that, how do you gauge the situation?"

"Pretty good, actually, if I look at it from the outside. I've managed to keep away from Fathom. She knows I'm here, no doubt of it, but I guess she doesn't want to push things any more than we do. Dr. LaPointe hit it off really well with their astrophysicist, Conley—turns out the two of them have published in some of the same journals and knew each others' work, so they had a common ground. One good thing about the time element is that it's given us a lot of chances for the initial suspicion to die down. Conley and LaPointe are both going over the alien data that they've been getting from the noteplaques. A whole bunch of them turned out to have astronomical-related data on them. That's a big break, I don't think I need to tell you."

"Indeed it is." The general nodded thoughtfully. While it was A.J. Baker who was credited with the first two discoveries, it was Conley who had discovered the third, and in the long run Hohenheim expected that it would be the astronomers and their allied fields that discovered the best leads to new alien finds. They were, after all, the ones most likely to be studying the right material.

"I'm more worried about Eberhart," Fitzgerald said. "Didn't mind him getting friendly with the locals. After all, it might make things a lot easier in the long run. But I'm worried about his developing relationship with that IRI engineer Secord, which has the potential to go way beyond 'friendly.' That could cause problems down the road."

"Horst is a very loyal and honest man. The latter makes it a bit difficult for him to do anything underhanded, true, but the former makes it so that I can depend on him to do his part when the time comes."

Fitzgerald shrugged, running a hand through his short graying hair. "I guess. And it's not like we're going to ask him to hurt anyone."

Hohenheim noted that there wasn't a trace of irony or self-persuasion in that last sentence. Richard Fitzgerald honestly did not see that from the point of view of people like Horst Eberhart or Anthony LaPointe they were going to be asked to harm their new friends. Might be, at least. In ways that were probably legal and not physical, and ones that they had intellectually accepted when they took the mission. But it would be harm nonetheless. The general expected the two would still carry through, but he was quite aware of the hard choices he might be asking his men and women to make. It concerned him that Fitzgerald appeared to be totally blind to that.

Granted, it could be argued that Fitzgerald's attitude was the correct one to take for a man in his position. The Irishman was not the *Odin*'s commander; he was its chief of security—which, being honest, meant that he also doubled as the informal head of whatever industrial espionage was carried out by the *Odin*'s crew. It wasn't his job to be liked, or to make people happy: it was to make sure that the entire mission succeeded.

That said, Hohenheim was still concerned. He was particularly concerned because he hadn't been allowed any say—any input at all—in the selection of the mission's head of security. That was... odd. Normally, a commanding officer on such an expedition, especially one as experienced as Hohenheim, would have at least been consulted in the matter.

The fact that he hadn't been led him to wonder if Fitzgerald had been given secret instructions. By... whomever. Hohenheim was not naïve. He knew full well that the power structure of the European Union's space program was complex and involved a number of sometimes antagonistic forces. It was indeed possible that some powerful people or agencies in the EU were using Fitzgerald as a tool.

"Secret instructions" was perhaps the wrong way of putting it. Hohenheim doubted very much that Fitzgerald had been told to do anything radically different from the mission Hohenheim had been given. The problem was more a matter of parameters. Two men can both be told to do the same task. But if one of them is also privately instructed to let nothing stand in the way of success, then the task itself can become transformed. Especially if the man involved is someone who has difficulty making distinctions or seeing limits to begin with.

He restrained a sigh. There was no point in brooding on the matter. In all likelihood, nothing would ever happen that might bring the underlying problems to the surface.

"What about the secrets?" he asked.

Fitzgerald grinned. It hadn't taken long for the crew of *Odin* to figure out that there were at least two major secrets that the *Nobel* personnel were trying to hide from them—and doing pretty well at it. One of Fitzgerald's priorities had been to find out what those secrets were. From the expression on his face, he'd clearly met with some success.

"I know what they're hiding now. Well, not all the details, but I know for sure one of them. Took me a while to figure it out, mainly because, well, they're damn good for civilians. Fathom's work, probably, but what I mean is that someone's briefed them on how to say a lot without actually revealing anything. I had to sort through a lot of nothing and get our analysts to go over the secondary and tertiary material before I could get a handle on what they were doing.

"Anyhow, the boffins involved are engineering and hard-sciences people, especially particle physicists and . . . but you don't need the details. Long and the short of it is that the aliens were melting ice here on a really grand scale for some project of theirs, and they think they've found the generators that let them do it."

Hohenheim froze. He could see his own reaction was gratifying to Fitzgerald. "Fusion."

"Fusion. They're virtually certain now, and from some of the work they're doing I think it may be something they'll be able to get working in some reasonable time. Not in weeks or months, but we're not talking twenty years, either. The E.U. or the U.S.A., now, you might be talking even less time. These boys and girls haven't got those kinds of resources, though." He pulled out a data stick. "I've got the outline of an op on there that should let us grab the critical data and send it to HQ. With that as a head start, we'd get working fusion ahead of these guys and could announce it as our own innovation."

General Hohenheim stared at the little data stick. The idea had its temptations. There was no fuzziness about whether such a discovery would be worth the effort. Working, efficient fusion technology would have essentially inestimable value for applications on Earth or in space. And Richard Fitzgerald's assessment was almost certainly correct, in that even with the considerable brainpower they had available, the IRI-Ares consortium simply didn't possess the resources to bring that technology out as fast as the E.U. could. If Fitzgerald's operation worked, the benefits would be immense.

However . . .

Hohenheim shook his head. "No, Mr. Fitzgerald. This isn't the operation we are supposed to perform, and there are huge potential risks. This well exceeds the level of duplicity we were intending to use. And without seeing your plan I can still tell you that there would be a significant risk of people being injured. You cannot be certain of obtaining this critical information without any confrontations."

"Very minimal, sir." Fitzgerald looked at him as though he wished to argue, but didn't. In some ways that worried the general even more, as Fitzgerald wasn't usually given to much restraint in speaking his mind. "But if you don't want it, fine. Might be some time before they find anything like what the head office was talking about, though. Going by the odds, looks to me like it might be another year or two. By then, I'm going to be worrying about whether we can count on our staff in a pinch, especially the ones getting really chummy with the locals."

He did have a point, much as Hohenheim didn't want to admit it. If they spent another year—or even a few more months—on station, pretty soon a number of his personnel would be seeing the people from *Nobel* as being as much their comrades as those of *Odin*. "What do you want, then?"

"Nothing much, sir. Just authorization to have some contingency plans in case I have to push things when we actually do make our move. I know you don't like it, General, but you know as well as I do that if we get loyalty issues, there may be some . . . incidents. I want to have some time to plan ways to neutralize the opposition without getting anyone hurt, and hopefully without them being able to prove we had much to do with it. But I can't guarantee that there won't be anyone getting hurt, if by 'hurt' we're including any and all sorts of emotional damage."

"Mr. Fitzgerald, I understand that it's impossible to avoid any type of damage when the interests of two parties clash. But we must avoid anything extreme. Any violence would seriously damage the claims the E.U. might get on our target, even leaving aside whatever disputes might arise from the use of industrial espionage."

"I understand that, sir."

Hohenheim studied him for a moment. To all appearances, Fitzgerald seemed the very model of obedience. The problem was that a man with his background and experience was inherently a very good actor. What did he really think? More importantly, what did he really intend?

There was no way to know. Hohenheim would just have to remain alert.

"Very well, Mr. Fitzgerald. Let me know as soon as anything new develops."

Once he was out of the general's office, Fitzgerald allowed himself a little smile. There was a certain delicious irony here. Nothing could be more plausible about "plausible deniability," after all, than the person in charge of a project being in fact ignorant of what was happening when his back was turned.

True, if and when the discrepancies surfaced, Hohenheim would be furious. But he was just the man in charge of the project. Which is not the same thing as being the man in charge of the payroll. The bonus that had been directly offered to Richard by Goswin Osterhoudt and more subtly implied by Commissioner Bitteschell was more than large enough—way more than large enough—for Richard to be quite willing to risk Hohenheim's ire. In fact, he was willing to risk a lot more than a mere general's wrath. With *that* bonus, Richard could retire a wealthy man.

Chapter 18

Anthony pushed back his hair, muttering, and then sighed, undid the ponytail, and shoved the escaping and offending strands back into it, tying it tighter. Ceres' gravity was enough to keep most items in one place, but had little effect on hair or other very light materials. "Larry, this plaque, it is for the linguists, not us."

Larry Conley glanced in his display, seeing the image Anthony was sending him. "Oh, yeah. About an acre of text and one little diagram that looks like it might be something astronomical. Maybe. Or it could be a Bemmie mating-dance diagram. They loved those little sketch-thingies. Maybe they were just better at figuring out each others' chicken scratches, I dunno. Send that one to Rich and Jane, that's for sure." Larry shook his head. "I swear, it's so totally frustrating. We *know* a lot of this is astronomical data, or maybe astrogation stuff, but anyway it has to do with the actual solar system and the stuff they did in it, but we can't read it. That damn Rosetta Disk is taking them a hell of a long time to crack."

"We are better off than we were before, at least," Anthony pointed out, stretching a bit before going on to the next image of a noteplaque. There were literally thousands of the devices to go through. Why the aliens had chosen to stack that many of them in the one area was yet another mystery. A.J.'s best guess was that it was a repository for spare noteplaques—a place where you'd dump them for reuse by someone else. Why none of them were wiped off—blank—was somewhat confusing, though.

Still, no one was complaining, least of all Jake. This was a treasure trove, and he'd been spending the last few weeks carefully excavating the room, cataloguing each plaque's relation to all the others around it, and with Rich and Jane's help sorting them into likely subject categories. Apparently, if A.J. was correct, there had been a lot of work done involving astronomical/solar system navigation or surveying early on, and they were going through the discarded notepaper.

Both Larry and Anthony's initial enthusiasm on the vast number of potentially useful plaques had...well, not exactly vanished, but become dampened as it became increasingly clear that it was going to take weeks to go through them and even decide which ones were worth more study by them, rather than by dumping them on the increasingly overworked linguists. Xenolinguistics was a new field, with several universities trying to produce graduates soon, but it would be a while before real help arrived in that area.

Anthony blinked, then grinned at the new image. "The Great God Bemmie is once more on this one."

Larry laughed. "I wonder if they were really religious?"

"Who knows? Maybe that was one of their debates. Wasn't something like that in one of the books A.J. mentioned?"

"Oh, yeah, a classic. *The Mote in God's Eye.* There it was a nebula that looked like a hooded man, though."

"The Great God Bemmie" was Jupiter. Apparently, while the Great Red Spot had not existed sixty-five million years ago, similar semipermanent storms had; three of them, to be precise, apparently connected to something on Jupiter's quasi-surface thousands of kilometers below the cloud tops. The three rotated along with the planet and maintained a relationship which was geometrically very similar to the trilateral structure of the Bemmies themselves, and several sketches had indicated that whatever else the alien's perceptions might be like, they could, like human beings, see similarities between themselves and even astronomical phenomena. They often represented the giant planet as having three eyes, and there were sketches of Jupiter as the front end of a gargantuan Bemmie with a fully functional third eye.

Exactly what it all meant, of course, they might never know. But it was an amusing thing to find one of the cartoony sketches; some of the Bemmie scientists or researchers actually used the symbol for one of their people as the symbol for Jupiter, along with a symbol meaning "very large"—leading Joe to say, "Ah, yes. The alien timekeeper of the system."

"Huh?" A.J. had replied.

Joe had given one of his fiendish grins. "Obviously, Jupiter was Big Bem."

This had resulted in Joe being hounded from the room.

Aside from Big Bem and a few notations on what Anthony thought might be Io, there wasn't much on this plaque, so he went on to the next.

Several hours went by. Larry finally got up and stretched. "Well, Anthony, I know you've got more endurance than I do, but I'm going to get myself some lunch."

"Oh, is it that time?" Anthony looked at the clock. "I suppose it is. But I started a little later than you, and I want to at least get through this set."

"No problem. Just flag anything you think might be worth looking at."

"Of course."

More plaques. More cryptic sketches and acres of wavelike Bemmie text flowing from outside in, to meet in those upward-sweeping curves.

"Oh, there's something. . . ." Anthony said to himself as the next noteplaque image appeared. Pictures of Saturn weren't nearly as common as those of Jupiter, but the few they had found had sparked rather acrimonious debates among the astronomical community, with even Larry and Anthony exchanging some pointed words occasionally on the subject. The famous rings had existed back then, but the sketches indicated some differences. That the number of clear ring segments would vary wasn't surprising. In fact, depending on exactly how one imaged the rings, from what angle, and in what spectrum, the visible number of segments in the modern era varied pretty widely.

It wasn't the fact that the rings appeared to be separated into three clear sections that was the problem, though. The problem was that several of the discovered sections—including the new one he was looking at—very clearly seemed to indicate that the rings were divided *vertically* as well—into three or four distinct layers, with clear spaces between. If that were to be interpreted literally, there were a number of models that would have to be totally revised.

Most of the rest of the plaque was text, though it appeared that one of Saturn's moons was also marked near the planet. The

Bemmies did appear to read from top down, as did humans, and near the bottom was a symbol crossing the centerline, which the linguists had said indicated something like a dash or "continued on next page." Of course, in many cases they were not able to find the next page. Knowing the pattern Jake had excavated in, though, Anthony decided to scout through the ones that were physically nearby this plaque, just to see if the continuation was obvious.

Upon viewing the noteplaque found just below and slightly to the right of the first, Anthony suddenly stopped. The top center column contained the inverted symbol, meaning "continued from," and just below this was a large sketch of some celestial body, a circle with various other symbols on and around it. He looked back at the first one, and saw small symbols next to the marked moon—symbols repeated next to this large sketch. A moon of Saturn, then. Or probably so. Which one? Titan would seem to be the obvious target of interest for anyone in the solar system. A moon with a thick atmosphere and all sorts of activity. But...

No, even displaying Titan's known characteristics in what Bemmie's range of vision would have given didn't seem to produce a correspondence with the markings. The symbols weren't too much help, either. While they'd determined a number of simple symbol conventions that allowed Anthony and Larry to read parts of the astronomical diagrams, too many things were still obscure.

Still ... that set of symbols, there, toward—he checked the symbology—what would likely be the moon's southern pole ... that set looked familiar. Very familiar.

Anthony became aware that he needed to breathe. He took a deep breath, realizing that he must have been staring without even breathing at that image for a long time. *This was it.*

His first impulse, surprising him, was to call in Larry. He got a grip on himself, already feeling guilty. But this was the reason he'd been brought along. Quickly he checked Larry's status in the on-duty tracker. Still at lunch. He uploaded the application Horst had given him, the last update being only a few days ago. He'd practiced with it many times, but for a minute he froze, unable to remember what he had to do. Then he closed his eyes and took a few deep breaths.

He was feeling intensely guilty. *Focus. Focus. It is not as though we will really be hurting anyone.* He felt bad that he would have to mislead them, but they already had three Bemmie bases. Besides, this new one was so distant that only *Odin* could possibly reach it anyway.

Just a little tweaking. No real erasure. Just some confusion.

Erasing data from the systems being used was an extremely difficult task. There were backups that even Horst's slow-viral approach probably would never reach, unless someone were foolish enough to mount them to the same system they were checking on. So the key was to make it so that they wouldn't bother to check correspondences with the backups until it was far too late. Just a minor transposition of relationships and a very small image edit. The tough part, handled entirely by Horst's app, was making sure that the check data was appropriately modified, so that any examination of the image would not indicate that any modification had been made. In essence, the internal "watermark" had to be modified and the records of the authentication data modified as well, so that all aspects of the system agreed that the modified image was, in fact, the exact original image that had been in the system from the beginning.

If someone were sufficiently suspicious and had access to the backups, of course, they could find the modification easily enough. But with luck, no one would be until it was too late.

Anthony sighed. It was done. He got up, just as Larry came in. For a moment Anthony froze, certain that guilt was written all over his face, that Larry knew he'd been tampering.

"Anything interesting?" the big astrophysicist asked.

"Nothing, really." Anthony's voice sounded strained and flat, totally artificial in his ears. "Time to get something to eat myself, I think."

If his tone was different, Larry didn't appear to notice. "Have fun. Back to the salt mines for me. See you later."

Anthony left quickly, almost bouncing into a wall in his hurry. He had to get this to General Hohenheim immediately.

Then, at least, the rest would be out of his hands.

Chapter 19

"Enceladus." The general pronounced the little moon's name carefully.

"Yes, General," Anthony said. "After I reported the initial find, I did continue my research. Since I knew of the connections, I was able to determine a few more facts to confirm the labeling."

Hohenheim nodded. "Very good. I had hoped for something in the Jupiter system, but we are provisioned for Saturn as a possibility. Tell me what makes Enceladus a good possibility, aside from simply finding markings on one of the diagrams?"

Currently, only Hohenheim and LaPointe were present, as the general wanted to evaluate the situation himself privately. Anthony activated the meeting-room display. A rotating image appeared of a mostly white sphere, covered with noticeably varying terrain ranging from small craters to faintly blue–striped cracks.

"Enceladus has been sort of an *enfant terrible* for us astronomical types in the past few decades," Anthony said. "It's much smaller than many of the really large moons like Ganymede, Europa, or our own Luna. In fact, at about five hundred kilometers across, it is quite a bit smaller than our Ceres here. According to many theories of celestial body formation, it should therefore be a relatively static body, a dead rock or iceball floating in space.

"Instead, it is one of only a very few bodies in the solar system with known volcanic activity. It has a surface indicating recent resurfacing—in some areas it may have the most recent surfaces in the solar system." He gestured at the faintly striped areas. "The false-color images overlaid here show what are sometimes whimsically called 'tiger-striping,' but what is significant about them is that they include crystalline water ice—possibly less than a thousand years old, or even newer, given our detection of cryovolcanism—and some organic compounds. There are, however, other areas of Enceladus that are much, much older on the surface."

A cutaway view of the miniature world appeared. Hohenheim frowned. He was of course familiar with cutaway views of Earth and other worlds, but this one was...odd. It appeared that the majority of the little moon was cold, but that at one point, near the south pole, it was significantly heated. Totally asymmetric and not at all consistent with anything he had ever seen before.

"I see your expression, General, and you're correct. That's called a *diapir*. The conventional description is that it is lower-density heated material rising to the surface near the south pole. Models of Enceladus have tended to converge on this structure, but what has *caused* the structure you see has been a matter of furious debate." Anthony paused. "Until now."

Hohenheim slowly turned to stare at the grinning scientist. "Are you saying...?"

"Where is the energy coming from, General? That's been the constant debate. Actually, it's been two debates. First, where the energy comes from, because not all models of the tidal forces active on Enceladus appear capable of supplying all of the energy needed. Second, why it's only apparently active in this one location. One can of course come up with all sorts of theories, and I assure you many have. Enceladus is very small, so perhaps it is not as differentiated as a larger body would be. But other evidence argues against this, such as the geological and chemical makeup. Tidal heating of differentiated magmatic chambers—which being liquid would flex more than the solid material around them—could explain the existence of isolated hot spots...if the tidal heating were sufficient. But many models don't show the tides as being quite sufficient.

"Yet there is clearly liquid water present in large quantities on Enceladus. Nearly pure water, in fact, as no ammonia or other materials were detected in many of the plumes. This is itself quite notable, as this means the liquid is at a temperature in the Earthly range—at least freezing point of zero Celsius or two hundred seventy-three Kelvin. That is a quite drastic departure in both expected temperature and expected chemistry for that part of the solar system. Much larger bodies, such as Jupiter's Europa, are known to have liquid water beneath the surface, but it was really quite unexpected to find evidence of it on Enceladus."

Anthony pointed again to the off-center southern heated area, the diapir. "The best models we've been able to make, however, have given us this considerable problem—the tidal forces just aren't quite enough. They're fairly close on a cosmic scale, but we're missing a terawatt or so."

"After all this time?" the general said finally. "That is not possible."

"With all due respect, General, it *may* be possible. The aliens used self-repairing redundant technology in a number of ways. If the device or devices in question were intended to operate for some unbounded amount of time, they may have simply continued to do so. Or, as I think more likely, they may have operated for long enough to create the current situation. On an astronomical scale, remember, even sixty-five million years is relatively short. If they had succeeded in creating a diapir or something similar, there is sufficient tidal heating to make it likely that it would still be slowly cooling to this day. We would not notice the change on our timescale. But if they did such a thing, somewhere on Enceladus would be a truly massive installation."

Hohenheim stared at the image, trying to envision it. The distant moon was indeed tiny compared to Earth, but he had spent more than enough time in space to recognize how vast even Enceladus was. Enough power to slowly reshape an entire small world...

He nodded sharply. "Very good. We must begin preparations. Subtly, of course. We must not alert the Ares people on Ceres to our new intentions. I believe I will arrange an apparent recall of *Odin* to Earth. Obviously we will not go there, but preparations for departure will be similar. Very well done, Dr. LaPointe. I am sorry you have been forced into duplicity with your colleagues, but in the long run I hope you will find it was worthwhile. At the least, you shall be the first on the site."

LaPointe managed a smile. "Thank you, General. I appreciate your sympathy. I'd better get back to work, though."

"Indeed. No point in failing to gather any additional data."

As the astronomer left, Hohenheim shook his head. Objectively, he was taking quite a risk. The symbols were undoubtedly those of one of the alien bases, and similar to those for Ceres—that is, the markings of the group of aliens who had lost their battle and apparently been evicted from the system. However, if some device capable of producing such power had been left running, it seemed to Hohenheim fairly likely that it could have destroyed the base when it finally broke down—as any device *must* have broken down after millions of years.

But he was also paid for his intuition, and his intuition said that this was *it*. And, he admitted, there was also the voyage itself. The course would take them through the Jupiter system, the massive planet's gravity well providing them with additional velocity. Hohenheim also knew that in the many months they had been on station, the mass-beam had not been idle. There were more surprises and demonstrations in store for those watching *Odin*, and he was looking forward to a bit of showing off. At the very least, the crew of *Odin* would be famous as the first human beings to ever visit the outer system.

Now, however, he had to have a long talk with Mr. Fitzgerald. There might very well be complications when the time came to leave, and he had to be ready to deal with them all.

Chapter 20

"Looks like the *Odin* is really getting ready to move out," Jackie said, sounding disappointed. She stared at the image of the huge E.U. ship in the Ares common-room monitor.

"Yes," Maddie said. "Why, I wonder?"

Jackie glanced sharply at her. "What's bothering you? After all the shadowboxing you've been doing trying to keep our guests from finding out anything, I'd think you'd be glad they were going."

Maddie couldn't help frowning. "It just doesn't make sense to me. The cost of sending *Odin* out here is . . . Well, it's actually rather hard to determine, but many millions of dollars, maybe orders of magnitude more than that. They could have had *Odin* doing a lot of other things that would have been potentially profitable, or at least a lot less of an apparent loss."

Bruce sat up a little straighter. "So what's your take, then?"

The former HIA agent shook her head. Being unable to answer Bruce's question in a clear, direct fashion was frustrating and upsetting. "I don't know, Bruce. Instinct tells me there's something wrong here. And I didn't survive some of the things I have by having bad instincts. My evaluation has always been that they came here to see if they could find out something that would give the E.U. a leg up. It only makes sense, given that the IRI and Ares have so far kept in the forefront, with the United States getting the main benefits after that. But . . .

"I know that Fitzgerald's managed to get a handle on what we've been doing in the fusion research—enough that I expected they'd try to suborn our systems or some of our people and send the data onward. With the resources of the E.U., they'd be easily able

134

to develop the Bemmie system to practical deployment far faster than we can, and according to you"—she nodded at Jackie—"and Dr. Vasquez, it's not so far from our own theoretical knowledge that the E.U. couldn't make a good case for having just come up with it independently after the discovery of the Bemmie superconductor, which shook up a lot of theoretical constructs anyway."

"But you made sure they couldn't do that, right?"

Maddie rose and drifted restlessly around the break room. Joe, as usual, was absent because he, Reynolds, and A.J. were still working on the dusty-plasma vessel and, in Joe's opinion, were close to making it work. "I actually made sure that they thought they *could* do it. And I'm about ninety-nine percent sure that Fitzgerald bought that line, but he ended up not taking the bait. Oh, I'd have shut them down and kicked them out when they tried." She shook her head and gave a faint chuckle. "Maybe I'm just a little full of myself. Richard Fitzgerald might just be smart enough that he saw the trap. I don't think he is, but maybe."

Jackie didn't look very happy. "You think all of them are here to, well, do industrial espionage? Really?"

Madeline laughed. "No, no, not all of them. Well, yes, in that I'm sure they were all told to keep their eyes open, but there's a big difference between that and actually stealing secured data. Your boyfriend is probably just fine."

Jackie blushed slightly—something barely visible with her dark skin. "Horst Eberhart is not my boyfriend. We went on exactly two dates—if you can even call them 'dates' in the first place. I barely know the man." After two or three seconds, she added a bit plaintively: "Only probably?"

"Only probably," Maddie said. "But that's from my paranoid worldview, remember. I get paid to assume everyone's up to something."

"So," Bruce said, "If I'm understanding you right, the problem is that you don't think these bastards got anything, so you're wondering why they're leaving?"

"Something like that."

"They couldn't have just decided you had things locked down too well and, after a while, it's not worth it?"

"Maybe." Maddie restrained the impulse to stomp her foot, which would have caused her to bounce off the ceiling. "But that just feels wrong. They're heading back to Earth. Why? Just to drop off people? No special cargo?" She hated feeling this uncertain. It was something so rare for her that it was unsettling. "Or are they even smarter than I thought? Did they get past all our security, including me, and so what they're doing is leaving *with* their prize?"

"Maddie, luv, you're the best there is. The only way they're getting away with something is if you didn't know there was something to find."

She froze. Her mind flew back, fitting together the dozens of pieces of the puzzle she'd encountered in the past year and a half.

Maddie turned and propelled herself toward the exit, bringing up her own VRD displays. "Bruce, I think you may be exactly right."

Control. Losing control will do me no good. The general took a deep breath. "Exactly what do you mean by 'insurance,' Mr. Fitzgerald?"

The security chief smiled. "The kind you didn't need to know about, General. It's my job, not yours. Plausible deniability and all that."

"I doubt very much if 'plausible deniability' is all that plausible here in the asteroid belt," said Hohenheim, his teeth almost clenched.

Fitzgerald shrugged. "Probably not plausible to the Ares people, sure. But that's hardly what matters, is it? What matters is simply what people think back on Earth. And for those purposes, we should be fine. I chose the right sort of men for this little jaunt."

Hohenheim suspected that his notion of "the right sort of men" and Fitzgerald's were kilometers apart. But...

He took a deep breath. What was done, was done. And he was the one who had set this all into motion in the first place, he reminded himself sharply.

"We are not...attacking them, I trust? Because that is directly contrary to our directives."

"Not attacking, no," Fitzgerald answered. "Just...making sure they can't do anything to stop us until it's too late. Which was what you wanted, right?"

Hohenheim reviewed their prior conversations. Unfortunately, he had said things which could, in their essence, be read that way by someone seeking to push the envelope. And Fitzgerald was nothing if not an envelope-pusher. He'd have to remember that in the future.

"What exactly is going to happen, then?"

"It's standard CCC technique, General—chaos, confusion, catastrophe. Very light on the catastrophe, of course. Modofori, Salczyck and Zaent are going for the fusion data, just the way I was going to have us do it before, except they think they're doing it as a sort of private side-gig for me. Personal profit, you know, with everyone getting a little cut."

"And you've actually framed them?"

"That's really such a cold word, General. If they don't get caught, they'll be rich men. And the paper trail—electronic trail, rather—doesn't even lead to me, let alone the E.U." He smiled cynically. "Of course, my guess is that little Goldilocks has so many tripwires and traps on that data that the first poor bastard who puts a hand on it is going to lose the hand. Figuratively speaking, at least. But that'll be enough to keep them distracted while we're leaving."

"Leaving our three crewmen behind?"

Fitzgerald nodded. "If that's the way it works out, yes. Their cover is that they're bringing the last of our own stuff back up in the *Hunin*. We're just doing maneuvers to get out of orbit, ready to do a main burn, far away from *Nobel*, right? So when they finally do make their break, we just let the IRI grab 'em. Sure, they'll guess that we were trying something cute, but they'll have no proof, and the neat part is that what we were *really* after they won't have a clue about."

"But when we start moving... You do understand that *Nobel* could catch us early on?"

"Right. It's smaller, they don't have nearly the load we do, they could catch us easy over the short haul, even if we can outdo anything else in the system on the long. So I've got something else set to make sure *Nobel* can't chase us."

"What?"

"Better you don't know. I think it's all covered, but the less you know, the less you can be accused of. Stop *worrying*, General. No one's supposed to get killed on this jaunt, and I'm not forgetting that. But giving them enough problems to keep them at home, that's not out of the mission parameters, now, is it?"

"I... suppose not," the general said slowly.

"Then I'd better get going. We're leaving in just a few hours, right?" Fitzgerald snapped a quick salute and disappeared out the door.

The commander of the *Odin* stared at the door, a rising sourness in his stomach. Fitzgerald was too eager, too capable in certain areas and too blind in others. Hohenheim shook his head, unable to fight the growing conviction that things were moving out of his control.

Too late now. Whatever Fitzgerald had planned, at least some of it was beyond any ability to recall. Time to play the hand he was holding. He headed for the bridge.

Chapter 21

Joe drifted in the long, dreamlike strides Ceres permitted, a cross between floating and walking that had taken some considerable getting used to. Usually, you had to guide yourself in mid-trajectory to some extent, because Ceres' puny gravity simply didn't get you back to the floor quick enough. But it wasn't quite puny enough to pretty much ignore. "Jackie, you're sure we have enough capacity for this?"

Jackie's voice over the link was amused. *"Joe, for the third time, yes. Do you think I'd have authorized it if we didn't? I'm just busy up here getting* Nobel *prepped. You've been around the power-distribution stuff enough to handle the install, haven't you?"*

"Oh, sure, that's not a problem. The setup's modular. I just know we've been using a lot more power lately, what with the research and our guests and all."

"Well, most of our guests are gone. All but three, I think, and they're getting ready. to leave soon. By the time you have the new main connection set and we can lay down the cable to the project, we'll have megawatts to spare. And if it does work, then we'll have enough reason to get another reactor out here."

"Okay. I'll stop bothering you, then." Joe continued along, knowing better than to hurry. In low gravity, hurrying just turned you into a pinball. But part of him still *wanted* to hurry. Setting up a major new power line was necessary so that they could test the repairs they'd made to the alien vessel.

After what was only about five minutes, but seemed like half an hour to Joe, he reached the control room for the reactor. The main power-connection modules were set on the far side of the room.

Fortunately, setting up a megawatt-capable connection was a lot easier now than it might have been thirty years ago, but he still had considerable work to do, and even following the procedures being projected for him in his own VRD it would take a little while. Obviously you didn't want to interrupt power to the whole base, so he had to arrange a cutout, install the new connection, then remove the cutout, without interfering with other operations.

This would only allow a partial test, of course. To run the ship—if it actually worked, something even A.J. stopped short of asserting as pure fact—would require most of the output of a reactor the size of this one, and of course it would have to be installed on board. But the important test was to see if, in fact, all the work they'd done would permit them to generate the necessary field in vacuum to hold the "dusty plasma" in place.

"How's it coming, Joe?" A.J.'s voice sounded in his ears.

"Not bad. Another half hour, I guess. By the way, we still need to figure out a good way to mop sweat out of people's eyes in these things."

"Yeah, I suppose so. I try to avoid all that sweating, myself."

Joe laughed. "You can't really fool us with that lazy-bum act, you know."

"It's the image. You know that's . . . Hey, what the . . . ?"

"What's up, A.J.?"

"One of Maddie's trip wires just went. Gotta go."

"Really? Okay, later, then." Joe went back to work. There wasn't much he could do in this case, and besides, as both Maddie and A.J. had been gleefully happy to point out in security discussions, there really wasn't anywhere anyone could run.

Well, not for long, anyway. There were miles and miles of Bemmie tunnels, rooms, and so on, only a fraction of them explored so far. But those were all in vacuum, so even if you had a shelter you could only last a short time. And in the open, well, you were obvious. Radiating heat energy like a beacon.

Them trying to get away with something *now*, that was a surprise. With the *Odin* pulling out in a matter of hours, already doing maneuvers to be ready to do a safe burn, who'd be stupid enough to try something?

At that moment, God brought a sledgehammer down on top of Joe Buckley.

"The fusion data?" Maddie asked, forehead wrinkled. "That makes no sense at all. Doing it *now*? When they were about to leave?" She glanced up at another portion of the VRD display, away from A.J.'s face and toward a data section. "Unless... There are only three members of *Odin*'s crew still here, on a last trip to retrieve material. If they're working solo..."

"You seemed to be surprised about what they were getting. Why's that?" A.J. could ask that in person now, as he had just come around the corner to the central monitoring area. "I got the impression you were about to call me anyway."

"I've found some possible indications that someone might have been tampering with our Bemmius data files, most likely in the astronomical data section. Which makes more sense to me."

A.J. nodded. "Well, you show me the traces, and I'll see if I can verify. Meanwhile you can track down our free-enterprise burglars."

Maddie nodded and sent her gathered data to A.J. He'd been correct that she had literally been moments from contacting him before the alert went off.

A subliminal shudder whipped through the room like a whisper of disaster. The lights flickered and went out, then backup, dimmer LED lighting came on. All her monitors blanked, but not before she had seen something to truly worry her. "What was *that*?"

"Umm... sensor analysis says... meteoroid impact. Significant one, too. Location... Oh, *shit*!"

"The reactor?" Maddie's heart seemed to go cold and stop. "But Joe..."

"Joe was there in the control room," A.J. said, voice disbelieving. "And the power's gone, which means it either took out the reactor itself or the control and distribution, which was what he was working on."

Madeline was halfway to the door before she remembered. "A.J., the three *Odin* crewmen—they'd gotten access through the bio library. And just before the monitors went out, I saw Helen there."

"Hold on, don't go *anywhere*." A.J. was clearly fighting down his own reaction to this news. "We need to coordinate. Suits on. The communication's going to be unreliable in here, but better than nothing. And you were right," he said, pulling on his suit, as Maddie did the same, "someone *did* mess with our files. It's going to take a while to figure out what they did, exactly, especially now, because I'll have to wait to get back online with the backup copies of our data and do a comparison."

The grim expression on his face was visible even through the faceplate in dim lighting. "I *can* tell you who did the erasing work."

Madeline took another deep breath as she fitted the helmet on. She knew A.J. was probably still analyzing what data he had available for her, even while he was talking. No point in interrupting. He'd known Joe even longer than she had. He was talking for a reason, but all she could really concentrate on was Joe. For the first time in her life, the only thing that mattered wasn't the mission. "Who was it?"

"Horst Eberhart. That glad-handing, smooth-talking, son-of-a-bitch Eberhart. He's the only guy they have who's that good—better than either of us—and this cover-up virus thingie he made, it's tailored to our setup. Be almost impossible to do by remote. Either he wrote it himself, or he sent someone else all the details on our setup—that he wormed out of me and Jackie, that *bastard!*—to someone else who did it."

A.J. made another set of control gestures. "Getting something here, now. I can get some of the independent sensor network up. Getting a low-bandwidth link to one of the satellites—dammit, I forgot. *Nobel* isn't in LOS right now."

"The timing sucks, you know that, A.J.," Maddie said. "Are you sure it wasn't a bomb?"

"Ninety-nine percent sure, yeah. The sensors would've *screamed* if a rocket or something was shot in this direction. Analysis shows a straight impact event at several kilometers per second, depending on the exact size of the impactor. That was just bad, bad luck on our part. Typical for Joe, of course."

Maddie couldn't exactly relax, but one of the many knots in her gut eased a bit. She really couldn't believe that anyone on *Odin* would be insane enough to start what would amount to war by blowing up the base. She'd gotten to know enough of them by now. General Hohenheim was a military man, and dangerous in that sense. But he was also a sensible man, not one to go off half-cocked. Even Fitzgerald couldn't be that stupid. She hoped. The three other men, though...

She pulled up her own copies of the files she'd managed to accumulate on *Odin*'s personnel. As she'd suspected, all three of these were on her red-flag list, which consisted of seven out of the ten people in *Odin*'s security force, including Richard Fitzgerald himself. All of them had proved to have some nasty histories when she'd used her old HIA contacts to dig on them a bit.

"Well, I've got a bit of good news, I think," A.J. said. "Looks like the impact didn't go straight to the reactor—must have hit the controls. But the tentative data left from the sensors in the area, just before they went down, seems to show that Joe was not in the precise point of impact. And I know he was in his suit." He patted her on the shoulder. "You go get the rescue party together. I'll go get these three clowns and bring them back."

She hesitated. "Are you sure? These people have backgrounds more like mine than yours."

"Like we said before, where are they going? Besides, I'm best suited to get the remote stuff that still has its own power working as I go along. I've got you a link to the satellites now—you should be able to get help. Go save Joe. I'll go make sure Helen's okay."

"Thank you, A.J." She watched for a moment as he went out. "Just be careful."

"These days, I am."

She activated the link. "*Nobel*, this is Madeline Fathom. Bruce, Jackie, do you copy?"

Bruce's voice came back immediately. "*Maddie!* It's good to hear a voice from you again. All telemetry and communications from Ceres just went dead a few minutes ago. What happened?"

"Meteor impact, A.J. says. Took out the control unit for the reactor. We're going to need your help on the ground to put things back together, Jackie."

"Ugh. Well, I think we can probably put something together, but it's going to take time."

"More importantly, Joe was near the impact site. We need to contact him, or find him. If he wasn't"—her voice threatened to do something humiliating like break, but she overrode it—"wasn't killed immediately, there's a very good chance the suit protected him, but he could be hurt or unconscious."

"And the suit can't keep him alive forever. Righto, then, we'll shift orbit around and get a look-see with the Beholders while we're on the way. Backup power working at all?"

"Some is, but the priority is of course for life support. And it won't last forever, either. That's why we have only voice communications and slow data links." She allowed her voice to leave the professional groove for a moment. "Jackie, please, let me know as soon as you get a look at the area. We have to find Joe."

"Don't worry, Maddie. I will. Why don't you get to the landing area, and as soon as we can get *Feynman* out the doors we'll come down for you."

"Thank you. I'll do that. In the meantime, I have to contact *Odin* on another matter." *Might as well do my job,* she thought as she headed for the other door which led more directly to the landing area. She adjusted the transmission frequency. "*Odin,* come in. This is Madeline Fathom, Ceres Base. *Odin,* do you read me?"

"This is *Odin,*" came the deep, warm tones of General Hohenheim. "Agent Fathom, is there a problem? We detected a sudden drop in communications."

"We have sustained a small meteor impact, General, but one which hit a critical location. One person who happened to be in the area may be injured, but we haven't verified that. I am calling about another matter, however."

Hohenheim's voice was puzzled. "Another matter? This seems to be one of considerable urgency—"

"If there is anything you can do, I am sure you'll be notified. However, just before this began, I had verified an attempt by three of your crew to obtain restricted information by criminal means. Specifically, James Salczyck, Leo Modofori, and Axel Zaent."

Hohenheim's voice hardened. "This is an extremely serious charge. You have evidence of this, I trust?"

"Our systems did not erase just because power was lost. And I have my own copies of my investigation. I have a great deal of evidence, and we have someone on the way to take them into custody. I intend to have them sent back for trial on *Nobel* once the immediate crisis is over. Do you have any objection?" This was the first test. If these people were acting under orders, the last thing the general would want is for them to be kept in the custody of others. He would offer to take them back in *Odin,* which would of course physically make more sense.

"Well...No, no, I cannot object. Obviously if it turns out your charges are of no merit, I—and the European Union—will be extremely disappointed in you, and it will have grave repercussions. On the other hand, if what you say is true, you have every right to charge them, and in the spirit of our cooperation I must allow you that right. Now"—his tone shifted slightly—"these three gentlemen did have one of our excursionary vehicles, the *Hunin*. Could you arrange to have it ferried to us after the crisis is over?"

The second test. "I'm afraid not, General. If these people planned it on their own, considerable evidence of what they intended to do with the information may be on board the vessel they were using, and I will not have time or opportunity to examine the vessel fully until after that time."

There was a moment of silence, during which Madeline reached one of the common areas which was now filled with worried people; she held up a hand to still the questions as the general resumed speaking. "Well . . . I suppose this is sensible. However, you do realize that the lander is an *extremely* expensive piece of the E.U.'s property, and that it must be returned to us as soon as is practical? Even our generosity has limits, and I assure you it does not extend to indefinitely giving away such a vehicle."

"I fully realize that, General, and as soon as a full forensic examination of the *Hunin* is complete, we will return it to the E.U. by the fastest practical means, even if we must use a considerable portion of *Nobel*'s capacity to carry it to Earth."

"Then," he answered, courteously, "I have no concerns. Your integrity is well-known. I will of course expect a formal document to this effect, outlining charges, actions to be taken, and the disposition of the *Hunin*, but deliver that after you have taken care of your emergency. Good luck, and please let us know if you require anything from us in assistance. *Odin* out."

"Thank you, General. Ceres out."

She looked around at the worried faces. Time to explain. And to hope.

Chapter 22

Helen was startled as the lights went out just as she entered the room. She'd been about to talk to the three men by the main bio console. They'd been clustered around, looking at something in a way that somehow didn't look right, but the sudden darkness distracted her.

A moment later, the emergency lights came on. She glanced around, puzzled. "What in . . . ?"

"Damn," said one of the men, a short, whip-thin blond.

"Just as well," said the second. His calm baritone voice and athletic build rang a bell. She knew this one somewhat—Modofori, that was it. "We might have tripped something, and—"

"Leo!" the third one interrupted, having looked up to see Helen standing there.

The three turned to face her. There was something in their expressions she didn't like, although that could just be the sinister tint from the reddish emergency lighting. "Wonder what took out the lights?" she said, figuring that was a relatively neutral topic.

"No idea," Modofori said. He looked concerned—and, strangely, a bit angry. "Um, Dr. Sutter—or would that be Baker?"

"Either will do, though I use Sutter professionally."

"Dr. Sutter, then." He looked around the room. "You know anything about the backups on this base? How long the air will last?"

That was an unpleasant thought. The lights had been known to flicker on rare occasion before, usually when someone was cranking up a high-power experiment or piece of machinery, but not stay out for any length of time. "Not offhand, sorry. If A.J. were here, I'm sure he'd have it down to the second."

"Maybe we'd better suit up," the third man said uneasily. He shifted his massive, squat frame to reach his spacesuit's case. People generally carried the suits with them, even though it was much easier to do work with them off in areas that were kept pressurized.

"Good idea, Jimmy," Modofori said. "But keep the helmets off. If air is going to be an issue, we want to save the stuff in our suits for last."

Helen, meantime, had been trying to reach the rest of the base. Her gut tightened. "I can't get through to anyone outside. Communications are down, too."

The three men looked at each other. The first man opened his mouth to say something, but Modofori gave a quick shake of his head. "That's . . . odd," he said. There was a moment of silence. "Well, we were just about to leave, anyway. Come on," he said to the others. "We've got stuff to take back to *Odin* before she leaves."

The one he'd called Jimmy glanced in her direction again and then whispered something to Modofori. Helen definitely didn't like the way this looked. She turned to the other door. "Nothing much for me to do here, either, not with the power off. Have a nice trip home."

The sound of movement behind her gave her a split-second's warning. She tried to move aside, but the reflexes of avoidance were still back on Earth, and she bounced more upward than sideways. Jimmy, his heavy form under more control, caught her leg and then spun, bringing her forcefully against the wall. She felt rather than heard a sort of crunching, cracking noise as her nose hit the flat surface, and blinding pain rocketed through her face. The concussion dazed her, and she wasn't quite clear on what happened next. By the time her eyes properly refocused, they were all in one of the corridors, a furiously heated discussion going on between the three men in a mixture of languages. She'd gotten used to this kind of discussion, and it wasn't that hard to translate. Unfortunately so, in this case, because as it turned out she really wasn't sure she wanted to know what they were saying.

"—asshole, we could have just walked." That was the shorter skinny one, dragging her by her right side.

"You saw how she was looking. She'd have sounded the alarm, if we hadn't tripped it already. And this can't be a coincidence." That was Jimmy, on her left. Ceres' gravity made her easy to carry, but two people could guide her more easily than one. Mass was not changed by gravity shifts.

"You think it's on purpose? How? And why? If it was a setup, what's to gain?"

"Shut up," Modofori said. The other two immediately silenced themselves.

Helen's communicator beeped. "Helen?" came the muffled voice of A.J.

Modofori shook his head. "Why does hers work when ours don't?"

"Helen? Answer me, please!" She was tempted to try to answer, but she suspected the result would be painful. Whatever these people were up to, they were serious.

Modofori fiddled with his radio. "Nothing on our frequencies. Don't know which one she's on."

A.J.'s tone changed, this time to the sharp, wiseass tone that preceded a truly heroic temper tantrum. "Modofori, Zaent, Salczyck, if you are there, better answer this, or you're not going to like it."

At their names the odd trio had stumbled, bumping into each other and jostling Helen. Something just brushed her nose, and she almost screamed in pain.

"Damn." Modofori grabbed the communicator. "What is it?"

She could just make out A.J.'s face on the little screen. "We know what you were up to, guys. Now it's over. Head to the main lounge and give yourselves up."

"I don't think so." Modofori looked like he was thinking furiously. "I'll call you back when *I* am ready to talk to you. And in the meantime, you remember whose communicator you were calling on. And stay quiet." He pointed the communicator camera in Helen's direction. "See? Now, I'll call back on this communicator when I'm ready. And if you play along, I think everyone can come out of this okay. If not..."

"I understand." A.J.'s voice was as cold as she had ever heard it.

"Good." Modofori switched the communicator to off, using the hard-off switch. And pulled the power cell for good measure. "There." He glanced at the others. "Let's move."

"I'm getting a very weak response from Joe's comm, mates."

"Thank God. His suit wasn't destroyed, then." Madeline allowed herself to feel a little hope.

"Apparently not. Whatever hit, though, did one scary lot of damage." Bruce's voice was grim. "Scattered debris over miles and miles in this low gravity." His tone shifted. "Okay, Maddie, we'll be landin' soon enough. Then we drop Jackie off at the site so she can assess the damage, and we can search for Joe."

"Thank you, Bruce." It occurred to her suddenly that she hadn't heard from A.J. in quite some time. "A.J., are you there?"

There was no answer for a moment, and she began to really worry. Then his voice came back, sounding oddly flat. "I'm here."

"Is everything all right? Did you get our fugitives?"

"It's not all right *yet*," A.J. answered. "But it will be."

"What's going on, A.J.?" She knew evasion when she heard it. "Don't try to handle this if you can't—"

"Don't go there." The cold reply brought her up short. She hadn't ever heard him use a tone like that, not even when he was furious at her. "I said, it *will* be all right. I'm taking care of it. You have my word. You just go find Joe and get things running again."

She thought a moment. "Is Helen all right?"

"She will be."

"Ah. Crazy bastards." She thought she understood now. But... "You're sure?"

"Absolutely. I gave you my word."

She knew that A.J. did not use that phrase lightly. It was acutely painful to her to not step forward, but...in his position, if she was sure she could handle it... "All right." She offered a short, silent prayer to whoever might be listening that A.J. really knew what he was doing, and then deliberately let the matter drop from her mind. Agent's training was what was needed here.

The *Feynman* was barely settling into place as she bounded out to meet it. "Let's go find Joe," she said to Bruce as the door opened.

"Righto."

The impact site was barely a hop away; in fact, using *Feynman* would have been overkill if they hadn't intended to use the shuttle as a search-and-rescue vehicle in the area anyway. Maddie sent several of the Locusts, which she could control nearly as well as A.J., on a survey of the area as Jackie made her way into the shattered hulk of the prefabricated building that had housed the control center for the reactor. Part of it had practically *splashed* on impact.

"That's bad," Jackie said matter-of-factly. "Punched through the main controls like a bullet. A bullet that must've been bigger than my two fists. And with atmosphere present..."

"Big boom." Maddie glanced around the room. It was actually startlingly clean in some ways, probably because the blast and air escaping had thrown everything *out*. There was still a film of dust here and there—and what was *that*?

On the floor, the dust showed a faint, odd pattern: light streaking, then two dark streaks like expanding cones, wide ends pointing toward the wall. The dark streaks, she saw as she bent closer, were really areas with a lot less dust. "Jackie?"

The dark-haired engineer saw the pattern, too. "Joe."

"He must have been standing here when the thing hit."

Jackie nodded. "Well away from the very center. I think I can get *Nobel* to give me at least an estimate of the force of impact. Hold on."

A few minutes dragged by like hours as Jackie set up the parameters for the model. Then: "Maddie? He could have survived. But it was awfully close. Depends on what he hit on the way out, where he landed, how exactly he was standing..." Jackie trailed off. "We'll just have to find him."

"Bruce!" Maddie said, pushing her emotions aside. "I've had the Locusts circling the area. Can *Nobel* tie in and compute a fix on Joe's location?"

"Sorry, luv, no joy. Signals seem to be bouncing off the base material, getting absorbed, multipath all over. No way of tellin' which of six directions to look in. If we can't narrow it down... well, he's got Buckley's of being found in time." Bruce got a dark amusement out of the fact that Joe's last name was, and had been for years, Australian for *hopeless situation*.

"Then," Maddie said briskly, "we'll just have to narrow them down, won't we?"

"We'd better do it quick," Jackie said. "The rest of the base isn't going to last forever without power. We have to get things running again."

"How long to replace the controls?" Bruce asked. "Do we even have the parts on hand?"

Jackie's gestures showed she was consulting her own database. "Actually, we do. But it's going to take four, five days at least. And that's longer than the emergency backups will last. We can probably save all the people, but there'll be major losses in other areas if it goes that long. We'll lose infrastructure to frozen pipes and all that kind of thing. We need to get at least minimal power flowing faster." She shook her head, gazing down at the immense hole punched through the area the consoles had occupied. "I might be able to rig something up, but I'm not sure. The reactor itself may have shut down when the controls went, which means I'll need the controls before I can start it generating again."

"How much juice do we need?" Bruce asked. "To keep things moving along until you can fix 'em?"

"More than a portable generator," she said reluctantly. "For everything, we probably want a hundred kilowatts or more. That won't run any of the heavy stuff, of course."

"Right, then. No worries—*Nobel*'s got that and to spare."

"Yes, but—" She cut off. "No, Bruce, you're crazy!"

"Hey, it's a fair sight better than losin' half the base, now, ain't it? And won't it be something to add to my resume?"

"And what about Joe?" Jackie demanded. "We're talking about saving the base, but what about him?"

"We have to narrow the search area," Madeline said. "And Jackie, I think you can do that."

"Me? How? Maddie, you know I'll do what I can, but I don't see what I can do."

She pointed to the tracks in the dust. "You were able to do a quick model to see how hard he was hit. But we assembled all of the stuff here. It's all in the engineering database. If you can get a good handle on the force of the explosion from A.J.'s sensor readings, can't you model what happened to Joe and find out where he went?"

Jackie froze, clearly struck by the idea. Slowly she straightened up. "Yes. Yes, we could do that. We can't get an exact answer, not even close. . . . But if we can even get a good sense of direction and distance . . ."

"Then do it fast, Jackie." She looked at the clock in the upper left of her field of view, a phantom row of numbers projected on her retina by the miracle of laser light. "If I guess right, Joe has maybe four hours left."

Chapter 23

"But . . . Look, Leo, what're we going to do?"

For the first time since Helen had seen him, Leo Modofori smiled. "A.J. Baker can get us past any of their security. He runs it, along with Fathom. With his help, we get what we came for. Then he gets us to *Hunin*. They'll have to let us back on board if we get close to *Odin*, and then, well, okay, they'll put us in jail for a bit. But if we've got what we're after, we'll be out and rich before you know it."

Jimmy Salczyck grinned back. "So, I did the right thing."

Modofori snorted. "Sometimes impulse and luck works, Jimmy, but we still should've talked. Anyway, it's over now. First we have to get somewhere we can hide out. Which isn't here. Baker knew where we were with the comm. We have to lose him so he can't set up an ambush, keep moving until he comes through."

"Won't he just have us nailed when we get to *Hunin*?"

"Not if we rig it right. He saw that we have his wife. We just make sure we get access to the monitors around the *Hunin* first. If it's all clear, fine. If not . . ." He didn't look at Helen, but it was obvious what was implied. "We need to cut through the unpressurized areas and come up somewhere else—the third lab, I think. There's a terminal we can use there, when the time comes. But we want to leave no trail for him to follow."

Zaent glanced about him uneasily. "These corridors seem narrower." He gave a nervous cough.

"This is not the time to develop claustrophobia, Alex," Jimmy said. He sniffed at the air. "Does feel kind of stale, though. . . . Now you have me thinking it!" He grabbed at his helmet with his free hand.

Modofori growled in his throat. "Exactly. Don't go putting ideas into your heads—or mine, for all that." He cleared his throat and then took a deep breath. "There's air enough down here to last us for quite a while. Hours of air. Houdini managed hours in something the size of a coffin, and we've got a mansion's worth, so cut it out. No, leave the helmets off until we get to the lock. Hold up a minute."

He moved in front of them with the smooth action of someone completely accustomed to the low gravity; even in her pain, Helen had to admire that. She wasn't that good, and she'd been here a lot longer. "Sorry about the rough handling, Doctor. Can I trust you to not try anything stupid on us? Because I promise you that if you do try anything, it will end up hurting a lot worse."

She nodded, trying not to look scared—although she definitely was. This was about as bad a situation as she could think of. The crash on Mars had been worse in some ways, but that was an accident. What might happen here wouldn't be.

"Good. Now, hold still a moment. This will hurt, but it will help in the long run." He glanced at Jimmy. "Hold her head still."

Helen closed her eyes. There was a moment of terrible, sharp pain, a twist, and suddenly much of the pain was fading away and she felt she might be able to breathe through her nose again. "Thank you," she said faintly.

"You're welcome. If your husband is half as smart as I have heard, we should all come out of this quite well. He *does* care about you, I hope?"

"Yes," she said. It was one of the things she had no doubts on.

"Good thing for us all, then. Now please get into your suit and don't give us any trouble. We have to move fast, and I can't afford the time to babysit you."

Modofori apparently had a VRD with a system that included a detailed layout of Ceres Base, because he led them onward with barely any hesitation, occasionally gazing into empty air before taking a particular turn. Shortly they came to an airlock, where he had them all appropriate additional air bottles.

Once through the airlock, there followed a bewildering series of twists and turns through alien-designed tunnels, the only signs of human passage being occasional marks in the eons-old dust and temporary markers on walls. Many of these tunnels actually had never had a human being pass through them, only one of the unmanned probes. And there were still many miles of corridors left unexplored. A.J. had once compared it to Mammoth Cave in Kentucky. "Except that we have to wear our scuba gear all the time here, and we probably won't have to wiggle through washtub-sized holes too often."

Helen tried to think of some way she might help out—get away from these guys and get somewhere she knew—but it didn't look hopeful. Impulsiveness aside, Jimmy Salczyck was as alert as a Doberman watchdog, and she already knew from personal experience how fast and strong he was. Despite the training both A.J. and Madeline had been giving her on the side, she doubted she could take on any of these guys, even the diminutive Axel Zaent. Her own VRD didn't have the extensive maps that Modofori's did, and with the main base systems apparently still down—something that clearly worried Modofori almost as much as it did her—she couldn't get any additional data out to guide her. So even if she did somehow give them the slip, she might end up wandering deeper into the base instead of getting out.

Finally they came to another airlock. Modofori brought out a small case and performed some complex set of operations on the controls and around the door seal. "What are you doing?" she asked impulsively.

He apparently didn't mind the query. "Making sure that it appears that this door does not open. It would be rather dense of me to spend this time in unmonitored corridors only to announce myself as I enter. Emergency power, while limited, does extend to keeping the door systems active and monitored, even if the full-scale hallway systems are down. I have no idea why power is still off, but for the moment it is an advantage I intend to exploit fully."

The airlock opened, and they passed through—Modofori first, then Helen, followed by the others. "Good. The lab I want is this way. The air's good, so unlock your helmets and save the tanks."

A few minutes later they were in one of the alien labs that had been used for what A.J. referred to as "bioforming" and which had been undergoing intense analysis. With whatever emergency was on, though, obviously no one was here now. And if the power came on, the remote location would give them plenty of time to get away before anyone else could possibly arrive. "Good enough. Time to get out of here for good."

Modofori took out Helen's communicator. Jimmy looked apprehensive. "Hey, Leo, won't he track us through that?"

"Probably. Almost certainly, in fact, since to make sure we could communicate with him no matter where we go he's probably had to key up low-power repeaters everywhere. But it took us a while to get here. Even if he can track us right away, he can't *get* here right away. If he's as good as I am at moving around, it'd take him at least half an hour to get here unless he just happened to set up in the area—and since I know where he was working, that'd be really unlikely. More like an hour away."

He put the communicator on one of the workbenches and put the power cell next to it. "Besides, I'm not exactly a slouch at this stuff. I don't doubt he can outdo me, but I can slow him down." From the little case he took another device which linked into his suit's datalink. "Mmm . . . yes, repeaters up. Not as secure as the normal link. I know this model—low power, self-contained, but only basic security on the ID. I can spoof them—make it look like our signal is coming from another location. If he gets suspicious, he'll be able to break through, but I think I'll catch that happening. Anyway, I don't intend to talk too long."

Satisfied, Modofori inserted the power cell, switched the communicator on, and spoke. "Mr. Baker, are you there?"

The little screen lit up immediately. "Yes." A.J.'s eyes were chips of blue-green ice.

"As I respect your abilities, I will not spend much time in conversation. I will talk, and you will listen. Currently you do not know where we are, and if you did you will not reach us before we move elsewhere. You are going to assist us in obtaining the information on fusion technology. You are then going to help us get to the *Hunin* unmolested. So that we may assure ourselves that we are not being ambushed, you will ensure that we have access to the sensors around the *Hunin*. While I am not your equal at sensors, I also assure you that I am capable of telling if you interfere with the actual data coming from the sensors in question, especially with the entire base apparently shut down. Once we are in the *Hunin* and ready to launch we will release your wife. Any deviation from this plan will result first in harm and finally in death for her. You must understand that while I have no interest in harming anyone, I can and will carry out my threats. We are in control in this situation, and you will do precisely as I instruct, unless you do indeed wish me to carry out those threats. Do you understand?"

A.J.'s expression had been impassive. Then it all of a sudden shifted, into a broad grin that somehow had very little humor in it. Even in the small screen, it gave Helen an involuntarily chill. "What I understand is that I don't think I have ever heard anyone manage to be more completely wrong more often in a single speech, even our current president."

One of the larger screens over the nearest research station flickered, causing all of them to jump, and abruptly A.J.'s face, twice life-size, was glaring at the three; even Modofori couldn't restrain a slight gasp. "I *do* know exactly where you are, and it will take me precisely three more minutes to get there. You will find you cannot go anywhere else. I will not assist you in obtaining any information, you are not getting to the *Hunin*, I'm giving you exactly zero access to anything except a jail cell, you wouldn't be capable of telling whether or not I was inventing anything if I told you I was doing it ahead of time, and most importantly"—his voice dropped to a low tone that still somehow carried with it a snarl—"you cannot, and will not, touch Helen, because *I* am in control of this situation, and you will do precisely as I instruct, or else I promise..." and suddenly he smiled with just a touch of actual humor as he quoted, "... 'You will know pain... and you will know fear... and then you will die.'"

At a gesture from Modofori, Jimmy grabbed her arm, forcing it up behind her back. "A nice speech, and I see we have less time than I thought. But I can carry out my threat."

A.J. raised an eyebrow. "I find your lack of faith... disturbing." His hand raised and gave a small gesture.

Helen felt Jimmy suddenly go rigid behind her. He gave a strangled cry and clawed at his throat. Helen knew she was staring, but doubted that her expression was any more dumfounded than Modofori's. Alex Zaent, his face pale, pulled out a knife and started for Helen. "You cut it out, you son of a—"

Another gesture—a rippling gesture, the one she knew well from A.J.'s use of virtual controls—and Zaent screamed and collapsed, the knife falling from a hand that seemed limp and useless.

Suddenly Helen understood. Yanking off her glove, she looked down at her hand.

Her engagement ring glinted dully next to the bright gold wedding band, its oversized setting empty of anything except air.

Modofori recovered slightly, but his voice shook as he spoke. "How are you...?"

"Ever wonder why a lot of the Faerie Dust technology is restricted? Now maybe you know," A.J. said. "The dust I'm using isn't meant for medical implantation, of course, so it won't last long—but it'll last long enough. It's actually going to take me another few minutes to get there, but I want you to know that I will know *everything* that is happening in that room. If any of you so much as twitches in Helen's direction again, I'll stop your god-damned hearts." The screen went blank. Jimmy, now able to breathe, slowly rolled to hands and knees—away from Helen. The others backed away from her as well.

By the time the door opened a few minutes later, Helen was alone in the center of the room, with the three men against the wall as far away as they could manage. A.J. didn't even look at them; he ran to her and hugged her tightly. "Oh, Jesus, Jesus, Helen, I thought I was going to lose you...," he whispered.

It was such a total change from the lethal man she'd seen on the screen just minutes ago that she just stood there, blinking stupidly, before hugging him back. "I was pretty scared myself," she said quietly. "And you scared the hell out of me just now, too."

"I scared the hell out of myself," he confessed. "I never knew what losing you would do to me until now." Without looking over at the others, he said, "Turn on the dataports on your suits, the three of you." Over his shoulder, Helen saw Modofori's suit suddenly go rigid as steel. "There, that'll hold you for a while. Someone will come down and pick you up in a little bit." He stood slowly. "C'mon, Helen."

"Wait," Modofori spoke. "The Faerie Dust in us?"

"Mostly nonreactive materials. I had to do major tricks to get it to the right places in you so it could do a few one-time zaps to the right nerves. I think your body's defenses will clean it all out just fine in a few days. I'll tell the docs to keep an eye on you until they're sure it's all right." He suddenly met Modofori's eyes. "I didn't want to hurt anyone, you know."

Modofori nodded, about the only movement the locked Tayler suit allowed. "I believe you. Thank you."

"Don't thank me. I'm still hoping someone else wants to hurt you later."

As they left, Helen caught at his arm. "What's going on with the base?"

"The base will be okay," he said. "If Bruce doesn't crash."

Chapter 24

Blackness slowly lightened to dim gray shot through with red pain. For a few moments he didn't even attempt to open his eyes, didn't even know who it was that would be doing the opening.

Joe. I'm Joe Buckley.

Joe tried to take a breath, felt knives in his chest and barely restrained a cough. The air was heavy, and cold. He tried to open his eyes, but they wouldn't open at first. Working his face, squinting and frowning and moving all the muscles, he felt something rough and sticky slowly giving. Finally, reluctantly, the eyelids came open, first the left and then the right.

Stars. Stars and dark roughness. Another squint, and he realized the roughness was rock. A lot of rock. *What the hell happened?* He could remember working on the power line for their lab; that was it. Then *boom*—nothing.

There were actual scratches across his visor, now that his vision was clearing. Something had hit him *hard*. Not that his body wasn't already informing him of that. He managed to move enough to get the self-diagnostics running. The suit was a mess, low on power, low on air, and some systems just plain not running. He wasn't in great shape, either. Broken ribs, possible minor internal injuries, concussion . . .

The comm unit was still active, at least partly. The antenna had been torn away. *Where the hell am I?* "Hello? Anyone there?"

Something suddenly moved in the circle of sky above him, a huge boxy shape of girders, cubes, and angles blazing with sunlight on one side, gliding with slow majesty across and, it seemed, downward. That was ridiculous, though. *Nobel* would have no business down that low, not even on a search-and-rescue for him. He closed his eyes, shaking his head to clear it even though that hurt. When he peeked again, there was no sign of the ship. No one answered his call. He tried to get the suit to boost the power and tried again.

"Hello, anyone there, this is..." He almost coughed again. "Joe. Joe Buckley."

Faint but sharp in his ears was the abrupt reply. "Joe? *Joe!* Thank God!"

"Dunno about thanking him, I think he *did* this to me."

"Bloke's right, act of God and all that." Bruce sounded distracted, though happy. "Glad to hear your voice, mate. Getting on a little eleventh-hour for you, if you know what I mean."

"What happened, anyway?"

"One hell of a lot," Maddie answered, unable to quite keep a teary-sounding edge from her voice. "For you, what happened was that a meteor smashed the reactor-control area and blew you...somewhere. We think we know the general location now, thanks to Jackie. Can you tell us anything to help narrow it down? Where are you?"

"Meteor? Now I'm getting hit by *meteors*? What, crashing in spaceships isn't good enough? Jesus!" Another breath did cause coughing, which definitely wasn't good. Once he could finally breathe again, he answered the question. "I'm in a hole. Pretty deep. I'm down at least fifty meters, I'd guess."

"That'd explain the diminished signal. And I'll bet there are side passages giving us multipath." That was A.J.'s voice.

"Still, now we know to look only in holes. Can you see the sky from where you are?"

"Yeah, I'm lying on my back looking just about straight up. Can't figure the constellations, though." He hesitated. "Um, the air's getting awfully thick."

There was silence for a moment. "How much air do you have left, Joe?"

"The recycler was kinda damaged, according to the readouts. I guess I have ten, twelve minutes before the stuff gets really unbreathable." When there was no response, he sighed. "Guess you don't have that good an idea where I am, huh?"

"No," Madeline said quietly. "No, Joe, I'm afraid we don't. But we might get lucky."

"I'll be prayin'," Bruce's voice said, seriously. "But I'll have to cut off, gents, because this last part is going to be very, very tricky."

"We understand, Bruce," A.J. said flatly.

Joe bit his lip. Ten minutes, and— "Wait a minute. Last part of *what*?"

"Of landing *Nobel*," Madeline answered. "We can't get the reactor back online right away, and we need power very soon."

"Maddie, look, I saw *Nobel* pass right over me. About ... call it three to five seconds before you answered me."

"Bruce! Jackie! Did you hear that?"

"I'm on it," Jackie said. "Hold on ... Got it! Depending on exact angles and times, that gives us ... this area."

"I see it." A.J.'s voice was energetic once more. "Concentrating all Locusts in the vicinity. Ignore any radio outside of that area. Maddie?"

"Combining with the maps ... there. It's one of those three."

The faceplate was slightly fogged now, and the air was sharp. He had to fight to prevent himself from gasping. Talking wouldn't be a good idea.

"Joe, hold on. We're—"

The radio went dead at that moment, and all that remained was the very dim lighting of the controls inside the helmet, and the stars, smearing into a mist of fog. And the pain, and breathing thickness ... and despite all efforts, the world going even darker ...

He was falling into pain, redness, cold, more pain ... sharper pain, as though he was struck, but his chest still ached. But the ache was fading, fading like everything ... almost gone, into warmer gray nothing....

Suddenly light blazed through closed eyelids and there was a hissing sound.... Pain screamed back into existence with consciousness, but he forced his eyes open, looking through a clearing faceplate into the airlock of *Feynman* and the tear-streaked face of the most beautiful woman in the solar system. "Joe?" she said, voice almost breaking.

He managed a grin. "Hey, it's like I always say. Seeing you is like a breath of fresh air."

Richard Fitzgerald entered Hohenheim's office. "You sent for me, Gener—"

With barely a shift of expression, Hohenheim grabbed Fitzgerald and slammed him against the wall, forcing a grunt of surprised pain from the Irish mercenary. "You complete fool. Do you realize what you have just done?"

Fitzgerald was too startled to reply immediately. He had not expected this violent a reaction, at least not once the operation was over. The general's vehemence had caught him unawares. So did his strength. Hohenheim was tall and broad, but much of that could have been the uniform. Richard realized now that he'd misgauged the man.

His immediate impulse was to disengage and counterattack, but that would be very foolish. *Careful, Richard, old boy. Just the overenthusiastic employee.* "General, please, calm down. We're getting underway now, and they haven't accused us of anything we didn't expect. It's all working out, so what's to be so angry about?"

The general slowly let him down, his fury seeming to ebb away a bit. "They have accused us of nothing *yet*, Mr. Fitzgerald. But you could have easily committed murder. Are you so callous and reckless you don't understand that? Furthermore, if they realize—"

"If they suspected us, they'd have said something right away, sir. Fathom isn't the sort to hold back. I tell you, the only chance they had to realize what was really happening was when it happened, unless someone spills the beans to them about our other capabilities, and that's not possible. Even Modofori wasn't in on that little part of the operation."

"He can cast suspicion on you, can he not?"

Fitzgerald shrugged. "I suppose he could try to say I sent them to do it, but he hasn't got a shred of evidence, and the others got slightly different conversations. They'll never match up. Oh, Fathom knows I sent them, and I think she's probably already guessed why. But with *Nobel* stuck on Ceres, they've got no chance of stopping us—and there's nothing in the system to catch us once we have a day or so running time, am I right?"

"True enough." The general turned away. "Mr. Fitzgerald..."

"Sir?"

"I thought I made it clear that I did not want them attacked. I consider this to have been an attack, however one may be able to argue otherwise. You did not—quite—disobey my direct orders, in letter, but in spirit I feel you have. In the future, I want you to understand that I will not look kindly on that kind of latitude. I will expect you to obey both the letter *and* the spirit of my orders, or I will have you relieved of duty, arrested, and sent back to Earth." Hohenheim's deep voice was as hard as iron. "And had Mr. Buckley died, Mr. Fitzgerald, I would have stopped this vessel, turned you over to them, and testified against you, no matter what that might have done to my career. Do I make myself clear, Mr. Fitzgerald?"

"Crystal clear, sir."

"Dismissed."

Richard paused once he had gotten some distance from the general's office. The back of his head throbbed where it had hit the wall. He'd also underestimated the general's ethical hang-ups, he now realized. That could be a problem in the future.

But there wasn't much point worrying about that now. Unless another emergency came along, there wouldn't be any reason to get into a pissing match with the general. Now, if all went as planned, it was going to be a matter of long routine and long-distance travel. Without Fathom or the others to bother them, he wouldn't need to worry.

Chapter 25

"A.J., you are such a geek. Going to your wife's rescue and you *still* couldn't keep from making cheap jokes?"

A.J. looked embarrassed. "That's how I keep from losing it, Joe."

Madeline nodded. "We all have our own methods. I'm . . . impressed, to say the least." Internally, she shivered. There were very few things that scared her, but the thought of the insidious way in which A.J. had dealt with the three renegade *Odin* crewmen gave her the creeps.

She was seated next to Joe's bed, where monitors were tracking his health. Dr. Brea didn't think Joe was in any danger, but he was to be monitored for the next day or so. A.J. and Helen, her nose bandaged, were in seats at the foot of the bed.

"Well," A.J. said, "I'm sure you knew the Faerie Dust could do stuff like that."

"Sort of," she admitted. "It's not as though no one ever thought of it before, but no one's quite gone ahead and weaponized it until now. And I had no idea you knew enough anatomy to do that so accurately. Especially using only the stuff from Helen's ring." That had been a point that was bothering her. There were an awful lot of the motes in the sparkling ring, but the power output and other aspects of the stunt A.J. had pulled didn't seem to jibe with what she knew of the Faerie Dust capabilities.

"Oh, I didn't just use that. I was able to get her ring to shed the stuff and get it on my targets before they suited up—as soon as Modofori answered, in fact, and I knew there was real trouble. If Helen had been wearing her suit then, it would've taken longer— I'd have had to work the things out of the suit when she had the helmet off, and so on. Anyway, once the stuff was all over them I was able to track them using occasional pulses from the marker beacons in the tunnels—had to override their power-conservation schemes, but that wasn't hard.

"Once I knew where they were going, at least in a general sense, I could spread a bunch more Dust in the area. When they took off their helmets, the first set from Helen's ring were able to guide the rest to the right points. It really doesn't take much if you're going to be triggering nerve and muscle impulses, but like I said, the stuff wouldn't last long. I had to move as soon as I was sure it was all set. The human body's a *terrible* environment for my little Faerie Dust motes."

He gave an exaggeratedly sympathetic look. "As far as anatomy, well, *I* don't know all that much, but the library files do, and Dust-Storm has been producing prototype medical motes, so I had to know something about it. And to be honest, I thought about these kind of techniques years ago, so finding the necessary nerve and muscle junctions was something I didn't have to work on just off the cuff. Guiding the motes to the right place, getting them to stay there, and hoping they'd all keep working long enough, that was the real pain in the butt."

"Now, alas, I have to start figuring out a defense against that kind of thing," Maddie said. "That really is quite frightening, even to me."

A.J. nodded. "To me, too. And the only defense I know of for sure is to already *have* stuff like that around, on, and maybe even in you that will intercept and kill off anything that doesn't belong there. That's how the human body works, you know. It's biological nanotech, and diseases are the attacking nanotech."

Maddie winced. "I think you and I are going to have to sit down and do some design brainstorming sometime soon. But not right now."

"*Odin?*" Joe asked.

"*Odin,*" she confirmed. "They're definitely heading for the outer system." Her communicator buzzed. "Fathom."

"Larry here, Maddie." The voice of the astrophysicist was grim, angry, and—through the tiny speaker—slightly tinny. "I went through the backups like you said, and I found it. Wasn't hard with the clues you and A.J. had turned up. They're headed for Enceladus. Judging by the course they're taking, probably going to use Jupiter for a course-correct and slingshot to push them to maximum controllable speed—and incidentally let them visit the big guy for publicity points."

"You're sure it's Enceladus and not somewhere in the Jupiter system?"

"Dead sure. That's the stuff that was hidden from the main systems, and the label on the Enceladus diagram is clearly for a major base—even if what we know about Enceladus didn't already tell me that." He summarized the peculiarities of the little Saturnian moon. "So yeah, I'm sure."

"How long before *Nobel* can't catch them?" she asked, trying to sound casual.

A.J. shook his head. "Too late already, even if we could spare *Nobel*. If we'd caught on right away, maybe, but they've gotten out into their mass-beam now. They'll be making eight kilometers a second already and accelerating every second. Judging on what our network's seeing on their course...Larry, can you give me a likely course-speed breakdown? I don't think they can crank it up much past one hundred sixty kilometers per second, based on what I've been able to figure out about their mass-drivers, plus they have to be able to make the corner and stop when they get to Saturn. It's going to be tricky."

"I can get you a rough guess...here."

A.J. stared into apparently empty space as he surveyed the data and imported it. "Yeah...they're full loaded. Rough guess, they'll be into Jupiter system in eighty days or a little less, then heading on to Saturn. Not sure what we'd do, anyway. They've got the right to make the claim, and there's no one else in the solar system who could get there."

Maddie almost said something, then stopped. There probably wasn't much point in it, at least not now.

Then Joe said, "But there is."

A.J. looked at him. "What are you...Of course!"

"You haven't even *tested* that thing yet!" Helen snapped, picking up on their meaning a split second after Maddie did. "And you'd have to stock it up for the trip, and figure out how you were going to get back, and..."

Joe opened his mouth to argue, and then—to everyone's astonishment—A.J. said: "She's right, Joe. It's crazy. We've got more stuff to work on with three bases—one of them, the one we have right here—than we'll manage to get done in a life-time. Why the hell should we take off and try to beat them to another one? I'm just glad we're all still kicking."

Joe's mouth slowly closed. Then opened again. "I'll be totally damned. A.J. Baker, Voice of Reason. What happened to the real A.J., you alien impostor?"

The blond sensor expert reached out and took Helen's hand. His gaze met Joe's, and Maddie saw Joe's eyes widen slightly. "Oh. Yeah, I guess that might do it. You just gotta stop this growing up, A.J. It's freaking us out."

"I'll do what I can." He glanced at Maddie. "Anyway, we've hung out here enough. I think me and Helen need to get some rest."

"Yes, let's leave you two alone for a while," Helen agreed. The two left, their drifting walk as close together as was practical.

Joe took her hand. "Thought they'd never leave."

She gave a slight laugh. His glance told her that he'd noticed something. Why she couldn't hide things from Joe now was a mystery.

"What's wrong, Maddie?"

She was silent for a minute. "Joe... When am I justified in *not* saying something, do you think?"

"Huh?" Joe stared at her. "I guess it depends on the things you aren't saying. Something about A.J. and those killer tricks? That scares the hell out of me, too. And A.J., if I don't miss my guess."

"I'm sure you're right. But that's not it, really." She tried to think of some way to put the question that didn't immediately lead to the next question and the inevitable answer. "I guess it's more a question of which right course of action I should take."

Joe thought about that for a minute. "You mean, if you have two courses of action that you can justify, but they each have something really bad as a potential result?"

"Something like that." She tried to keep her gaze level and unrevealing.

Joe was silent and thoughtful for a long time. She waited patiently. In some ways she'd learned to trust Joe's judgment more than just about anyone else's. Glendale or Hughes would have been good to ask, too, but not by remote; not by transmissions that took hours per exchange.

"Well... without more specifics, it's kinda hard to say, Maddie. But I guess I'd say that you have to look at what the costs are to you. You're almost always worried about other people, so I don't think you look at yourself as much. If one choice is going to cost *you* more than the other, maybe that's the only way you can tell them apart. Is one of them going to hurt your career? Your friends? Our marriage? Is one of them legal and the other not? I really don't know, Maddie. I know you don't ask me stuff like this lightly. And I could tell something's bothering you. But I know you don't make these decisions lightly, and you've always made the right ones before, so I think whatever you decide is probably the right one." He grinned suddenly. "It's like a test, Maddie. Keep your first answer—don't second-guess yourself—unless you have a real honest-to-god reason that you *know* you were wrong with the first one."

Maddie shook her head in bemusement. Joe's suggestions were simple stuff—direct, obvious advice that any agent already knew. But they were the kind of thing that any agent could often forget, and she *had* forgotten. Forgotten that it's not just your paranoid instincts, but your warmer ones, that you had to follow. You had to remember that you needed the support behind if you were going to face the danger in front.

Sometimes that meant *not* protecting the people you were responsible for, if the protection would be to lie and lose trust. And what she knew, or guessed, was something that would certainly do that, if she was right.

"You're right . . . as usual, Joe," she said slowly. *Then . . . there's something I have to tell you. Tomorrow. After you and A.J. rest.*

Because there'll be no rest afterward.

PART V: SPACECRAFT

Pursue, v: 1) to follow in order to overtake, capture, kill, etc.; chase 2) to follow close upon 3) to strive to gain; seek to attain or accomplish.

Chapter 26

"They *caused* the meteor strike?" Joe nearly lunged out of his bed.

"I didn't say that," Madeline said sharply, forestalling even more incandescent invective from A.J. "I said that there is a way in which they could have done it—technically possible, and my intelligence on their designs says it could be actually possible to have hidden the necessary components."

"What about our prisoners?" Bruce said, all his normal good humor totally absent. "You've interrogated them a time or two, I know."

"Nothing conclusive. They certainly don't know anything about those kinds of capabilities, but I know their type—they wouldn't be told anything like that. They all implicate Fitzgerald, but their stories don't exactly match. I think that's probably deliberate on Fitzgerald's part, but unfortunately what I think doesn't mean squat in legal terms. They'll be sent up, but there isn't a shred of real evidence we can use against Fitzgerald, Hohenheim, or anyone else. Basically, it's the word of a group of known criminals against someone in a lot better position. And their actions in turning over the evidence to us would be circumstantial evidence that they're really not worried about being prosecuted. What I know about Fitzgerald tells me he's more than capable of something like this. But I can't prove it."

"I can," A.J. said, voice grim. "At least good enough for me. I did vector calculations based on the modeling Jackie had to do in order to locate Joe, then refined them based on where we actually found Joe, connected 'em all into the timeline. If I project the probability cone of the impactor outward, it goes

171

right through *Odin* at about the time *Odin*'s long axis is oriented straight toward us."

"Show me."

An animation appeared on her VRD and those of the others in the room—Joe, Helen, Jackie, Bruce, and Larry (and presumably A.J.'s as well). The *Odin* turned slowly, majestically, a few hundred kilometers from the surface of Ceres, where the reactor control unit was marked. After a short time, the control enclosure exploded. It froze, then began to reverse, this time showing a very narrow cone expanding out from Ceres, to envelop *Odin* at the moment the vessel's long axis appeared to point directly (or nearly so) at Ceres.

"Did we recover samples of the actual impactor?"

"Some," Jackie said. "But it appears to be nickel-iron—perfectly reasonable meteoroid material."

"Hold on there," Bruce said. "That bastard hit at several klicks a second, right? Wouldn't that make *Odin* accelerate, at least a little?"

Jackie nodded. "Newton's still in charge here. Action and reaction. A.J.?"

"Wish I could give you a definite answer. Problem was that they were doing a lot of little burns around that time—a lot more fiddly and erratic than the last time they turned, I'll note—and that makes it hard to tell. There *looks* to be a spike around the right instant, but I'd have a hell of a time proving that it didn't come from some part of their clumsy maneuvering." A.J. shrugged. "The fact is that even a few kilometers per second on something weighing a few kilograms amounts to a centimeter per second or less on something the mass of *Odin*. That thing's a brute—over ten thousand tons loaded."

"So...what can we do, Maddie? Call up Glendale and have him lodge a direct protest, drag *Odin* back?"

"We can do that," Madeline said carefully. She really didn't want to push decisions one way or the other here. No matter what her own preferences. "And I think we have enough circumstantial evidence that they'll at least have to tell the general to bring her back for an inspection."

"But the fact that you haven't done that already," Helen said, "tells me that you're not sure that's the best course. Why not?"

"Because as we're the ones doing the accusing, the *Odin* won't be inspected here. We'll *all*—or at least those of us pressing charges—have to show up at Earth or, barely possibly, Mars, for the inspection and possible trial. And if Fitzgerald is even half as smart as I know he is, he'll be spending all that time having every trace of wrongdoing erased from the ship."

"How?" Jackie demanded. "You can't throw stuff away easily in space, and a weapon's not an easy thing to hide, not if it can..." She suddenly stopped, grim understanding dawning.

"Exactly," Maddie said. "It shouldn't be easy to hide a weapon capable of firing something at the speed of a meteor...but apparently they did just that. What kind of weapon fires nickel-iron projectiles at several kilometers a second, Jackie?"

"A coilgun. A magnetic-acceleration-based projectile cannon," Jackie answered slowly. "Which is not at all far from what they have for their main drive. If they're using it to accelerate, they obviously *can* use it to throw stuff away. In whatever direction they want. All they'd need would be some kind of structure they could extend out that would allow them to concentrate and focus the fields for throwing single large objects, maybe right along one or all of the main mass-beam ring supports. Which might account for the slight off-centeredness of your cone projection, A.J."

"Would we be able to see that?"

"Doubt it, luv," Bruce answered. "We weren't watching them doing the turn. It's not like we haven't already got about a billion pics of *Odin* from every bloody angle, so the only images we got of them from then wouldn't show anything even with A.J.'s tweakin' that would let you know if there was anything there that wasn't bloody obvious."

"So," Joe asked, "what are our alternatives?"

"Only two I can think of," Maddie answered. "We can drop it entirely—but let them know privately that we know what they did, and that we'll expect them to remember that, but basically be politically tactful. We'll end up getting Modofori and his group convicted without much of a fight and probably get some useful shipments and concessions. Remember that if we sent out this accusation, we'd definitely sever relations with the E.U. and lose a lot of potential friends and resources that we really need. If we keep quiet and use it on a subtle political front, we could lever a lot more out of them."

"And the other?"

She glanced between him and A.J. "We go after them and beat them to Enceladus, or, if we can, stop them from getting there."

Bruce frowned. "In a ship you haven't even tested? You're starkers."

"She'll work," Joe said. "And if she doesn't, we don't lose much. Just the time it takes to get ready and then unload her."

"What about supplies?"

"Already figured it," A.J. said. "*Odin* sort of gets a backhanded thanks. With the E.U.'s help, we've gotten a lot more stocked up than we would've otherwise. We'll want to take as much with us as we can stuff into the ship, of course—enough for many months. I'm actually figuring two years or so. The real trick will be getting back. But I've got some ideas for that, and I think I can show you that they'll work. The critical part is that you'll have to call *Nike* or someone in to do a supply run to get *Nobel* back off the ground, because we'll need to take the reactor with us. Plus a big fuel tank and one of *Nobel*'s spare rocket nozzles."

"I don't know that I like that whole idea," Bruce said. "I can't go with you, even. You'll have to fly her on your lonesome."

"Not a major issue," Jackie said. "The dusty-plasma sail isn't like any other ship ever made, even the mass-beam *Odin* uses. Anyone flying it is going to be breaking new ground."

"You talked to Director Glendale about this?"

Madeline nodded. "I arranged the tightest beam I could to him and encrypted the conversation. It was something of a risk, but we can't make decisions like this without his input and blessing. Joe and A.J. are able to make decisions for Ares, at least in this kind of situation." She switched in the replay of Nicholas' reply.

Their screens showed the dark-haired director gazing seriously into the camera. "Madeline, Helen, Bruce, A.J., Jackie, Joe...and anyone else who may be listening. You are in an extremely delicate situation. I can't pretend that I like the idea of confronting any of our allies at this time—but I also am not two hundred and fifty million miles from Earth and recovering from what appears to be the first interplanetary attack in our history. All of your alternatives seem to me to have negative as well as positive sides. While I find it acutely painful, I do not feel that I am in a position to decide for you. You must make the choice of action that you feel is right for this time and place. I will back you fully in whatever course you take. Just make sure that it's the one you can live with the best. Good luck."

"So," Madeline said. "It's up to us."

"Then I guess it's down to a vote," Bruce said. "We're all the senior officers and representatives, and there's . . . seven of us. Three choices. I think we need to get a clear majority, so we need four or more of us voting for one of the three. That seem fair?"

The rest nodded, Maddie included. "I don't think we need to do secret ballots, either. All the choices are acceptable, and I don't see why we shouldn't let discussion of the choices happen during the votes. We want this to be the best decision we can make." The others nodded, and they looked again at Bruce, who, as the captain of *Nobel*, was the closest thing they had to a real commanding officer.

"Right. Well, let's see now. I guess we'll just go around the table and vote for our choices, starting with me and ending with Maddie. Or do we want to knock the choices down to two first, making it sure that in the second vote we get a decision?"

"I like that one better," A.J. said. "How about we first vote for the choice we *don't* want?"

"Good enough. Suits the rest of you?" Bruce looked thoughtful. "Well, I'll tell you, mates—the one I don't like is the first one. We lose our allies by accusing them, and give the buggers a chance to clean up and make us look like chumps."

A mutter of agreement went around the table. The vote went quickly, with five votes against the first approach—accusing *Odin* and having her brought back in for examination—and two against the second, politically careful, approach. "Well, now, that was pretty clear. So we're down to two choices—be politically smart, or chase the bastards down in a Bemmie ship they didn't know we had ready. If it works." He looked torn. "I think I'll let someone else go first. Then I'll take my vote."

A.J. spoke up. "Beat the sons of bitches. I want to chase 'em down, pass them, moon them as I go by, and grab the *fourth* base for us, dammit. That bastard Horst suckered me, and they almost killed my best friend. I'm not pretending they're still my pals."

"I vote for letting it drop," Helen said, drawing an outraged look from A.J., who nonetheless managed somehow to keep his mouth shut. "Even if we can beat them out there, we don't have the resources to really take advantage of another base.

The E.U. really feels left out. I don't like what they did—to Jackie, to Joe, or the rest of us—and I think to be honest that we should blackmail the hell out of them because of it. But charging out after them in a ship older than some mountain ranges is just insane."

"I agree," Larry said. "Sorry, guys, but you'll get more flies with poisoned candy than a flyswatter. And you'll be chasing down an *armed* vessel, remember, and we haven't even got a peashooter."

"Screw that," Joe said with quiet venom. "*They shot me with a meteor.* I say we go after them, not pretend we're so stupid we couldn't figure out the scam."

"I'm with you, Joe," Jackie said. "And I'll help you get there if I have to get outside and push."

Jackie's voice was level, but Madeline could hear the fury in her undertone. The young woman could insist, as she always did when teased by Joe or A.J., that Horst Eberhart was not her boyfriend. Technically, that was perhaps true. Given the tight and crowded conditions aboard spacecraft, romance was difficult to develop. But that there was a mutual attraction between Jackie and the German astronaut had been obvious.

Now . . . Jackie obviously felt betrayed on a deeply personal level, not just professionally. Madeline couldn't blame her.

Bruce sighed and looked around, then sighed again. "Look, mates, I understand the anger. I feel it myself. But I've got a family and a career, and so do most of you. Sometimes you've got to take it instead of dish it out. My vote's that we do the quiet blackmail route. No crazy heroics."

As the others looked at Maddie, she realized *it's three and three. I'm making the decision in the end. Just like I didn't want to.* She looked at Joe, and his anger suddenly faded. He looked at her, saying nothing, but the brown eyes softened and said to her, as clearly as if he spoke, *You know what I want to do. But you tell me what you want, and we'll do that.*

For a moment, tears stung at her eyes. Because she knew that's what he would say, and that he would mean it, and he'd never reproach her on any choice. *I'm a lucky girl.*

She was free to make the decision. For herself. For Joe. For the rest of her friends.

"Down to me, I guess. There are good arguments on both sides. If it was an easy choice, we wouldn't be voting." Maddie studied the others in turn. "Are all of us ready to go along with whatever the final decision is—even if it's not the one each of us wanted?"

All the others—even A.J.—nodded. It was that, as much as anything, that decided her.

"Well, some of my attitude is probably just personal. Or maybe it's wounded professional pride. Whichever it is, I just can't see looking at myself in the mirror and thinking that I let that bastard Richard Fitzgerald stick his tongue out at us all while we pretend nothing happened. But there's not just my hurt pride involved—though that's there—and it's not even because the son of a bitch almost killed my husband. The fundamental issue, to me, is that we can't allow people like that out here. Space is dangerous enough without adding sleazy political games into the mix—and this probably isn't even political anyway. I'm willing to bet that if and when we discover the full truth about what happened—and especially *why* it happened—we'll find nothing more sublime than the usual money-grubbing. I'm almost sure this is just industrial espionage run amok. It doesn't even have the twisted dignity of evil empires at work."

She sat up straighter. "So I say we put a stop to it. Hard. They can't be allowed to get away with it. Ever. Not even once. I'll play politics, but I won't play patsy, and I'm not going to start playing blackmailer so that I can be on an even lower level than they are. We will go after them. We will catch them. And we will beat them, if we have to chase them across half the solar system to do it."

Bruce let out a long breath. A.J. grinned. Helen closed her eyes. Larry shrugged. Joe looked at her with sympathy.

Jackie just looked satisfied. "Let's get started, then," she said.

Chapter 27

Helen stared in stunned amazement, so riveted by the sight in front of her that she forgot to move out of the way; A.J., caught off-guard, bounced into her, shoving her into the cavernous hangar that was home to the alien vessel.

"Hey, you could at least have moved—" A.J. began, then noticed her expression. "Oh, that's right. It's the first time you've seen the ship in the flesh, so to speak."

"I'd seen pictures, but...Holy Bug-Eyed Monsters, Batman, that's bizarre," Helen said finally.

The alien dusty-plasma vessel seemed to float in the center of the vast room—which was ridiculous, given that Ceres did have a significant gravitational field. It took Helen a few moments to spot the cables that were suspending the gigantic hull over the hangar floor. The alien spaceship looked like a beetle held in a spiderweb.

Vaultlike material glinted dully in the bright work lighting, a sheen of metallic luster with hints of structured striations, something like spun aluminum but with a bronze color that somehow carried a bluish undertone. The color shifted subtly depending on the angle of the light, which meant that as you moved around the ship, the hull showed strange, almost-invisible moving patterns. The shape overall was made of sweeping curves in trilateral symmetry, like the ship's makers. There were no sharp edges except the trapezoidal outline of the airlock entryways. It was streamlined and organic-looking, small spikes like points of bamboo shoots curving over areas that looked like ports or vents surrounding the entire vessel at its midsection. And the size...

"It's huge," Helen murmured.

"Well," Joe answered from the other side of the ship, "partly that's because you're up so close and it's inside. Compared to *Nobel* or *Nike*, it's pretty tiny; mass of the hull and interior bracing and assorted structural elements is about a hundred and ten tons or so."

Helen blinked; to her, the almost-living, streamlined shape seemed colossal, at least the size of *Nike*. But she knew that *Nike*, even empty, massed around two thousand tons.

"That's a little deceptive, though," A.J. said. "That Vault material is tougher than anything else we've ever seen, and that made it possible for them to make this thing bigger than it might be otherwise. This little beast measures about sixty-five meters long and is about fifteen meters across at the widest part there. And, like *Nike* or *Nobel*, it's got a lot of empty space inside. Which is good, because we're gonna need it all."

"Really?" Helen studied the ship, which was somewhat more elongated in what she thought was the front, coming to three slender points at the very end; the rear of the vessel flattened out into an almost tripartite tail. Somehow it reminded her of a cuttlefish or squid in swimming posture. "There's only six of us going. And you're vandalizing the thing to make more room, it looks like."

The "vandalism" Helen pointed to was the addition, at the four cardinal points around the vessel's girth, of long backswept rods ending in slightly curved blocks. The four jarring additions, clearly human-built, were attached just behind the circle of bamboo-shoot–shaped spikes.

"I'll admit they're aesthetically displeasing on this ship," Jackie Secord said, entering the conversation as she exited one of the ship's locks. "However, those four habitat modules will—once we get her outside—extend out and allow us to spin up for gravity, just like *Nobel*, and we'll definitely need that to stay healthy on the way."

"And," Joe said, "we will need every bit of space we can get. We can't get nearly as good recycling gear set up for this ship as we could for the ships we had years to design, so we have to take a lot more consumables. Normally we can make do with slightly less than two tons of consumables per person per year, but with the systems we're dealing with . . . Well, I think we'd probably be able to get away with three or four, but I'm going with six, and figuring on at least a three-year trip. So that's nearly a hundred and ten tons of consumables—food, water, and air. To run the ship needs power—lots of it—which is why we're taking the base reactor. That's about seventy tons right there. Add in twenty tons of lander and various equipment, and we're around three hundred tons main payload. And then we need seven hundred tons of fuel capacity."

"Fuel?" Helen was puzzled. "I thought the point of this dusty-plasma sail was that it didn't *need* fuel. Well, a few hundred kilograms of dust and gas, but not fuel."

"True," Joe said, "But to do fast course changes—or to change direction 'against the wind,' so to speak—you need a rocket, or something like it. We may need to do an Oberth around Jupiter, and when we want to come back, we'll *definitely* want to use that approach to head back in-system."

"You're talking about a NERVA-style drive, like the *Nobel*, right?"

Jackie nodded. "Exactly. We're saying 'fuel,' but really it's just reaction mass. Heat it up with the reactor, throw it out the back."

Helen frowned. "But...if I remember right, the base reactor's rated at something like thirty or fifty megawatts. I'm sure that *Nobel*'s engine reactor is a lot more powerful, maybe ten or twenty times more powerful. Is the base reactor going to be enough, Jackie?"

The dark-haired engineer grinned. "No and yes. If I had to use the reactor straight, no, I could redline it and still only get a pretty puny rocket. I want something close to the real deal. What I *can* do is basically create the equivalent of a fast-surge accumulator—a big bank of superconducting batteries that gather up a few hours of the reactor's output and then release it in a relatively few seconds. For those few seconds I can essentially pretend I've got *Nobel*'s reactor driving this rocket instead of our base reactor. And I really do have to be able to push the rocket to basically the same level of performance that it would have for *Nobel*, because I'm going to need to do a real fast burn as we pass Jupiter, if we end up intercepting *Odin*, or as we pass Saturn, if we just try to beat them to the punch."

"You can't do it over a longer stretch?"

"Nope. The whole point of the Oberth maneuver is timing. At perihelion you do the delta-vee burn, and depending on whether you do it to speed up or slow down, you either speed up or slow down a lot more than you would otherwise. Basically you're either gaining or losing the energy equivalent to throwing your fuel down the gravity well you're maneuvering in. It's a squared function, so even a relatively small delta-vee will get you a pretty big change."

She pointed to a huge funnel shape just visible past the flattened fins of the aft portion of the vessel. Helen recognized it as one of the spare NERVA rocket nozzles for *Nobel*. Meters across, the spare nozzle had been jury-rigged to the rear of the alien vessel. "And that will handle the load just fine."

"If," Joe noted, now inside the ship, "our calculations are all correct. If that thing's significantly off from the center of mass when we fire, we could be in trouble."

"That's why we've done the calculations and designs six times, Joe. But we can't wait much longer. Even with all the tricks we can pull off, A.J. doesn't give us more than another six days before there's no way to catch them at Jupiter, and not all that much longer before we would just have to give it up entirely."

"I know. Just pointing it out. I've crashed before, you know. Twice. I'd rather not do it again, this time almost four hundred million miles from help."

"You can't launch from inside Ceres, though. Not without using your fuel, right?" That was A.J.'s voice; he was working on the control systems deeper in the vessel.

"We *will* use some of the fuel that way. I want to test her before I go out that far. Do I look crazy?" Jackie said. "I want to fire the engine long enough to get into orbit around Ceres. *Feynman* or *Einstein* will refuel us—I'm using mostly water, which isn't the best fuel for a NERVA rocket by a long shot, but it's stable, easy to get here, and useful for a lot of other things—and then, if everything looks good, we'll take off. If the dusty-plasma drive doesn't work, well, then we go to plan B. That's *B* as in blackmail."

"I could settle for that, if I have to. But I am confident she'll fly," A.J. said. "And we need to think about publicity here. Dusty-plasma drive doesn't sound sexy."

"What would you suggest?"

He told them. "But I'm waiting until I see it running. I think that you'll agree I'm right, and if so, we've also got the name for our ship."

Jackie nodded. "Provisionally accepted. We'll see when she launches. How about the gas and dust supply for the sail itself?"

"Got it. I'd thought of this wrinkle earlier, but the fact that our friends on *Odin* were actually using it kicked me into getting it set up. We'll be using Faerie Dust for a lot of it. That will give us quite a bit of control over the sail, even more than the Bemmie magnetics. Of course, Bemmie probably used that, too, given that they were even using nanotech for their notepads, but there's no way for me to tell. We'll be able to vary the reflectivity and the geometry to some extent. Much more maneuverable than the base version. So I can say with some confidence that I'll be able to put you on any course you want pretty reasonably quick. We can make our final decisions once we see how she performs."

Jackie nodded. "Thanks, A.J. I really didn't want to be locked into one course from the start."

"It wasn't likely, but now it's not a problem. If she works at all. Which I hasten to add she will, Captain."

Helen saw Jackie wince at the title of address. As the engineer for the drive and the one most familiar with the operation of an actual vessel in deep space, Jackie had ended up with the two "hats" of captain and engineer. Madeline Fathom was willing to be an emergency pilot of sorts, but she refused to take command.

"On the ground, or in combat itself, perhaps," she'd said. "But you're going to be the one in charge in space, Jackie. A.J. isn't suited to it, and neither is Joe, while neither Helen nor Larry is qualified. Larry can help with the navigation and investigation of anything in the astronomical arena, but he's got minimal technical knowledge. As we can't really take any more people, that leaves us with no other choices."

"Come on, Jackie," she said. "It's not *that* bad."

Jackie shrugged and then gave an unwilling half smile. "Well, yeah, I guess. If by a miracle this eons-old alien vessel does rise from the dead, I'll be the commanding officer of the fastest ship ever built." The smile widened. "And then I get to prove it by catching the *other* fastest ship ever built."

Helen saw the smile widen even more, becoming somehow sharper, and it wasn't a nice smile at all. But then, she'd feel the same in Jackie's position. She almost felt sorry for Horst and *Odin*. Almost.

NEBULA STORM (Modified)

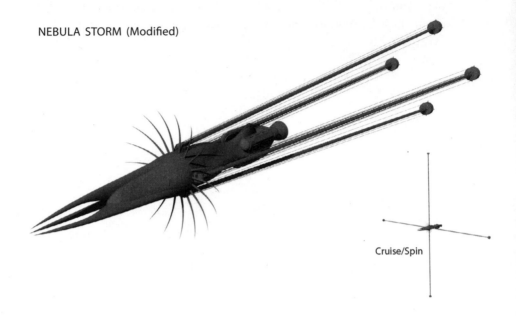

Cruise/Spin

Chapter 28

"All clear?"

"All clear, mates," Bruce's voice responded from *Feynman*. "Got clear images comin' in from all the Beholders in range, too. Includin' the one you put on the long orbit, A.J."

"Thanks, Bruce. I think we'll appreciate the long view if this thing works."

"All right, Bruce," Jackie said, voice somewhat tense. "We're in orbit around Ceres right now at an average altitude of fifteen hundred kilometers. I'm going to have Joe and A.J. try to kick in the drive as we start coming around in the direction away from the sun. If it works, we'll be able to accelerate for about half of each orbit and break free into the outer system pretty fast. A few orbits will do it. If it doesn't work, no major problem. Eventually, we'll have *Feynman* drag us back in."

"Right, just as planned. How are the control systems looking? You got out all right, but is the geometry set?"

"Very good, actually. We can keep even this much water liquid with the waste heat from the reactor and the insulation we already have, and that allows us to use the water as a sort of balancing agent. We can move it around in response to minor changes of the center of mass during acceleration. Lots of calculations involved, but the design models seem to be working out."

"Good. So, how's your feeling on running her dry out near Jupiter or Saturn, then?"

Jackie gave a strained laugh. "Not totally relaxed about it, but I feel a lot better than I did. All the other systems are working well. We do have auxiliary radiation shielding set up just in case, but

Larry and Joe assure me the dusty-plasma drive should shield us pretty well. We've got all the food you could spare, entertainment stuff to keep us from getting bored, and all the equipment we could squeeze out of the research staff. According to Madeline, Nicholas has promised that he'll get *Nike* out here with another reactor as soon as possible, no matter how many favors he has to call in, assuming this thing works."

A blinking light showed at the edge of her vision. "A.J.'s just signaled. Coming up on sail deployment."

The screen showed a view of the long, tri-ridged alien vessel, tentacular sail-control vanes extending from the midline, four Earth-designed habitat modules on long booms just aft of them, with the bulky Earth-built fuel tank and NERVA rocket nozzle easily visible at the rear. The clash of engineering styles was jarring; the Bemmius preference for almost organic-appearing curves versus the squar-ish, sharp-edged Earthly add-ons. The interior was in some ways worse, she mused, watching the control vanes continue to reach out. The main supports and parts of the hull remained, but much of the rest had been replaced, chopped, modified; you could still see the lower Bemmie-style designs in some areas, where others clearly were high-headroom designs forced into the space of one and a half or two Bemmie rooms. The resulting vessel might be spaceworthy, but she suspected that neither human nor Bemmius passengers would be entirely comfortable in the setting.

Enough musing. "All right, A.J. Set sail!"

"Deploying dusty-plasma sail, aye, Captain," A.J. said, perfectly seriously. "Main magnetic field now generated. Releasing gas now."

Jackie thought she saw a faint shimmer in the areas of the release nozzles, but that might just have been imagination. The status graphics in the upper right, however, showed the sudden expansion of the magnetic field, ballooning outward at incredible speed. "Field inflation confirmed. Releasing Faerie Dust."

Now she was sure she saw something. And wasn't the view of the stars around them a little . . . dimmer? A tiny bit washed out, almost fogged?

"Ionization of plasma confirmed. Energy consumption within calculated limits. Everything holding, Joe?"

"We're doing fine. Field's just about expanded to maximum." The professional tone disappeared for a moment. "Just *look* at that, will you?"

The long-range images, taken from a Beholder nearly five thousand kilometers away, showed what short range simply could not. The vast tenuous sail was nearly invisible to those within it, as a mist or light fog may only slightly dim the light and soften edges to those viewing it from within.

To the Beholder's view, projected on the screens of the alien vessel, *Feynman*, and Ceres base, the tiny dot that was the actual ship suddenly seemed to radiate a mist, a mist that expanded outward vastly, covering more than eleven degrees of the sky, looming up like a pearlescent stormcloud. The mist shimmered, and as more light and energy impinged upon it and the Faerie Dust dispersed within, delicate hints of color and interplay of light glowed out, became a spectral shadow occulting the entirety of the immense asteroid Ceres itself.

"Magnetosail? Dusty-plasma? Bah." A.J.'s voice held a combination of awe and triumph. "We are riding one of the living forces of creation, a miniature version of the cradle of stars. Captain, ladies and gentlemen, I give you the legacy of *Bemmius secordii* to their namesake Captain Jacqueline Marie Secord. I give you . . . the *nebula drive*."

Jackie found her voice a moment later. "You were totally correct, A.J., and I'm glad. Joe, is the champagne ready?"

"Rigged for breaking!"

A.J. continued, overdramatic lines being his specialty, and in this case, somehow appropriate. "We're giving chase to the King of the Gods, in a ship drawn by a cloud lit by the power of the sun and of the thunderbolt."

Jackie nodded. "And so we christen thee—the *Nebula Storm!*"

A faint additional sparkle of glass and mist was visible from the bow of the vessel. "Dramatic, but I like it," Bruce said. "Is the sail actually working?"

"If you can see it, it's working. We're getting several percent reflection. Acceleration is . . . about half a percent of gravity. We'll reach Ceres escape velocity by the end of this orbit, I think, and then it's outward bound." A.J. turned from his seat to look at Madeline, who had been quietly watching the launch. "Maddie, you can send the go-ahead. We're on our way to Jupiter, and we are going to catch *Odin* just about the time they get there." He grinned over at Jackie. "And wouldn't I just *love* to see their faces whenever they finally look over their shoulders and see what's coming after them!"

✳   ✳   ✳

Horst sat impatiently in front of the screen. It had taken some time to work around the idiotic communications blackout that Fitzgerald had seen fit to impose. Had it been the general's direct order, Horst might have felt more inclined to either obey, or at least to make a polite inquiry as to exactly *why* they weren't supposed to communicate directly with other organizations. As it was, though, Fitzgerald had been such a *scheisskopf*—as Horst's grandmother would have called him—that Horst took a positive pleasure in ignoring him. Especially since he had promised Jackie that he'd send her a message every day after they left, and the blackout was making him break his word.

Having managed to finally send a message back to Jackie at Ceres, he was now waiting for the response. Nervously waiting. Their relationship when he left had been at that twitchy stage where nothing was entirely clear. At this range, assuming she replied pretty promptly, round-trip would still be less than ten minutes. But it had been more than thirteen days, and if the people still on Ceres had guessed what was going on, Jackie could have more than one reason to be angry at him.

He was pretty sure she'd eventually understand. After all, taking the information didn't hurt anyone directly, and she must have guessed what he was supposed to do for the E.U. He'd even—sort of—told them. His best bet, he guessed, was to just admit that what they did was a sleazy trick and throw himself on her mercy. If they'd guessed. No point in borrowing trouble.

Of course, that didn't sit well with him, anyway. Sneaking around wasn't his idea of the way you were supposed to behave, especially to friends. Which was another reason why he didn't like Fitzgerald and his cronies. Odd, too, that there were other areas of the system he'd run into that seemed to have security on them he didn't remember installing. He might have to look into that himself. Well, no, he should probably ask the general.

What was taking her so long? She should be off-shift but not asleep now. He noodled around with some of the data he had on the secure areas. Some looked like they had to do with the engine controls, which made no sense at all. He'd *done* all of that, and there wasn't any need for more security on them. But it was there, nonetheless.

The screen suddenly flickered, and he leaned forward eagerly.

Then sat back in startlement as the face of Bruce Irwin appeared, looking none too friendly,

When he spoke, his Australian accent was thicker than usual. "Mr. Eberhart! So sorry to be the one respondin', but Jackie isn't here. I'm not sure that she'd even want to be speakin' to you, but you might try just waitin' a bit. She'll be catchin' up to you lot around Jupiter way." The transmission cut off as abruptly as it had begun, leaving Horst staring at the blank screen in total confusion.

Catching up to you lot . . . What could he mean by that?

The astronomical telescopes were accessible with a little work, since they weren't being used as much at the moment. One could be focused back the way they came on Ceres. That wasn't hard now that they weren't even doing much catching of the mass-beam.

He drew in a breath, startled. *Something* was visible behind them, something monstrous. At nearly fifty million kilometers, it was still visible as a pearlescent disc in the high-power telescope, implying a size beyond comprehension, and giving no clue at all as to what it actually *was*.

Who to call? The general eventually, of course. Not Fitzgerald. Anthony! He was the astronomer. He might know what it was.

Internal communications, of course, worked just fine. "Anthony, it is me, Horst. I was looking through one of the telescopes, and I have seen something very strange. Could you take a look and tell me what it is?"

"Of course, Horst. Give me the coordinates."

A few minutes later he heard Anthony LaPointe curse. "Good God! Moving on our own course, or near to it . . . and the size—it is huge, a thousand kilometers across."

Horst could not avoid thinking of a line from an old movie. *That's no moon. It's a space station.* "A thousand kilometers? It is bigger even than Ceres!"

"Yes. And moving in what appears to be a powered orbit, acceleration roughly on the same order as our own. Now, how . . ." LaPointe trailed off. Then: "Ahh, let us see the spectrum . . . reflected light and ionized gas . . . ingenious. With traces of manufactured material. And with enough enhancement I believe I can make out something at the center. No detail, but . . . it is a ship. A variant of magnetosail, I believe. I may have heard of such a thing before."

"A ship a *thousand kilometers across*?"

"The ship itself is small, Horst, smaller than ours by far. Perhaps five hundred tons, a thousand tons, no more. What we see is a cloud of gas and dust, held by a magnetic field. A nebula, one might say, chained to the ship."

Horst laughed suddenly. "So *that* was the other secret they were hiding, the one that Joe and A.J. didn't talk about. Their *Nobel* couldn't catch us, but they fooled us anyway. I think we need to talk to the general."

"Indeed. Let me record this data and bring it with us. I will meet you in a few moments."

Horst shut down the terminal and laughed again. This was getting exciting. And perhaps he might see Jackie again sooner than he thought.

If they were going to catch up, she wouldn't really have much to be mad about at all. Things were looking up!

"It would seem, Mr. Fitzgerald, that your little plan has not quite worked out as expected. We are being pursued."

Fitzgerald barely registered the general's acid tone. He was too busy staring in disbelief at the screen. The bloody bastards had pulled a new *ship* out of nowhere. Well, not nowhere. He'd known they were working on some kind of ship, but none of the prior alien vessels had been of any use to anyone. The idea that these boffins could have made something older than mankind workable was utterly ridiculous.

But ridiculous or not, it was clearly coming after them, and according to the data from LaPointe it could almost certainly catch up to them at Jupiter. Fitzgerald shook himself mentally. Gaping was undignified, and dignity mattered. It mattered a great deal. Moreover, it was time for, what was the term? Ah, yes, spin control.

"Well, now, that makes it interesting, doesn't it, sir?"

"That may be one way of putting it. I find it less amusing than you appear to find it. Perhaps you can help me find the humor?"

"Can certainly make a good try at it, General. Sure, they can probably catch us around Jupiter, but have you asked Dr. LaPointe if they can beat us to Saturn—given what we know and they don't?"

The general tilted his head. "If they're faster than we are..."

Fitzgerald grinned. So, for once he was actually ahead of the tech curve. Not always easy to do. "General, you know better than that. We could be going twice as fast as we are now if we could've arranged the right braking material ahead of time. But it won't quite be where we want it if we cranked the speed up right now. It *will* be there when we get to Saturn on our current schedule, and we've already got surprises hanging out in Jupiter system. So we'll be heading out on our second leg a lot faster than we're going now, and they can't go much faster because whatever tricks they have in mind, that ship of theirs is basically a sail in a storm. If they do more than a passive slingshot, they'll have nothing to use when they brake around Saturn, which doesn't have as big a gravity well to play with."

Hohenheim nodded slowly. "True. But then..."

"Then either they have to try to stop us somehow, or we're in a real race. Which *Odin* is almost certainly going to win."

Hohenheim's brow wrinkled. "And if they *do* try to stop us, that's an attack. On us."

"Exactly, General. Oh, they wouldn't be coming out after us if they weren't sure we shot 'em, but they've got nothing for proof. If they had *proof,* they'd have just sent a message to Nicholas Glendale back at Mars, and we'd all be heading home to some unpleasant times right now. They've got nothing. And me and my boys, we have everything planned out on how to get rid of the evidence if we did get pulled in."

"*Can* they stop us?"

Fitzgerald thought for a moment, sorting through the technologies he had a reasonable grasp of—which was quite a few, so it took a little time to be sure of his answer. "I don't really see how, General. We know the inspections aren't all that easy to get around, and these boys and girls weren't planning on fighting a war anyway. Even darling Madeline was looking for espionage, not naval battles. No doubt Secord and Buckley could come up with some kind of missiles between them, but nothing we wouldn't sense coming, and without some kind of really impressive terminal guidance we'd be able to avoid them just by a couple of random course modifications—which we can more than afford."

Hohenheim let out a long breath. "All right, then, Mr. Fitzgerald. We continue as planned. It's a very good thing that they are not armed, however, since we are not."

"What? I don't get you, sir."

Hohenheim gave him a cold smile. "Mr. Fitzgerald, if they do attack us, we cannot return fire. If we were to return fire, they would have the evidence they need that we did, in fact, have the motive, means, and opportunity to destroy their power-distribution center, as we in fact did. They will be watching us *extremely* closely and will not miss a single piece of evidence. You can be quite sure they are prepared to record everything, also."

The point had not occurred to Fitzgerald before, and the realization was a punch to the gut. The *Odin* was armed with a weapon potentially more destructive than any ever built, save for nuclear warheads, but it couldn't be *used* now.

The general's smile widened, and got even colder. "I see that aspect of the situation had not yet suggested itself to you, Mr. Fitzgerald. Firing back would prove our guilt, and would result in further tragedy. Therefore, to protect my people and my ship, if it *does* turn out that the Ares vessel—which has rather ominously, I will note, refused to reply to any messages we have yet sent—does somehow have the capability to damage or destroy *Odin*, I will not fight back, but will instead surrender and hand you and myself over to the authorities." He dropped the smile. "However, as you say, it appears that we will not have to worry about that. So . . . you're dismissed, Mr. Fitzgerald."

Fitzgerald found himself in the main hallway of *Odin* without even a clear memory of walking out the door. *Never thought he'd be the type to give anything up without a fight,* he mused. *Then again, he has been showing a lot of conscience lately.* He shrugged. No point in worrying about it. The likelihood that the Ares vessel could pose any threat to them was pretty small, especially now that *Odin* knew to keep an eye on them.

But even if the chance was very small, he'd better be prepared. Just in case.

The general knew military tactics and politics. But he didn't know nearly as much about espionage and sabotage. Richard Fitzgerald grinned. He'd already surprised the general before with that. He needed to have a serious heart-to-heart with his boys right away. This kind of a party needed advance planning to make sure all the guests played their parts properly. And as one of the guests might be named Madeline Fathom, only the very best planning would do. It might soon be time to really pull out all the stops.

Chapter 29

"We have a problem."

A.J. turned to face both Maddie and Jackie, who were looking grim. "What's wrong?"

Jackie answered. "I realized that we'd been making some unwarranted assumptions, so I had Maddie do some inquiries. It took a while, but we confirmed something that I hadn't wanted to confirm. The E.U.'s mass-beam setup *wasn't* idle a lot of the time. It's been running pretty much nonstop. I have no idea of the cost, but it must be huge."

A.J. frowned, puzzled. "But that makes no sense. Most of the time, *Odin* was sitting still around Ceres."

"I'm afraid," Madeline said, "it makes altogether too much sense. I had Jackie run the numbers. With reasonable assumptions about their capabilities, if they were running it that much, by the time *Odin* gets to Saturn, there will be a large amount of their drive-dust in the Saturn system. Enough so that they can afford to boost their speed radically for the Jupiter-Saturn leg."

A.J. stared at them blankly for a minute, then went through one of his fits of typing on invisible keyboards, grunting half-comprehensible audio cues, and staring at things invisible to others. "I see what you mean. And if the stuff's even half as smart as it probably is, you can do all sorts of tricks with it in terms of when and where you use it. They'll have fuel galore left after they stop, and so they can use *Munin* to land on Enceladus, and then after they get their team down they can even explore other parts of the Saturn system. Dammit!"

Maddie nodded. "It also means we might have to assume that

they're not limited when they get to the Jupiter system, either. No reason they couldn't have stuff waiting for them there."

"Or even have it being sent on its way now," said Jackie. "This trip they might not use it, but they have to be thinking of some Jupiter trips in the near future, maybe with the next set of mass-beam ships. Maybe sending out a mass-beam relay station."

"This really screws up everything," A.J. grumbled. "I would've bet that we could beat them to Enceladus. They can't go much faster than they are now without trouble, or rather they couldn't if they didn't have an ace in the hole. Now it's clear what they were up to. They guessed that the best chance for exploration finds would be in the outer system and set it all up that way. The E.U. bets big, and looks like they're going to win that bet, too."

Maddie, meanwhile, was studying files from the data they'd accumulated on *Odin*. "Jackie, you actually did manage to gather some considerable intelligence on how their drive worked. If they're using something like cut-down, massively duplicated Faerie Dust, couldn't we—through A.J., I'd presume—keep them from using it? Shut it down?"

"I don't know." She glanced at A.J.

The sensor expert reluctantly shook his head. "Not without knowing a lot about the design. Which is kept seriously locked down, I'm sure. If I had some samples, no problem, but not as it stands."

"Then why don't we get some samples?" Maddie asked.

"Huh? I suppose we could try to figure out the exact trajectory they're sending the stuff along—it's going in the same general direction, I'd guess—but we don't have the energy figures, so we don't know how fast it's going. And a rough guess won't cut it."

Jackie suddenly leaned forward. "But we don't have to guess. We can make it come to us!"

"How—damn, yes! We saw their signal laser!"

Maddie caught their sudden enthusiasm. "Can you duplicate it well enough?"

A.J. drew himself up with comic exaggeration. "Can you *doubt* me, woman? A.J. Baker, master of all things technological? Even if they did laugh at me in the Academy! But I showed them all, I did. Yes, I can. It's basically a green laser with a very simple pulse pattern that makes it easy for the nodes to verify that it's actually the laser and not something else. Hmm, you know, if we were doing this while they were still accelerating, it'd be like real honest-to-God sailing, trying to cut each other off from the wind. Yes, yes, I can! If any of their Drive Dust is still anywhere near our path, I'll get a sample!"

"Will that allow us to stop them?"

A.J. thought a minute. "I dunno. Not directly, really. The stuff we'd need to control is off in Saturn system, or at least scattered around Jupiter, and there's no way I'm managing that. It doesn't leave an easy way to trace it, and it's not going to be all *that* smart, so doing any fancy programming . . . nah." He looked a little deflated.

"We still may be able to use it," Maddie said. "I think I have an idea. But first let's see if we can actually get a sample." She smiled, and A.J. gave a delighted grin back as he saw the glint in her eye. He knew she'd come up with something truly entertaining. "This race is not yet over."

Horst felt cold and gray. *So that's what they were doing. All this time, and I thought I knew them.* Fitzgerald wasn't so much a surprise, but he'd thought better of the general.

The modifications were extensive, yet subtle, hidden from any casual inspection, and with the proper preparation able to be disposed of with virtually no trace. The control software left no doubt as to the capabilities or purposes of the modifications, and the software logs left no doubt whatsoever of what had happened in the hours before their Ceres departure.

No wonder they don't respond. I wouldn't want to talk to me, either, after that. Buckley was one of Jackie's best friends, and we nearly killed him. Stealing information was one thing, but this—

"Something very odd, Horst."

"What is it?" he said dully, remembering that he was on watch with Anthony. Not that there was much to watch. Interplanetary travel was basically very boring.

"It is the Ares vessel. She is doing something odd."

That got a bit of his attention. "What do you mean, odd? Turning back? Accelerating? Shutting off?"

"Nothing so drastic. It seems to me that they are doing some kind of light experiment."

Horst looked at the enlarged image that Anthony sent him. "I don't see anything—oh, wait." The translucent cloud had seemed to show a faint shimmer, just a bit different than the usual slight shifts of lighting. "Let me see . . . The enhancement we should be using . . . Let us try to isolate the moment. Focus on that . . . enhance . . . What is the spectrum here, Anthony?"

"It seems normal, except there is a spike in the green region of the spectrum."

"Hmm." Horst rubbed his chin. He was still angry and depressed, but this was interesting. "I wonder why. Have you seen this before?"

"There are at least three occurrences so far."

Green. What is that making me . . . ?

"Anthony, is that spike centered on five hundred and twenty nanometers?"

"Why . . . yes, it is. How did you guess?"

That clever fellow. "Not a guess, a deduction. We may be seeing the start of some trouble. I must go talk to the general."

"Go to him? Why not call him?"

Horst unlocked from his chair and drifted to the exit. "Because I wanted to speak to him privately anyway."

Anthony, knowing his friend's recent moods, didn't ask any more. He just gave Horst a concerned look as the slightly younger engineer dropped into the tube connecting the bridge with the habitat ring.

Horst pretended not to notice Anthony's gaze. He didn't need sympathy right now. It took him only a few minutes to make his way along the connecting tube and arrive in the full-gravity corridor. He sent a query ahead of him; by the time he reached the door, it was open.

Hohenheim was sitting at his desk, going over daily reports. "Yes, Mr. Eberhart?"

"I believe that the Ares vessel is preparing to move against the *Odin*, sir."

That got the general's attention. Hohenheim sat up straighter and removed his VRD glasses. "How so, Mr. Eberhart?"

"We have detected regular spikes of emitted green centered on five hundred and twenty nanometers, sir."

Hohenheim gave a slow nod. "I see. They are attempting to draw the Smart Fuel Dust toward them. But we are done accelerating. This cannot affect our current course, can it?"

Horst shrugged. "I am not sure, really. Light can cross the space far faster than we. If Mr. Baker does obtain a sample, I suppose it is possible he could program it—or, more precisely, have someone with access to more powerful lasers program it by remote. If they are close enough to us when in the Jupiter system, however, they may be able to interfere with our maneuvers by drawing off a significant portion of the fuel. We have more powerful dedicated lasers, but there is at least some risk, I would think."

The general seemed to turn the matter over in his mind. "I thank you for this information. I will have to have it examined. Would you be so kind as to model the possible scenarios along with Dr. Svendsen? I would like to know as soon as possible if there is any likelihood of such an event."

"Yes, sir." Horst stood there a moment longer, and as the general looked up again, said, "May I speak to you frankly, General?"

Hohenheim's gaze was unreadable, but he sat back in a way that somehow made Horst nervous. "Please do."

Horst hesitated, then took the plunge. "Why did we attack Ceres?"

Hohenheim studied him expressionlessly for what seemed like an hour, even though it could only have been a few seconds. "Clarify your question, Mr. Eberhart. How exactly do you mean 'attack'?"

"I mean that we hit them with a projectile weapon. There was no meteor at all, sir."

"Ah," said the general, in the tone of someone who's been expecting bad news for a long time. "Might I ask how you came to this conclusion?"

"I found a set of control applications that did not look familiar. When I examined them, I was able to determine what the exact systems were that they controlled."

"I see."

Horst waited.

Finally the general stirred. He looked into the distance, as if he saw things in the air beyond Horst. "I do not like to either rehash the past, Mr. Eberhart, or to seek to set blame on others for actions taken here. For these purposes, I think the best I can tell you is that it was decided as a matter of policy, to ensure that there would be no pursuit. Whether that policy was a wise one I do not wish to discuss, as there is no practical reason to do so." He met Horst's gaze. "I am personally very sorry for the trouble it has caused, but we must accept the situation as it stands. If it makes you feel any better, that weapon shall not be used again. I have already given the appropriate orders."

It wasn't much, but Horst could tell it was as much as the general was going to say. And in some ways, it told him an awful lot. "Thank you, General. I will begin the analysis at once."

"Very good. You may go, Mr. Eberhart."

Horst proceeded toward the engineering section, where a status query had shown him that Mia Svendsen was located. His mind was far from settled. The general's speech had avoided a number of statements, but he thought he could read between the lines. Fitzgerald had thought up the attack; maybe he'd carried it out without orders.

And if he'd done that, what were the odds that he'd follow orders not to fire again? Horst figured he might be well advised to make some preparations of his own. Anthony would help, he was sure. Mia might, too.

Better safe than sorry.

The tiny mote glittered under the microscope. The faceted angles of reflectors and lenses, darker areas of solar-energy conversion, active-material actuators, and other components made a sort of geometric, three-dimensional cityscape as A.J. zoomed in. "A nice bit of work, actually. Simplistic compared to a lot of Dust-Storm's designs, but making it too complicated would be a waste of resources and increase the problems with manufacturing it in large lots. And, boy, have they needed large lots." The sensor expert shook his head in admiration. "I still find it mindboggling, actually. Masswise they've outproduced everyone else in the world on this scale. Sure, it's all been one model for one purpose, but that's still an awful lot of Smart Dust."

Joe was impressed by the image. He'd seen earlier designs, but he'd forgotten how very much stuff was compressed into the microscopic motes. "Tons of it. Manufactured partly with 3D component design and fabbing, and partly assembled by assembly micromanipulators. They've kept the exact procedures and techniques a dead secret, too."

"So," Maddie said, "does this actually get us anywhere?"

"Sure does. I can program this stuff easily, within the limits of what it can do. Which is pretty limited. Even my Faerie Dust isn't particularly brainy—each of the motes doesn't have much more processing power than a 1980 desktop. These suckers are more like late 1970s programmable calculators. Working on things like this you come to understand what the old-time programmers had to go through and why they were concerned about using an extra bit here or there.

"Of course, I can play some tricks they couldn't. I can split tasks up among many different nearby motes so they can perform overall computation and related active operations that no individual mote is up to. To cut to the chase, I can make this stuff work for us."

"How much of it can we catch?"

A.J. raised an eyebrow. "Well, relative to what they sent before, not all that much, but from our point of view, a lot. We've got well over another month before we end up in Jupiter system and start getting to the critical moments. In that time I could get hundreds of kilos of the stuff. Why?"

"I was wondering if we could replace your dust with theirs in our sail."

A.J. looked scandalized. "*Could* we? Well, sure, we could. It's not like the operation of the sail needs tremendously complex work. But why would we want to swap?"

Madeline's smile was the devilish grin that both scared Joe and, sometimes, turned him on. Not the time for that, though, so he should probably be scared. "Because, A.J.," she said, "we can put yours to a much better use."

A.J.'s offended-dignity pose vanished, replaced immediately by keen interest. "Such as...?"

"Such as sending it to our friends on *Odin*."

A.J. stared at her for a moment. Then he burst into a laugh that was very near to that of the mad scientist of bad science-fiction movies. "As Dr. Gupta would have said, indeed, *indeed* we can, Miss Fathom!"

"Whoa, whoa, slow down," Joe said, confused. "They're like millions of miles ahead of us. How do we get the stuff there?"

"Nebula sail, Joe, nebula sail." Jackie was catching the excitement. "The motes are *meant* to catch light and guide themselves with it. They can also accelerate with it, though at a slug's pace. But what we can do with the field is shape it so that it serves as a large, pretty weak accelerator—something like what the *Odin* does, on a less efficient scale—and shoot the stuff ahead of us. A sort of dusty-plasma rocket. It'll slow us down a little bit, but we just replace the lost gas and dust and adjust the course. Meanwhile we've given A.J.'s motes quite a kick, and they can accelerate a bit more and guide themselves straight to *Odin*, especially once *Odin* starts using its fuel-control laser again."

"She's got it," A.J. said. "And if I can get it to the right places, I might be able to pull off several tricks."

Maddie nodded. "This being the tactical area, I hope you have no problem with my directing the action, Captain?"

"None at all."

"Guys," Joe interjected, "I just want to point out that this would definitely be counted as an attack on them. If we start messing with their ship in flight, that is."

"Didn't they start this, Joe?" A.J. asked.

"Sure, but we haven't officially said anything about it. And if you're going to be trying to control the stuff, you won't want to be a long distance away. I've been trying to figure out the range and accuracy of that weapon of theirs, and it's awfully hard to be sure—given that we don't know the exact design, firing rate, all that—but you can bet they'll start shooting back."

Madeline shook her head. "I don't think they will, Joe. They're in a Catch-22 situation, you see. If they shoot at us, they'd provide us with the proof we need that they have the weapon we suspect them of having. We could break off combat right then, maneuver to make it hard or impossible to hit us at any range, and then send the record of that short battle home. They'd be completely screwed. And if A.J. can manage to mess with their systems at all, they'd have other problems."

Joe chuckled. "Okay, I see what you mean. Count on you, Maddie, to already have figured why it doesn't matter that you're chasing a warship in a rowboat, and made sure that the warship can't shoot at you."

"*Sail*boat, please," Jackie said. "A four-masted ship of the line, at least."

"And by at least one measure the largest ship ever made. Telescopes on Earth can probably see us, even at this distance, though they probably couldn't figure out what they're seeing."

"So, what's the plan, Maddie?"

"A.J., you get ready to catch us a lot of replacement Dust. We'll need more anyway, since the sail's expanding as we get farther out. Joe, you and Jackie do the modeling to figure out the best configuration for the sail to discharge our smarter smart dust and get it refilled. After we send A.J.'s Faerie Dust off, we don't do anything until we can be sure it's in place. The problem is that even with the best advance programming, we won't be able to get back the data from the Dust—and know what we can and can't do with *Odin*'s systems—without active communication. And if we appear to be actively beaming them without actually talking, they'll know something's up."

Jackie frowned. "Yeah. And Horst isn't anything like stupid. That jerk could probably figure out counters to anything we could do by remote, once he gets the idea. Unless we do something permanent to *Odin*, which we don't want to do."

"You might be being too harsh on Horst, Jackie," Maddie said mildly. "The messages he's been sending have been pretty friendly, and I don't think he's so stupid that he'd believe you wouldn't be angry about them attacking. It's possible he may not have known about anything but the information theft. Which is annoying, but it *was* his job, and as I recall he even basically admitted as much."

Jackie's intense, pretty face twisted into a grimace. "I wish I could believe that."

A.J. snorted. "Me, too. Except the fact that he was the system-programming engineer for their drive system, which just happens to incorporate the weapon in question. There was no other way for them to smuggle that by the inspectors. He had to know, so far as I can see."

"I suppose it doesn't look good," Madeline conceded, with a glance at Helen. Helen was older, Maddie more experienced, and both of their instincts seemed to agree that Horst had been genuine. But the facts didn't seem to bear that out. "In any case, you're certainly right about his capabilities. For that reason, we will probably only be able to use the trick once, when we are ready. We will open communications with them once we are in reasonable range, and while I attempt to convince them to cooperate, A.J. will find out what sort of tricks we can play. Depending on which scenarios appear possible, we will adjust the negotiations to reflect what we can do."

"If they don't fight back?"

"If they don't, I think we would be well advised to work out the compromise that should have been worked out when they found the base to begin with. A joint custody between the E.U., Ares, and the IRI, and let the E.U. conduct the first landing and get priority. That's provided, of course, the people specifically responsible for the direct attack on our Ceres base are turned over to us. Otherwise we will do our best to beat them to Enceladus, and we can probably arrange that by disrupting the right systems for long enough."

Jackie nodded. "I'd still rather kick someone in the nuts, but that really does make more sense. And I'm sure Nicholas would approve."

"So am I," Helen said. "And I've known him a long time. He'd be very much in favor of it. It's the best approach, and if Maddie's right, it will achieve what we're really after—getting the people who shot us locked up, while not embarrassing the E.U. too much and giving us a stronger alliance."

"It's settled, then," said Maddie, pleased. "Let's get to work!"

Chapter 30

Helen woke up slowly, realizing A.J. was no longer lying next to her. She glanced sleepily around their bedroom and saw his figure silhouetted against the lazily spinning stars. She got up and went over to him, sliding her arms around his waist. He jumped slightly, but then hugged her arms to him. "What's up?"

He was still staring out. Less than ten days from the effective edge of the Jovian system, Jupiter was visible almost dead ahead of the *Nebula Storm* as a brilliant not-quite-point, a tenth of a degree across and the brightest thing in the sky except for the Sun, now shrunken behind them to the same size—an intolerably bright near-point of light. "Just thinking."

"What were you thinking about?"

He gestured out the window. "A lot of things. Partly marveling that my sense of wonder is still holding out. We've seen so many that you'd think I'd be blasé about it, but...I still look out there, sometimes, and think *I'm on a spaceship going to Jupiter!* and realize that I'm like four hundred million miles from Earth, and I get a chill, just like I used to when I was a kid and saw something incredibly awesome.

"And partly marveling that I'm actually getting tired of living in little spaceship cheeseboxes. Even pretty luxurious ones. I used to think when I was a kid that I could live perfectly happily in a ten-by-twelve room for my entire life, as long as I had the right gadgets. Then I expanded that to several rooms because I had to have space to put my stuff, but still..."

She hugged him. "So, what, you want to go back to Earth and follow me on a dig?"

"The frightening thing is that right now the thought of pitching a tent on Earth, without a single air filter or wiring conduit for fifty miles, so I can use toothbrushes and jewelry picks to dig out a five-foot bone, sounds downright appealing."

She laughed. "I'm tempted to hold you to that, whenever this crazy mission gets done. But I know you'd regret it after the first week." She sighed, hugging him tighter. "I do miss blue sky, grass, and all that kind of thing. We've been out here in space for... My God, it must be seven years."

"Closing in on eight. I actually got back to Earth for a few months, so it's only been, what, four or so for me. Still, that's a long time. I'm glad all of us don't get vertigo easily, since it let Jackie spin us up to a full G. I griped at first, but honestly, we needed to get used to full gravity again. Partial seems to prevent the direct bone loss and other effects, but I felt like a rag doll for a lot of my one visit home."

"Like we all did for the first few weeks of this trip. You're right, though. We need real gravity, or at least a full-bore simulation of the real thing. I suspect long-term Mars residents may have problems."

"Dr. Wu is doing studies on that. He's also pushing everyone back on Mars to spend more time in the centrifuges. We really do need to do the research to make sure we don't kill ourselves settling other worlds."

They were quiet for a moment. "Anything else on your mind?"

He turned to face her. "Just wondering... We've sort of tap-danced around the subject before." He took a deep breath. "Children?"

"*Now?*"

"Well, of course not *now*. Anyway, it takes time—nine months, last I heard. And I know your implant's got at least another year on it. But... well, you're older than me, and so I figured..."

"If I wanted any, we really should be talking about it now." She smiled and kissed him. He really was adorable when he looked so nervous. "Thank you, Adric Jamie Baker. I love you, you know."

"I love you, too. So..."

She shook her head. A few decades ago, her age would have already answered the question in the negative, but no more. So... "I really don't know yet. I suppose... yes, probably. When we go back to Earth. Which we should do, I think, after this is over. Watching Bruce's little girl did make me a little wistful about having my own. But I don't want to raise her out here. Or him, if it's a boy. We've both done enough, haven't we?"

He glanced out the window, to where the stars still turned and Jupiter gleamed. "Yeah. I guess we have." He kissed her and let his hands slide down a little lower. "Maybe we should get in some more practice on the kid-making thing."

She giggled. "Why not?"

"They'll be passing us very close by, General."

Hohenheim nodded. "That is still some days in the future. What do you mean by 'close,' Dr. LaPointe? In space, that can be a rather broad term."

LaPointe brought up a display of the Jovian system and the orbital paths. Those present—the general, Mia Svendsen, Richard Fitzgerald, Horst Eberhart, and a scattering of other *Odin* crewmembers—studied the image and its animated paths.

"Both of us are on a course to slingshot around Jupiter. While they started out several days after us, they have been moving faster and correcting their course to close in on us. We performed our first correction burn—effectively slowing ourselves down—just a few days ago. We are accumulating the replacement fuel, but they are now catching up quickly. Either of us could try to change that to some extent, but it should be remembered that at the critical moments we *must* be following the exactly correct trajectory, or we will be very far off our final destination. At any point up until relatively shortly before the Oberth Maneuver, even small deviations in course could drastically affect our final course, so any changes we make will have to be adjusted for."

"No offense, Andy, m'boy, but it seems to me that doesn't answer the general's question at all. How close?"

"I am sorry you are dissatisfied, Mr. Fitzgerald. I was trying to make clear that we could easily affect the answer by a very large amount, or that they could, if either were to maneuver. But, assuming there are no further maneuvers, the Ares vessel will pass us at a distance of ten thousand kilometers."

Fitzgerald sat up straighter. "Bloody hell, that *is* close for out here. You think they're planning to attack?"

Hohenheim held up a hand. "I believe we have discussed this before. If they attack us, they would be initiating a war, which I think is highly unlikely."

Anthony noticed an exchange of glances between the general and Fitzgerald, and a flicker of unreadable expression on Horst's face. It took some effort to keep his own face from showing a bitter amusement. *We are still all trying to keep the others from knowing that we know.*

"They have no weapons capable of firing across such a distance, and the fact that we stole—let us not dissemble on this point—important information from them is not at all sufficient justification for them to attack. It is, however, sufficient motive to attempt to beat us to our goal. I confess to being somewhat surprised by this, but I suspect it may be a matter of offended pride, at least in part." He looked back at Anthony. "Can they beat us at this point?"

This was of course the sticky point, and one over which he had spent some sleepless nights. "General, I cannot say for certain. Just as we have capabilities of which they do not know, so I would be cautious in assuming that we know all of theirs. It is an alien vessel which they have adapted. It is true that we have determined the basic principles on which it operates. And excepting for the one short containment failure they suffered a month ago, the dusty-plasma sail has been functioning very well." He noticed the impatient look of the others and hurried on. "In any case, the answer depends on what I assume, General. If they have nothing but a dusty-plasma sail, I cannot see that they can. In fact, at their peak speed they were in danger of leaving the system if they could not stop.

"Because of that, I think they have arranged something else. They may do an Oberth Maneuver, if they were able to arrange a rocket of some kind. They have been slowing—much more quickly than I would have expected—by interaction with the Jovian magnetosphere. The acceleration in question is still very small indeed, but the control they have over the magnetic bubble and its shape permits at least an order of magnitude greater deceleration capability than we could possibly have expected. Still, they will have to do something when passing Jupiter, as we do. Their final velocity will be the deciding factor. Unless they have some particular surprises in store for us, their speed when leaving Jupiter will tell us how fast they believe they can afford to go to Saturn."

He sighed and spread his hands. "I wish I could be more

certain. If I must guess, I would say no, they cannot. While some minor points of their vessel have surprised me, they would need some very effective means of slowing down in order to make it practical for them to match the speeds we expect to reach."

"There's the problem for me," Fitzgerald said. "You think that Fathom, Baker, Buckley, and Secord can't do the same figuring between them?"

"They do not know what we can—"

Fitzgerald made a savage cutting gesture. "Bollocks. Maybe not before this, but you can bet your insurance that once this turned into a chase, little Miss Supergirl called in all her old chums and started digging. And tell me that I'm wrong when I say that once they figured out the mass-driver was running, they'd put the rest together very quickly, eh?"

That was a painful jab. LaPointe had never liked Fitzgerald even before Horst let him in on certain secrets, and sarcasm like this didn't help engender feelings of warmth and brotherhood. Especially when Fitzgerald was right. "No, I cannot argue that. They are very good at their jobs, and if they knew the mass-beam was being constantly in use, then they would be guessing the truth very quickly."

"So then, if they know that much, they must know they can't beat us. So either they've got something up their sleeves to pass us, or they have something figured that they can use to slow us or stop us."

The room was quiet as everyone tried to figure out a way of looking at the situation that didn't come out to that answer. From the expressions on the other faces, Anthony saw that no one else was getting anywhere with that. Richard Fitzgerald had a darkly satisfied look.

General Hohenheim shrugged finally. "Your logic appears sound, Mr. Fitzgerald, but the other facts remain. I find it hard to imagine that they have any weapons capable of harming us at such a range, and even less that they would be willing to use them on us at this point. While they may hold a grudge against some of our people for our trickery, none of them are monsters. They would not condemn a hundred of us to death for that. It is, I suppose, possible that the alien vessel itself has some unique trick that will allow them to match our speed, but that is something we can only wait and see. Even if we had weapons capable of firing upon them, we could no more use them than they could. It is a race, and we shall see which of us shall win. I would hope, however, that they will be courteous enough to talk when we reach a closer approach. We may learn much more in conversation."

He glanced around the table and fixed on Mia Svendsen. "On the very remote chance that they do intend some form of attack, I want things arranged to minimize damage, along with a complete set of scenarios for redundant controls, escape using *Munin*, and so on. Even if the scenarios appear ludicrous, they are worthwhile to consider. One day I am afraid they will not be so ludicrous."

"Yes, sir," Mia replied. "I will have them to you before closest approach."

"Good." Hohenheim rose. "Thank you, that will be all."

Horst caught up with LaPointe near his cabin. "You know they *do* have reason to think we are a real threat, Anthony."

"Yes, I do. It seems that we have at least three and possibly four factions on board. The general and those immediately involved in the attack on Ceres Base, you and I and our friends, and the rest of the crew of *Odin* who as yet know nothing of the outrage we have perpetrated."

Horst looked puzzled. "But you said four?"

"I am not convinced that General Hohenheim and Mr. Fitzgerald are a single faction. The security chief was responsible for the selection of a large number of our crew, and that is a concern to me."

Horst's dark eyebrows drew down. "Are you saying he is working against the general? That the general did not order the attack? Why would he not say so?"

Anthony found his friend's straightforward naiveté endearing but, in this case, a bit frustrating. "Because this is not Earth and he cannot just fire someone and send them home. He needs to maintain a unity in the crew, and at least outward harmony. If Fitzgerald did this in any way that could be justified by something the general said, then the general would be forced to give him the benefit of the doubt. But the relationship between them, it is not the same as it was when first we started, that I am sure of. It seems much more tense."

They entered Anthony's room. "Mr. Fitzgerald is not happy with our captain, I think," Anthony continued. "And while he has the same general need to keep some apparent peace, he's more than likely arranging to protect himself."

"But that would be mutiny!" Horst protested.

"It has happened before. In a sense, have we not been planning just that?"

The young German engineer looked pained. "Not really. I mean, we are just planning on how to keep from committing another crime."

Anthony spread his hands. "But it is the same thing, isn't it? If the order comes from our general or his designated representatives, disobeying and obstructing them would be mutiny."

Horst slowly nodded his head. "But Fitzgerald..."

"Oh, I agree. If he is planning something, it is much more likely to be something bad. But I do not think we should be sitting here ignoring the fact that we, too, may be considering the same basic crime."

"It's just an ugly word."

"And it would be even uglier were it to come to pass. Let us hope, that it does not, and all we see here is a race." He handed a surprised Horst one of the small bottles of wine he had brought as budgeted luxuries. "In fact, let us drink to that hope."

Horst nodded. "I will drink to that." After each had a glass, they tapped the plastic rims together. "To peace in our journey."

"Peace."

As they drank, Anthony could not help but notice that he saw Jupiter go blood-red as the *Odin*'s rotation took the planet behind his glass.

PART VI:
TRAJECTORIES

*Catastrophe, n: a great
disaster or misfortune.*

Chapter 31

"Are we ready?"

"All ready," Maddie confirmed to Jackie. "While you talk with *Odin* directly, A.J. will be able to query the Faerie Dust that should be all over the *Odin*. The low-bandwidth transmissions involved should be easy to hide in the noise, as long as no one actually is looking for it."

Jackie winced. She hated unknowns like that. "And how likely is it someone will?"

Maddie shrugged. "I don't think *I* would be doing it in their position. I honestly don't think this idea would have occurred to me if Darth Baker hadn't pulled off that trick on Modofori and his pals. So I think it's pretty unlikely. I just don't make one hundred percent assumptions."

"Joe? You and A.J. ready?"

"Sure am," Joe said. "If they do go nuts and fire on us, we'll have quite a few seconds' warning. Even at closest approach, assuming they can manage a firing velocity of thirty kilometers per second—which I don't think they can, not even close—we'll still have five minutes or so. In that time, even with our effective acceleration cut by ten times because Jupiter's magnetosphere's squeezed us down, we can change position by four hundred fifty meters. Since the actual width of the *Nebula Storm* is only about a thousand feet, they almost certainly can't hit us at all."

"And," A.J. put in, "we've tied the engine system into our radar. If the radar plot shows something coming at us that my sensors say we can't avoid for sure by using the nebula drive, it'll give us a little kick from the main engines, however much it calculates

213

it needs to get to full safe range. That still shouldn't be enough to change our main maneuver program, I hope. There's some leeway in the system."

"Just in case, we are all suited up, right?" Helen put in. "And I'm standing by with patch kits and a pair of hands to help. This isn't really my gig."

"Not mine, either," Larry pointed out. "But being ready to be damage control's better than just sitting in a chair waiting to see what happens."

"All suited up, Helen. And Joe says he's got damage-control programs in place."

"And of course," A.J. pointed out, "we also happen to be inside a ship made of the same material the Vault on Mars was. A thirty-kilometer-per-second projectile would probably get through, but much less might not."

Jackie nodded. "Still, let's hope none of that happens. On this pass, at least, everything should stay friendly." She looked around once more. "Okay, here goes."

She activated the radio, aiming toward the *Odin* for the first time in this journey. "*Odin*, this is Captain Jacqueline Secord of the Ares Exploratory Vessel *Nebula Storm* calling you, overtaking from approximately two hundred fifty thousand kilometers astern. Please acknowledge."

Twenty seconds passed with no return. Since the radio signal crossed the distance in less than one second, this indicated either someone wasn't listening, or there was some delay in responding. Jackie tapped her finger on her chair arm. It was hard to judge how long she should wait.

Just as she was about to repeat the message, the screen shimmered to life, showing General Hohenheim in what was apparently his office. "*Odin* returns your call, *Nebula Storm*. Welcome to Jupiter System. You have come fast on our heels, Captain Secord."

She relaxed fractionally; it looked like diplomacy would at least begin the day. And with that transmission, A.J.'s data had begun flowing. The programmed contingency allowed the Faerie Dust to transmit only when *Odin* itself was transmitting, so the longer they talked . . .

"We know where you are headed, General. And it is my intention to beat you there."

After a second and a half passed, Hohenheim smiled. "Of course you do, Captain. While I admit to being—well, let us not be petty—utterly astounded that you had the audacity to take such an alien antique out into space on such short notice—and quite impressed by how well the vessel performs—I cannot pretend to be surprised at your intentions. You will, of course, forgive me if I say that it is my intention to beat you to Enceladus by a significant margin and claim the world, or as much of it as possible, for the European Union."

"Naturally."

"Might I ask why you have waited so long to call? We have—as I am sure you are aware—been trying to contact you since we first noticed the astonishing phenomenon of a nebula chasing us."

Jackie shrugged. "General, we had no warm feelings for any of you at the time, and direct communication with reasonable time lag wasn't really possible until now. You know how frustrating communication is with delays of more than a second or two. But consider this a courtesy call. We shall be passing *Odin* at a range of nine thousand, nine hundred and fifty-six kilometers and will then precede you farther into the Jupiter system."

"We had of course noted that, but your information is appreciated." The general studied her for a moment. "Captain, of one thing I wish to inform you—the actions taken to remove and conceal the information we have taken were done directly under my orders. There are members of my crew who were friends of yours, and I would find it sad to think that these friendships would be ruined by actions which—in truth—must have been at least somewhat expected by both sides."

Jackie didn't dare look around for support or hints. *Were we wrong? Was it just a terrible coincidence, an accident, something that just barely missed the* Odin *and hit us? Or is he trying to find out if we know. After all, no one's said anything about it.*

That must be it, she decided. Hohenheim had to pretend nothing had happened. But she wondered what he was trying to say. *If we* do *know, or discover it ...*

"General, I suppose I agree, in principle," she said slowly. "But if you have spent considerable time with someone and they have used some of that information against you ... That's a rather nasty betrayal, don't you think?"

Hohenheim nodded. "I would not blame people for being angry. But remember that there is duty, and these people had agreed to do what was done long before they met any of you. I assure you, it was not easy for them to do what they did, and it became harder with each day."

Images of Horst flashed in her mind: of him laughing next to her; the time he'd held her hand much longer than he needed to, after helping her through a hatch; the hours they'd spent talking. *All a fake?* It did seem hard to believe. Even Maddie and Helen had expressed their doubts.

She reminded herself sharply that keeping someone on *Odin* talking was the important point here, anyway. "I suppose it must have." She cut in the privacy switch. A.J. could still tell she was having a conversation, but now the images and sound would be projected to her VRD and into her suit alone.

"Since we will remain in reasonable communication range for a limited time . . . I know it may be slightly out of standard procedure, General, but might I talk with Horst Eberhart?"

Hohenheim's expression softened momentarily, in a startlingly warm way, and there was a faint twinkle in the brown-gold eyes. "Of course, Captain. I am sure Mr. Eberhart will be willing to give you a few moments of his time. Please stand by."

Perhaps a minute went by, although it seemed longer than that. Then Horst's face was in front of hers, blue eyes wide, uncertain, and . . . almost frightened? Could that really be an act? And if it had all been an act, why continue now?

"Hello, Horst."

"Jackie . . . I am very sorry." The apology was the first thing he said. "For everything. I had promised . . . they hired me for this. If I had known before . . ." He shook his head. "But then I wouldn't have been hired, and I wouldn't have met you. So it might have worked out badly either way." He took a deep breath and suddenly met her gaze directly, with an intensity that startled her. "But I never lied to you. Never. Not once. About anything."

A crazy part of her actually believed him. The sane part just *wanted* to believe him more than anything in the whole world. "Horst . . ."

"They didn't even want us calling back for a long time after we left, so it took me days to find a way around it. And then you didn't talk to me."

"You used me, Horst!" she snapped. "The program that hid the data—A.J. told me how it worked. You couldn't possibly have done that without everything you learned from me, and him for that matter."

"I know! I know, Jackie. But it was what I was there to do. I wasn't . . . wasn't there to . . . to get involved with anyone. But I did anyway. And when Anthony got that information and we covered it up, both of us felt . . . dirty."

He's telling the truth. Dammit, he has to be! "Really?"

"You do not know how many times we have talked about how much it sucks, Jackie."

The dry, precisionist tone in which he said the line made her suddenly burst out laughing. She felt like something was letting go inside her, opening up like a flower. "It sure did. . . . Horst. Did you mean what you just said?"

"That it sucks?"

"No. That you got 'involved.' We never talked about it."

He smiled, quite shyly. "Hard to do—get involved, I mean—on a spaceship crammed with people. Privacy is usually required. But it is how I felt, certainly."

She blinked back suddenly startling tears. "So did I," she said softly. "That's why I was so hurt by what happened."

The change on Horst Eberhart's face was astounding. Lines seemed to vanish from his face, and she really understood what people meant when they wrote that someone's face shone with happiness. There was nothing, for that instant, but pure crystal-blue joy in his gaze, and it was that which cut the last knot binding her heart. That look couldn't possibly be faked. Somehow—impossible as it seemed—Horst *hadn't* known about the coilgun attack. Maybe he'd known the gun existed, but someone else must have fired it, and he had never known they'd done so.

A green light blinked on in her line of sight. That meant that A.J. felt he'd done all he could at this point. Time to wrap up. She hadn't thought she'd be so reluctant to do it, but then . . .

"I have to go, I'm afraid. I guess I'll be seeing you again, at Enceladus. One way or the other."

"Yes," Horst said. "Is it all right if I don't wish your ship good luck, or will that get me in more trouble?"

She laughed. "Sweetie, that's just fine, because while I wish *you* all the luck in the world, that ship you are on isn't getting any of it!"

❊   ❊   ❊

"So, how did we do?" Jackie asked finally.

A.J. could not restrain a triumphal grin. "We are *in*. We are so totally in that you would not believe it. Operation Bungee is a go."

"You are sure it will work?" Madeline asked.

He was used to Madeline questioning him. And of course it gave him a chance to brag more. Which was still fun, if not quite as much the absolute necessity as he seemed to remember it being back when he was younger. "Maddie, it will most certainly work. My Faerie Dust was all over their outer surfaces, and there are places where it could get inside the control runs. There's control gadgetry all along the main accelerator ribs, and I'm slowly co-opting control of it. The most important question was whether I could find a way to get inside the ship itself, which I managed while you were talking—a vent valve in the NERVA system which they hadn't changed in their design. A bunch of the dust can get in that way, then through the filtration system. It's meant to handle impurities, but not impurities that are smart enough to avoid being emptied out."

"And then you can run the engines?"

"The NERVA engine, damn straight. Jackie knows more about that thing than anyone other than Gupta. She worked on every part of its design. Between her and Joe, I could figure out how to basically shortstop any commands they give and substitute my own. And I really just need to do a couple of things to make 'em swing ship before blasting.

"Controlling the mass-beam and the coilguns—that's a little trickier. I can mess with the control nodes on the outside, but me, you, and Joe are going to have to go over what I've managed to learn about the control parameters and designs with a fine-toothed comb to figure out exactly what I can and can't do. I can't take control of every system in that ship, at least not without a lot more Dust or a lot more time, and if someone catches on, we're in real trouble."

"Were you able to verify the existence of the coilguns?"

"Not yet. On our next close approach, I will. I can say there are a few anomalies along the accelerator ribs, but none that a fast-talking engineer couldn't explain away at this point. The motes will keep trying to work their way in, try to gain access, but they've got to do it as subtly and conservatively as possible, or they'll trip something."

Madeline looked satisfied. "So the whole plan doesn't need to be changed?"

A.J. shook his head, confidence filling him as usual. "Not a thing, really. We do our braking maneuver at closest approach—just about scraping atmosphere off the big guy—and then make sure they do theirs. With the right vectors we should be able to close on them again and give them the chance to make a deal."

"What if they fire?" Larry asked. "People whose ships were suddenly hijacked have been known to do that."

"I think I can screw that up even now," A.J. said. "And by that point, we'll also have the proof we need, I think. So shooting us wouldn't accomplish anything, right?"

"True enough. And it's not like we'll be offering them nothing."

"Then," Jackie said, smiling in a more natural way than she had since they started, "in a few days this should all be over."

"Just a few. Then, of course, we'll have to actually get to Enceladus, but we can both do that, especially once we're cooperating instead of competing."

A.J. had to admit, he was glad it was almost over, at least on the cloak-and-dagger side.

But he did have one more bit of fun in store for himself at the expense of the *Odin*. Harmless overall, but it would be his little reminder to Horst—and especially the unseen Mr. Fitzgerald—of just *who* he'd been messing with.

He couldn't wait.

Chapter 32

"Maximum power burn will commence in approximately fifteen minutes," General Hohenheim said, his voice resonating throughout *Odin*. "All stations, report readiness."

"Engineering, all ready," Mia Svendsen's voice replied.

"Security, all ready," said Fitzgerald from his position to Hohenheim's far left.

"Damage control, all ready."

"Living quarters, all secure."

The remaining groups also reported readiness. Hohenheim leaned back in the command seat. The acceleration of *Odin* would be relatively small, but after months without noticeable acceleration, there were still many potential chances for minor and even major disasters. "Dr. LaPointe, is all ready?"

"Yes, General. Ready for Oberth Maneuver in . . . ten minutes."

Jupiter loomed before them, covering more than half the sky. The planetary lord of the solar system and the king of the Norse gods were speeding toward a rendezvous, a brief dance of power in which Jupiter would gift them with three times the delta-vee of the rocket burn they performed, energy drawn from a gravity well of nearly sixty kilometers per second—fifty, at the altitude the *Odin* would pass.

"Any sign of *Nebula Storm*?"

LaPointe shook his head. "She had drawn considerably ahead, sir. We will not see her again until we clear the other side of Jupiter."

"Can you tell if she performed any powered maneuvers, or a simple flyby?" The Ares vessel had preceded them toward Jupiter, collapsed its dusty-plasma sail, and disappeared into darkness some hours before.

The French-English astronomer studied other readouts. "It appears that she will have two unique accomplishments to her credit, at least. From traces of water vapor I can tell that she did indeed perform powered maneuvers. She has the first manned flyby of Jupiter, and the closest."

Horst turned at that, startled. "Closer than we will pass?"

At LaPointe's confirmation, Horst gave a soundless whistle. "They must be practically scraping the cloud tops. No wonder they had to retract the sail."

"Impressive," said Hohenheim. "Perhaps they need every bit of speed they can get. But let them have the small triumphs, as long as the end of the race is ours."

"We will know that when next we see them. Their final velocity will be our answer. Either they will be faster, and will almost certainly win, or they will be slower, and we have won," LaPointe said. "Not long at all now."

The general checked the chronometer. "Coming up on five minutes. Mia, the engine is ready?"

"As ready as possible, sir. No one has ever attempted to run these engines at this level of output before, so nothing is quite certain, but I am confident."

"I can ask no more." The Oberth Maneuver depended on accomplishing the change of velocity as much as possible at perigee. Ideally, of course, it would be instantaneous, but absent reactionless drives and mythical acceleration compensators, some compromise had to be made. In this case, they were "redlining" the NERVA assembly to produce the absolute maximum thrust for this burn. Modeling showed it should do no real damage for this one burn. Hohenheim knew full well, however, that models were not the same thing as the real world.

Jupiter was closer now, no longer a planet but a gigantic cream and brown-striped wall, a mass of churning clouds beyond human comprehension. The Great Red Spot was close enough to show its true nature as a titanic storm, a hurricane large enough to swallow three Earths.

Alarms buzzed, and red lights suddenly appeared on LaPointe's console, just as a faint quiver ran through *Odin*.

Hohenheim leaned forward. Jupiter was moving, the entire field of view in the forward screen rotating. "What is it, Dr. LaPointe?"

"I do not know, General! The lateral thrusters, they have fired!" LaPointe's hands moved over the controls. "I am getting no response. We are continuing to rotate."

Horst Eberhart brought up his displays. "It looks like a reversal of vector. But it's not accepting the cancellation codes."

"Dr. LaPointe, if we are even slightly off when we make this burn, it could seriously impact our outward course."

"Yes, I know, General." LaPointe was now working virtually every control in sight.

"Mr. Eberhart?"

Eberhart shook his head. "Our commands are not getting through to the thruster systems, General. It will take time to figure out why—and I don't have that much time."

"Dr. Svendsen," Hohenheim said calmly. "Are you following this situation?"

"Naturally," Mia Svendsen's cool, controlled alto replied. "I will go to manual control. This means that your controls will be cut out, however."

"They do not seem to be of much use at the moment. Get us back on course, Dr. Svendsen."

"Yes, sir."

Jupiter and the stars outside appeared to have completed approximately half a rotation when the lateral thrusters rumbled again. The rotation stopped. Hohenheim waited, but no additional movement commenced. "Dr. Svendsen, we are waiting!"

The voice was now no longer so cool or controlled. "They are not responding to manual control. The problem appears to be in the embedded controller code itself."

"Damn!" Horst cursed. "That will take hours, maybe a day or two, to figure out."

"We have two minutes," Hohenheim said. "I think it would be wiser to troubleshoot with maximum fuel for course correction in case of emergency. Since our controls are still cut out, Dr. Svendsen, please cancel the main burn. Shut down the NERVA drive for now."

"Yes, sir."

He leaned back slowly, thinking. "Dr. LaPointe, obviously without a powered flyby our course will be quite different. Please begin to—"

The entire ship shuddered, and the thundering roar of a NERVA rocket at full power filled the air.

"*Svendsen!* I told you to shut the engine down!"

"I *did*, General! The reactor is refusing to respond! I entered all the commands, I got all the regular acknowledgments, and then it went right ahead with the burn!"

Hohenheim pursed his lips, then sighed. *Nothing to be done now. All I can do is try to salvage the mission.* He waited until the entire burn completed itself. "Mr. LaPointe. I would presume that in this orientation we lost, rather than gained, velocity?"

Looking somewhat shell-shocked, Anthony LaPointe nodded. "Approximately thirty-six kilometers per second, sir."

"Please recalculate our orbit and determine whether we are headed for immediate disaster—and if so, what we can do about it." He rose. "Mr. Fitzgerald, I will see you in the briefing room in five minutes."

No one said anything as he left.

"Horst Eberhart, General," Richard Fitzgerald said. "It can't really be anyone else."

He could see by the grimness of the general's face that Hohenheim had already reached the same conclusion. "Can we be sure?" the general said.

"Look at the facts, General. He *was* control systems. He and Svendsen together, but Svendsen isn't a programmer. Oh, she can code all right when she has to, but not a patch on him. He had a hand in every single bit of control code written, from the firmware in the bloody control nodes to the main user interface. So he's got the opportunity. Motive, well, you were the one who let him talk to his little skirt over on the Ares ship. First thing out of his mouth is how sorry he is, and the two of 'em are going sappy a few minutes later. Eberhart's just the kind of guy to figure that he could make it all right by letting them get ahead of us."

He could see Hohenheim's grimace of distaste, both at the bluntness of his commentary and the fact of his eavesdropping on a private conversation. Well, too bad. That *was* his job in such delicate circumstances, and in this case it looked to have been bloody good he'd done so.

"Horst is a good man," Hohenheim said finally. "He wouldn't risk the ship just because he felt guilty."

Fitzgerald waved that off. "He isn't the type to kill anyone, I know that. But there wasn't much risk in this. He just screws up the whole mission, but no one gets killed. He knows we can get home eventually."

"Ares had motive, too, of course."

"Too right on that. But they never had access to our systems. Sure, if even one of them had ever been on board I'd be looking real close at our friends on the alien ship, but there's just no way. They'd need time to get into the systems, figure out how to cut out the right areas, and they'd have to do that *without alerting our friend Horst*. I don't believe that last part one little bit, unless we go the whole way and make him a double agent. Which"— Fitzgerald held up a hand, forestalling Hohenheim's protest—"I don't believe, either. He's not sneaky enough for that."

He stopped and waited. He didn't need to say any more. The general knew what had to be done, no matter how much he liked the young engineer.

General Hohenheim nodded. "Have him brought here."

It only took a few minutes before Horst arrived. He looked startled when he saw Fitzgerald as well as the general. "Sir?"

"Sit down, Horst," the general said. When the system engineer hesitated, Fitzgerald stepped forward and shoved him down.

"The man said sit, boyo, and sit you will. And listen, and then talk when we say. Now, why don't you just come out with it?"

Horst stared at him in apparent disbelief. "What are you talking about?"

"Don't go playing an idiot, Eberhart! There isn't anyone else on this ship that could've messed with the drives like that, and you know it."

"Calm down, Mr. Fitzgerald," Hohenheim said. "Horst, please. I can understand why you did it, but denying it will do no good."

"You think *I* caused the drive failures?"

"Well, *somebody* bloody did. And it sure wasn't me, and it wasn't the general, and I'd like to ask you who else *but* you could do it."

Horst glared at Fitzgerald, but said nothing.

"Mr. Eberhart . . . Horst. You have been an excellent member of the crew so far, but you cannot deny appearances are very much against you. One odd drive failure, in one drive system, could be accident. Two, under these circumstances, are entirely beyond the pale of believability. And, again in these circumstances, I really cannot afford to take risks. However, there is one other obvious group of suspects. If you can only tell me how they could have done it."

"You mean the *Nebula Storm*."

"Exactly. Is there any way that they could have done this, given what we know about the access they had to our vessel?"

Moments passed slowly as Horst thought. Richard smiled inwardly as he saw, by the young engineer's expression, that there was no way out. "Sir . . . No, I can't see one, not even for A.J. Baker. If he had access to our system designs, or any interior access . . . or if he had his Faerie Dust on our ship, yes, he could. But there's just no way I can think of he could have done that. If they'd had that on board our ship near Ceres, they'd have stopped us long since—they'd have had plenty of chances"—he glanced at Fitzgerald narrowly—"to find out what we did, and how we did it. They wouldn't need to do this—they'd just have transmitted the evidence." He looked desperately at Hohenheim. "But . . . Sir, I didn't do it!"

The general shook his head. "I truly wish I could believe you, Mr. Eberhart. But I can't." He nodded to Fitzgerald.

Fitzgerald grabbed Eberhart's arms, forced them behind his back, and slipped on the cuffs. "Horst Eberhart, you're under arrest for suspicion of sabotage and possible espionage. Come along with me." He hustled the stunned Horst out of the general's office, toward the security area. Weeks back, anticipating possible problems, he'd had his security team set up three tiny holding cells. It was a jury-rigged arrangement, but it should do the job well enough.

This was working out well. While Richard had never had any personal animus against Eberhart, he'd always known the idealism of the young man could be trouble. And here the trouble was.

"Once this crisis is over, we'll have a longer time to talk. And talk you will, boyo. Talk you will."

Chapter 33

"Are we a go?" Jackie asked.

"No sign of *Odin* yet. And if she'd stayed anywhere on original course, she'd have come blazing out of there quite a while ago," A.J. answered.

Jackie glanced at Madeline, who nodded. "If our guesses were right, Jackie, they would have been accelerating on that leg, and we reversed that."

"Of course, if we'd been wrong and they'd been planning a deceleration, that would have meant we'd have sent them accelerating out of control, wouldn't it?" Jackie asked with sudden concern.

A.J. gave her a hurt look. "Do I look that simple-minded? We planned on *emulating* a glitch that reversed the vectors. I wasn't actually putting in something that boneheaded and unadaptable. If they were planning on decelerating, Larry and I had figured out specific changes to their profile. No way was I taking chances on doing that, because then there really wouldn't be anything in the system that could catch them, at least not without getting lost itself." The sensor expert shrugged. "Anyway, it doesn't matter. The fact that we haven't seen them tells us what happened. They had to have decelerated."

"Larry? When will we see them?"

"Unless celestial mechanics have changed, I'd say we can expect our guests to pop into view in about...twenty minutes."

"Once we establish contact, A.J., how long until you will be able to confirm the existence of the coilguns?"

"A few minutes, no more. I've already got a lot of contingency

226

programs laid in for establishing a no-go lockout on them. That shouldn't take too long."

"What if they *do* fire on us?" Helen asked.

"Same drill as before," said Joe. "But remember, we've already done the calculations. There's no way they can hit us. That goes double now that we'll have the Faerie Dust in the systems. Even if A.J. can't do anything to stop the firing, we'll know exactly when it fires, and even sluggish as *Nebula Storm* is down here, we can get out of the way. We still have enough reaction mass for a short emergency burn on the main engine, too."

Maddie frowned. "So this weapon is useless in space?"

"Hardly useless," A.J. retorted. "Worked damn well on Ceres. If you don't know it's coming, it's effective over a pretty long range. Beam weapons would be a hell of a lot better, but those would be hell to hide. Not that they'll be able to hide weapons like this now, either, but it was a useful trick the first time, just like the original Trojan Horse. A projectile weapon of that kind is useful against fixed targets or targets that either don't know it's coming, or that really can't accelerate out of the way. You could probably even put a little bit of terminal guidance into the shell to predict and adjust for target accel that wasn't too large."

He looked abstracted for a moment. "In this case it wouldn't make much difference. We start with a regular sail maneuver. If the shell shows a shift in course, we do a bigger burn. It can't have much maneuvering capability, since there's a limit to what you can stuff into a projectile. And especially a projectile that's going to go through a coilgun. The combination of electromagnetics and radiation will fry anything except very, very hardened or shielded electronics, or some MEMS/NEMS or optical units."

"Radiation?" Maddie asked.

"The way the accelerator works, you tend to get X-ray or gamma pulses out as a side effect. If I'd suspected anything of the sort before the fact, I'd have been able to prove they used a coilgun just by being able to localize a radiation pulse to the *Odin*. That's why they'd have to have the things out on the drive ribs anyway, now that I think about it. You want to keep the gun away from habitable areas, no matter how good your shielding is."

"And magnetic shielding is useless against X-rays and gammas," Joe noted. "So the only shielding that would work is a lot of mass. The same arguments would apply to the main drive, if not as intensely, so it wouldn't have been hard to justify the design to maximize the fuel tankage and reactor shielding along that arc. It'd make sense, given that you're putting the NERVA engine in that area anyway."

"All right, everyone," Jackie said. "It'll be showtime in a few minutes. As we discussed, we're basically going to our old choice number two, except this time we're the ones in the stronger position. We'll have proof they had the means to perform the attack on Ceres—a weapon deliberately concealed from the IRI and other powers—and that we can now probably beat them to Enceladus."

"So, then we make them the deal that should have been made all along—for all three groups to work together. We'll even let them be in on the first landing on Enceladus. Yeah, we know, Captain," A.J. said. "And we blow the whistle on them if they tell us to screw off."

"Exactly. And that would take us just a few seconds, right?"

"Well, longer than that," A.J. said. "Not normally, but remember, we haven't even completely cleared Jupiter yet, and Io's going to be getting in the way. I figure it'll be another . . . what, six or seven hours, Larry?" The astronomer nodded. "Six or seven hours until we can punch through a message to Ceres, let alone Earth or Mars."

"But it's only a few seconds of transmission, anyway. And they can't stop us from transmitting, correct? Jam us or something?"

"Not a chance," said Joe. "At a range of thousands of kilometers, tens of thousands? Nope. We'll get through. They can't shoot us, and they can't jam us. They'd be crazy or stupid to do anything other than cut the deal."

Jackie glanced at A.J. "You wanted to open the conversation. You wouldn't tell me why. Are you going to embarrass me?"

"*You* might be embarrassed to do it," A.J. said. "But it's nothing too bad. I thought of a lot worse. Besides, all of you have been complaining about how I've been growing up too much. Consider this my one last great hurrah of immaturity."

Jackie studied him, then smiled and shrugged. "I got my personal phone call on company time, I guess I can give you one last A.J. stunt, as long as you promise it's not *too* extreme. And you know what I mean by that."

A.J. gave a little seated bow. "I do. And it will in fact be very much extreme, but not extremely embarrassing. And"—he gave the trademark A.J. grin—"extremely apropos to the situation, I assure you."

"Then take your places, everyone," Jackie said. "We've got about seven minutes."

"When will *Nebula Storm* be in view?" Hohenheim asked.

Anthony LaPointe shrugged. "I would expect very soon, General. However, we do not know exactly what reaction mass they had to expend, what ISP they could manage to obtain from their necessarily improvised nuclear rocket, or exactly what course they intended to take. These will affect the exact point at which we will regain line-of-sight on the Ares vessel."

LaPointe was clearly ill at ease, with his best friend currently held in the *Odin*'s tiny brig. Hohenheim couldn't spare the time to reassure him—and if there were others harboring similar thoughts of sabotage or collusion with the Ares vessel, this would certainly make them reconsider. Hohenheim hated having to think this way, but despite Eberhart's appearances of sincerity, there did not seem to be any other reasonable explanation for the *Odin*'s drastic misbehavior. He connected to Engineering. "Mia, how are things?"

"I am trying to trace the faults, sir." Mia Svendsen's voice was tired and harried. "It really does look like the problem with the laterals is in the control nodes, probably in the firmware driving them. That's the only way I could see something being able to intercept and abort the commands from here. I've sent two people up to take one of them out of the housing, put in one of the replacement units, and bring the old one down for a full examination."

"What about the NERVA systems?"

"I only have so many people, sir. The NERVA engine is essentially out of the picture in terms of useful—or even nefarious—applications. The laterals, which share controls with our ion drive, could still be of very significant use. I am personally performing some pre-use testing of the control systems on the mass-beam, in case..." She hesitated, then went on. "In case the same person has managed to compromise those as well."

Hohenheim nodded. "Any results?"

"At the moment, all seems to be functioning normally, although I have been detecting slightly higher than normal RF noise, which I am trying to localize."

"*Nebula Storm* in view, General!"

Hohenheim turned. "Range?"

"About ninety thousand kilometers, General. We are slowly overtaking them."

Hohenheim breathed a sigh of relief, glancing at Fitzgerald. If the Ares vessel had been moving faster—had accelerated, rather than decelerated, strongly—the mission would have been almost certainly at an end, and probably his career with it. It seemed, however, that the *Nebula Storm* had no special tricks available to decelerate at Saturn, and therefore, even with the loss caused by the reversal of thrust on their Oberst Maneuver, there was a good chance that they could still beat the Ares vessel to Enceladus. It would just be a much, much closer race.

He studied the viewscreen. This deep in Jupiter's magnetosphere, the *Nebula Storm*'s captive nebula was vastly compacted, only a few tens of kilometers across; the vessel appeared as a tiny dot of light. "Any sign of communication?"

"Not yet, General. Do you wish to initiate contact?"

"In a moment. Let us take a closer look at our competition and see how they are doing from the outside."

LaPointe brought the powerful telescopes of the *Odin* into play. The view dissolved, then reformed, the dusty-plasma sail of the vessel now filling a large portion of the screen. LaPointe gave a faint French curse of disbelief as the image came into focus.

The *Nebula Storm*'s sail was no longer an abstract mixture of light and fog; a great shield-shape was formed from the dust and plasma, a huge badge with a rising sun behind some tall building and the number "714" at the bottom. At almost the same moment, the *Odin*'s speakers blared out with a simple fanfare, four emphatic notes followed by five more, and A.J. Baker's voice filled the bridge. "*Odin*, this is the Ares-IRI vessel *Nebula Storm*. You have the right to remain silent, but I don't think it will do you much good. Instead, I think you'd better talk to our captain. Captain?"

"General Hohenheim, this is Captain Jacqueline Secord. Are you receiving me?"

Hohenheim's mind was racing furiously. "The right to remain silent" was a phrase familiar to almost anyone who had followed any American entertainment, especially police dramas. The implications...

"*Odin* receives you, Captain," he answered. To shape the material of the sail that way ... He did not believe it could be done simply with the magnetic fields, even assuming the aliens' control mechanisms were indeed advanced. The material of the sail itself would have to be mobile, which now made all too much sense. "Am I to assume, from your rather unexpectedly confrontational contact, that you are responsible for *Odin's* current difficulties?"

"We are, in fact," Secord answered. "My overly melodramatic sensor engineer will take the credit for much of that, of course."

"Captain Secord," Hohenheim said carefully, "such actions are clearly an assault upon my vessel. Is it truly your intention to attack the European Union and, in effect, declare war between a small corporation and a U.N. agency and one of the most powerful political units on Earth?"

Secord's smile was not comforting. "General, it was not Ares or the IRI which began this. And as of this very conversation, I now have incontrovertible evidence that the E.U., or at least some components of it associated with the final design and outfitting of *Odin*, have deliberately and with malice aforethought armed the *Odin* with a weapon—a coilgun—capable of firing projectiles at meteoric speeds. Combined with other evidence, we have sufficient justification to state with conviction that it was an attack by *Odin*, and not a meteor, which disabled the power station on Ceres and led to the injury and very nearly the death of one of Ares' personnel."

Hohenheim felt the grim weight of the trapped descend upon him—but at the same time, a paradoxical lightening of his heart. "I see."

"Do you deny these charges?"

The general shook his head. "I would be a fool to do so, Captain Secord. If you had sufficient control of my vessel to force us to do what we have done, it would seem obvious you must have the evidence you mention. Yes, *Odin* did indeed fire a single projectile at Ceres. Is it your intention that we now proceed back to Earth?"

"That is one possible path," Secord said. "However, we don't think that this is the best choice for all concerned."

"What are you proposing, Captain?"

"A compromise, General. One that should have been done the moment Dr. LaPointe discovered the Enceladus connection. A joint venture, with Ares, the IRI, and the E.U. having equal shares of the discoveries, and perhaps even with E.U. personnel making the first landfall on Enceladus."

She spread her hands in a pacific gesture. "We really *don't* want enemies, General. We are, as you implied, not nearly large enough to play with the big boys if they get rough. Certainly we could get you dragged back and arrested. But that would still be so completely embarrassing to the E.U. that we would be lucky to ever get any cooperation from them ever again—at least for years. And we don't have the resources to explore, catalogue, and properly exploit another alien installation, anyway. We've been running on a shoestring ever since this thing began."

She laughed, and the sound made the bands of tension around the general's chest loosen for the first time in months. "Hell, look at our expedition here, flying after you in a sixty-five-million-year-old antique. We can't afford this kind of crap, and neither can the human race."

General Hohenheim nodded thoughtfully, vaguely aware that Anthony LaPointe seemed to have slumped back in relief at his console. "I presume that this logic was what convinced Horst to cooperate with you?"

"Horst?" For a moment, Jackie Secord looked completely taken aback. Then she laughed. "Oh, no, poor Horst! You think *he* sabotaged your systems?"

The general blinked. The connection had seemed obvious, as well as the methodology he could have pieced together: signals hidden within the main transmissions, with Horst having the key in his own head or personal data unit. But her reaction...

"Then how, please, did you manage to suborn my own systems? No member of Ares has ever been on board *Odin*, and, in fact, if you had managed to infiltrate the systems prior to our departure, this chase would never have been necessary."

A.J. Baker's image joined Jackie's on the screen. "Thank Madeline Fathom for the idea, General, and me for my Faerie Dust, which is all *over* your ship."

Anthony LaPointe sat up suddenly. "My God!"

A.J. chuckled. "Yeah, I think you just caught on."

Hohenheim understood suddenly. "Your supposed drive failure. It projected your Faerie Dust toward *Odin*, and eventually caught up with us." Hohenheim saw the sensor expert's grin widen. "And then, when you were close enough, you initiated contact to gather data and program the maneuver. And by now your Dust is spread throughout the main systems."

It made sense. Horst Eberhart had been as blameless in this as he had been in the attack on Ceres. It appeared both sides would owe the earnest engineer an apology.

"It seems that you do indeed hold all the cards. So, I agree in principle, Captain Secord. What would be the terms of this agreement?"

"I am not a lawyer, General. The agreement would be based on the one currently existing between the IRI and Ares Corporation, which has been very satisfactory so far. The only additional stipulation is this." She looked suddenly stern, a judge passing sentence. "The people directly responsible for the attack on Ceres will be arrested and, whenever practical, sent back to Earth for punishment. And you and your crew will provide full statements as to their actions and complicity."

And so ends my career. Well, it will be in a good cause. And I will at least be able to look at myself in the mirror. "I will allow you to choose the exact level of guilt that this encompasses, Captain. But I agree to your terms."

"Level of guilt?"

Hohenheim shrugged. "Such actions are taken by, and known to, different people at different times, and the responsibility for actions can be direct or indirect. For example, I myself did not directly order the attack. It was, however, done to accomplish ends which I had agreed to. And while it was from my point of view unnecessary and extreme, as commander I take the ultimate responsibility for those under my command, especially as I obviously colluded with those responsible after the fact. I will permit you the judgment of how widely you wish to spread your net."

Secord nodded. "I see what you mean. I will—"

The screen went blank. With sudden sinking conviction, Hohenheim glanced to his left.

Richard Fitzgerald was nowhere to be seen.

Chapter 34

Once the talk-talk had started, Richard had realized that Hohenheim would be going along with anything the Ares captain suggested. The *Odin*'s commander had always been unhappy with the whole situation, and this was just the kind of honorable exit the bastard was looking for. Unfortunately, that exit would inevitably include sending one Richard Fitzgerald up the river, and that would never do.

But he'd prepared for this contingency, along with many others. While attention was focused on the Ares group, he'd slipped out, down the main shaft toward Engineering. The controls for the ship were still locked down in that area, with Mia doing the troubleshooting and all. The bridge might be the main control area, but it wasn't hard-connected. That was his first goal. Well, first after establishing all the control he could manage by remote.

That bastard Baker. That would certainly complicate things; Richard's prior arrangements hadn't assumed a Faerie Dust wrench in the works. The real question was how many people were going to be a major problem. Eberhart wasn't even a question mark. He'd have to be dealt with. Hohenheim, the same, and *that* was the real pain in the arse. With the general on his side, even the straight arrows would probably have fallen into line, but with Hohenheim trying to make deals with the other side, it was going to get really sticky.

First things first. He opened a channel that his people would be monitoring. "Code seven. Repeat, code seven." They'd spent a long time going over the various scenarios, but he had to admit he'd really never thought he'd have to go to code seven—taking control of *Odin* directly. If it didn't work out, he was going to be in for a long prison sentence. Even if things did work out, the situation would be chancy. But he thought the resounding success of seizing a major Bemmie base on Enceladus, even if some lives were lost as a result of violence, would satisfy the powers-that-be in the European Union enough to allow Richard to slip through the legal cracks—and now as a very wealthy man.

Johnson replied. "Code *seven*, sir?"

"You heard me. Seven." He cut off. It was remotely possible that his team would back out on him now, leaving him pretty much alone, but he didn't think so. The potential rewards were still extremely attractive, and the immediate risks were fairly minimal.

The first thing to do was cut off the discussion. He'd arranged a pretty foolproof cutoff for communication—a major issue for any security chief, and in this situation doubly so. He triggered that code, saw it register. Good. No more talking with Ares.

Now, what next? As he thought of the next step, General Hohenheim's voice suddenly boomed out, echoing throughout the entirety of *Odin*. "Attention all personnel. Attention all personnel."

Silencing in-ship communications was of course another contingency, which Fitzgerald triggered immediately. Hohenheim was cut off in mid-sentence, before he got to the crucial point of informing the entire crew that the security chief was a mutineer.

Not that Richard liked to think of it that way. He felt that he was simply doing the job he'd been hired to do, and assuring the success of the mission. It wasn't his fault that the commander of the expedition did not have a spine to match his reputation. Hohenheim had lost sight of the essentials.

The biggest essential of all, of course, was to prevent *Nebula Storm* from talking. They'd said they had just found their evidence. That meant they hadn't had a chance to send it yet, and until they cleared Jupiter and Io there wasn't going to be a chance.

He triggered his own controls. As he'd expected, the ship responded. Baker and the other Ares crew weren't trying to keep total control of *Odin*. That would be rude, a pain in the ass to handle, and they didn't have the crew to spend watching things anyway. Nor did they have the programming time to be able to trust it all to automatic. The *Odin* would line herself up for a shot right nice, especially since *his* control protocols were separate from the others. Sure, Baker and his damn Dust would figure a way to cut it off, but if they didn't manage it in the next few minutes, it'd be too late.

He just had to get to Engineering in time to make sure the deployment and loading worked right. The *Nebula Storm* crew weren't idiots; they'd be ready in case *Odin* fired on them. He had to anticipate that, and deal with it, and he'd been working on that issue for months.

First, though, a clear and simple immediate task. He keyed his communicator. "Dominic."

Alescio responded immediately. "Here, sir."

"Deal with Eberhart. Code *seven*, remember."

"Yes, sir."

The main corridor running down the center of *Odin* was normally empty, especially under running conditions, which was why Richard had chosen this route—that and the fact that in zero-gee he could practically fly along, and could outmaneuver anyone else in the crew. The monitors would of course usually be able to pinpoint anyone's location, which is why he'd taken those out of the picture, too. He could use them, of course, but not on the run.

A technician—Erin Peltier, that was it—popped suddenly out of a side passage. "Chief Fitzgerald, what—"

Bugger. I don't have time *for this.* Peltier wasn't one of the mission-criticals, but she could have been useful, especially as they really didn't want to lose many people at this stage. But he couldn't afford someone who might talk to the wrong person at the wrong time, either, at least not for the next few hours. He kicked against the wall, hooked the shocked Peltier as he passed, and used leverage and angular momentum to slam her into the wall. The impact clearly stunned her. He gripped her throat, cutting off the carotid artery, and thus bloodflow to the brain, until she went unconscious.

What now? That wouldn't keep her out long. He thought a moment, hands moving to a position that would snap Peltier's neck like a straw. Then relaxed his grip. He wanted to avoid killing except where it was absolutely necessary, and it simply wasn't in this case. With code seven in effect, most people on the ship would figure out what was happening in a few minutes, anyway.

He stuffed Erin into a crawlspace. A bit tight, and she might suffocate in there if she couldn't work her way out, but probably not. He'd have someone check on her later, once the situation stabilized.

Another call came in; this one more favorable. Engineering was under control—and he was almost there. Fitzgerald allowed himself a quick smile. Give him a few minutes more, and the inevitability of the results just might even convince Hohenheim that there was no point in fighting. If not, they'd at least get more of the crew to give it up.

Especially once *Nebula Storm* was no longer in the picture. That was now the critical task.

Madeline stared at the suddenly blank screen, her gut tightening. Hohenheim's reactions, the attack on Ceres, her own inside knowledge of how certain people worked, it all fit together. "Jackie, I am assuming command. We are about to come under attack."

Jackie nodded. "Are you sure? The general seemed almost relieved by our contacting him."

"I'm sure," Madeline said. "General Hohenheim may not be in command over there any longer. If he is, I suspect he is currently preoccupied with trying to keep that status."

A.J. winced. "You think there's a *mutiny* on board? That's crazy, isn't it?"

"Undoubtedly crazy," she answered, keying in commands and looking over scenarios. "But people like Richard Fitzgerald are only technically sane. Jackie, I want our rotation stopped. We don't need any additional stresses on the ship if we need to maneuver, especially with damage."

"Slowing rotation. Won't take that long to stop—a few minutes."

"A.J., I need some intelligence. They know about the Dust now, so there's no need for subtlety. Talk to me."

The blond head nodded as A.J. fixed his helmet on. "I'm on it. At this range it may take a while—remember how much interference there is, and how very low-power the Dust's transceivers are. Even *en masse* they're not up to significant broadcast strength. But—" His tone sharpened. "I can confirm something's very not right. *Odin* is swinging ship, which would bring the coilguns to bear on us."

"Have you managed to cut their controls to the weapons?" Madeline asked.

"Not yet. I was starting to get in there during the conversation.

Then the Dust went to sleep with the cessation of their transmissions. I've finally got it woken up again, and I'm starting the process. Damn this separation! I've got actual speed-of-light delay on everything I'm doing, and I feel like I'm typing my commands out on some stone-age three hundred-baud terminal. And the bandwidth sucks, since I have to duty-cycle everything to match the available scavenged power."

"They are closing with us, correct?"

"As planned," Larry said. "But not all that fast. We've got a differential of less than four kilometers per second. It'll be hours before we reach near approach, which isn't going to be all that near anyway. We cross each other's courses, heading..." Maddie saw the slight shift of the astrophysicist's posture.

"What's wrong, Larry?"

There was a pause, as Larry seemed to be checking something. When he spoke, his voice was grim. "*Odin* had better get its personnel issues sorted out reasonably soon. Near as I can tell, they're headed for a landing on Io. And *Odin* isn't meant for landing, even if you could do it on Io, which I'm not sure any ship could."

"What about us?"

"We'll be quite a ways from Io, though still in spitting distance in astronomical terms. Our really close approach will be Europa. But it's not looking like a dangerously close approach."

Jackie looked pale. "But with their communications out..."

"We can't warn them right now. I know. They have their own navigators on board, of course, but if Maddie's right and there's a mutiny going on, they're not going to be looking at that aspect yet. Hell, they probably already *know*, but if this goes on, they may not maneuver in time." Conley shook his head in bemusement. "What are the odds? Space is practically empty. A random course change should have almost zero chance of sending you on a collision course with anything."

"Someone's definitely running out the guns," A.J. interjected from his own position. "And he's using his own protocols and controls, different from the ones normally in place."

"Fitzgerald," Madeline said, her tone of voice making the name a curse. "Just the type to do that."

"Hey, it's not all that different from what you did on board *Nike*," A.J. pointed out mildly.

Maddie restrained a sharp reply. After a moment, she shrugged. "You're right, of course. The difference is that I think Richard Fitzgerald is doing this for himself, not for the mission. Like a lot of people in my profession, he's a past master of justifying any action that he takes."

"It's still insane," A.J. said. "He can't possibly believe he can get away with it."

Maddie laughed bitterly. "How I wish I could agree with you. But he probably does believe it, and if he can get rid of us, he may even be right. It's not as if there are any police out here to check the crime scene to see if it matches the suspect's story."

"I'm getting into the coilgun control systems," A.J. announced. "Damn slow work, comparatively, but it shouldn't take too much longer."

"You'd better hurry," Larry said bluntly. "*Odin*'s just about finished lining up for the shot."

"But there's no real danger, right?" Helen said. "You guys told me that."

Maddie looked at the screen with gathering foreboding. From everything she knew, Helen was right. There wasn't a chance in hell that the coilguns could fire anything effective at this range. Even the molasses-slow reactions of the *Nebula Storm* would be sufficient to evade, or should be.

The problem was that she found it difficult to believe that Richard Fitzgerald didn't know that as well as she did. His actions so far might be reprehensible and even crazy from some perspectives, but he'd been playing in her league all along.

"There *shouldn't* be any danger," Madeline Fathom said finally. "But I'd feel a lot better if they never got to fire at us anyway." She looked at A.J. "Shut them down."

"Working on it," A.J. said absently. "Just a few more minutes, and we can all relax."

Chapter 35

Horst Eberhart sat quietly in the tiny, almost featureless cell. Outside he looked calm, but inside he was raging. And, he had to admit, afraid. He didn't know what was going on outside, but the situation couldn't be good.

It was still gnawing at him how he'd managed to end up here in the first place. He *knew* he hadn't touched the controls and ruined the *Odin*'s maneuver, yet he also had yet to figure out a plausible alternative.

Fitzgerald? Could *he* be doing it? Horst was intrigued by the idea, now that he thought of it. Wasn't one of the classic intelligence-agent ploys to make allies look like enemies? If Fitzgerald was really on Ares' side—working *with* Madeline Fathom, and just making it look like they were enemies—that would explain what just happened.

But, no, that didn't make sense. If he was working with them, there was no way that Joe Buckley would have been within a kilometer of the power-control facility when *Odin* blew it to powder. Fitzgerald might be cold-blooded enough to think it'd help things look more convincing, but there was no way Fathom would have done so.

Besides, if Fitzgerald were on their side, they'd have known what they were up to from the beginning. He shook his head. There had to be another explanation. Mia Svendsen? As the engineer, she could have pulled that off. Maybe. Certainly after the overrides were authorized—by the general. But before that... and again, the same objections applied to her.

The reason it made all too much sense for him to have done

it—and he gave a weak grin as he realized that he was now arguing the prosecution's future case—was that he'd developed a personal relationship with an important member of the Ares/IRI group *long after* the mission began. And while his relationship with Jackie Secord had remained undefined, it had been getting increasingly close—certainly enough to give credence to the charges against him.

Added to that, he had discovered the treachery of *Odin* considerably after they'd left. In this scenario, he would have gotten guilty over his initial, smaller betrayals, and then, after finding out that his own people nearly killed Buckley and did cripple the base, would have decided to turncoat. It was neat and made perfect sense, and even fit with Horst's gut feelings on the whole situation.

"The real problem," he said finally to empty air, "is that I didn't do it!"

Given that this was true, though...what happened? Horst didn't believe it was an accident, any more than did the general or Fitzgerald. It was too exact, too carefully timed and totally unstoppable by any ordinary means, to be a random glitch or set of glitches. There had been a couple of other close friendships between Ares/IRI and *Odin* personnel, like that between Dr. Conley and Anthony LaPointe, but none of the people there were capable of the "black ops" programming necessary to pull this off, as Horst was.

He leaned back and folded his arms, then continued to think on the problem, as there wasn't much else to do in his current situation. Since he'd basically eliminated any possibility of a traitor on board *Odin*, that left only one answer.

A.J. Baker. Horst had spent more than enough time around Baker to know that in some ways he'd underestimated the sensor genius. Yes, A.J. was not quite his equal in the programming arena, especially the systems programming that Horst focused on, but he was as smart as his reputation made him out to be, and the Faerie Dust he had was beyond cutting edge and right on the bleeding edge of capability.

Faerie Dust. Horst sat up as a possibility burst in on him. They had security procedures, of course, but with the capabilities of that Dust, Baker could have smuggled some on board *Odin* by using the personnel as unwitting mules. You'd practically have to examine each person as they entered under a microscope to have a chance of detecting the stuff. Self-powered and self-mobile, the motes could hide and might well be able to spoof many forms of sensors if properly programmed—and there was no one in the solar system who knew more about programming such things than A.J. Baker.

But, again, that theory fell under the weight of his own argument, given to Fitzgerald months—no, well over a year ago. It would be totally out of character for Baker to do something like that. After the fact of the attack, yes, he might be able—make that, he *would* be able—to justify doing it as a wartime necessity, but not while everyone was cooperating. It would be a temptation, but one that Baker would resist.

Yet it made so much sense otherwise. It was the ideal answer—if Horst could only figure out a way that the Faerie Dust could have made it all the way to *Odin* without anyone noticing.

It was the exact phrasing of that thought—placing the Dust itself in the active role—that suddenly crystallized his thoughts into a clear and perfect vision of what had happened. He laughed aloud, both in relief that he understood and in the sheer devilish brilliance of the approach.

At that moment, the speaker overhead suddenly spoke in the general's voice: "Attention all personnel. Attention all personnel." The words were filled with tension and anger. "The *Odin* is currently under—"

The silence that followed was objectively no different than the silence that preceded those cryptic lines, but it now seemed filled with menace. *What was going on out there?* Horst stood in the middle of the little room, tense and uneasy.

Without warning, the door slid open, revealing Dominic Alescio, one of Fitzgerald's men, holding one of the specially-modified shotguns designed for shipboard use. Time seemed to slow to a crawl, adrenaline stretching every perception to breaking limits. That was the last horrid piece of the puzzle, and in that moment Horst Eberhart knew he was going to die, as Alescio, without so much as a change in expression, began to pull the trigger.

Barreling in from the rear, a third figure plowed into Alescio. The gun went off, the explosion deafening in the confined space, and shot ricocheted and whined like a cloud of enraged bees throughout the room. One pellet grazed Horst's cheek, but his location in an adjoining but separate room had shielded him. From the cries of the other two, both combatants had gotten worse.

Horst Eberhart charged from the tiny cell toward the others. With shock he recognized the bloodied form now underneath Alescio as Anthony LaPointe. Alescio, also bleeding but clearly in far better shape than the astronomer, rolled aside just before Eberhart reached him and came to his feet, trying to bring the gun to bear.

But Horst was close, he was furious, and he was younger and faster. He was also very strong. Before the other man could pull the trigger or even get the shotgun decently lined up, Eberhart smashed the gun aside and slammed a full-strength right into Alescio's gut. The shock of impact screamed red agony through his fist—of course the guard was wearing armor.

Still, the impact was enough to make Alescio grunt in pain and stagger backward, trying to get into a combat stance. Horst ripped the gun out of Alescio's hand and spun it around, pulling the trigger.

Nothing happened. Nothing except that Alescio, bloodied and furious, started backing Horst up with a series of kicks and punches that the engineer could barely ward off even with the gun as a makeshift shield. *Idiot!* he snarled to himself. The guns were individualized, with a personal-characteristic lock; if the wrong person or persons were to get hold of the weapons, they were useless.

As guns, anyway. Horst took a kick to his own gut which made him glad he hadn't eaten anything recently, but he'd known it was coming. In the moment of contact, he brought the gun barrel down.

Alescio gave a high-pitched scream as the metal barrel shattered his kneecap. Horst jumped back and stared incredulously as the other man somehow tried to shrug off the pain and move in on him again. But the pain and injury to his knee—as well as other wounds from the earlier ricochets—slowed him by too much.

This time the gun barrel cracked heavily against Alescio's temple. He went down like a dropped sack of potatoes and didn't move. Horst paused a moment, breathing hard and letting some of the shaking die down. He was lucky this had happened in the habitat section of *Odin*. Without gravity, he was pretty sure he'd have lost the fight. He thought he felt the deck quiver under his feet, but there was no way to be sure right now.

He went over to LaPointe. "Anthony, are you crazy?"

"So it is crazy to be rescuing your friends? Then, yes, I am completely mad." The English-French astronomer's left arm was bleeding profusely from multiple holes; clearly he'd taken the edge of the initial shot. There were several other small wounds, mostly on his scalp and face, that Horst presumed were the result of ricochets. Fortunately, most of the energy had been lost by those projectiles before striking LaPointe. Only one of them was bleeding, and not badly. The other ricochet wounds were bruises.

Horst bound the arm tightly, tying a tourniquet high up on the bicep. The bleeding appeared to stop. "Thank you, Anthony. I would have been dead."

"That is exactly what I was afraid of once I saw Fitzgerald had taken off. So I left the bridge and came here as fast as I could. It did not take a genius to know what he would want done to you." He grunted in pain as Horst pulled him upright, but he stood reasonably steadily.

"So it's happening. I can't believe it." Horst peered out of the doors. No one in sight at the moment. "We've got to get to your cabin, then find out how we can help the general...unless he's working with Fitzgerald?"

"No, not a chance. He was about to make a deal with the *Nebula Storm* that would have saved the mission—but not, obviously, Fitzgerald's career. In fact, the bastard would probably have wound up serving a long prison sentence once we returned."

Now, there was a pleasant surprise. Too bad he didn't have time for the story yet. "Then let's see what we can do to make sure that happens. Can you keep up?"

"I think I shall have to. Lead on."

Gun still gripped in his hand, since it was the best club he had available, Horst Eberhart moved out into the corridors of the mutiny-wracked *Odin*.

Chapter 36

"Either help me or get out of the way, Svendsen," Fitzgerald said. "Or I'll bloody well have you shot."

The Norwegian engineer glared at him. "You can't afford to shoot me."

Say whatever else you would about Svendsen, she was not cowardly—and there was enough truth in her statement that Richard wasn't about to kill her casually. He sighed as he continued to maneuver the heavy cylinders toward the loading area. If it had been in an area with acceleration, he'd have needed forklifts and assistants. As it was, he had to be careful not to end up crushed by them.

"You're right. I can't quite be shooting you when I'll be needing the engineering talent to run this beast," he conceded. "But I *can* have my boys work you over and lock you in a closet. Which I'll do if you don't either help or sit down and shut up, because I have to get this done fast." He had no doubt that Baker and the rest of the Ares crew were working hard to shut down the coilguns.

Mia Svendsen glared again and looked like she was going to spit at him. Instead, she settled for something presumably insulting in Norwegian before strapping herself into one of the seats—away from any critical controls. He nodded at Johnson, currently the only other person present to keep Engineering secure. There were about a hundred people on board *Odin*, and he had less than ten percent of them on his side. Admittedly, they had all the weapons and most of the combat training, but right now things were stretched really, really thin.

He glanced at Mia again and shrugged. *I could have used the* help but I suppose it's just as well; she might have tried to bugger things up at just the wrong moment. And with *these* loads for the coilguns, it would not be a good thing to have anyone screw up.

The other concern was Eberhart. Poor Alescio was still out, so no one knew exactly what had happened. But it was clear that either he'd screwed up and somehow Eberhart had gotten the drop on him—unlikely, in Fitzgerald's opinion—or that someone else had arrived in time to turn a simple execution into a fight. Since no one had reported securing LaPointe, Fitzgerald was willing to bet that it was the astronomer who'd buggered up that little part of the plan.

But the most critical thing was the *Nebula Storm*. She had the data, and in a few hours she'd be transmitting it. The whole mission would then be over—unless she never transmitted. *I'll bet you think you're nice and safe, thousands of kilometers away. Well, old Richard and his friends have a few more surprises for you.*

Weaponry had been one of his specialties from way back, in his days in the military. As soon as he recognized the limitations of the coilgun, he'd had people looking for ways to at least minimize those. And then he'd tailored the best ideas for application in the scenarios he thought might eventually emerge.

It was nice when your careful planning paid off in the end.

Anthony and Horst burst into Anthony's cabin. Horst glanced around, looking for something to tend to Anthony's arm. Something about the window caught his eye. He drew in a shocked breath as he realized that he had not, in fact, imagined the deck quiver under his feet as the ship's orientation changed. As if to confirm his realization, another rumble passed through the *Odin*.

"Oh, God," he breathed.

"What is it, Horst?" Anthony followed his gaze. "Do you think . . . ?"

"Fitzgerald's going to fire on *Nebula Storm*!" Leaving Anthony to search for his own bandage materials, Horst sat before the room's terminal and brought up his own access.

"But does it matter?" Anthony said painfully, starting to clean out the wounds with the cabin's first-aid kit. "You know how little they must move to avoid the projectiles."

"Yes, I do. But Fitzgerald knows that, too." He brought up the work he'd begun weeks ago. Now that there was no more need for subtlety . . . "Time to disable the guns for good."

But when he saw the results, he hissed. "That bastard has his own application suite!"

"Yes, he would. Not taking chances with General Hohenheim locking him out."

"It just means I'm having to improvise a bit more, and on a lower level, with the shutdown." Horst frowned in concentration, then began to grin. "But I think I will beat him. He's still loading the guns. Just a few more minutes."

Fitzgerald slammed the port shut, sealed it, and activated the loading cycle. "Now we're ready to go, my friends. A little gift from the *Odin* for you all. Actually, four little gifts, each with something extra."

The coilguns—one on each of four support ribs—signaled readiness. Even as he pressed the final button that started the firing cycle, Richard's eyes registered that one of the status lights had just gone amber. But his finger was already in motion, and sluggish neural impulses could not be recalled.

The first coilgun cycled, magnetic fields synchronizing in perfect timing, grabbing the shell and accelerating it outward with immense force, hurtling directly toward the *Nebula Storm* at over fifteen kilometers per second. The next gun also cycled, neither A.J.'s Faerie Dust nor Horst's last-minute interventions quite able to affect it. The third would not have fired at all if Fitzgerald had relied on the original control suite, which was by now totally crippled by Horst and by the general, who had just locked the system down. As it was, one of the embedded controllers failed and the acceleration rings associated with it shut down. As the firing cycle had already begun, however, the following rings tried to compensate, mostly successfully. Now it was the fourth and final shell's turn, and it too began to accelerate at hundreds of gravities. But there were now no fewer than three different agencies trying to control the coilgun, at levels ranging from parts of the hardware up, and the embedded controls were no longer receiving reliable signals.

Halfway down the acceleration ring, the field inverted, unstably reversing twice. The shell's own controller, minimally complex in order to survive the hellish environment, miscued and took the sudden deceleration and heat to be impact. And did what any good armed shell should do in that situation: it detonated.

The explosion tore apart the *Odin*'s fourth mass-driver support rib like a firecracker on a straw, blasting shrapnel throughout the area. Some of that shrapnel was from the rib itself, but the rest was payload—high-density depleted-uranium pellets, coated to enhance penetration. The semi-smart shell had not had time to set for a directed blast, but at that short range the *Odin* still covered a huge fraction of the sky; there was no way to miss, and thousands of pellets did not.

Like the blast of a monstrous shotgun, the storm of armor-piercing bullets ripped into *Odin*, both the main body and the wide-flung habitat ring. Never meant for atmospheric entry, *Odin*'s hull was strong enough to take micrometeorite impacts. It also had design contingencies, alarms, safety features, and emergency procedures meant to deal with one or two unexpected larger holes. But this was not just one or two holes, and the personnel who might normally have been in a position to respond were busy with a mutiny, on one side or another.

The explosion and impact were puny compared to the mass of the huge ship. It did not reel under the blow, was not sent spinning and fracturing; it continued relentlessly on its way, outwardly almost unchanged.

But the interior of the *Odin* had become a charnel house.

Chapter 37

"Almost..." A.J. suddenly sat up. "Oh, that's bad."

"What?" Jackie looked worried.

A.J. ignored her for the moment. The status reports for the coilguns had stopped abruptly. The Faerie Dust was probably cycling, looking for more data, until it met another contingency to act on. But the last data he'd gotten...

"Something bad's happened. I can't tell what, though. I *think* we've been fired on, but something went wrong with the fourth shot."

"They got off *three shots*?" Madeline said, in a tone of mild reproof. "You seem to be slipping, A.J."

"Gimme a break," he muttered as he tried to redirect the motes on *Odin* to new assignments. The responses were not encouraging. "Fitzgerald had his own control protocols, as well as the original layer, and someone—I'll bet Horst—was trying to shut him down on their end. The combination was like having a four-way duel with blindfolds."

"I got them on radar," Joe said. "The shots, that is. They're pretty darn close for quick shots, but none of them are coming anywhere near us. Well, on a cosmic scale Fitzgerald was dead-on, but on a personal scale he's still way off."

"How close?" Madeline asked.

"Kilometers off, all of them. We won't even have to dodge. My guess is that even though A.J. and Horst weren't able to stop the firing, whatever they were doing probably screwed up the targeting. Even just a little nudge would be enough."

Some of the Dust finally responded with some data. And it looked like...

"Larry, give us a close-up of *Odin*," A.J. said, feeling a coldness begin to seep into his chest. "Fast."

"Second that." Joe's voice suddenly had no humor in it. "I'm picking up other targets near *Odin*. Looks like debris."

The screen blanked, then returned. At the current range, even with the highest-resolution imagers A.J. had been able to put in *Nebula Storm*'s systems, the huge ship looked like a diatom. But they could make out enough detail to see that the perfect symmetry of *Odin* was no longer perfect.

"What happened, A.J.?" Jackie demanded. "Are they going to be okay over there?"

"I can't be sure what happened, exactly," A.J. said. "Not at this range. Not with all the other crap going on, when I'm having to get low-bandwidth answers to my questions. Something went badly wrong on the last shot. I'd guess that Fitzgerald's last shell blew up in the middle of firing, probably because we were all screwing around with the controls at the same time. Hell, it might not even have been the shell. If the magnetic drivers went wrong, they could probably have fired the shell the wrong way or something like that. I don't know the details. Everything that was going on shut down a lot of the Faerie Dust, too. I've lost a lot of it—I knew it'd happen with it being that close up to the firing, but still . . . Anyway, I'm trying to get more info. I'm really worried by the fact that they haven't reestablished communications. That means that whatever Fitzgerald set up wasn't just a temporary glitch."

"You can't tap into their comm systems and get them working?" Helen asked.

"I wish. I know I pull off a lot of crazy stunts sometimes, but there really are limits. It's not like TV and movies where the super hacker is really a magician who uses techno-jargon. Wish it was. I could just spout off some obfuscating phrases and hey, presto, I'm running all their systems. But all I have access to right now is Faerie Dust which isn't even in the right locations and that can't communicate anything to me except in short low-bandwidth pulses, and we're still far enough off that we've got fractions-of-a-second comm lag, though that's shrinking. I've given the Dust some instructions to concentrate in some of the other systems I know something about. But since the Dust doesn't come with jet engines or rockets, it's going to take a while for it to get there."

"I see." Madeline's brow furrowed for a moment. "Can you get anything out of our sensors?"

"Lemme see what I can coax out." He shifted to the onboard sensors of *Nebula Storm*, which included visible, ultraviolet, infrared, radar, and a number of others. A picture of the space around the distant *Odin* began to build up. Filter . . . spectroscopics . . . Oh, not good.

"Definitely worse than just the one accelerator rib. I'm getting significant gas and vapor around the ship. She's leaking atmosphere, reaction mass, maybe other stuff like a sieve. Best guess—when it happened, it shredded a large part of the rib and blew pieces of it into *Odin*."

"And they're still headed straight for Io," Larry added.

"You'd think they'd have been able to calculate that right after the main burn, though," Jackie said, puzzled. "Why didn't they shift orbit? They can't be *completely* out of fuel."

"No, they probably have a little left," A.J. agreed. "I dunno why they wouldn't have shifted."

"It's obvious," Madeline said. "Given the amount of time, we know that dodging even something the size of Io wouldn't take much effort from them for quite a while. They don't need kilometers per second of delta-V for that, just a relatively few meters per second, and they have enough for that. So, instead of correcting right off, they were waiting to find out where *we* were. They needed to know the strategic and tactical situation before making that move."

"Except that the longer they wait, the harder it's going to get," Joe continued. "And with a mutiny and now what looks like major damage, I'll bet no one's thinking about that right now."

Jackie looked at Larry and Joe. "Can we match up with *Odin*? Do anything to help them?"

Larry sighed. "We're closing at about four kilometers per second. We can bias that for a closer approach at course intersect if we want, but we don't have the power to make up the delta-vee difference. If they manage to *miss* Io . . . taking just the right orbit flyby, they might be able to come close to matching up with us at Europa. Maybe." The Ares astronomer shook his head. "I think they'd still have to do a minimal Oberth even there, and I don't think they have that much left. I think it'd take at least a kilometer-per-second burn."

Joe looked depressed and angry. "Even if we did...I really don't know what we could do. We can't tow them clear. Even almost dry in the tanks, *Odin* masses something over ten thousand tons. We don't have the room on board to take more than a few refugees, and I don't know how far we could push life-support."

"Then the only thing we can do is keep trying to warn them," Madeline said decisively. "Jackie, I want you to broadcast a warning to them, with details of exactly when they will impact and a constantly updating timetable of how much they have to shift their current course to escape. A.J., keep trying to get information out of their systems...and find *some* way to deliver a message. Can you do that?"

A.J. studied the meager data he was getting back, compared it with what he knew of *Odin*, its systems, and its crew. "I think so. I just hope I can do it fast enough."

Alarms screamed throughout the *Odin*, almost deafening Horst and Anthony. Horst's display flickered, paused in mid-update, and then went to local. "The shipboard net just went down."

"But I thought that was impossible!" Anthony said with a stunned look.

Horst felt the back of his neck prickling as though something horrid was creeping up on him. Which maybe it was. "Nothing is impossible. But that is a very improbable thing to have happen. A distributed network it is, not so centralized... Some nodes are coming back. I am trying to find out..." As he managed to force some kind of status evaluation out of the crippled network, the full horror began to sink in. "Dear God," he breathed.

Most of the habitat ring had suffered some kind of damage. A few cabin segments—including Anthony's—had been in the shadow of *Odin*'s hull, shielded from the debris and shrapnel, but the vast majority of the habitat ring, standing so far out from the main hull as it did, was in line of sight of the explosion. Damage ranged from single punctures to shattered composite viewports to segments so riddled with holes they looked like a section of sponge. The entire facing side of *Odin*'s hull was riddled with holes, random punctures through hull, support networks, power conduits, and stored supplies. One of the external cameras showed an image that Horst quickly blanked out: an image of debris slowly moving away from the *Odin*—debris that showed several human silhouettes.

Anthony was looking over his shoulder, muttering something that sounded like prayers. "Horst, how bad is it?"

"I am trying to get more accurate information. Connecting to the controllers for the main systems. But it is very bad." Horst knew that most members of the crew, during the last few hours, had been in their cabins or in the hab-ring laboratories. The main hull was for command or bridge crew and engineering, for the most part, especially during maneuvers. Which implied something he did not want to think about. "Connected, finally. A lot of discontinuities in the network . . . Well, one good piece of news—the *Munin* is undamaged and can probably be launched."

"But it cannot hold that many people, yes?"

Horst hesitated for a moment, but there was no reason to evade the issue. "There may be not that many people left to load on," he said grimly.

Anthony stared at him, wordless for a moment. "You . . . you cannot mean that."

"I am very afraid that I do," Horst said quietly. "We need to get into our suits now. According to the data I am getting, any route we take out of here will take us through vacuum."

Anthony nodded silently, and began—painfully—to pull on his suit. "Where do we go?"

"To the *Munin* first. It has independent systems, including its own communications, life support, and power. We need to be able to tell *Nebula Storm* what has happened. Maybe they can help. And we can use *Munin* as our own fortress, if Fitzgerald and his people survived. Assuming, at least, that the bastards are not yet on board it." He went to shut down the terminal, but stopped as an unusual signal was highlighted by his application. He sat back down. "Who . . . ?"

The signal was coming from one of the surviving controller units on the *Odin*'s driver-support ribs. But it wasn't a normal control or update signal. It looked like . . .

Suddenly he understood. Decoding the signal didn't take long. Reading it, however, he almost wished he had taken longer. Anthony saw it in his face as he turned. "Horst, what is wrong now?"

"I just got a message from A.J. Baker, through some of the Faerie Dust he still has on board. And he tells us that soon we will have a much worse problem to worry about."

Anthony froze. "Oh, God, I had forgotten! Io!"

"Yes. Io."

The astronomer resumed putting on his suit. "We must find a way to get control of *Odin* very soon."

"We will have to use the laterals. The NERVA drive is no longer usable."

"What?"

"Oh, the reactor and so on is basically intact," Horst said bleakly. "But the thrust nozzle is shredded. Try a burn with that kind of damage, and it will vaporize. I have no idea what would happen after that."

"Then," Anthony said, clumsily forcing his wounded arm to cooperate, "we have even less time than I thought."

Hohenheim struggled slowly back to consciousness. *How long have I been out? What happened?*

He tried to move, but found that something impeded his movement. Opening his eyes, he gasped.

Below him, space rotated slowly, majestically. Jupiter passed him, and other distant objects. Nowhere was there a sign of the *Odin*. He was alone, spinning through the void, four hundred million miles from Earth.

Not while still feeling gravity, I am not. He moved his head; everything seemed to be working. He looked around, trying to ignore the vertigo of space all around him.

Looming above him like a constantly falling skyscraper was *Odin*. Looking down his body, he could see that he lay facedown across one of the habitat support ribs. The part of the cabin unit that would have been under his upper body had been blown away somehow. His legs and abdomen were trapped under wreckage that had fallen on top of him rather than being sucked out into vacuum. He was hanging, in effect, off the edge of a cliff that dropped off into infinite space.

Do not move yet. It seems stable for the moment. I do not seem to be badly hurt. What happened?

It came back in a rush: the *Nebula Storm*'s victory and face-saving offer, Fitzgerald's treachery . . . Yes, and then he'd realized that real fighting might break out, since Fitzgerald controlled the armory. So he ordered the bridge crew to prepare, and...

Disaster. He'd gotten into his suit, but the others had not yet finished when the doors opened. The lockdown had been subverted. They hadn't managed to kill him, but he'd forced them to split up. He hoped that they hadn't killed the few people remaining on the bridge. So he'd diverted them away in one direction, managed to take down one who'd relied more on guns than bare-hand skill, and...and come to his cabin. And then there had been a shockwave and impact....

Something had gone dreadfully wrong. Looking down the length of *Odin*, he could see the mangled ruin of the fourth support rib. To the right and left of him, the habitat ring curved down and away, riddled with holes, missing pieces as far as he could see. Some of the drifting debris he could make out was not mechanical or structural in nature, either.

He wished he could believe that this meant most of the mutineers had perished, but he knew better. They'd been wearing their armor, almost certainly ready to put on helmets. Some might have already been wearing the helmets. Maybe one or two were dead, but a far larger number of the main crew were now gone.

He realized there had been no chatter of communications. The shutdown Fitzgerald had imposed was either still working, or the damage had been extensive indeed. In either case, it occurred to him that it might be even more useful to be thought dead. He could access the communications and update software... Yes, he could do it. Reception should remain, and deliberate communication, but anyone doing a regular search would not get operating-status data from his suit.

He studied his position. The wreckage that pinned him must weigh at least three hundred kilos—in this case, a good thing, because otherwise he'd probably have slowly slid out of its grip and plummeted off into the deep. The problem was going to be getting out from under it without possibly causing worse problems. He had no way of knowing how strong, or fragile, the wall on the other side of the support was. If he moved wrong, put stress on the wrong place, it might fracture, leaving only the main support he was sprawled over intact. This might get him out from under—but it could also drag him overboard with the rest of the debris, and there was no swimming back to this ship. He wasn't wearing a suit with reaction jets.

An idea struck him. He reached down to the area of his belt. Yes, the safety line was still there. That should work. Carefully, he managed to force the safety-hook end out of its place underneath him. Once that was out, the slender composite-metal combination line slid out with minimal effort. With great care he managed to loop the line entirely around the support, which was almost—but not quite—small enough to get his arms around. He had to try whipping the hook end from one hand to the other several times before he managed to catch it, but after that it was easy to pull it the rest of the way around and hook the line to itself. He tested the loop to make sure the hook was locked shut, then started wiggling, tugging, and pulling.

The suit moved a fraction of a millimeter. Then a centimeter. He pushed and grunted and swore and gave a mighty heave.

Abruptly the pressure holding him shifted, tilted, pulling him back and down as the other wall cracked. But the looped line prevented him from falling, while the carbonan suit shrugged off the glancing blows and scrapes as the remaining debris fell away from *Odin*. Hohenheim dangled from the main support for a moment, then grabbed the support and clambered onto it. Standing up, he slid the loop of safety line with him, looking for a higher point to fasten it to. There was no floor left to this room now except the pieces remaining on the support beam, but the main door was visible. And so was his wall safe, still securely fastened to the wall.

The wall safe was what he had come here for. He studied the situation. The safe was about two and a half meters from the door. Maybe a bit more. He couldn't reach it standing in the doorway. He looked up. That was more promising. Some of the ceiling had been ripped away when the cabin depressurized, and there were pipes and cables visible. Taken together, they should support his weight. If he climbed up the main support . . .

It was not nearly as easy as it looked. Without the little safety line, he was not sure he could have managed at all. But eventually he was suspended from the plumbing and air tubing and slowly lowering himself to the safe. A code and verification later, and the safe opened. Hohenheim reached in, found what he was looking for, and pulled it out.

A few minutes later he stepped through the doorway into the silent vacuum of the corridor beyond and made his way, gingerly, to the nearby connecting tube that led to the main hull. He paused a moment, looked down at his waist, where the gun now rested, waiting, and gave a nod of satisfaction.

Alone in the silence of space, General Hohenheim crawled toward the body of his wounded ship.

Chapter 38

"Anything new, A.J.?" Madeline asked after a long period of mostly silence.

The blond sensor expert nodded. "Getting something finally, with Horst's help."

Jackie's head snapped around. "Horst's alive?"

A.J. grinned, the first normal smile any of them had managed in a while. "Sure is. Alive and kicking, in fact. He and Anthony are headed to *Munin*, their other lander. It has separate comm systems, so hopefully we'll have communications going soon."

"Taking them a while," grumbled Larry. "Do they know about their deadline, emphasis on *dead*?"

"Yeah." A.J. looked serious now. "But they're having to try to get past Fitzgerald's people—and *Odin*'s very badly hurt."

"How badly?" Maddie asked. Something was starting to nag at her. "Do we have any idea how many people they have left, and what the condition of the ship overall is?"

"Starting to get the picture," A.J. answered. "And I don't like it. The NERVA engine's workable, but the thrust nozzle is toast, and so is some of the venting around it. The mass-beam's totally screwed right now. Even if we could work around the lost support beam, the software's going to have to be reinstalled all through the thing after what we did to it."

His lips tightened in an almost-white line; Maddie could tell he was both furious and upset. "The habitat ring's the worst, though. There was damage all through it, and people weren't ready for this. It's...bad. Really bad."

Madeline felt her eyes narrow as a tight, cold feeling crept up her spine. "A.J., Jackie, give me a model of an explosion on that support rib. I want to see how it did that much damage."

"Okay." A.J. worked for a few minutes, asking Jackie to help him on some points. "Here we go . . . Hmm, no, that didn't do it. Some damage, but nothing like what I see. Okay, boost the power . . . Nope. Hmm. Well, we've got . . . but no . . ."

Maddie raised her head, looking at the image of *Odin*. "A.J., try putting fragmentation in the shell itself—say five hundred kilos of armor-piercing, maybe ten to twenty grams each."

"Okay." A few moments went by, and he sighed heavily. "Yeah. Yeah, Maddie, that does it, all right." His voice sounded leaden.

Now she knew. "A.J., give me a plot—where are those shells from *Odin*'s salvo going to be when they miss?"

"Son of a bitch . . ."

The screen lit up, showing the courses of the three shells and *Nebula Storm*. Madeline leaned forward tensely in her seat, already knowing what she was going to see.

At closest approach, the three shells bracketed the *Nebula Storm*, the alien ship at the nearly precise center of a triangle. The third shell seemed to be lagging slightly, but not much.

"Damn him. If we hadn't had so much going on, I probably would have thought of this sooner. Jackie, Larry, get us out of here."

"Don't have much fuel left, and they're gettin' kinda close," Larry said. "But . . . let's see, we need to get probably well over a hundred kilometers from them to make sure not too many of those little beasts hit us. Yeah, we've got enough to do that. Stand by—we're doing a burn. Toward the side of the third one there. That one's a little behind the others." *Nebula Storm* began to pirouette, bringing its drive to the proper alignment to take them out of the path of the oncoming weapons.

"That won't take us *into* anything else, will it?" A.J. asked.

"Not likely, but lessee . . . No, it'll take us closer to Europa in the end, close enough to do quick sightseeing from far up, but not dangerous. Jackie, drive ready?"

Jackie looked up from her controls. "Accumulators charged. How much of a burn?"

"Get us a delta of one hundred sixty meters per second. That'll do it."

"Wouldn't want to do much more than that. We're kinda tapped right now," Jackie said. "Firing in three . . . two . . . one . . ."

The adapted NERVA drive thundered briefly, shoving the *Nebula Storm* sideways. A.J. watched as the trajectories diverged. "Yeah, that'll do it. We'll be over two hundred kilometers from the nearest one when it goes off. I don't know if we'll avoid all the damage, but I don't think it can concentrate fire enough to really screw us at that range."

"Probably not," Maddie said, slowly starting to relax. "Not with a simple explosive shell. You can do a shaped and directed charge for some reasonable directionality, but there's a big difference between hitting a two-hundred-meter target at one kilometer versus hitting it at two hundred kilometers. I—"

"*Course change!*" A.J. suddenly shouted. "The three shells just did a burn! They're matched with us again!"

"I was afraid that might happen," Maddie said in careful, precise tones. "I've been underestimating Fitzgerald all along. He's a sociopath, but a very smart one. I wonder how much delta-V they can carry."

"Can't be much more than that," A.J. said. "I know what the approximate mass of those shells was. Can we do another burn?"

"One more," Jackie said. "Then we're on fumes, so to speak."

"Here's the vector."

Nebula Storm roared again, dodging from the path of the closing shells.

Maddie watched, tensely. *Please be out, please be out...*

"Shells doing another burn..."

"Oh, hell." That was Helen.

"But they ran out of juice."

Maddie relaxed a bit. "How far short?"

"They'll be...well, closer than I'd like, but a lot farther away than they were going to be if we hadn't moved. About ten kilometers, give or take."

"They'll have to blow a little before actual closest approach," Joe pointed out.

"Yeah, probably about thirty or forty seconds. Maybe a little less, depending on how fast the explosion makes them go. I doubt they're going to hit much more than a couple of kilometers per second from the boom."

"It's a moot point anyway. Our closing velocities are almost ten times that."

"How long until they hit?" Madeline asked.

"Or until they miss? We've got about ten minutes."

"Seal off all doors now. Can we lower the hab sections?"

"You mean lying flat, like before we first launched?" Jackie asked. "Yes, since we're not rotating. It'll take a few minutes, but we have enough time. I don't know if that's going to be better or worse."

"Most of the vector is forward. If we lower the hab sections, we present a smaller overall target. Lower them." She glanced at Joe. "Retract the sail and pull in the control cables."

"Understood."

A waiting silence descended upon the *Nebula Storm*. Slowly the four hab sections at the end of their long booms descended to lie as flat as possible against the hull of the alien vessel. Like a deflating balloon, the nebula sail began to shrink.

"Don't suppose going through the nebula sail would affect them?" Helen asked.

"Don't think so," Joe answered glumly. "Doesn't matter now that we're retracting it."

"Five minutes."

The great glittering nebula had faded, and the Smart Dust retracted within the hull, along with the tendril-like control cables.

"One minute."

Seconds passed. Simple calculations were made. The decision reached.

The three shells recognized the only possible target in range and adjusted shaped charges. The range was distant, but there was still a chance. The first two detonated, the third just fractions of a second behind them.

"Incoming targets," A.J. said. "Uncountable on radar—it's like a goddamn cloud. Impacts possible in . . . thirty seconds . . . twenty . . ."

Maddie braced herself, even though she knew the impacts would likely be nothing to the ship as a whole, as A.J. counted down to zero.

A storm of armor-piercing bullets ripped through space. Focused to as narrow a cone as their configurable explosive propellant charges could manage, they had still been much farther than optimum from their target. The vast majority of the man-made meteoroids streaked harmlessly past *Nebula Storm* and on into empty space.

A few, however, did not. Fourteen thumb-sized projectiles with a relative velocity of twenty-one kilometers per second slammed into *Nebula Storm*, each carrying the energy of a small cannon concentrated in an item the size of a small thumb. Even the Vault material of the alien hull, tough as it was, could not simply shrug such impacts off with impunity. The impacts, even at poor angles, ripped gouges down her sides, punched into the interior, bored through composites and metals like a bullet through butter. But the *Nebula Storm* was huge, and the chances that a handful of hypersonic bullets would hit anything critical over a two-hundred-meter-long hull were miniscule, and none of them came close.

Except for one.

The alien hull suddenly chimed to multiple impacts, blows so close together that they almost sounded as one: a high-speed machine gun. Alarms screamed out, and the bridge went black, the blackness just as abruptly relieved by red emergency lighting. "That doesn't seem good," Larry said.

"It's not," Jackie said. Her voice had a hollow, shocked quality to it. "What happened?"

Jackie didn't answer for a moment. Then she chuckled, a laugh that carried an almost creepy overtone.

"Jackie, no offense, but what the hell are you laughing about?" A.J. demanded. Madeline stared at the dark-haired engineer with rising concern.

With apparent difficulty Jackie got herself under control. "Sorry. It shouldn't be that funny. But it is. Remember where we get our main power from? Well, that's the *second* time that goddamn E.U. ship has shot the same goddamn reactor!"

Maddie felt her lips tighten along with her gut. "The reactor itself?"

"I think so, this time. The safety seals tripped and all—I don't think we're looking at a radiation hazard—but it's totally scrammed itself." Jackie shook her head, looking grim now.

"Can we fix it?"

"I'll have to find out what's really wrong first. Give me a few minutes. A.J., Joe, help out here."

Helen and Larry nodded to Maddie. "We've got holes to patch."

"Understood," Maddie said. "Stay away from the engineering area until we know what's going on there, though."

"You got it." The two scientists cycled the lock out of the bridge.

A few minutes later Jackie sat slowly up and turned to face Madeline. Her expression gave the answer. "No."

"No chance at all?"

"Not really," Jackie said. "It didn't actually punch the core, but the amount of work we'd have to do ... At the least we'd need a big dock or a big, flat area to work on—one with enough gravity to keep things in place, or else someplace sealed off. And without the reactor, we can't even sail around very long. We don't have the fuel to set down anywhere, even if somehow I could get enough energy."

A.J. looked at her with a horrified expression. "You're saying we're going to drift through space until we just run out of power and die?"

"I ..." She looked momentarily defensive, then suddenly sighed. "Yeah. We are."

"I don't suppose," Maddie said, feeling unnaturally calm now that the worst news was delivered, "there's any way we could get help."

"No," A.J. said. "Not unless *Odin* can pull off a miracle."

"How long do we have?"

"Well ... that'll take a little while to figure out. If we can get to the lander ..." Jackie and Joe went into a combination live and electronic conference. Maddie glanced over at A.J.; the sensor expert was staring bleakly into space. "How are things on *Odin*?" she asked quietly.

A.J. shook himself and bent back over his controls. "I'll find out. Can't be any worse than it is here."

Maddie looked at the screen, which still showed the image of the huge E.U. vessel surrounded by debris. "I'm not so sure."

Chapter 39

Fitzgerald cursed. "Move it, you bloody fat-arsed bitch!"

Mia glared at him again, probably more from the personal insult than from his giving her orders. The insult was completely unjustified, in point of fact. The Norwegian engineer had quite an attractive figure.

Richard couldn't believe how quickly it had all gone wrong. He still had a few of his people left—Johnson, Desplaines, Feeney—but the explosion and subsequent damage had wiped out over half of his team along with most of the *Odin*'s crew. It had also damaged the systems all over the ship, although the vessel's material structures had taken a lot less damage than human bodies.

Still, as serious as the situation had become, it was still not desperate—*provided* that he'd succeeded in taking out the *Nebula Storm*. Or at least disabled their ship and its communication equipment, if not killed them outright. Without a functioning and mostly intact spaceship, no one could survive the orbital environment of Jupiter and its hellish magnetosphere for very long.

If there were no Ares and IRI survivors left—or wouldn't be, before they could send a transmission to the inner system—Richard thought he could still salvage the situation. Well enough, at any rate. Other than his own people, no one still alive aboard the *Odin* had any idea what had caused the catastrophe with the exception of Horst Eberhart and Anthony LaPointe. If Richard could take them out of the equation, he'd have plenty of time to remove the evidence of the coilguns and plant evidence that indicated the disaster had been caused by enemy action coming from the—now happily destroyed—*Nebula Storm*.

That evidence probably wouldn't fool a really good and determined forensic team, once they returned to Earth orbit. But Richard was quite sure his patrons at the ESDC and in the E.U. Commission of Enterprise and Industry would see to it that whoever investigated the affair would be safe and reliable.

There was still Mia Svendsen, of course. She'd have to be silenced also, eventually. He still needed her expertise, but he couldn't allow her to mingle with other survivors of the crew. That was going to be a tricky situation, but he was confident he could deal with it. Right now...

And then he thought to check the *Odin*'s course. Straight for Io, possibly the least hospitable spot in the solar system outside of Jupiter itself or the surface of Venus. He growled and gestured to Jackson to keep an eye on Svendsen; he moved ahead of her, with Feeney ahead of him taking point.

God damn them! That spineless Hohenheim, A.J. Baker and Horst Eberhart. Together they had managed to bugger *everything* up. He'd had the situation completely under control until they'd created a total cock-up in the coilgun systems. Baker, well, he could understand that, but couldn't the general at least realize that taking out the *Nebula Storm* would end up being for the good of everyone in the long run? Fitzgerald had been hired to do a job—so had the blasted general himself, for the love of Christ—and then bloody *everyone* had to keep getting in the way. To put the cherry on top, they'd managed to get the *Odin* turned into a colander. Mia Svendsen had told him that it was going to take her weeks to get the engines back on line—and they didn't have weeks before their up-close meeting with the most volcanic body in the system.

That left only one option for anyone who wanted to stay alive: the *Munin*. The lander/transport—and its missing twin, *Hunin*—were the largest pieces of cargo ever transported between planets, each massing five hundred tons fully loaded. And for convenience and efficient use of space, the *Munin* had been loaded with maximum supplies as soon as they had set out. It would hold up to ten people, and that would be more than enough, it seemed. Of the total of one hundred or so original crew of the *Odin*, there probably weren't more than a dozen left alive. Twenty, at most. But most of them were cut off. He couldn't afford to spend hours dragging possibly injured people out of *Odin*'s wreckage, or arranging spacewalks to reach them.

And, being realistic, at this point the fewer people from the expedition who survived, other than his own team, the better. There would be no way now to continue on to Enceladus, so the original mission was in the crapper. The only thing left to do was to survive until they could be rescued, which would probably take years. Then, perhaps, he could cash in eventually on the inevitable fame that would accrue to him from being the surviving officer of the ill-fated expedition.

The prerequisite for that, however, was that no one could survive until rescue other than himself, his team, and whatever crew members were completely ignorant of what had happened. So those of them who were already dead or would die soon were simply saving him the trouble of disposing of them later.

It was an unfortunate situation, certainly, but Richard was no stranger to hard times. He'd get through it well enough, he thought. And there was one bright spot at the moment: Hohenheim had apparently not survived. The general's life signs had gone to zero shortly after the disaster. *Shame that, but you brought it on yourself, boyo. If you'd only just listened to old Richard, we'd both be sittin' pretty right now.*

The sporadic connection to the formerly seamless shipwide network sputtered back to life. He could access data about the hangar area now. *Oh, bugger me.* "Feeney! Hold up."

"What is it, Chief?"

"Someone else got to the hangar bay first," he said calmly. He really should have predicted this, but then, there hadn't been much time. "And they're trying to talk to our old friends off on *Nebula Storm.*" He queried the net, using his security authorization. The answer was, in its own way, rather gratifying. "Well, well. It's Horst Eberhart and his sidekick, LaPointe."

Vanna Desplaines looked concerned. "If they're already aboard *Munin,* that's a problem. We can't force the doors."

"Of course not," agreed Fitzgerald. "But there are ways to convince 'em to come to us." He grinned. "There are always ways, you know."

"—ing *Odin.* You are on a collision course with Io. You will need to change course. The following is the most efficient..."

Horst glanced at Anthony, who nodded. "They are accurate."

"A shame that we cannot do that," he said. Once they'd managed to access the *Munin*'s communications gear, it hadn't taken long to pick up on the *Nebula Storm*'s automated warning. He activated the transmitter. "*Nebula Storm, Nebula Storm*, this is Horst Eberhart on *Odin*. There is no point in continuing to broadcast. We can do nothing."

A few moments later, Jackie's voice responded. "Horst! How bad is it?"

"It is hopeless, Jackie," he answered soberly. "The NERVA drive is damaged and would take weeks to repair out here. Lateral thrusters cannot produce the delta-V we need, even if enough of them were intact, which they are not. There are maybe twenty of us left alive. If that."

"Jesus Christ." That was A.J. "Eighty percent of you *died?*"

"Everything went wrong at once, A.J. Some must have been killed by Fitzgerald's people. A lot of them were in the habitat ring, which was shredded by the blast. Most of them wouldn't have been in suits, so they'd have been killed by the decompression even if they'd been otherwise uninjured. And getting to whatever survivors there might still be on the ship would be hard, if it was possible at all."

"And of those twenty," Anthony put in, "at least four are Fitzgerald and his people."

"Marvelous," Maddie said. "So he's got all the weapons, and the survivors are divided."

"But we are on *Munin*, which is the only escape," Horst said with a touch of grim satisfaction. "If he wants to live, he's going to have to play our way. He cannot force the doors on something this size, especially if he wants it intact."

"Don't get cocky," Maddie said. "He may have overrides or other plans. If there's nothing else we've learned about Fitzgerald by now, it's that he's a cunning bastard."

"I will try to remember that," Horst answered. "Once we get *Munin* out, we will be able to escape from Io. I believe the *Nebula Storm* could then tow us eventually to safety, with the right computations, yes?"

There was silence—silence for so long that Horst thought for a moment that they must have lost the connection. Then Jackie's voice came on, this time heavy with regret. "I'm afraid not, Horst. We could have...but Fitzgerald got us."

"*How?*" demanded Anthony LaPointe. "It is too far, and you

are too small. It is beyond belief that you could have failed to see the attack or avoid it."

"Fitzgerald was a smart one," A.J. said. "Those shells weren't like the little fat bullet he shot at Ceres. These were big, relatively smart cans of armor-piercing BBs the size of my thumb. He bracketed us with his shots, and then the damn things *chased* us when we tried to dodge. So . . . short story is, he got our reactor."

"No way to repair it?"

"Not without at least a place to sit her down. Or a spacefloating drydock. I need a place that either has gravity or that's enclosed so I can work on the ship opened up without worrying about where stuff might drift off to," Jackie said quietly. "And we haven't got what it takes to—"

Her voice dissolved into a mass of static. Horst blinked, then swung toward the instruments of *Munin*; Anthony was doing the same thing. "Horst—"

"Yes. I do not think they suddenly stopped transmitting, and that means we are being jammed. Which would need something very close."

The external ramp cameras came on. Standing in the doorway of the hangar were three figures: Richard Fitzgerald, security officer James Feeney, and Mia Svendsen. Fitzgerald gave a cheery wave. "Why not say hello, boyo? It's the friendly thing to do."

Chapter 40

Richard saw the furious face of Horst Eberhart materialize in his VRD. He let Horst give vent to a considerable range of epithets. Most of them were in German, some in French, two in English, one in Italian, and one in Czech. He hadn't realized the lad was such a linguist.

Shame he wasn't in any position to actually *do* anything. "Yes, yes, let's take it that you've told me what you think of me and my ancestors. We're wasting valuable time here, since our dear friends on *Nebula Storm* have sent us heading straight for a very un-soft landing on Io."

"*Nebula Storm*? It is *you* who have doomed us, Fitzgerald!" Anthony LaPointe almost shouted. "Had you never attacked them, had you not tried again, then all of us would still be alive!"

He shook his head. Of all the wrongheaded things to be arguing about! "I was doing a job. You don't *have* my job, and innocents like you never do understand how things work, anyway. It's simply a waste of time to argue about who did what to whom. The real question is how those of us still alive can stay that way.

"Now, it seems to me that *Munin* has more than enough room for you two, the four of us, and little Mia here. She's all fueled, she's loaded, she's ready. And I happen to be qualified to pilot her, too, which I don't think either of you two are."

"I have flown some," Horst said. "In space. Between myself and Anthony, I think we can fly it."

"Maybe so. But it's a lot different in real life than the simulator, don't you forget that. Still, I won't force you to trust my flying. Just open up and let us on board."

Horst laughed. "Let *you* on board? You must be joking!"

Richard shook his head. "Now, that kind of talk gets us nowhere, Horst." He nodded, and Feeney pointed his pistol at Mia's head. Behind him, Johnson and Desplaines emerged, flanking him on either side. "Do I have to draw you a picture? Surely you're bright enough to see the bargain. Or do you think we won't hurt her?"

Horst was silent, clearly trying to think of some argument he could make, or of some other threat which wasn't immediately cancelled by the threat to the *Odin*'s chief engineer. "We'd be outnumbered four to three, counting Mia. That's bad enough. No one's coming on board armed."

Richard considered. He liked having weapons, but he really couldn't afford to shoot anyone at this point, even Eberhart and LaPointe. Eberhart might also be able to get around the guns' personalized locks, in which case bringing them on board could end up putting a weapon in the German engineer's hands. "I suppose I can give you that, for the sake of some small goodwill. You're not silly enough to think that us getting rid of the guns will mean we can't hurt Miss Svendsen, are you? Didn't think you were." He gestured. "Lose the guns, mates. And any other toys we brought along. We shouldn't be needing them."

Johnson stared at him. "Chief, are you *sure* about this?"

He cut out his transmitter. "Seven of us having to survive somehow is none too many," he said, voice low but carrying to the others. "And besides, if two engineers and an astronomer can beat the four of us in unarmed combat, we're nothing but a bad joke and that's the truth."

The other three looked reluctant, but followed orders. Richard collected the weapons—six firearms, three knives, and an explosives kit—put them in one of the mesh holding bags used for loose items in weightless spaces like the hangar, and held it up. "There they are," he said, transmitter active again. "I am putting them over here."

He went to the wall, clipped the bag securely, then rejoined his group, where Johnson was keeping Mia in a restraining hold. "Satisfactory? Now open up."

"How do I know you don't have anything concealed inside your suits?"

Richard rolled his eyes. "You *don't*, boyo. And I don't think I'm getting out of my suit just to make you feel better. Sudden decompression without a suit doesn't appeal to me, and the shape old *Odin* is in, that could happen just about any time. You take what you see. Now open up."

Horst hesitated, but Richard could see that he knew he'd run out of options and delaying tactics. The younger man began to reach for a control out of sight of the camera.

Something warned Richard Fitzgerald; perhaps it was a very slight shift of Horst's gaze, a widening of the eyes; perhaps it was an intake of breath on the part of Anthony LaPointe. Perhaps it was just more than a quarter-century of instincts honed in lethal conflicts around the world. Whatever it was, he found himself suddenly diving forward and up, launching himself across the hangar toward the support and loading mechanisms—just as the thunder of a large-caliber handgun blasted out from behind him.

Johnson never had a chance to even scream. One second he was stolidly holding Mia immobile, the next his head exploded in a spray of red. Feeney, startled, tried to whirl, actually managed to complete a quarter-turn before the gun roared again, blowing a hole in his neck. Vanna Desplaines made a desperate dive toward the net bag holding their guns. Two more shots echoed out, deafening in the enclosed room. The first *spang*ed off her carbonan suit, sending her into an uncontrolled spin to smack into the wall. The second hit her just as she began to rebound, and took her right between the eyes.

Richard stared down incredulously at the shadowed doorway, searching for some sort of weapon—a crowbar, a hammer, something. Four shots, three dead? Even *he* would have had a hard time pulling that one off. Who in the name of...

An involuntary chill went down his spine as the figure in the doorway moved into view. Looking directly at him, golden eyes gleaming cold as dead men's treasure, General Hohenheim raised his pistol.

Chapter 41

"General! You're alive!"

Hohenheim found the relief and genuine pleasure in Horst's exclamation warming. But he didn't have time or luxury for enjoyment at the moment. "I am. Mr. Eberhart, while Mr. Fitzgerald stays extremely still, I would like you to open the *Munin*'s hatch and allow Mia to board." He looked down at the wide-eyed engineer, who was pale and shaking—and covered with blood and other remnants of her former captor. "My apologies for being unable to warn you, Miss—*do not move, Mr. Fitzgerald!* I have excellent peripheral vision, and I believe I have demonstrated my accuracy with this weapon. As I was saying, my apologies, Miss Svendsen. I hope you are unharmed?"

Mia swallowed, then nodded. "I . . . I am all right, General. They had said you were dead."

He smiled grimly. "That is what I intended them to think." The *Munin*'s hatch opened. "Now get on board."

Mia stood, a bit shakily, and moved toward the ramp. Her boots gripped the deck and allowed her to walk and keep her balance despite being at the edge of collapse.

It was at that moment that everything went wrong. Vanna Desplaines' body had continued to ricochet gruesomely in slow-motion around the docking area, and at that crucial instant she passed between Hohenheim and Richard Fitzgerald.

The speed of Fitzgerald's reaction showed that he had already anticipated exactly that turn of events—had watched everything, estimated angles, movements, timing. He dove toward the body, her armored corpse making a shield that Hohenheim's single reflexive shot did not penetrate. He then spun his body around, flinging his associate's toward Hohenheim and gaining a change in vector that caused him to sail directly to the wall he had just recently left. Before the general could get a clear shot, his former security chief had ripped the mesh bag from the wall and bounded away, back into the shadowed reaches of the support and loading mechanisms.

And now he is fully armed, and I have one gun, Hohenheim thought grimly as he pulled himself back into the doorway from which he had entered. He gestured savagely to Mia, who had frozen and tried to drop to the ground—a gesture which had ended with her floating mostly motionless near the boarding ramp. "Get on board *immediately*." As she moved to comply, Hohenheim continued: "Once she is on board, Mr. Eberhardt, you will close the hatch."

"Sir?" There was concern in the young engineer's voice. "Are you not coming on board?"

"No, Mr. Eberhart. I doubt if Fitzgerald is less of a marksman than myself, and in order for me to reach the ramp I must cross a considerable empty space. He will have an excellent field of fire and cover, while I would have to give up all cover in order to board.

"On the other hand, *you* must get out of here immediately for two reasons. Firstly, because if you go to these coordinates"—he transmitted a location on the wreck of *Odin*—"you will find a few more survivors whose time is running out. And secondly, because if I do not keep Mr. Fitzgerald busy"—he suited actions to words by firing two shots in the general direction of the renegade security chief—"he will almost certainly find a way to disable or control the launching mechanisms, and then no one will leave here unless he allows it."

"Only . . . a few survivors?"

"Five, when I left. One was . . . not well. I believe there are no others left that we could reach in time. The radiation shielding was badly damaged in most areas, in addition to the general decompression damage and the many people killed or injured directly by projectiles. I am afraid that even if there are people left alive currently, other than in the location I gave you—which is still shielded—they are simply breathing dead."

"Dear God. I had forgotten about the radiation hazard."

"As did I, at first, until my radiation alarm went off when I tried to enter one of the cross corridors. We are being reminded again, and now as savagely as possible, how deadly the environment is so close to Jupiter. Now go, pick them up. You are no pilot. It will take you some time to master the controls and reach that location, and we have no time to waste."

"But, General—"

"*That is a direct order,* Mr. Eberhart. Get yourself and the remainder of my crew to safety."

"Are you insane?" Fitzgerald finally burst out. "*Munin* can handle at least ten people! There's plenty of room for both of us!"

He could not make out the former Irish mercenary, but looked in the direction of the outraged voice. "Mr. Fitzgerald, there is no room on any ship under my command for a mutineer, a traitor, and a murderer, and you are all three. While I live, *Odin* and *Munin* remain under my command. And since I sincerely doubt that you are ready to nobly allow me to board *Munin* and go down with my ship in expiation for your crimes"—Hohenheim carefully inserted another magazine into his weapon—"it appears that we are about to play out the final act of a melodrama. Carry out your orders, Mr. Eberhardt."

After a moment's pause, Eberhart replied. His voice was strained and thick. "Yes, General."

"Good luck, Horst, Anthony, Mia. It has been an honor having you on my crew."

"It's been an honor to serve under you, sir," Anthony said quietly. The noises in the background indicated that perhaps the others simply could not speak.

"Not so honorable as I might have been, I'm afraid. Please tender my apologies to the *Nebula Storm* and, when the time comes, to my superiors. I accept all the responsibility for the mission's failure. I am now carrying out my final duty as the captain of this vessel." He triggered the airlock, which shut behind him and Fitzgerald. "Launch, Mr. Eberhart."

Fitzgerald's angry voice came again. "So, we're both going to just bloody sit here and watch the only hope we've got *fly away?*"

As the ramp of *Munin* locked closed and atmosphere began to vent out, Hohenheim chuckled. "Yes, Mr. Fitzgerald, we are going to do exactly that. Because if you make any move to stop them, you will show me where you are. And then"—he braced himself against any backblast from the shuttle—"I will most certainly shoot you dead."

※   ※   ※

I can't bloody believe this. Fitzgerald saw the doors opening, and very nearly *did* try to make a dive for the manual cut-outs that would have forced the launch bay to close back up. If the *Munin* left without him, he'd only live another few hours on the dying *Odin* before being shot by Hohenheim, killed by a radiation overdose, or—oh, happy day!—making landfall as a meteor on Io.

But Hohenheim had demonstrated the deadly accuracy of his microgravity firearms skill. Someone had slipped up on part of his background, obviously; the file Fitzgerald had on the general hadn't indicated anything like that kind of skill. While none of the other deaths appealed to him, even less did Fitzgerald like the idea of being shot down like a desperate dog leaping for something he knew he'd never reach. Better to die stalking each other than like that. Dignity mattered.

And there were still some other angles possible. He'd heard the coordinates Hohenheim had given Horst. Although he knew the rudiments of handling the landing craft and had been given some basic training, Eberhart was a programmer and system engineer, not an experienced pilot. It would take him some time to get *Munin* under enough control to be able to dock with the right area of *Odin* to rescue the other refugees. If Fitzgerald could somehow get past the general, he could cut *through* the ship to get to the refugee area and once more pull the ancient but still effective hostage approach. And once he was on board, Hohenheim would either already be dead or be as good as dead.

So he watched—not without considerable concern—as *Munin* lifted and drifted out the doors, which closed once the shuttle was well clear. *Time to get things moving. And talking is always a good distractor.*

"Well, now, that was bloody brilliant, General Hohenheim. You've sentenced us both to death, and for what? A little overenthusiasm on my part in carrying out my orders? In trying to make sure we actually succeeded in our mission? Which, if I might remind you, was to find the treasure and get it for ourselves, not share it out to those who were already awash in wealth."

Hohenheim sighed. "You see, that's the problem. I see now that it's always been the problem, Mr. Fitzgerald. You see everything about you in simple terms, no matter how complicated it really is. To you, this is about you doing one simple job—no matter what. I suppose it was Bitteschell who gave you your directives?"

"He hired me. He set the general terms." Fitzgerald saw no reason any longer to dance about. Either he or Hohenheim or both would soon be dead anyway. "But the specific orders—not to mention the offer of a monster bonus—came from Osterhoudt at the ESDC."

"Ah, that company's chief operations officer. That makes sense, now. I had been puzzled by the thought that Bitteschell had given such ruthless instructions. That's really not like him. But Osterhoudt does have such a reputation."

Fitzgerald didn't really care what Hohenheim said; it was simply important that he be kept responding, because the more he focused on the conversation, the less he might focus on other things. As he got out one of the charges, Fitzgerald said: "I'm amused by your use of the term 'simple.' It *might* have been simple, if you hadn't kept making it harder. Though I have to give you credit, sir. That was impressive shooting you did. I wouldn't have expected it from a man in your position."

"Even good intelligence usually misses things, especially when they don't seem important at the time. Fifteen years or so ago, when I was stationed in America for a while, I was friends with some people in their Special Forces. I spent considerable time learning something about small arms and their military uses. I was quite a marksman, in fact. Of course, using those skills in space poses its own challenges. But I have as many hours in space as any astronauts in the world except a handful of Americans and three Russians."

That explained a bit. But there was a great deal of difference between being a marksman with small arms, even one trained by elite military forces, and being what Fitzgerald himself was. He eased himself along the support as slowly as he could. There were shadows here, and some cover, and he knew that Hohenheim still had to be in the cover of the doorway. If Hohenheim remembered that...

His instincts warned him again, pulling him entirely around the loading arm as two more shots rang out in air that was just starting to return to the landing bay. *Thank engineering for nicely redundant and independent support, at least.* "Bloody hell!"

"Yes, I remembered to try infrared sensing this time, Mr. Fitzgerald. A shame I didn't remember that earlier, but most of us are used to visible light. You stand out quite nicely. I can make out your glow even behind that support."

I'll bet you can. Fitzgerald could see the shadowed infrared glow of General Hohenheim too, if he cared to risk a glimpse at the door. It was nice that sensor suites cut both ways. "And so we'll just be sittin' here for the next, what, day or so until we meet the friendly face of Io?"

"Actually, Mr. Fitzgerald, I intend to leave that contemplation for you. I have another engagement." Dumbfounded, Richard heard the door open and then close.

Understanding came immediately. *That clever bastard.* Hohenheim had realized the same thing that Fitzgerald just had. Fitzgerald had to get past the general, but the general didn't have to get past Fitzgerald. If he succeeded, of course, Hohenheim would have to take back that lovely melodramatic farewell, but Fitzgerald supposed he'd get over it. The general could always console himself with the fact that he'd left Fitzgerald here to die.

On the other hand, the new situation meant that Hohenheim was also no longer an immediate threat. Richard dove straight down for the doorway, bringing boots finally back into solid floor contact and hitting the control. The door, however, did not open. He had rather expected that, of course; the general didn't want him leaving.

But Hohenheim probably hadn't known exactly what Fitzgerald still had on him at the end. The one charge he'd selected before might not be quite enough, but adding a second one should do just fine. He set the timer and moved well away to the side. A moment later the shaped charges gave a dull *bang*, and the door blew to pieces.

He restrained himself from going right through. Time was of the essence, but he didn't put it past Hohenheim to have waited for a few minutes to see if, in fact, Fitzgerald did have a quick solution to the locked door. The general might be sitting in ambush outside.

Richard sidled up to the area and took out a small mirror— amazing how useful a polished piece of metal could be. He scanned the area carefully in the reflective surface and caught a faint shape in one of the now-black monitor screens on the wall.

Hohenheim was there, all right. And obviously he knew Fitzgerald was coming out.

Bloody hell.

However, the general didn't know exactly *when* his opponent would come out, nor how. Hohenheim would have to react, while

Fitzgerald would be acting. The problem was that there was a lot of straight corridor outside of this door.

He could take a dive that would force a hand-to-hand confrontation if Hohenheim didn't get him instantly, but he remembered the general's unexpected strength. While Fitzgerald was not afraid of facing just about anyone in a *mano-a-mano* confrontation, Hohenheim was in surprisingly good condition for a commanding officer, and he outweighed Richard by many kilograms. It was always possible that he'd gotten some training in hand-to-hand combat from his special forces friends, too. Quality generally outweighed quantity, but, as others often said, quantity had a quality all its own. While he was undoubtedly a more skilled fighter than the general, Richard saw no reason to test whether or not his extra skill would outweigh the general's superior size and possibly superior strength.

But he *did* know where Hohenheim was. Which meant...

Seconds later, a body dove headlong from the doorway. General Hohenheim fired twice, hitting both times, before it registered on him that the body had been flying oddly limp to begin with. But by that point, Richard Fitzgerald had already gotten a good bead on him from his position at the bottom of the doorway and shot twice.

The angle was bad, though. Richard would have preferred to do this standing, but that would have exposed him too much. The two bullets ricocheted from the carbonan suit, one very narrowly missing the faceplate, sending the general tumbling. That did, however, give Richard the opening to get out of the launch bay.

He continued to shield his escape by shoving Feeney's body down after the general. Another bullet whined by him, and another, but by then he was to the end, and through! His security override code locked down that door. For the moment, he was safe.

And, now that he thought about it, the situation was better than he'd realized. General Hohenheim had guessed Fitzgerald had remembered the location of the others, figured out his plan, and had set himself up on the *other* side of the corridor from the direction that led there, figuring that Fitzgerald would be heading in that direction and thus leave his back exposed.

So, he'd outthought himself. Now Richard was already heading in the direction he needed to be, and Hohenheim was the one who'd have to take the long way around—if there was a safe way around at all.

The *Odin* was still partially intact, but the combination of damage and the fact that nothing had been done to neutralize her spin before the disaster meant that she was still turning. With pieces now no longer connected as they were supposed to be, the giant ship was wobbling on her axis, stressing components in ways they were never meant to be stressed. Things were getting worse, and Richard had to move quickly. By now, Eberhart would have gotten his craft under control, and he only had to make one stop.

Richard swiftly made his way along the corridors. He knew what route the general must have taken; there were only so many ways to get where they were going. Momentarily there was a flicker of connectivity, and he was able to get a partial outside report.

There's Munin! *Not where she's going yet. Good, good. I have more than enough time.*

He opened the next door, leading to the radial corridor up to the hab ring—and his radiation alarm screamed. Reflexively, he slapped the door shut and backed off.

Shield failed . . . That would cover the whole radial.

His suit would reduce the dosages, but at this range from Jupiter and Io, even inside *Odin*, he wouldn't have that much time. Normal radiation flux inside this region was over thirty-six hundred rem per day, and right now the sensors had been measuring doses of almost twice that, which meant that half an hour's exposure would start making you sick, and a few hours would make you a dead man.

He'd gotten a quick glimpse up the radial before the door closed, and there was no possibility of making it up in time. It would be a thousand-foot crawl through a tangle of wreckage which could shift and fall at any time. But there might still be a way. There were a couple of maintenance access shafts that provided a shortcut through parts of the main hull, and one of them was just a little ways back the way he had come. He could move over to the next section through that, and then go up to the hab ring where Eberhart would be trying to dock.

He backtracked, found the access tunnel, and wormed his way in. It was a tight fit in the suit, but he could make it. Another hundred feet and he'd be clear.

Even as he thought that, the *Odin* quivered again, and something snap-crunched behind him. Simultaneously, radiation alarms began and an automatic cutoff door slammed down only twenty feet behind. Still, his suit would protect him easily for the next hundred feet, and once he was past this section the other would, hopefully, be shielded.

It was darker up ahead than he'd expected; he should be seeing light coming from the central corridor. He had to hurry. The dosage meter was slowly moving. That wasn't an immediate concern yet—wouldn't be for at least a half hour, actually—but he didn't like any exposure. Richard didn't fancy coming down with cancer eventually, assuming he survived all this.

As he continued, it became clear that something was blocking his path. He shone a suit light at it, and realized it was a body. He felt his lips stretch in an ironic smile as he realized it wasn't just *a* body. It was a body he had put there himself—that of the technician, Erin Peltier.

Peltier hadn't been dead when he left her, but she was dead now. That much was obvious by the fact that there was no air left in this section of the tunnel. Something, probably one or more of the armor-piercing pellets, had punched a hole through a nearby area of the hull.

Too bad for the technician, of course. Fitzgerald hadn't intended to kill her—but it was of no major concern to him, either. What *was* of concern was that her body blocked his exit and, in vacuum, had swelled and securely wedged itself into the tunnel.

Since she was already dead, however, there was no need for delicacy. A quick set of efforts showed that he couldn't budge her by hand, especially without any weight or leverage. But he still had what was left of Johnson's kit. Explosives... Richard sometimes thought there were no problems they *couldn't* solve.

He squirmed backward and made sure he covered his head as well as possible. The detonation slammed into him through the floor and walls. Doing his best not to dwell upon the nature of the mess all over, he was able to shove past the remains and come out into the central corridor, back behind still-operating shielding.

Only to find that another sealed door was cutting off access to the central corridor, one that had been concealed by the dead woman's body.

Bloody brilliant. Of course there would be. No decompression of the central corridor would go unsealed.

He was running out of explosives, but there should be enough for this last door. He'd just have to hope there were no more obstructions.

He felt, rather than heard, cracking and groaning noises from around him. *Whole bloody ship's coming apart soon.* A blast shook the maintenance corridor, and he started moving forward immediately. Air whistled past him now, and abruptly everything spun around him, accompanied by screeching, shattering sounds in the thin atmosphere.

Weakened by impacts, stress, and two successive nearby explosions, a section of the main hull suddenly blew out under the return of air pressure. Richard Fitzgerald was hurled outward from *Odin*, scrabbling desperately to catch hold of a cable, a support stay, *anything.* Something loomed up and struck him a heavy blow; he blacked out.

When he came to, he realized he was falling, falling through space. The jets on his suit managed to stabilize his spin, and he looked around.

Jupiter loomed over him, enormous, its roiling surface filled with storms beyond imagining. In one direction, receding slowly but surely into the distance, lay *Odin*. Ahead, a small dot of yellow-orange waited. That would be Io. He couldn't see it growing slowly yet, but he knew it would soon enough.

Richard quickly checked the fuel remaining for his jets. Not enough to return to the *Odin*. Not nearly enough.

He sighed. It was over, then. All hope, all struggle, all effort. All life. Done, over, finished. He was a dead man.

So be it. Oddly, perhaps, he had not lost any of his equanimity. He'd been a lot more depressed on his fortieth birthday, actually.

Besides, there was still time for sightseeing. He'd visited the Grand Canyon once and found himself getting bored after gazing upon the magnificent vista for an hour or so. He wondered how long Jupiter would keep its interest.

Considerably longer, as it turned out. The Grand Canyon had been created by the infinitesimally slow forces of erosion. The thing was grand, certainly, but also static. You saw one part of it, for a while, and you'd pretty much seen it all.

Jupiter, though . . . The giant planet was *alive*. Richard found it fascinating, the way those immense storms worked their way across the face of the great globe.

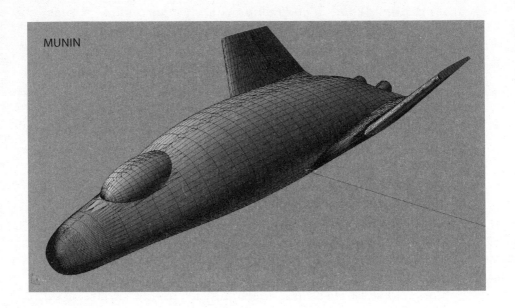

Chapter 42

Hohenheim stared in frustrated chagrin at the locked door. He'd been outwitted on his own ship.

But it should not be a surprise, really. This sort of operation was Fitzgerald's specialty. Perhaps Hohenheim should not have delayed, but simply gone on ahead. Yes, Fitzgerald would have been in pursuit, but perhaps it would have worked out better.

Enough recriminations. He would have to try to work his way around and intercept Fitzgerald, though it seemed unlikely he could catch up unless something slowed his former security chief down. Still, there were many things that might happen. And his presence here did give him one advantage.

That advantage, was that Hohenheim knew that the way in the other direction—which led toward Engineering—was passable. Or had just recently been, at least. If he could make it there, he could take the central corridor straight to the radials.

"Passable" was, of course, a relative term. It turned out that Fitzgerald and his party must have had to squirm past a number of obstacles, which now slowed Hohenheim's progress considerably. With every passing moment, he grew less optimistic about catching up with either Horst or Fitzgerald.

Abruptly he emerged into the main engine room. Despite the damage done to the rest of the ship, this area looked deceptively intact. The armor, water, and other bunkerage around the reactors, as well as the angle from the explosion, had combined to protect it. Only the huge number of red telltales and alerts gave away how very little of *Odin* was still functional.

However, all the general cared about at this moment was the

central corridor. Engineering, of course, had a direct passageway straight to the central corridor, which he followed. But just as he opened the door, new alarms screamed through his mortally wounded ship, and the door resealed itself against a sudden decompression. Something had blown out the side of the main hull somewhere.

He would have sat down heavily, had there been gravity, for he knew now it was hopeless. If Fitzgerald had followed the right path, and nothing had changed along the way, he would already be where the final survivors were. Perhaps Horst would have picked them up by then, or perhaps not; but whatever was passing there was now beyond the general's ability to influence.

Communications were essentially out on the ship. Given some time, especially here, Hohenheim might be able to cobble together a transceiver that worked, even in this part of Jupiter system. But for what purpose?

"At least I will be comfortable," he said to himself. Main engineering retained power from the main reactor. Storerooms nearby were still pressurized. Despite the damage, there were supplies here that could keep him alive for a long time—weeks, certainly; perhaps even months.

That was another ironic taunt of the universe, given that he had only the relatively few hours remaining before...

How had Mr. Buckley put it once, in a conversation at dinner on Ceres? Ah, yes: *deceleration through lithobraking.* That would be happening to him on Io very soon.

It was hardly a terrible way to end things, though. There would be none of the lingering horror of radiation sickness, and he had done what he could to restore some of his own honor. A quick flash of light and no pain; there were many worse ways to die.

Except...

That didn't sit well with the general. He drifted over and looked at the consoles. *Damage to the main thrust nozzle and its cooling systems. Self-sealing tanks prevented us from losing all the remaining reaction mass.* There was minimal connectivity left even in the most basic health-maintenance systems, but the main engineering computers were able to produce a good estimate of conditions throughout *Odin.*

He shook his head dolefully. The situation was worsening by the minute. The spin, the imbalance—each time something broke,

it weakened something else. It was quite possible the whole ship
might come apart before they reached Io.

Come apart...

He suddenly had a dim memory of a long-ago conversation
with Dr. Castillo, the chief engineer on *Odin*. It had been after
he had first boarded the great vessel and Castillo had been giving
him a final internal guided tour. *What was it?*

"Severable sections," he said to himself slowly. The *Odin* was
made such that in emergencies some components could be separated from the others. The major concept had included being able
to remove symmetrical sections of the hab ring in case one of
them was damaged, causing imbalance.

At the time, he had wondered what the point was, given that the
probability of actual collision with a meteor was so low as to be
not really worth considering. Now, of course, he understood that
the designers had been thinking of...far more directed disasters.
The ship's main contractor had been the European Space Development Company. From the very beginning, undoubtedly operating
under the directions of the chief operations officer, Osterhoudt,
the company's top engineers had seen to it that the *Odin* was far
more of a warship than she appeared to be. And then, adding
insult to injury, had hidden the fact from the *Odin*'s captain but
given it to their hand-picked chief security officer.

The most extreme variant of "severable" would remove the engineering and mass-beam drive—essentially the entire rear of the
ship—from the rest, leaving the forward section of the main body
and the hab ring drifting. That made perfect sense for a military
vessel. Such a separation would concentrate power, leaving the
concealed weaponry and drives operable and getting rid of any
excess weight. True, maneuverability would be terrible, given the
geometry. But the ESDC's engineers hadn't really had any choice,
if they were to keep the hidden design a secret.

But in *this* case, the problem of poor maneuverability was
irrelevant, since Hohenheim couldn't possibly keep the ship intact
anyway.

The general initiated a search for the triggering systems. With
his command overrides, it wasn't hard to find. He couldn't reach
many of the hab-section controls, but for his purposes it didn't
matter. He was going to use the extreme variant.

First things first. He checked his chronometer. *Munin* must long since have left for its rendezvous with destiny, and hopefully survival. It was possible that there were one or two other survivors on board *Odin*, but Hohenheim had managed no contact. At this point, he had to assume that only the dead remained with him.

And he had to hurry. Every passing hour brought him closer to Io and made any desperate attempt to evade that hellish globe that much less likely to succeed.

The lateral thrusters... Some still operative. Enough, he hoped. He modeled the current movement of the ship on the main console, thanking whatever gods there were that modern interfaces did not require him to do the calculations. Then he ordered a precisely timed sequence of thrusts.

Slowly, slowly, he began to feel a sense of turning that was separate from the ship's earlier axial spin. *Odin* was now spinning, more and more quickly, about her lengthwise center of mass as well as the axial. He could feel a faint pressure toward the wall in that direction, as the *Odin* now tumbled like a thrown bolo instead of a rifled bullet. It was an end-over-end spin that would normally signify disaster. But the *Odin* was doomed anyway, and there was a purpose for this tumbling.

The tumbling sent Io spinning smoothly around the cameras' field of view. Once more he input the model, then incorporated the vectors of their approach to the moon. Taking a deep breath, waiting for the designated conditions... Hohenheim ordered, "Separate."

The concussion of separation would have knocked Hohenheim off his feet if he had not strapped in; as it was, his head slammed painfully into the back of his helmet. There were other distant sounds and vibrations that did not bode well for even the section of *Odin* he had kept with him. But he did not care about that; what was important was whether his desperate maneuver had worked.

Spinning on approach, when the two pieces separated they retained the same total momentum. Their center of mass would remain in the same place, barring some form of acceleration placed on one component separate from the other. But the center of mass was merely a geometrical and physical construct, one that now occupied empty space. The shattered hab ring and most of the main body hurtled off in one direction, while the engine and drive section spun off in the opposite direction—away from the meeting with Io.

By itself, that would not be enough; Hohenheim had known that before he started. But he needed all the help he could get; at least it started him edging away from direct central impact with the deadly moon, and drastically reduced the mass of *his* part of the ship.

Now...

First the spin had to be brought back under control. The laterals left on this section would be driven past normal design limits, but—again—he didn't need to worry about long-term endurance. No, his main worry was something else entirely, the major remaining question mark in this enterprise, one that might render everything he was doing futile. But it was better to die trying than not to try at all.

Finally, *Odin*—what remained of her, rather—was no longer tumbling or spinning. She sat with her mass-drives pointed almost directly away from Io, the blunt-nosed engineering section almost facing toward the pockmarked moon. Almost, but not quite.

And now, the moment of truth.

For there really was no other choice. Mangled though the nozzle was, the NERVA-based drive was still operative. It might work for a second, or ten seconds, or longer. It might, possibly, have some failure mode that would blow the control room into shrapnel. But if it worked—even for just a few moments—it just might give him enough thrust to send them plunging around Io instead of into it, hurtling out into the Jupiter system, probably to never encounter another solid object again for years or even centuries.

He would not get home. But the maneuver might give him the time he needed to report home, and to make his peace with family and friends left behind, before he died. He would die on *his* terms.

He checked the vectors one last time. The nozzle control systems were ... shot. He would have to hope that the imbalance from the missing section of number four driver rib would not be too significant for the time the main drive fired. He offered a silent prayer. *Let me not have entirely wasted my last few hours in this world.*

Then he activated the drive.

For its last time, *Odin* came fully alive, the thunder of the NERVA rocket delivering a million pounds of thrust, shoving the now greatly lightened vessel forward. Amber telltales lit, then shifted to red, and he could see the drive nozzle starting to come apart. He overrode automated shutdowns. *Run until you can run no more, or until you reach the limit of reaction mass I have allotted.*

The power of the rocket vibrated through Hohenheim's bones, a defiant cry of the wounded ship against the approaching destroyer, and he brought his head up proudly. The great ship, the largest ever built by the human race, had done well. One last effort, one final task, and *Odin* could rest. The ship had been done a great disservice, but it would still give its best to save the last living human being aboard.

And then, with a doomsday roar that echoed throughout the wrecked vessel, the main engine's nozzle blew entirely off.

Chapter 43

"The best hope we have is that someone figures out a way to come get us. And is willing to spend the hundreds of millions to do it," Joe said gloomily.

"That bad?" Helen asked.

"It's not good, that's for sure. We were cramped for equipment space, you know that. Our lander has a little reactor on it, but nothing like what we'd need to run the drive. Jackie and I think we can rig it to provide us with power to live on, but that's about it. I can do some slow maneuvering if we have to with the few ion jets we've got, but those do use reaction mass and power, so we sure ain't going home on them. We can't deploy the sail, and we can't refuel the engine, and even if we could refill the reaction mass tanks, without the reactor we couldn't *use* it."

"It's ironic," Helen said after a few silent moments on the bridge of *Nebula Storm*.

"How so?" asked A.J.

"Well, usually in the lost-in-space kind of stories, the real problem is either not knowing where you are, or running out of air or food or water. But we've got close to two years of all of that, if we manage to keep power going at all. And we know exactly where we are and where we want to go."

Jackie, Helen noticed, was still silent. She'd been waiting quietly at the console ever since Horst had been cut off by a burst of static that A.J. had localized to somewhere onboard *Odin*—a deliberate jamming transmission. That implied that Fitzgerald had caught up with them. No one knew what to say to Jackie. Knowing that Madeline Fathom saw Fitzgerald as someone dangerous, and knowing what Maddie was capable of, no one wanted to raise false hopes.

The screen suddenly lit up with a transmission. "*Nebula Storm*, *Nebula Storm*, this is *Munin*. Please answer."

Jackie, of course, answered first. "*Horst!* Is . . . are you all right?"

The German's voice was solemn. "I am all right, and so is Anthony. We have six other members of *Odin*'s crew on board. The general asked me to pass on his apologies to you all."

"General Hohenheim is alive?"

"He was when we left. At his orders."

A.J. closed his eyes. "Oh, Jesus."

"What about Fitzgerald?" Madeline asked.

"The general stayed to deal with him, Madeline. There is no other way off the ship."

Maddie nodded slowly. "I see. I hope . . . that you have considerable supplies on board?"

"We have better than that." Anthony LaPointe's face was actually smiling, a startling contrast from the last few conversations. "I think that I have a way for us to all go home."

"*What?*" Everyone, even Horst, seemed surprised. "Why did you not tell me, if that is true?" he asked.

"Because until we were able to see whether our friends were still alive, there would have been no point. We will need both of our ships and talents."

"All right," Larry said. "What's your idea?"

"Our orbits, they are not terribly different. We can match with you, I think you will agree, by doing an Oberth around Io at the right time."

"If you put yourselves on the right non-collision course first . . . sure."

"Do you still have any reaction mass on board?"

"Yes," Jackie answered. "In a pinch we've got actually quite a few tons of water to spare, too. So, what do we do?"

"It will be risky."

Helen laughed. "Right now we're all marooned and likely to die really slowly in the end. Screw the risk. What are we going to do?"

Anthony grinned. "We are all going to land on Europa, my friends."

"Wait a minute," Jackie said. "*Nebula Storm* isn't equipped to land anywhere, and even if we were, we haven't got an engine to do the landing with."

"That is why you need us. We have the engine. *Munin* was designed to be a SSTO capable of reaching low Earth orbit. We will need to use about two kilometers per second total in shifting our orbit to match up with yours en route to Europa. If we refuel from *Nebula Storm*—'top off the tanks,' as they say—we will have more than enough to counter the remaining one or two KPS differential with respect to Europa and land. Remember, *Munin* is more than half as big as *Nebula Storm*."

Jackie and Joe looked at each other. "That's going to take some tricky flying," Joe said finally. "And we'll have to make connections that'll take the strain. And . . . Jesus, I dunno. We sure can't do VTOL in this, and we haven't got landing gear. And keeping it balanced . . ."

Maddie nodded. "It's going to be hellish. But it probably is our only chance. Europa isn't like Io. It's frozen, but a lot of water ice—which we can use for fuel—relatively smooth, and no volcanoes or other immediate threats. If we *can* set down and live through it, we can fix *Nebula Storm*, right?"

Jackie frowned. "Probably. And we'll have the *Munin* for a reactor, too, if it turns out that we can't get ours running again—which we may not."

"And once you are running again," Horst said, "your Nebula Drive can be used—with the right kind of sailing—to get us heading home, yes?"

"Yes, indeed," said A.J., sliding an arm around Helen's waist and hugging her in relief. "Yes, we can."

"Then let's start designing," Jackie said. "Is Mia there?"

"Yes, she is one of the survivors."

"Good. Because we're all going to have to work on this, and when we finally match up, we'll only have a few hours to figure out how to lock our ships together well enough to take the stress of landing. At least it's not in an Earth gravity well, but it's still going to be a hell of a ride . . . and a lot of stress on any link we make." She started bringing up the plans of the *Nebula Storm* and prepping them to send to *Munin*.

Helen took A.J.'s hand and pulled him up.

He looked startled. "What? I have to—"

"Get some rest, that's what you need to do. They won't need

your super-sensor skills for the planning. They'll need them when we get to the installation and when we do the landing. So we're going to go get food for everyone, have a dinner, try to relax, and then get some sleep."

"An excellent idea," Madeline confirmed. "I will be doing the same thing in a little while. Because I think I'm going to end up the pilot on our side."

"And aside from a few calculations, we won't be needed until docking, either, Tony," Larry pointed out. "Sorry, guys, but you engineers work out the details. We'll be getting up in time to do the work."

"And try," Madeline confirmed, "to get some rest yourselves, if you can. We will probably *all* want to be wide awake when we get to the landing."

"Yes," agreed Horst. "We will be busier than you, though. First we have to make burn to pass Io—which will be in a few minutes—and then Oberth as we reach it."

"Good luck on that, then."

Helen waved at the screen. Then the two of them made their way to the galley. "You don't even sound scared," A.J. said.

She turned and pressed into him. "I'm terrified, A.J. But there's nothing a xenopaleobiologist—whatever I am—can do. If anyone can get us out of this, it's the people on this ship. And then I just have to not make you, or anyone else, worry. It's bad enough—I don't need to make it worse."

His hands held her tightly. One moved up and stroked her hair. "I won't let you die."

"I hope not. I married you for the miracles." He laughed softly and hugged her even tighter. Finally she let go and turned. "Now, let's get out the Joe Dinners. If this *does* have a chance to be my last meal, it'll damn well be a good one."

Chapter 44

Eventually, Fitzgerald thought to check the time. Then he checked his radiation meter.

He'd died fifteen or twenty minutes earlier. Perhaps half a hour, depending on his body's resistance to radiation. But whatever the specific moment it had happened, his life had ended. Even if, by some miracle, a spacecraft arrived to rescue him now—it would have to be the *Munin,* perhaps because Eberhart had been overcome by unlikely mercy—it wouldn't matter in the least. No doctor, no hospital, not even on Earth, could have saved him after this much radiation poisoning.

But dignity mattered. It always mattered. Richard Fitzgerald had been slain by Jupiter himself, had he not? No one since the time of Homer could make that claim.

He stopped gazing upon his murderer and looked ahead, toward Io. The huge moon was clearly visible now, clothed in its bright and fatal colors.

So, as it turned out, there was still one last hope left. Perhaps Richard could last long enough to die on one of the solar system's true hell planets, after being struck down by the lord of the gods. Wouldn't that be something to boast about, if there turned out to be an afterlife? Richard didn't think there was, but . . . you never knew.

It was not to be. When he felt the first twinges of nausea, some time later, he reached to his belt and took out a gun. It looked like one of Vanna's, so he made sure it unlocked to his key code.

Dignity mattered. It always mattered. Richard Fitzgerald was not going to go out suffocating on his own vomit in a spacesuit. He took one last look at Jupiter and fixed his eyes on Io. The moon was close enough now to see the details of its surface—which consisted mostly of volcanoes, it seemed.

He pressed the gun to his faceplate, centering the barrel between his eyes as best he could. Then, looking straight onto the face of hell, pulled the trigger.

Chapter 45

Blotched, pockmarked, scarred with orange-yellow blotches, Io's hostile surface streamed by *Munin* a scant hundred kilometers below. Bombarded by radiation so intense that it would be almost instantly lethal without shielding, shrouded in a sulfurous atmosphere just barely thicker than vacuum, with a surface constantly reshaped by stupendous eruptions of molten rock, the tortured moon's leprous face wrung an involuntary shudder from Horst. In a short time, *Odin* would meet its end—out of sight of *Munin*, as the lander would at that time be making its own Oberth Maneuver near the other side of Io. The orbital adjustment *Munin* had made to avoid hitting Io had sent her ahead of the doomed E.U. ship, passing some other debris along the way.

"We are on course, Andy?"

"All is ready. You just keep on with your design work."

Horst studied the designs that he, Jackie, Mia, and Joe were working on.

The fundamental challenges were really twofold. First, fastening the two vessels together so that the power of the *Munin*'s rockets could be applied to both vessels. Second, determining where the *Munin* and *Nebula Storm* could be fastened together that wouldn't cause the thrust from the rockets to be applied off-center, thus turning what should be straight thrust into a spin.

"The positive side is that we don't have to do most of it fast," Joe had pointed out. "We don't have to build these links to hold under ten Gs or anything."

Mia shook her head. "There will be maneuvers that may well have significant peaks. Not ten gravities, but more than one."

There were some points suitable for anchoring at least part of *Munin* on *Nebula Storm*. The most obvious were the attachment points that were originally used to suspend *Nebula Storm* in Ceres' gravity. Those had been heavily overengineered, and Joe was confident that they could take just about any strain that was likely to be encountered. Horst thought Joe was probably right. The obvious orientation to anchor the two vessels was one that placed their airlocks in as close proximity as possible. A couple of the tiedown locations were close, and if they could put a connecting tube between the vessels, they could use the internal supports of *Nebula Storm* as an anchor to the front landing gear of *Munin*.

Jackie had come up with the best way to adjust the center of mass: extending two of the four habitat sections on *Nebula Storm*, the two which would be on either side of *Munin* when locked down, and putting as much heavy stuff—including water—in them as necessary to mostly balance the center of mass. The main rockets of *Munin* had some slight ability to deflect and adjust their angle of thrust, which would—they hoped—make up for minor deficiencies.

To minimize vibration and movement during thrust, Mia wanted to use several tons of water. Freezing in place at the interface between *Munin* and *Nebula Storm*, the ice would probably help. How long it would last no one could tell, but they didn't have many alternatives.

The real sticky point was exactly how to manage the connections and the landing itself. "I do not see how we can pull off this landing," Horst said finally. "*Munin* is designed to land. *Nebula Storm* is not, and together—especially in the configuration we will need to maneuver in—I cannot imagine even Miss Fathom bringing us down uninjured."

Static crackled in his ear before Jackie answered. Even with the best selection of frequencies and top-notch signal enhancement, the storm of electromagnetic noise around Io made conversation difficult. "*Yeah. I've got a possible fix for that, but then we can't do the welding we were talking about. We need to separate the ships just a few minutes before we come down.*"

"Jackie, if we are separated, you are falling. We can land, yes, but what about you?"

"*Look, what we do is run a cable from your reactor to our engines. I get the accumulators partly charged, we'll have enough power to do another burn or two. Not big ones, but if we're slow enough—down at the hundred-meter-per-second range or so—then* Nebula Storm *will be able to land itself, if I retract the hab sections. It won't be pretty, and we'll probably get bumped around, but it's livable."*

"Yeah, that'd work!" Joe said. His enthusiasm dropped. "But that *really* throws a wrench in the works. First, we can't tie ourselves together through the airlock link—we don't want the airlock open. And...If we don't weld everything together..."

"Cables," Horst said suddenly as he finally found what he'd been looking for in the *Munin*'s extensive onboard manifest. "For exploring parts of Enceladus, or wherever we ended up going, as you had to on Mars. We had exploration vehicles with very strong cable to hold and lower large loads very long distances. These are combined metal-composite-carbonan cables, Jackie. If we use several of them at each connection point...?"

"Give me the specs." There was silence as she ran her models. "That...should work. How do we detach, though?"

"Blow the cables," Joe answered promptly. "Have Maddie make appropriate demo charges. It's one of her specialties, remember. And we could rig something—a big cable, a rocket, whatever—to heat the connecting area where the ice is, weaken it so we can break free."

Horst chuckled briefly. "This is going to be the most...what is that name—Goldberg? Yes, Rube Goldberg–inspired operation I have ever imagined. Are you sure that we do not need to trigger it all with a hamster on a wheel?"

"I dunno," Jackie said. *"Do you have a hamster on board?"*

"Let me check the medical supplies..."

She laughed. *"Oh, I needed that. Actually, the cables are a better idea if you guys can prepare most of that ahead of time. Welding in vacuum is a pain, and we will only have a few hours to get all this done."*

A roar of power thundered through *Munin* and shoved Horst down in his seat. "We are doing our Oberth now."

A few moments later the rocket went silent. "Anthony?"

"One moment...Yes, everything is good. We are catching up with *Nebula Storm*. In a few hours we will have to match up. Then we will have to work like demons."

Horst signaled Jackie to shift frequencies. "Jackie...at least I will see you before—"

"*—before we might end up killing ourselves in this crazy stunt. Yeah. I'm glad.*" Her static-fuzzed image still was clear enough for him to see a hint of tears in her eyes. "*But let's live through this, okay?*"

"I would much prefer that." He unstrapped and stood. "Now, I am sorry, but we all have to go and get the materials ready."

"*Yeah, I'm going to have to get everyone up soon to start prepping on our end. Especially A.J., since he's going to have to run our Locusts. They'll be invaluable for doing the outside work, even if the rest of us all do have suits.*"

"Then I say good-bye for now."

"*See you soon!*" She gave him a gleaming smile, and then disappeared.

Horst turned to Anthony, Mia, and the others. "Okay, you can stop grinning at me. We have work to do."

Anthony shook his head. "The things a man will do to get a date."

"They're both engineers," said Mia. "What do you expect?"

Io loomed before Hohenheim, now. It was no longer a disc but a monstrous wall, a wall of pustulant yellow touched with oranges and greens and whites, toward which *Odin* hurtled unstoppably. The general recalled that some had compared the surface of the Jovian moon—often imaged with a brighter orange shade—to that of a pizza. But the hideous surface before and below *Odin* looked more like decaying flesh, the peeling face of a horror-show zombie with a death-rictus grin and the stench of the grave.

Uncertainty precludes answer.

The simple phrase on the screen showed why he was staring as though enraptured. The combination of the damage done to the ship—the change in mass, in geometry, the failure of the nozzle which had not been performing per normal specifications, all of that and more—meant that there was still some element of uncertainty in the precise path of *Odin* around Io. Around Io—or into it.

This was of course made worse by *Odin*'s need for radiation shielding. Hohenheim had not dared tamper with those settings, and so wherever the system could maintain a shield, there one remained. But as Castillo had told him long ago, that meant there would be some small, and in this case unpredictable, forces exerted by the mighty magnetic and radiation fields of Jupiter on his smaller but concentrated shielding.

And so Io grew, and grew, and was not even a planet with a curve easy to identify. He could see individual mountains now, one belching a cloud of yellow-black that, it seemed, would nearly reach *Odin*'s current altitude.

I should turn away. There is no need to see.

But instead he stood. The surface of the moon was approaching rapidly. Coagulated sulfur and craggy, savage mountains seemed to cover everything. What would happen, would happen soon, and he would face it head-on.

Odin screamed silently out of the black sky of the Jovian system, as though riding eight-legged Sleipnir down upon some inconceivably monstrous Jotun—or, no, a fire giant, great Surt himself. The drive-spines, three remaining, traveled before *Odin* like a three-pointed spear: Gugnir as a pitchfork. Ahead, Hohenheim saw a great ridge of mountains, higher than Everest, looming before his ship. He braced himself. There, in all likelihood, was his tombstone.

One mountain in particular, a vapor-belching cone, lay directly in *Odin*'s path. Hohenheim could not keep from sucking in his breath as *Odin* bore down on it at literally meteoric speeds.

There was a sharp, shuddering *snap* that echoed high and low. Hohenheim was swept off the floor even with his boots and the grip he had had on his chair. He smashed into the ceiling, around and around, tumbling...

Tumbling? He should have vaporized on impact!

Even as that thought came to him, the spin began to reduce, the remaining laterals fighting the tumble. He glimpsed, weaving drunkenly by in the screen, the great ridge of mountains, receding now, the surface dropping away below him.

Projected path clear blinked on the screen in front of the main engineering console. Hohenheim felt a great burst of relief, and wonder, and, yes, triumph.

Whatever else, he would die on his own terms. And he would now have plenty of time to prepare those terms.

Chapter 46

Madeline strapped herself into the control seat. "Are all connections secure?"

"*As secure as we can make 'em,*" A.J. answered her. "*Got Faerie Dust all over them to give me warnings if anything happens.*"

Not that this would do me much good, Maddie thought but did not say. After all, once they committed to the landing, there would be really no chance to change their minds. If things started to come apart, they'd just have to do the best they could...which would probably be not enough, and they'd all die. But trying was a lot better than just waiting until something ran out. "Jackie, are the accumulators charged?"

"*Off the topic, do you realize how old-fashioned that name sounds? Accumulators, that is? Used to read it in like 1940s SF,*" A.J. said.

"*Shut up, A.J. Yes, Maddie, they're charged. Not nearly fully, but with our limited reaction mass, more than enough.*"

"Disconnect power-cable connection, then, and seal the airlocks. A.J., all disconnect charges placed?"

"*Placed. They're under your control and codes. No one else can trigger them.*"

"Good. Network?"

Horst answered. "*You have control of our rocket until disconnect, Madeline. The telemetry is triple-redundant to make sure we don't glitch during landing.*"

"Balance?"

"*Got tons and tons of mass stuffed into the extended hab areas. We've modeled both ships, and the center of mass for acceleration is now pretty close. We can use the automated system on* Nebula

Storm *to do some minor adjustments, and the main rockets on* Munin *have enough thrust-deflection capability."*

"What about our hull?"

A.J. shook his head. *"Don't worry about it. The part of our hull that might get hit by the rocket wash is all Vault alloy. Sure, keep the rocket on it long enough and we'd probably damage something, but we're not firing it that long."*

Maddie nodded. *"Munin,* are your reaction mass tanks fully loaded?"

"Yes. Glad that where we are going there is a lot of ice, because otherwise we would all be very short of water when this is done."

"Good. Everyone strapped in?" The others reported in. "Mia, I want you and Jackie to keep a really close eye on everything. We can't afford glitches."

"Understood. We are watching."

Madeline rubbed her eyes and took several deep breaths before putting her helmet on. This being a critical maneuver, she'd also taken a stimulant. She simply hadn't had enough sleep, and this was not the time to have slowed reflexes. There were only two good aspects to the situation. One, obviously, was the low gravity of Europa, less than one seventh of Earth's, which meant a gravity well of just slightly over two kilometers per second—within *Munin*'s capacity to handle even with the added mass of *Nebula Storm*. That was critical, because not only did they need to land, they needed *Munin* to be able to lift them off of Europa eventually, because the nebula drive wasn't capable of lifting off from anything larger than a smallish asteroid.

The second good thing was that Europa had no atmosphere to speak of. This jury-rigged double ship had the aerodynamics of a falling bridge, and were there any atmosphere—even one as thin as Mars'—the pressure variations during reentry would probably rip them apart. Aside from the gravity well itself, she'd be able to treat the maneuvers as being the same as in deep space. That gave them a chance. *Not a great one . . . but I'd better make it good enough,* she thought.

"All right, everyone. We are almost there."

Europa now loomed before them, eclipsing even Jupiter in size as the combined *Munin/Nebula Storm* overtook it in its orbit at a differential of less than a kilometer per second. Smallest of the Galilean moons, it was still immense, half again as wide as

Luna, far more massive, far more complex. From their current altitude, it looked as smooth and polished as a billiard ball, an ivory cueball with multiple browned lines like cracks from age covering its surface. Somewhere below that surface, Maddie knew—depending on the scientist you asked, anywhere between two and fifty kilometers below—there was a dark ocean that covered the entire moon to a depth ten times greater than the deepest parts of Earth's ocean.

The smoothness was deceptive. Europa might be the smoothest object in the solar system, but there were still plenty of ridges, blocks, edges, hills, and chasms, and they had only minimal control over their landing site. In the few hours they had, A.J. and Larry had gone over the available imagery and what they could make out with the onboard instruments and picked their best guess as to a landing trajectory that might offer decent landing topography...but it was still a crapshoot.

"About to begin maneuvers. I'm going to ask everyone to either cut out radios or stay quiet unless they have something I need to hear. This is going to take all my concentration, and I don't need even a gasp, a curse, or a prayer distracting me."

"*Understood,*" A.J. acknowledged. She saw some people drop out of the network—mostly the former *Odin* crewmembers that she hadn't had time to get to know yet, and who weren't engineers involved in this maneuver. Helen and Larry also dropped out. Larry had done all he could, and Helen was not going to be able to do anything more, either, now that the gruntwork of putting the whole contraption together was over.

"Here goes..."

Munin's rockets coughed and then began a low, rumbling roar at minimal power. She wanted—needed—to get a feel for the clumsy dual ship before she kicked in full power. It was sluggish... wobbly...still some imbalance...but there, A.J. and Horst's programming was kicking in, automatic compensation based on the accelerometers all over the ships. The departure from projected optimal course was minimal. "Working so far. Full de-orbit burn coming up in three, two, one..."

Now the rockets gave vent to full-bore thunder, sending a shudder of vibrations throughout *Nebula Storm*. "*Ice seal under stress...holding, but I'm seeing cracks starting to build. Think it will hold, but be ready,*" A.J. said quietly.

"Cables?"

"All well within limits. No shifting yet. The torque on the hab section connecting tubes and supports is getting awfully near their design limits, but doesn't seem to be increasing any more."

"Burn almost done...in five, four, three..."

Just as the *Munin* ceased its rumbling, there was a reverberating *crunch*. "What was that?"

"Ice seal shifted and broke. We're only held together with the string and duct tape now. On the positive side, we don't need to worry about making sure that part breaks when it comes to the time to separate."

"Any advice?"

Horst answered. *"When we do the other burn for landing preparation, begin very slowly, as before, then taper slowly. This will let any slack be taken up and stress the cables least. Backing down slowly will let the strain off the cables evenly—I hope—so there will be no great shifts."*

"I understand." She leaned back. "It will be a while before we come to the landing decision. Larry, A.J., I want you to keep watch ahead of us and refine our landing site as much as possible. As we know from our little landing in *John Carter*, you don't have to hit at kilometers per second to ruin your day."

"We're on it. Take it easy for now."

She reached out and took Joe's hand. Even though the contact was just glove-to-glove, it felt good. "You okay?" he asked privately.

"Scared to death. I practiced a *lot* after that crash, and Bruce said I was getting pretty good, but I'm not half as good as he is, and I think he'd find this a hell of a challenge."

"You're my Supergirl. You'll do it."

She giggled. "Yeah, I'll just fly out and catch us if something goes wrong."

"I almost believe you could." He smiled at her fondly.

"I'd try, anyway."

"Maddie, all that matters is we're doing our best. And if anyone can get us down safe and sound, it's going to be you."

Once more his words made all the difference. She stopped worrying. If the worst happened, it happened.

Chapter 47

It was no longer a moon. Europa was *down*, now; a planet of ice, of jumbled ridges, occasional craters, scattered blocks the size of *Odin* stuck in the center of smooth, featureless frozen white, all rolling by underneath them at a tremendous speed. "Without atmosphere, we're having to kill our speed directly. According to Larry and A.J., we will be landing near the area called the Conamara Chaos. There's no good way to predict smooth landing spots, if any, so we just have to wing it. Everyone make sure they are securely strapped in." She did not allow her voice to betray any uncertainty. Her review of the Conamara region didn't encourage her; "chaos" was a good description of the area, but outside of it wasn't much better. On a planetary scale, Europa was smooth; on a human scale, it was some of the most rugged-looking terrain she'd ever had to look at. Plenty of areas of Mars were smoother to land on. But . . . there were a few possibilities. If she could just get lined up right.

"Combined landing burn coming up."

The rocket came on again at minimal power, slowly building to maximum. Scraping noises and vibrations echoed through both ships as, despite the cables, the two shifted slightly with respect to each other. Horst and A.J.'s balancing application was strained to its limit, and Maddie could feel the combined ship moving toward some catastrophic adjustment that would send them spinning out of control. Instinctively she eased off on the thrust, watching the projections of time and velocity. She had to get their relative velocity with respect to Europa's surface down to less than a hundred meters per second. Five hundred meters per second, and descending. Altitude ten thousand meters. Four hundred meters per second. Something moved slightly, and the entire mass of strung-together high technology seemed to wobble in the sky before a combination of programmed adjustments and Maddie's gut-level instinct managed to damp it down. Three hundred meters per second, and they were below five thousand meters altitude. Ridges and many-meter-high scarps loomed below them, ice frozen metal-hard in vacuum at a temperature of one hundred sixty degrees below zero—more than two hundred and fifty below, in Fahrenheit. Two hundred meters per second and they were lower than she liked, but she had to take her time; A.J. and Horst both indicated silently, in messages on her VRD, that the cable links would shift if she went to full power again—shift and perhaps let go. One hundred fifty. Forty...thirty...twenty... One hundred ten...

"One hundred meters per second relative. *Munin*, we are detaching from you. Horst, are you ready?"

"Ready to take controls. Good luck."

"Separation in five, four, three..."

Multiple demolition charges—specifically designed for vacuum use here in the outer system—detonated on cue, severing the cables at precisely selected locations. *Munin* peeled away from *Nebula Storm* with a very small burn from its lateral thrusters.

"*Munin* away. Retracting hab sections." The overloaded sections would slightly unbalance *Nebula Storm*, but she could use that to keep them oriented in what amounted to a "right side up" attitude when she did the braking burn. The automated balance application was adjusted to deal with the current situation; she could see A.J. watching it like a hawk.

"Altitude is about a thousand meters. Hold on, everyone. One way or another, we're almost done."

She cut off outside imagery for everyone but herself. No one else needed to see this, and right now it was not even vaguely comforting. A shattered chaos of icebergs hundreds of meters high, small but sharp-edged ridges running for kilometers, not a single smooth area larger than a football field in...

Wait. What was that? She concentrated the imaging systems in that direction. Alongside that long, wider ridged valley...parallel to it, a wide, smooth area. And it might...barely...be in range.

She let a lateral jet bias them in that direction, saving the main engine's accumulators for the very end. The ground rose up . . . closer . . . closer . . .

She couldn't restrain an intake of breath as the peak of a great block of ice passed *above* her. Above her and to the side, no more than sixty meters away. The terrain below her now was jagged, fangs of ice reaching for the ship. She had to clear them, but they were coming up to meet *Nebula Storm*.

The vague dark patch of smoothness was barely visible at this angle, but approaching. But she wouldn't make it. Unless . . .

Another lateral burst, tilting them up. She fired a short, sharp pulse from the main engines, then fired the laterals to bring them back into the proper alignment. There was a faint jolt, but she maintained control, seeing that the very tail of *Nebula Storm* had clipped the top off one of the blocks of ice. But the ice was still rough below them, still clawing up—and then suddenly she saw darker ice, still no skating rink but not a mass of frozen teeth. She cut in the main engines. The accumulators dumped their hoarded power into the reaction mass, sent it roaring out the NERVA nozzle at many, many kilometers per second, making every gram of mass work to slow *Nebula Storm*.

Fifty . . . forty meters per second . . . Altitude eighteen meters . . .

The rocket died off, power exhausted, with speed at five meters per second, altitude seven meters. A second or so later, *Nebula Storm* landed on Europa.

Munin was trailing *Nebula Storm*, a considered choice based on wanting both vessels close together on Europa and knowing that *Nebula Storm* had neither the maneuverability nor design to control its landing. Horst and the others watched, almost holding their breaths.

"Almost down . . ." Horst breathed. Only a tiny bit more, and the ship would be down and still, as perfect a landing as could be imagined with such a vessel.

And then the *Nebula Storm*'s rocket died.

Five meters per second sounded so slow—barely a brisk jog, nothing compared to the meteoric speeds the ship had possessed but a few days before. A man on Earth could easily have outrun it now. But the *Nebula Storm* massed nearly a thousand tons. This was no aircraft, but a solid mass the size of a patrol ship, a small runaway train. A plume of white dust and tumbling shards blasted from beneath the careening spaceship as the *Bemmius*-made hull carved a remorseless path through the ice of Europa. Ponderously, majestically, the great ship bounced, rear end coming up, front down to score another massive dashed line in the face of the Jovian moon, then rear end down again, both down, sliding, ripping through ice like the blade of a titanic ice-skate. The *Nebula Storm* skidded, turning slowly from end-on to broadside. One of the habitat extensions caught suddenly on a projecting ridge, crumpled, and tore free. The ship rolled slightly, trapping the connecting tube underneath its mass, shredding the composite and steel, steam erupting as the water inside boiled outward in vacuum, shrouding the careening vessel in white fog. To his horror, Horst saw, casting knife-edged shadows across the ice, a forty-meter ridge cutting across the relatively smooth ice like a wall, dead ahead of the out-of-control Ares-IRI vessel. He pointed, wordlessly.

"I see it. But the *Nebula Storm*, she is slowing..."

It takes immense force to stop a thousand mobile tons, and with only Europa's feeble gravity to provide the pressure, the *Nebula Storm* would not stop quickly. But stop it would, in the end, and already the five meters per second had become three and a half, three, cutting an interrupted gouge nearly a hundred meters wide across Europa in a stupendous fountain of crystalline white. Even as Horst began bringing *Munin* in for a landing, he could barely tear his eyes from the ponderous, deceptive grace of the *Nebula Storm*'s slow-motion crash. He could hear someone praying in the background. "Stop, stop, God, please stop..."

Two and a half meters per second now, dropping, just a brisk walk—but there was no more room. Broadside on, the *Nebula Storm* smashed irresistibly into the immovable bulwark of steel-hard ice, sending a blast of steam, ice dust, and boulders of crystalline water spurting into the black sky of Europa. The cloud settled, unnaturally fast with no atmosphere to keep the dust suspended, and all was still. For a few seconds, no one said anything as Horst gave his full attention to bringing *Munin* to ground as close as possible to the crashed *Nebula Storm*. Only when he felt the huge lander settle with crushing solidity onto the ice did he speak. "*Nebula Storm*! Jackie, Helen, A.J.—are you all right?"

For a moment there was no answer, and he thought his heart might just stop. But then the voice of Madeline Fathom answered, as calm and collected as though she were sitting back on Earth. "Munin, *this is* Nebula Storm. *That probably looked worse than it was. We got a bit shaken up, but we are all fine. Joe's got a slight bruise on his forehead and Jackie got whacked across the shin by something that got loose in that last jolt, but her suit kept that from being anything serious. No leaks, all major systems still operating, and the hab unit we lost had the stuff in it we could most afford to lose. You can see that one of the others extended a little on impact, just over the top of this ridge, and it's twisted some, but Jackie doesn't think it's beyond repair."* Her image appeared on the screen, and they could all see the entire crew of *Nebula Storm* behind her. *"It's a good landing, because we're all going to walk away from it. And one day, we'll all be walking back into this ship and going home."*

"Speaking of walking away . . . ," A.J. said.

"Yes. No better time, I think; we'll all have plenty of work to do, and until we get this over with, we can't really get to it. Horst?"

He took a deep breath. "Give me a minute."

"Hold on!" Maddie's voice cut across all frequencies. *"A.J., Horst, I appreciate the quick spirit of cooperation, and that you want to do* something *after all this tension. But is getting killed your main priority?"*

"Getting . . . ? Oops."

"Oops, *indeed.*"

Horst almost smacked the side of his head. "Sorry, sorry. Radiation again."

"Radiation. Yes, we're at less than a thousand rem per day here at the surface of Europa, and so stepping out for a few minutes won't really hurt anyone. Except that we may be here a long time. We cannot afford any avoidable exposure. Jackie?"

"Give me a minute . . . All systems show good. I think we can do it."

A faint shimmer appeared near *Nebula Storm*. Horst looked at *Munin*'s instruments and could detect the expansion of the magnetic field which guided gas and nanodust up and over them. Gravity and the immense magnetic pressure of Jupiter would keep the size of the dusty-plasma field severely constrained, but it would still spread kilometers across and protect both ships and the space around them from the invisible, deadly radiation. They'd have to run a cable from *Munin* to keep it running, with the *Nebula Storm*'s reactor down. But Jackie said that they should be able to keep it running for long enough. Whatever radiation still got through the field should be survivable.

A few moments later, he stepped out onto the boarding ramp of *Munin*, which rested on the white-dusted ice a short distance from *Nebula Storm*. Across from him he could see two figures, side by side on the ladder extending from *Nebula Storm*'s airlock. His VRD showed Jackie's smiling face and Larry Conley's easy grin next to the appropriate suit. "Ready?"

"Ready!"

Horst began, and the others joined in.

"By the authority vested in us as representatives of the European Union—"

"—of the Ares Project—"

"—of the Interplanetary Research Institute—"

Three boots extended and touched, as one, on the surface of Europa, twin dim shadows cast by mighty Jupiter and distant Sol coming together on the contact.

"—as the first human beings to set foot upon Europa, we claim all rights, privileges, and responsibilities pertaining therunto for us, our heirs, and assigns, and for the human race as set forth in the laws to which all of us are bound."

For a few moments they stood quietly, gazing up at the brown-streaked immensity of Jupiter in the star-filled sky and the distant, blazing near-point of light that was the Sun. Horst felt a chill run down his spine that had nothing to do with the cryogenic temperatures around him. Only now did he truly grasp it: he was standing on the surface of a new world, the first (along with the two others) to ever do so.

Then Madeline Fathom's voice broke into their reverie. *"Good work, and thank you, everyone. Whether anything worth discovering comes from Europa or not, this is the spirit of cooperation we want them to hear about back home."* Her face appeared in everyone's view. *"And now, let's all get to work—because we're going home, every one of us!"*